Joel Tyler Headley

The Life of Ulysses S. Grant

Joel Tyler Headley

The Life of Ulysses S. Grant

ISBN/EAN: 9783337333867

Printed in Europe, USA, Canada, Australia, Japan

Cover: Foto ©Raphael Reischuk / pixelio.de

More available books at **www.hansebooks.com**

THE LIFE

OF

ULYSSES S. GRANT.

BY

HON. J. T. HEADLEY,

AUTHOR OF "WASHINGTON AND HIS GENERALS," "NAPOLEON AND HIS
MARSHALS," "SACRED MOUNTAINS," "FARRAGUT AND OUR
NAVAL COMMANDERS," ETC., ETC.

ILLUSTRATED.

NEW AND ENLARGED EDITION.

NEW YORK:

E. B. TREAT, PUBLISHER, 805 BROADWAY.

IRA S. SMITH, CHICAGO; RANDALL & FISH, DETROIT; H. C. WRIGHT
& CO., ST. LOUIS; A. L. BANCROFT & CO., SAN
FRANCISCO, CAL.

1872.

PREFACE.

IN a former work, composed of biographical sketches of the distinguished generals that shared the fortunes and the triumphs of General Grant, we gave a brief outline of the military history of the latter. The object of the present work is to fill up that outline, and present him not merely as a great military leader, but by a careful collection and faithful narration of the facts and events that go to make up his history, from his boyhood to the present hour, furnish to the reader the materials for obtaining a correct estimate of his character as a man.

Immediately after the war, things were in that state of chaos that it was impossible to get hold of those details so necessary to the proper understanding of this. These have since come to light, which enables the biographer not only to give his complete history, so far as it illustrates his great qualities, but also to explain much that was hitherto wrapt in obscurity. This is especially true of his early struggles in the West, against secret persecutions and open hostility. In his varied fortunes whilst serving under Halleck, much that is new and strange has been learned which not only reveals Grant in a more attractive light than even his great deeds, but also the mysterious path by which Providence finally led him to the exalted height which he so much adorns.

Such a complete history of him is desirable, not only because of the prominent place he holds in our military annals and national history, but because of the important position he at present occupies in the civil affairs of the republic.

If he is destined in these turbulent times to take the helm of the government, it is of vital consequence that the people should know his character as illustrated by his acts, other than as a victorious general.

We believe a calm perusal of the following work will enable a just man to form correct conclusions, and that he will rise from it convinced that a more unselfish, patriotic, or purer man was never entrusted with power.

In reference to Grant's military life West, we wish to acknowledge our great obligations to Col. Badeau, who, as a member of the General's staff, had access to his private papers, and hence was able to reveal what was before unknown, or only conjectured.

ILLUSTRATIONS

FINELY EXECUTED ON STEEL,

From Photographs and Original Designs.

CONTENTS.

CHAPTER I.

CHAPTER II.

CHAPTER III.

CHAPTER IV.

CHAPTER V.

CHAPTER VI.

CHAPTER VII.

CHAPTER VIII.

CHAPTER IX.

CHAPTER X.

CHAPTER XI.

CHAPTER XII.

CHAPTER XIII.

CHAPTER XIV.

CHAPTER XV.

CHAPTER XVI.

CHAPTER XVII.

CHAPTER XVIII.

CHAPTER XIX.

CHAPTER XX.

CHAPTER XXI.

CHAPTER XXIII.

CHAPTER XXIV.

CHAPTER XXV.

CHAPTER XXVI.

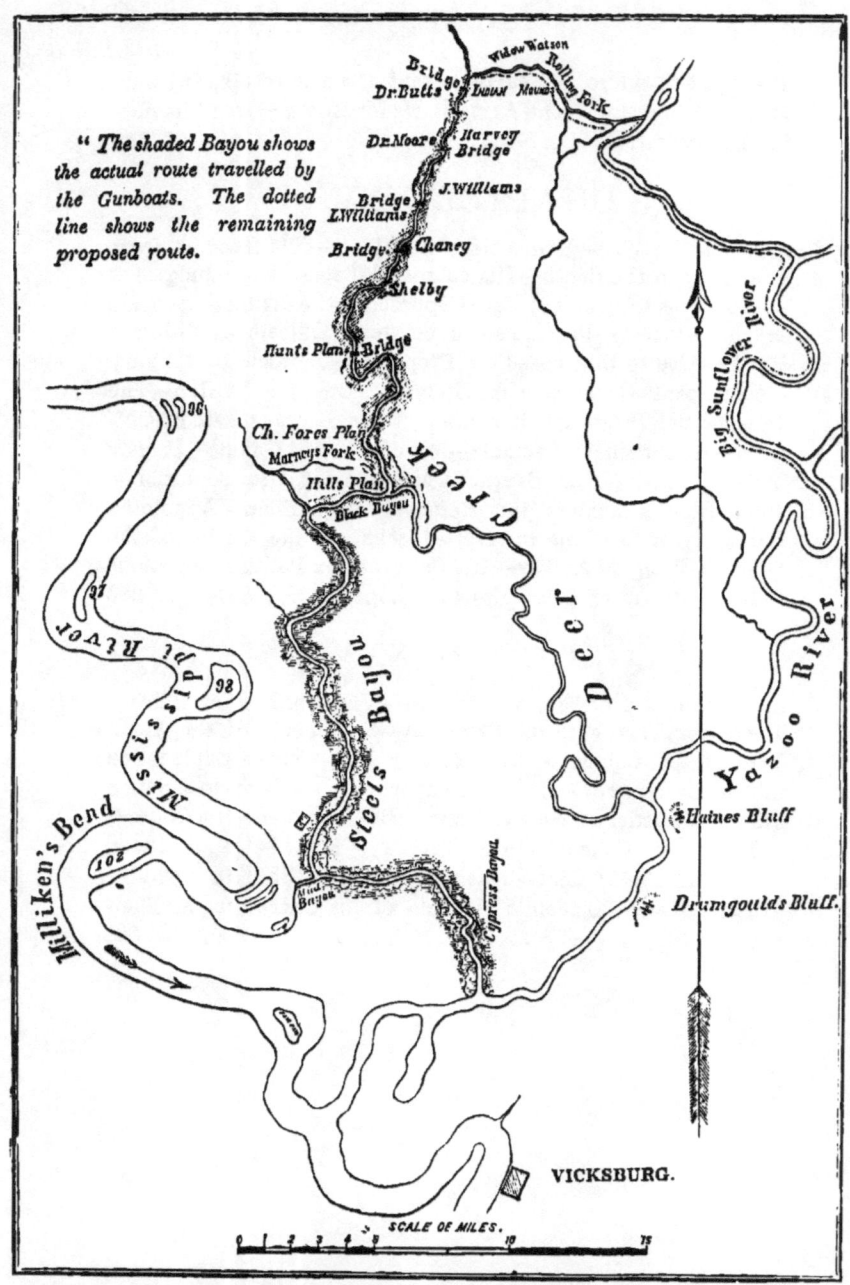

" *The shaded Bayou shows the actual route travelled by the Gunboats. The dotted line shows the remaining proposed routes.*

THE LAST INLAND ROUTE OF GEN. GRANT TO REACH THE REAR OF VICKSBURG

LIFE OF GRANT.

CHAPTER I.

BOYHOOD.

Childhood of Great Men—Influence of Circumstances—How Generals are made—Grant's Ancestry—Nativity—Early Life —Apt at Figures—Examined by a Phrenologist—His love for Horses—Early management of them—Rides a Circus-Pony— Sent alone on business to Kentucky—Ingenuity in loading heavy timber—Dissatisfied with his position—Resolves to go to West Point.

THERE is always more or less desire to know something. of the early life of great men, in the expectation of finding those traits or qualities of character, in boyhood, which afterwards rendered them so distinguished. Sometimes the wish is so strong to find these early revelations, that every floating rumor is caught at, and accepted as true, if it goes to establish precocity of genius. Thus, the boyhood of Napoleon and Washington has been turned into a romance, in the eagerness to show how, almost in their infancy, they gave indications of their former greatness.

But the truth is, *circumstances* make men— not that circumstances can make a strong man

out of a weak one—a wise one out of a fool—
but that men are *educated* by circumstances.　A
man of well-balanced character, strong common
sense, and good mental capacity, is capable of ex-
panding to meet any of the exigencies of human
life ; that is, he will grow to his condition, adapt
himself to the sphere rapidly enlarging around
him.　Washington, for instance, but for the Revolution, would doubtless have been distinguished
only as the first man in his county, of excellent
judgment, and worthy of any position of trust
or responsibility.　But he had the capacity for
greater things ; and when the momentous struggle of the colonies was thrown upon him, he rose
to meet the great responsibility.　As the war
advanced, he advanced in military knowledge
and skill.　In short, he was capable of being
educated by the circumstances and events into
which he was thrown.　There are great geniuses
in history that were born such—who seem to be
endowed with a sort of inspiration that enables
them to leap to results which others reach only
by patient labor and slow experience; but they
are rare as comets in the solar system.　The
great truth, that but few men are equal, *at once*, to
any and all emergencies that may arise, was one
that our government, at the outset, was slow in
learning. ˙ In ordinary wars, the general that has
been educated for the very position of trust in

which he finds himself, and shows by his failures
that he is unequal to it, proves his incapacity, and
his removal is a matter of imperious necessity.
But no one in our country had received the
training requisite to fit him for the wide field of
operations, and the distracting circumstances presented by the awful civil war that was precipi-
tated upon us.   That military leaders should
blunder, as well as the government, which was
equally unprepared for it, was inevitable.   To require, as some did, an immediate change of government—even going so far as to hint at the removal of the President—was insanity.   We were
all children, and had, like children, to learn to
walk, by repeated stumbles.   Ignoring this important fact, in military matters, made the government present the spectacle of throwing dice, as
it were, for a general.   One after another was
sacrificed, and Grant and Sherman narrowly
escaped the same fate.   The latter was removed
from the Department of Kentucky, as a crazy
man; while nothing but the most strenuous efforts
of a single friend saved the former from disgrace,
after the battle of Pittsburgh Landing; yet both
proved themselves to be eventually the greatest
captains of the age.

But though it is true that the child seldom exhibits any indications of the future greatness to
which he attains, yet, in many respects, the old

maxim is true, that "the child is father to the man."

A child of weak and vacillating will never becomes a man of great decision and executive force; nor one who exhibits a total lack of perseverance and energy in every thing he undertakes be distinguished for marking out a course, and persisting in it, over all obstacles, and amid the greatest discouragements. Those qualities of character for which Grant is so remarkable, he exhibited as a child. He confronted difficulties with the same dauntless resolution then, that he did afterwards.

His father, still living, loves to recall and recount the events in the childhood of his distinguished son; hence, there is no public character of modern times, of whose early life so much is known.

He is of Scotch descent; and though much effort has been made to trace his lineage to Connecticut, we can find very little that is reliable, beyond his great-grandfather, who settled in Westmoreland county, Pennsylvania, where, in in 1794, the father of Ulysses was born, and, five years after, emigrated to Ohio—then the far west. Here he in a few years died, leaving his son, eleven years of age, an orphan, and nearly penniless. There were seven children in all, the oldest of which was but twelve years of age when the family was broken up. When sixteen years old he was apprenticed to his half-brother, in Maysville, Kentucky, to learn the tanner's trade, and served out his time, and then went back to Ohio, and set up in business for himself, at Ravenna, Portage county. Compelled by illness, after a few years of toil, to abandon his trade, he finally settled down again, for a while, at Point Pleasant. He shortly after became acquainted with Miss Hannah Simpson, who had emigrated from his native county, in Pennsylvania, and married her.

Ulysses, their first child, was born here, on the 27th day of April, 1822. The mother was a Methodist, and trained her child to respect religion, to avoid profanity and strife, and to love truth, industry, and honesty. The · father was poor, and Ulysses was early taught to help him, on whom a rapidly increasing family pressed hard. Thus, at eight years of age, we find him driving team for him ; and at ten he was accustomed to drive a pair of horses alone from Georgetown, where he lived, forty miles, to Cincinnati, and bring back a load. Like many farmer-boys, he was very fond of horses, and, though a mere lad, showed great skill in managing them, and acquired a knack, no one knew how, of breaking them to pace. Most of the incidents of his boyhood differ but little from those which make up the life of boys of poor parents, whose necessities compel them to work instead of play. Some of them, however, exhibit those traits which have since distinguished him—in fact, have led to his success. That tenacity of purpose, which no obstacles or dangers can shake, was illustrated in the persistency with which he once clung to a circus-pony that he was induced to mount in the ring. The trained little animal could not, with its utmost efforts, shake him off; and the ring-master, disappointed to see him succeed, where others always failed, let loose a monkey, which sprung up behind him and mounted on his shoulders, and began to pull his hair. The spectators shouted, and the pony struggled still more frantically to get rid of its rider; but Ulysses, with his face wearing the same imperturbable expression it in after-years wore in battle, rode on, until pony and ring-master had to give it up.

That quiet, fixed resolution, which is such a marked feature in his character to-day, he possessed when a mere lad. His father possessed great confidence in his ability to take care of himself, and once sent him, when but twelve years of age, to Louisville, alone. We give the incident in his own language. He says:

"It was necessary for me to have a deposition taken there, to be used in a law-suit in which I was engaged in the State of Connecticut. I had written more than once about it to my lawyers, but could not get the business done. 'I can do it,' said Ulysses. So I sent him on the errand alone. Before he started, I gave him an open letter that he might show the captain of the boat, or any one else, if he should have occasion, stating that he was my son, and was going to Louisville on my business. Going down, he happened to meet a neighbor with whom he was acquainted; so he had no occasion to use the letter. But when he came on board a boat, to return, the captain asked him who he was. He told him ; but the captain answered, 'I cannot take you ; you may be running away.' Ulysses then produced my letter, which put every thing right ; and the captain not only treated him with great kindness, but took so much interest in him as to invite him to go as far as Maysville with him, where he had relatives living, free of expense. He brought back the deposition with him, and that enabled me to succeed in making a satisfactory adjustment of my suit." *

The father remembers also the following incident, of which doubtless similar may be related of hundreds of others who never reached any eminence, yet it has a peculiar interest in the light of after events. He says, " I will relate another circumstance which I have never mentioned before, which you may use as you think proper. He was always regarded as extremely apt in figures. When he was ten years old a distinguished phrenologist came along and stayed several days in the place. He was frequently asked to examine heads blindfolded. Among others, Ulysses was placed in the chair. The phrenologist felt his head for several minutes without saying any

* Written for the " Ledger."

thing; at length, a noted doctor asked him if the boy had a capacity for mathematics. The phrenologist, after some further examination, said, ' You need not be surprised if you see this boy fill the *presidential chair* some time.' " *

Now, whether the opinion of the phrenologist was worth any thing or not, or whether it was a mere piece of flattery, or a scientific opinion, may not, perhaps, be of much consequence; but one thing is certain, if he had not been different from the ordinary class of boys of his age he never would have been selected as a subject for public examination. This fact alone shows that he was a marked lad, possessing certain positive, distinct qualities which distinguished him from others. If it were not so, the examination of his head would have been without significance. Another anecdote is told of him when a little older, showing that great self-reliance which also formed so remarkable a trait of his manhood. Sent once to the woods with a team to bring some pieces of timber, where his father supposed there were workmen to do the loading for him, he, on his arrival, found no one there. Instead, however, of returning with the team and reporting the state of affairs, he immediately set about performing the herculean task himself; and unhitching the horses, he with their help hauled up the pieces of hewn

* "The Hero Boy," by Rev. P. C. Headley.

timber on a half-fallen tree, that served as an inclined plane, the ends projecting over. He then backed the wagon under them, and hitching a chain to the ends, pulled them one after another in, and started for home with his load.

The means for securing that mental discipline and culture necessary to fit him for any position of eminence were wanting in the little town where he resided. His moral training, however, was excellent. Though his parents were not the old rigid Scotch Covenanters, they had the Scotch probity and prudence, and inculcated right principles into the boy, and it is said of him what can be said of few lads, that he was never known to tell a lie or use a profane word.

He devoted himself to his father's business of tanning leather with reluctance, preferring to drive a team instead.

But while he was thus growing a strong, broad-shouldered young man in an obscure western village, he was not satisfied with his lot. Besides, his father felt that he ought to have the benefit of a better education than could be obtained at home. It was a subject of much anxious thought with him, for he believed that his son had capacity for a more important position than that which the trade of a tanner would give him. But his means were limited—the want of money, which chains so many gifted minds to the mere effort to obtain a

2

livelihood in the dull routine in which they have been brought up, stood sadly in the way of young Grant being placed in the more enlarged sphere for which he seemed to be fitted.

There was, however, one way of securing an education, and that was by adopting the profession of arms and obtaining the appointment of Cadet at West Point. Besides, Ulysses had a strong inclination for a military life, and so it was decided to apply for a situation in the United States Military Academy.

Thus, in the early struggles of this Western youth—in the discussion and balancing of various plans and projects, fate was silently weaving the first threads of that web on whose completion hung most important destinies.

CHAPTER II.

IN accordance with the plan finally adopted, the father applied to Mr. Morris, member of the Senate from Ohio, to obtain the desired situation for his son. But he was unable to assist him, as his promise had already been given to another applicant; but in stating the fact to Mr. Grant, he informed him that there was a vacancy in the congressional district of Mr. Hamer, and advised him to apply to him. He did so, and Mr. Hamer at once interested himself in the case, and on his application Ulysses received the appointment. Mr.

Grant had another son named Simpson, the mother's family-name, and in some way Mr. Hamer got the idea that this was the middle name of Ulysses; hence in his application for the appointment he gave the name of the applicant as Ulysses S. Grant, and it was so entered on the books at West Point. Ulysses tried several times to have it changed, but at length gave it up, and he became U. S. Grant. Thus, by mere accident he acquired those initials which, according to the conceit of this or that person, have been made to stand for so many different things: Uncle Sam Grant, United States Grant, Unconditional Surrender Grant.

It was a trying position for the awkward, rough, Western youth of eighteen to be thrown suddenly into the company of a hundred young men, many of whom had received the advantages of a good education and a wide intercourse with the world. He saw at once that he must make up for his deficiency by close application. Acquainted only with the first rudiments of the difficult mathematics he must become master of, ignorant of French and drawing, he had to begin at the beginning. Taking patiently the fagging still permitted at West Point during the Freshman year, to the disgrace of the institution, he applied himself diligently to the arduous work before him. His aptitude for mathematics was now of great service to him, and learning thoroughly what he undertook, he made slow but steady progress, and soon distanced many who with the same application and energy would have been far in advance of him.

At the close of the first year, after the examination, the usual thinning process took place by which many were thrown back to go over again the studies they so little understood; but young Grant, notwithstanding the difficulties he had labored under, took his place with the successful ones in the next class. Passing through this year in the same studious way, he was made in the subsequent class of 1841 sergeant of battalion.

In the examination of this year more cadets were thrown back, and the Western boy found himself in a class dwindled down to nearly half of its original number. The last year he was promoted to the position of officer of cadets, and finished his course successfully. Though not, like the brilliant McPherson, graduating at the head of his class, he stood No. twenty-one, which was above the average.

His acquisitions were of a solid, substantial character, but in no one thing did he evince any peculiar excellence, except in horsemanship. He was a bold and skillful rider, and showed here his boyish fondness for horses and knowledge of their character, which to this day distinguish him.

He could talk "horse" then as well as now when badgered by politicians.

Only thirty of the original number that formed the class with which young Grant began his career graduated with him. Some of those successful ones he afterwards served with under a common flag, and still later met them as foes on the battle-field.

Brevetted as second lieutenant of the Fourth Infantry, he now joined his regiment at Jefferson Barracks, in Missouri, empty yet of any actual command. He had little to do beyond the routine of daily duties, except now and then to accompany an expedition along the frontiers, to look after troublesome Indians.

In 1844 his regiment was ordered to the Red River, in Louisiana. His life here was dull and dreary to one ambitious of distinction.

But the rumors of hostilities between the United States and Mexico, growing out of the boundary line, roused every young officer into new life. The right or wrong of a war troubled them but little, so that the road to distinction was opened to them.

In 1845, when Gen. Taylor was sent to the Rio Grande with an army of occupation, Grant's regiment formed part of his force. In the meantime he was transferred to the Seventh regiment, but this change was so repugnant to him that he applied to the government for permission to remain with his old regiment. This request was granted, and in 1846 we find him a full second lieutenant, lying with his regiment at Matamoras. Marching with Taylor to Point Isabel, he, on the return of the little army to relieve the sore-pressed garrison of Fort Brown, took his first lesson in practical war, at Palo Alto. In this, his first battle, he acted with that settled coolness and promptness which have always characterized him. The shout of victory rolling over the field had hardly died away before the sharp, decisive action of Resaca de la Palma completed the discomfiture of the Mexican army, and it fled over the river in confusion. Then came the long, joyful shout of welcome from the manned ramparts of Fort Brown, as the liberated garrison saw their deliverers marching gayly forward to the sound of triumphant music.

The war had now fairly begun, and Taylor took up his line of march for Monterey. In the desperate fight for this place Grant's regiment bore its appropriate part.

The young soldier had now received the full baptism of fire necessary to his introduction into the stern realities of his profession.

When Scott organized his force for the invasion of Mexico, Grant's regiment was among the number of those he withdrew from Taylor.

After the fall of Vera Cruz, the army started for the Mexican capital, and Grant received the appointment of quartermaster of his regiment, and at the same time acted on the staff of his general.

The long and toilsome marches, the bloody battles, the splendid strategy of Scott, that make up the history of the weeks and months that followed, were an important part of the training of Grant, the results of which were to be seen in future years.

At the battle of Molino del Rey his gallant bearing won for him promotion on the spot, as first lieutenant, though Congress did not confirm the appointment.

At the battle of Chapultepec, which followed in a few days, he had an opportunity to especially distinguish himself. Nearly half way up the slope to the foot of the castle's walls, stood a strong field-work, so flanked by ravines and chasms that its capture was a most hazardous enterprise. But it must be carried before the storming parties with fascines and ladders could advance, and the battalion ordered to take it marched boldly forward, under a fierce, withering fire. The ranks were frightfully thinned and more or less disorganized, especially when they got in close musket-range of the redoubt, and success became doubtful. At this critical moment Grant rallied a few men of his regiment, and with Captain

Brookes, who did the same with that of the Second Artillery, suddenly wheeled to the left, and enveloping the enemy's right flank with their rapid fire, rolled it back in confusion. Other regiments now coming up to their support, the Mexicans fled, and the redoubt was carried. This flank movement was a brilliant conception in the heat of the battle, and was carried out against overwhelming numbers, and in the face of a deadly fire. It was mentioned in the various reports of the officers, and among others by Col., subsequently General Garland, who after describing it says, "I must not omit to call attention to Lieut. Grant, who acquitted himself most nobly upon several occasions, under my observation." It would be interesting to know the details of the events in which he " *acquitted himself most nobly.*" But this much is on record, that in galloping all steadily through storms of shot and shell to deliver orders, and rallying a handful of men right under the enemy's guns, and heading the desperate charge, "he acquitted himself most nobly."

One of the occasions referred to by Garland, was in the battle of Molino del Rey, which occurred a few days before that of Chapultepec. The thrilling scene was described to us by General Garland himself. After the battery midway to the mills on the top of the slope was carried by the desperate charge of Major Wright, with a handful of men, the Mex-

2*

ican forces were divided, and the battle resolved it
self into two separate attacks. Garland commanded
one of the columns, which now, with Drum's battery of only two pieces at its head, took up its
desperate march for the works on the top of the
hill.   The advance was slow and toilsome, for that
slight battery had to contend against overwhelming odds, and its progress gauged that of the column.   Covering the infantry, it had to make a path
for it to the walls of the mill.   Garland watched
with the deepest anxiety the effect of its fire, for
should it be silenced he would be compelled to
march over the wreck of the guns, and push the
uncovered, naked head of his column up to the very
muzzles of the Mexican cannon, or retreat.   He
did not mean that any contingency should force
him to the latter alternative, for when the moment of decision arrived he had resolved to charge
with the bayonet, over barricades, guns, gunners,
and all.   At length, weary with the slow and
deadly effort, he, while Drum, after a short and
rapid fire, was advancing his pieces, called a drum-
mer and bade him place his drum on the ground
for a seat, on which he might rest for a moment.
The instant after he was seated, a grapeshot
struck the cap from his head, and grazed the skull
so closely as to carry away his wig.   Had he been
standing erect it would have passed through his
body.

At length, under the overwhelming fire of the enemy's batteries, every gunner attached to Drum's pieces was killed or wounded. Garland then called on the infantry to supply their places, but not a man volunteered. They had one and all toiled bravely forward to the spot where the bayonet must decide the conflict, and they would not throw aside their muskets at such a critical moment. But those guns must be served, for every shot was worth a whole regiment of men in demolishing the defences preparatory to the final assault. A few young men seeing the dilemma, sprang forward, manned the pieces, and rolled them forward through the iron hail till they were within a hundred yards of the hostile batteries, and there played on the foe with a rapidity and power nothing could withstand. *Each one of those gallant youthful artillerists was a West Point officer.* Right there in the blaze of the hostile guns they loaded and fired as coolly as though on parade. Carried away by such a noble example of self-devotion, the soldiers charged with a high and ringing cheer, and clearing every obstacle that opposed their progress, swept the defences with resistless power. No wonder Garland could say of such officers, " *they acquitted themselves most nobly.*"

At the outset of the campaign Scott had called the West Point officers about him, and told them that he was entering on it " with a halter around his neck," with " *the end of it at Washington*," and said he, " I expect you, my young *friends, to get this halter* off for me." Grant was one of the brave officers who *did* get it off.

At length, Grant had the proud satisfaction of riding into the grand plaza of the Mexican capital beside his commander, and seeing the stars and stripes hoisted on its public buildings. That young officer, standing proudly in the heart of the conquered city, and the tanner's son with his pole and hook fishing out hides from his father's vats, present a striking contrast, and yet such, in some form or other, our republican institutions furnish every year, to the astonishment of the old world.

The siege, the toilsome march, the consummate strategy exhibited in every important movement, the bloody battles, furnished a school in which young Grant was trained for a position of which he then little dreamed. He was one of those who in time of war, if death spares them, rise rapidly in rank. But the proclamation of peace soon ended his dreams of preferment, and the army was scattered through the various posts of our wide country.

Young Grant returned home, and in August of 1848 married a Miss Dent, daughter of a merchant in St. Louis, Missouri.

His regiment being stationed at Detroit, he,

after a short furlough, joined it there, still holding the position of quartermaster. It was afterwards transferred to Sackett's Harbor, on the
northern frontier of New York State. Subsequently the regiment was ordered to California,
where, after its arrival, a portion was detached
for duty in Oregon, then almost as much out of
the country as our new possession of Alaska now
is. Nothing could be more dreary than life in
this remote region, far away from his family—
through summer and the long winter, day after
day, and month after month, the same monoto-
nous round of duties. The morning reveillé—
the drill—the evening tattoo—these constitute
the excitements of a soldier's life on one of our
frontier posts. No places of amusement, no so-
cial circles in which to spend an hour, no libraries,
papers and letters coming only at long intervals,
combine to make an officer's life at one of them
dismal and lonely in the extreme. For two years
Captain Grant (for his rank had been confirmed),
was thus shut up in that then remote, thinly settled territory.

The Mexican war had promoted so many young
officers that there was no probability that Grant
would get beyond the rank of captain till his head
was gray. He had now served more than the
eight years required by the government to pay for
four years of education at West Point, and hence

felt at liberty to consult his own interest in future. Other officers had resigned, and were already on the fair road to wealth and competence, and there was no reason why he should waste the best part of his life in idleness. There seemed no prospect of his services in the field ever being needed by the government; besides, if they were he could volunteer them. In fact, there was every motive to induce an active, enterprising young man to leave the army at that time, and many, especially northern officers, did. Grant followed their example, and, resigning his commission, returned home to try his fortune in civil life. Taking a small farm near his father-in-law, in the vicinity of St. Louis, he settled down to the quiet life of a western farmer. A person familiar with this part of his life says :

It is well known that when he resided in Missouri he was very poor, and lived in a small, uncomfortable house, cultivating a farm of a few acres. His chief income was derived by hauling wood to the City of St. Louis. He used to supply Hon. Henry T. Blow, of that city, with his fuel. Mr. Blow was elected to the Thirty-ninth Congress, and on one occasion went with his wife to one of Gen. Grant's popular receptions. Mrs. Blow wondered if General Grant would recognize her as an old friend or acquaintance, under the different circumstances of their relative situations in life. Well, Mrs. Blow had not been long at the General's before he came to her and said, "Mrs. Blow, I remember you well. What great changes have taken place since we last met!" "Yes, General," said Mrs. B., "the war is over." "I did not mean that," he replied; "I mean with myself. Do you recollect when I used to supply your husband with wood, and pile it myself, and measure it too, and go to his office for my pay?" "Oh, yes, General, your face was familiar in those days." "Mrs. Blow, those were happy days; for I was doing the best I could to support my family."

He afterwards endeavored to add to his income by the collection of debts for others, though dunning delinquent debtors proved neither a pleasant nor a profitable business.

The ex-captain was not getting along very prosperously in his new vocation, and his chances of obtaining even a competence were very doubtful. His father learning the unfavorable condition of affairs, wrote to him, proposing that he should come on to Illinois and assist in the leather trade. It promised to be far more lucrative than his present occupation, and he accepted the offer and removed to Galena. In 1859, over a modest store, the sign of "Grant & Son, Leather Dealers," could be seen. It is said that he did not prove a very active merchant. Handling sides of leather was very different from handling a sword, and chaffering with customers came rather hard after being so many years accustomed to command. Still the business was in a flourishing condition, and to all human appearance his occupation was fixed for life. He expected to be leather-dealer, nothing more, and his highest ambition could reach no farther than moderate wealth.

Here the history of his life might have ended

but for the civil war into which we were plunged. Although like McClellan, and Sherman, and Hooker, and Slocum, and others, he was out of the service, no sooner did the country need his experience and aid than his civil pursuits were cast aside. It is to the everlasting honor of West Point, and a complete refutation of the slanders uttered against it, that though so many officers had resigned their commissions, and a portion of them were on the high road to wealth, every one, to a man, abandoned at once his profession or business and took up his long-neglected sword, and offered his services to his country. From the counter, from the law-office, from the engineer's room, and from the school-room, they came swarming at her call.

CHAPTER III.

A BRIGADIER-GENERAL.

His Politics—Raises a Company and takes it to Springfield—He offers his services to the Government—His letter unanswered—Assists Governor Yates in organizing the troops—Made Colonel of the 21st Regiment—Endeavors to get on McClellan's staff—Serves in Missouri—Made Brigadier-General—Amusing Anecdote of him—Makes Cairo his Headquarters—Occupies Paducah—Proclamation to the People—Correspondence with General Polk—Battle of Belmont—His congratulatory Order—Letter to his Father, giving an account of the Action—The Cairo Expedition—Order respecting it—Retaliatory Order—Proposes to Halleck to seize Fort Henry—Rude treatment by the latter.

Though opposed to the election of Mr. Lincoln, because he believed that it would intensify the hostility already existing between the North and South, he took no active part in politics, contenting himself simply with voting. Then, as now, he thought little of party—his country was his party, her welfare his only object, and hence he watched with the deepest anxiety the gathering elements of civil strife on every side.

The news of the fall of Fort Sumter—of the insult to the flag he had so often battled under, aroused all the slumbering fire of his nature, and he immediately organized a company of volunteers and took it to Springfield, Illinois. He then wrote a letter to the adjutant-general, offering his services to his country, but it was never even acknowledged.

With that modesty which always distinguished him, he did not, like others, apply for a high rank, but was willing to serve in any capacity the government might select. But he was too obscure to be wanted when so many eminent civilians offered themselves as commanders.

His name was in the meantime presented to Governor Yates, by a friend, who spoke of his military education and his gallant record, acquired during the Mexican war. The governor needing some one to assist him in arranging the quota of the State, that had been called out, commissioned him as adjutant and set him to work.

A short time after, the governor, receiving a request from the President to send on two names for the position of brigadier-general, proposed to Grant to send his. The latter, however, declined the offer, preferring, he said, to earn his promotion. Having completed the work required of him to meet the first call on the State for troops, he was in the middle of June commissioned a colonel of the 21st Regiment, that its own colonel could not manage. Below the medium height, and shabby in appearance, the new colonel did not make a favorable impression on the regiment, but the men soon found they had a character to deal with that would not admit of trifling. He was now,

at last, in the army of the Union.   He had offered
his services to the general government, but no
notice was taken of it.   He had also tried to get
on the staff of McClellan, but failed.   Hearing of
the latter's appointment as Major-General of Ohio
Volunteers, he modestly thought, as an old army
friend, he might offer him a position on his staff,
and went to Cincinnati to see him.   He called on
him twice, but finding him not in either time, and
seeing a crowd of applicants around his headquarters, he became discouraged, and returned
home.   On what slight events a man's destiny
sometimes turns!   Had Grant obtained an interview with McClellan, he doubtless would have received the coveted appointment, and shared that
commander's fortune and fate, and been lost to the
war.

However, it will be seen that the whole credit
of putting Grant in the field belongs to Governor
Yates.

Grant's regiment was first assigned to Pope's
department in Northern Missouri, where his duty
was to guard the Hannibal & St. Joseph Railroad.
Other regiments were in this region, and he became for a time acting brigadier-general.   On the
7th of August, 1861, he received his commission
as brigadier-general, for which he was indebted to
E. B. Washburn, a fellow-townsman, though
scarce an acquaintance, who ever after, as member

of Congress, stood nobly by him when all others seemed ready to desert him. He was now sent to Southern Missouri, which was threatened by Jeff. Thompson. He marched to Ironton and Marble Creek, fortifying and garrisoning the latter places, and thence to Jefferson City, which was reported to be in danger.

The following incident, which occurred on this long and tedious march, illustrates one phase of Grant's character. It is said that he is as "distinguished for his eccentric humor, as for his skill and bravery." In this case there was a certain grimness in the humor, for while it raised a laugh on one side, on the other it cut like a sword, for it administered a stern rebuke.

A member of his staff says :

"When Grant was a brigadier in Southeast Missouri, he commanded an expedition against the rebels under Jeff. Thompson in Northeast Arkansas. The distance from the starting point of the expedition to the supposed rendezvous of the rebels was about one hundred and ten miles, and the greater portion of the route lay through a howling wilderness. The imaginary suffering that our soldiers endured during the first two days of their march was enormous. It was impossible to steal or 'confiscate' uncultivated real estate, and not a hog, or a chicken, or an ear of corn was anywhere to be seen. On the third day, however, affairs looked more hopeful, for a few small specks of ground, in a state of partial cultivation, were here and there visible. On that day, Lieutenant Wickfield, of an Indiana cavalry regiment, commanded the advance guard, consisting of eight mounted men. About noon he came up to a small farmhouse, from the outward appearance of which he judged that there might be something fit to eat inside. He halted his company, dismounted, and with two second lieutenants entered the dwelling. He knew that Grant's incipient fame had already gone out through all that country, and it occurred to him that by representing himself to be the general he might obtain the best the house afforded. So, assuming a very imperative demeanor, he accosted the inmates of the house, and told them he must have something for himself and staff to eat. They desired to know who he was, and he told them that he was Brigadier-General Grant. At the sound of that name they all flew around with alarming alacrity, and served up about all they had in the house, taking great pains all the while to make loud professions of loyalty. The lieutenants ate as much as they could of the not over-sumptuous meal, but which was, nevertheless, good for that country, and demanded what was to pay. 'Nothing.' And they went on their way rejoicing.

"In the meantime General Grant, who had halted his army a few miles further back for a brief resting spell, came in sight of, and was rather favorably impressed with the appearance of, this same house. Riding up to the fence in front of the door, he desired to know if they would cook him a meal.

"'No,' said a female, in a gruff voice; 'General Grant and his staff have just been here, and eaten every thing in the house except one pumpkin pie.

"'Humph,' murmured Grant; 'what is your name?'

"'Selvidge,' replied the woman.

"Casting a half dollar in at the door, he asked if she would keep that pie till he sent an officer for it; to which she replied that she would.

"That evening, after the camping ground had been selected, the various regiments were notified that there would be a grand parade at half-past six, for orders. Officers would see that all their men turned out, etc.

"In five minutes the camp was in a perfect uproar, and filled with all sorts of rumors. Some thought the enemy were upon them, it being so unusual to have parades when on a march.

"At half-past six the parade was formed, ten columns deep and nearly a quarter of a mile in length."

After the usual routine of ceremonies, the acting assistant adjutant-general read the following order :

HEADQUARTERS, ARMY IN THE FIELD.

SPECIAL ORDER NO. —.

Lieutenant Wickfield, of the Indiana Cavalry, having on this day eaten every thing in Mrs. Selvidge's house, at the crossing of the Trenton and Pocahontas and Black River and Cape Girardeau roads, except one pumpkin-pie, Lieutenant Wickfield is hereby ordered to return with an escort of one hundred cavalry, and eat that pie also. U. S. GRANT,
Brigadier-General Commanding.

One can scarcely imagine the astonishment which the promulgation of this order caused, made as it was with all the seriousness of one just preceding a battle, nor of the uproarious merriment and laughter of the soldiers as the true state of the case became known. Shout after shout rolled over the field as the astounded lieutenant ordered up his escort and trotted out of camp. There was no evading the order. Back along the road he had just travelled so wearily, he made his way to the widow's house, and deliberately ordered out the solitary pie he had been so kind as to leave for his general a little while before.

It was carried off as a grand joke, yet there was a sting to it. It required no explanation. Each officer learned two things by it he would not be apt soon to forget. First, not to

forage right in front of his commander without
any reference to his needs; second, to be careful
how he assumed his character and authority anywhere.   The last was doubtless the chief lesson
Grant designed to inculcate.   Reports and slanders of all kinds against a general who was compelled to march through a divided country were
rife enough, without having any act that a subordinate might commit charged to him.   We venture to say Lieutenant Wickfield has never eaten
a pie since, without thinking of that one which
required an escort of a hundred men to dispose of.

The district of Southeastern Missouri was
placed under his command on the 1st of September, by Fremont, who succeeded Pope, and included such portions on the borders of Kentucky
and Tennessee as he might deem best to occupy.
His headquarters were at Cairo, a most important
point strategetically, for here the four rivers, Mississippi, Ohio, Cumberland, and Tennessee, unite.
The two first kept open his own communications,
and the two latter carried supplies to the enemy.
Grant early saw how vital the occupation and holding of it was.   Kentucky claimed to be neutral
territory, thereby forbidding the establishment of
any military post within her boundaries; yet Columbus and Hickman, both in the limits of the
State, and situated on the banks of the Mississippi, had been seized and held by the rebels, as well

as the central position of Bowling Green. Grant
felt that it would not do to regard a neutrality
which allowed the enemy to seize all the important points in the State; and Paducah, at the
mouth of the Tennessee, commanding the navigation both of it and the Ohio, being a most important place, he determined to seize it before it
fell into their hands. Delay was dangerous, and
if he waited until the vexed question of occupying
neutral territory was thoroughly discussed, it
might be too late. He did not even apply for permission to his immediate superior, Fremont, but
simply notified him that he was going to move at
once, unless he received a telegram to the contrary.
He did not delay a moment longer than necessary, but on the 6th of September despatched a
steamer loaded with troops to occupy it. To
make it as little offensive as possible, he issued
the following proclamation to the people, explana-
tory of the motives that governed him:

PADUCAH, KY., September 6, 1861.

To the Citizens of Paducah:

I am come among you, not as an enemy, but as your
fellow-citizen. Not to maltreat you, nor annoy you,
but to respect and enforce the rights of all loyal citizens.
An enemy in rebellion against our common Government has taken possession of, and planted his guns upon
the soil of Kentucky, and fired upon you. Columbus
and Hickman are in his hands. He is moving upon
your city. I am here to defend you against this enemy,

to assist the authority and sovereignty of your Government. *I have nothing to do with opinions,* and shall deal only with armed rebellion, and its aiders and abettors. You can pursue your usual avocations without fear. The strong arm of the Government is here to protect its friends and punish its enemies. Whenever it is manifest that you are able to defend yourselves, and maintain the authority of the Government, and protect the rights of loyal citizens, I shall withdraw the forces under my command.   U. S. GRANT,
Brigadier-General Commanding.

The legislature of the State remonstrated against the seizure of Paducah as an act of aggression, and a correspondence followed between it and Grant, in which the latter vindicated his course in a courteous manner, and quietly held the post.

The next month he received a communication from Gen. Polk, proposing an exchange of prisoners—several having been taken in portions of his department. To this he sent the following short reply:

HEADQUARTERS DEPT. SOUTHEAST MISSOURI,
CAIRO, October 11, 1861.

General:

Yours of this date is just received. In regard to an exchange of prisoners, as proposed, I can of my own accordance make none. I recognize no "Southern Confederacy" myself, but will communicate with higher authorities for their views. Should I not be sustained, I will find means of communicating with you.

Respectfully, your obedient servant,

U. S. GRANT,
Brigadier-General Commanding.

To Major-General Polk, Columbus, Ky.

During this month Col. Plummer obtained a victory over Jeff. Thompson in Southeast Missouri, which brought out a highly complimentary order from Grant.

Columbus, only a few miles below the mouth of the Ohio, was the first of a series of defences erected by the enemy along the Mississippi to prevent its navigation by our steamers, and the whole country, especially the Northwest, were clamorous for its capture. In the meantime, word having been received that troops were about being moved from this point to coöperate with Price in Missouri, Grant was ordered to make a demonstration against Columbus to prevent it.

The enemy at this time had a large force under Polk at Columbus, also a camp and garrison opposite, at Belmont. Grant, finding his force too small to attack the former place, determined to break up the camp at the latter. In order not to be overwhelmed by the garrison at Columbus, he asked Gen. Smith, commanding at Paducah, to make a demonstration against the former place, which he did, by sending a small force, that was not to advance nearer, however, than twelve or fifteen miles. He also despatched another detachment on the Kentucky side, for the same purpose, with directions not to advance nearer than Ellicott's Mills, twelve miles from Columbus.

The force under his own command was two

thousand eight hundred and fifty strong.   These
were embarked in transports on the evening of the
6th of November, and moved down to the foot of
Island No. Ten, within eleven miles of Columbus,
where they stopped for the night, and tied up to the
Kentucky shore.   At daylight next morning the
transports passed quietly down-stream till almost
within range of the rebel guns, when they were
quickly pushed to the Missouri shore, and the
troops landed.   The gunboats Tyler and Lexington accompanied them.

The cannon were hauled by hand up the steep
banks amid dropping shot and shell from the
rebel encampment, from which, as it occupied an
elevated position, Grant's movements could be distinctly seen.

The troops, after landing, passed through some
cornfields and halted, preparatory to an advance.
Colonel Buford was ordered to make a detour to
the right, and come down on the rebel camp in
that direction.   The main army then moved forward till it arrived within a mile and a half of the
abatis that the rebels had piled in their front.
This was composed of trees, that for several hundred yards had been felled with their tops pointing
outward, and the limbs sharpened, so that a dense
breastwork of points confronted any force advancing down the river.   The gunboats in the meantime were engaging the batteries at Columbus.

As the columns advanced, the dropping fire of the skirmishers showed that the enemy had been met, and was determined to dispute every inch of ground to their encampment. The Thirtieth and Thirty-first having been sent forward to relieve the skirmishers, a spirited action was commenced, which lasted for half an hour, in which our ranks were thrown into disorder. Colonels Foulke and Logan, however, soon rallied them, and drove the enemy back for a quarter of a mile, where, being reinforced, they attempted to turn McClernand's left flank. Being defeated in this by a prompt movement of Colonel Logan, and suddenly swept by a fierce fire of artillery and musketry, they began to show signs of wavering. Foulke and Logan, sword in hand, shouted to their men, urging them forward by stirring appeals, which were answered with cheers, and these raw troops stood up like veterans to their work.

The officers, however, had to set the example of exposure, for now, added to the fire in front, the batteries at Columbus, which had ceased firing at the gunboats, sent their huge projectiles crashing through the tree-tops overhead. Grant and McClernand were both in the thickest of the fight, exposing themselves like the commonest soldier. The latter, while leading a gallant charge, received a ball in his holster ; and the horse of Grant was killed under him. While this struggle was going on, a tremendous fire from the Twenty-seventh broke over the woods, to the right and rear of the rebel encampment. The other regiments having now worked their way into line through the brushwood, the whole closed sternly up on three sides of the abatis at once, and sweeping rapidly forward, drove the enemy pell-mell through it. Following close on their heels, our excited troops dashed through and over with a cheer. The sight of the Twenty-seventh in the open space beyond roused all their ardor, and they, too, soon stood in the clear ground around the camp. The artillery opened on the tents, not three hundred yards distant, and the rebels broke for the river and the woods like a flock of frightened sheep.

The torch was then applied to the tents and baggage, and in a moment the spot was wrapt in flames and smoke. The enraged enemy across the river at Columbus now turned their batteries on the smoking camp, and soon shot and shell were hurtling through the air on every side. Grant saw at once that he could not stay here; and to make matters worse, he was informed that the rebels had thrown a large force across the river, directly in his rear, and between him and his transports.

Without showing the least surprise or anxiety, he quietly said, " Well, if that is so, we must cut our way out as we cut our way in." Soon after, in reply to an expression of anxiety as to the result, by an officer, he said, "We have whipped them once, and can whip them again." Ordering the artillery to the front, he gave the command to advance, and his little army moved straight on the astonished enemy, and reached the transports waiting to receive them.

It was a spirited contest. The Seventh Iowa especially fought gallantly, losing their lieutenant-colonel and major, the colonel himself being wounded. Our total loss was about five hundred, while that of the rebels was nearly a thousand—a great disparity, especially when it is considered that we were the attacking party, and the former fought a part of the time behind defences. Two guns were brought off, and two more spiked, and some battle-flags captured, together with many prisoners. Grant was delighted with the conduct of his men, and issued the following congratulatory order to his troops, the first he ever penned after a battle:

HEADQUARTERS DISTRICT, S. C., Mo.,
CAIRO, *November* 8, 1861.

The General commanding this Military District returns his thanks to the troops under his command at the battle of Belmont on yesterday.

It has been his fortune to have been in all the battles fought in Mexico by Generals Scott and Taylor, except Buena Vista, and he never saw one more hotly contested, or where the troops behaved with more gallantry.

Such courage will insure victory wherever our flag

may be borne and protected by such a class of men. To the brave men who fell, the sympathy of the country is due, and will be manifested in a manner unmistakable.

U. S. GRANT,
Brigadier-General Commanding.

Though this action was gallantly fought, it injured, rather than helped, the opening prospects of Grant. It being generally thought that the object of the expedition was to take Columbus, it was regarded as a total failure, and so reported by the rebels.

Since the war he has written a full and complete report of the whole movement, and requested it to be substituted for the one that he made at the time. In this, which is given in the Appendix, he shows that he simply executed orders ; so that whatever blame may attach to the expedition, it does not rest on him.

More interesting, however, than this report, is the following private letter to his father, giving an account of the battle, and showing his feelings at its result. He says that he can assert " with great gratification, that every man, without a single exception, set an example to their comrades that inspired a confidence that will always give victory when there is the slightest possibility of gaining one. I feel truly proud to command such men.

" From here we fought our way from tree to tree, through the woods to Belmont, about two and a half miles, the enemy contesting every foot of ground. Here the enemy had strengthened their position by felling the trees for two or three hundred yards, and sharpening their limbs, making a sort of abatis. Our men charged through, making the victory complete, giving us possession of their camp and garrison equipage, artillery, and every thing else.

"We got a great many prisoners. The majority, however, succeeded in getting aboard their steamers and pushing across the river. We burned every thing possible, and started back, having accomplished all that we went for, and even more. Belmont is entirely covered by the batteries from Columbus, and is worth nothing as a military position,—cannot be held without Columbus.

"The object of the expedition was to prevent the enemy from sending a force into Missouri to cut off troops I had sent there for a special purpose, and to prevent re-enforcing Price.

"Besides being well fortified at Columbus, their number far exceeded ours, and it would have been folly to have attacked them. We found the Confederates well armed, and brave. On our return, stragglers, that had been left in our rear (now front), fired into us, and more recrossed the river and gave us battle for a full mile, and afterward at the boats, when we were embarking.

3*

"There was no hasty retreating or running away. Taking into account the object of the expedition, the victory was complete. It has given confidence in the officers and men of this command, that will enable us to lead them in any future action without fear of the result. General McClernand (who, by the way, acted with great coolness and courage throughout) and myself each had our horses shot under us. Most of the field-officers met with the same loss, besides one third of them being themselves killed or wounded. As near as can be ascertained, our loss was about two hundred and fifty killed and wounded."

This battle took place on the 7th of November. Four days after, General Halleck superseded Fremont in the Western Department, and Grant's district was enlarged. He now began to assemble troops at Paducah, preparatory to some general movement of the forces under his command. It was generally supposed its objective point was Columbus, and great hopes were entertained that this stronghold, whose occupation by the enemy was a source of such constant irritation to the West, would be captured.

The Cairo expedition, as it was called, commenced in the very heart of winter, and three grand columns, under Paine, McClernand, and C. F. Smith, in all nineteen regiments of infantry, six of cavalry, and seven batteries, moved off into the interior. McClernand, with some five thousand men, made a march of seventy-five miles over ice, and through snow and mud, while the cavalry marched a hundred and forty, and came back again, reporting that some new roads had been discovered, foolish reports exploded, the inhabitants impressed with our military strength, &c., and that apparently was all. The movement, however, was in accordance with Halleck's order, and the object of it was to prevent the enemy from sending reinforcements to Buckner at Bowling Green.

An order, designed to guide the conduct of the troops in this expedition, reveals that even balance of Grant's judgment and feelings under all circumstances which forms one of the brightest traits in his character. Swayed neither by false logic nor carried away by passion, he sees the right, and has the firmness to pursue it.

He says, "Disgrace having been brought upon our brave fellows by the bad conduct of some of their members, showing, on all occasions, when passing through territory occupied by sympathizers of the enemy, a total disregard of the rights of citizens, and being guilty of the wanton destruction of private property, the General Commanding desires and intends to enforce a change in this respect."   *   *   *   *   *

"It is ordered that the severest punishment

be inflicted upon every soldier who is guilty of taking or destroying private property, and any commissioned officer guilty of like conduct, or of countenancing it, shall be deprived of his sword, and expelled from the army, not to be permitted to return," &c.

It will stand recorded to his enduring honor, that, amid all the exasperation, public clamor, and private temptations, that carried so many beyond the limits and laws of civilized warfare, he maintained a character above reproach. Many of our officers were guilty of atrocious violations of private property, whose conduct has thus far escaped public condemnation; but when the present chaotic state of affairs has wholly given place to calm reflection and Christian feeling, they will stand side by side in history with those epauletted marauders that disgraced the English flag, both in our first and second wars with England.

Grant's record in this respect is untarnished. What he was at first, he continued to be to the last, temperate in judgment, dispassionate in feeling, and forbearing in the hour of victory.

But while he could be thus forbearing, and show himself superior to petty revenge and a false public sentiment, he could be severe and relentless in the discharge of duty, no matter what suffering it might cause, or charge of cruelty it might provoke.

Hearing that his pickets were shot by the inhabitants who sympathized with the rebels, and yet whose property he was protecting, he issued the following order:

HEADQUARTERS, CAIRO, January 11, 1862.

Brigadier-General Paine, Bird's Point:

I understand that four of our pickets were shot this morning. If this is so, and appearances indicate that the assassins were citizens, not regularly organized in the rebel army, the whole country should be cleared out for six miles around, and word given that all citizens making their appearance within those limits are liable to be shot.

To execute this, patrols should be sent out in all directions, and bring into camp, at Bird's Point, all citizens, together with their subsistence, and require them to remain, under the penalty of death and destruction of their property, until properly relieved.

Let no harm befall these people, if they quietly submit; but bring them in and place them in camp below the breastwork, and have them properly guarded.

The intention is not to make political prisoners of these people, but to cut off a dangerous class of spies.

This applies to all classes and conditions, age and sex. If, however, women and children prefer other protection than we can afford them, they may be allowed to retire beyond the limits indicated—not to return until authorized.

By order of   U. S. GRANT,
                       Brig.-Gen. Commanding.

There is the true Cromwellian ring in this order. A Carlyle would say, here is no "rosewater surgery." Those who have mistaken his leniency for mawkish sensibility, or any sympathy with those who are warring against a common government, may read this with much profit to themselves. It is worth pondering upon. This man, so quiet and moderate, and careful of the wants and rights of peaceable citizens, can strike with the relentless severity of a Nero when outraged justice and humanity require it. His heart, ever open to kindly feelings, delights to mitigate the horrors of war, but it does not prevent his grasp from tightening like steel on the throat of the guilty who abuse his forbearance, and mock his authority.

Smith, one of the commanders of the Cairo Expedition, reporting on his return that Fort Henry, on the Tennessee river, could be easily taken, Grant immediately forwarded this information to Halleck, and soon after asked permission in person to attack it. Halleck, however, treated the proposition with contempt and positive rudeness, which took Grant by surprise. It is difficult to determine what motive prompted this treatment, for the plan to capture this fort had been thoroughly discussed the fall before, in Washington, previous to the departure of Buell for the west.

CHAPTER IV.

FORTS HENRY AND DONELSON.

It has been supposed that the movement against Forts Henry and Donelson originated out West —some giving Halleck, others Grant and Foote, the credit of it; but it had its origin much farther back than the suggestions made by those commanders.

Notwithstanding Halleck's rude treatment of Grant's proposition to seize Fort Henry, he soon found that Government had determined to send an expedition against both it and Fort Donelson, the one on the Cumberland and the other on the Tennessee river. Fort Columbus, deemed so impregnable, was to be flanked by their capture, and a way opened into Tennessee.

Fort Henry was the first object of attack—which was to be a combined one of the naval and land forces—Foote commanding the former and Grant the latter.

A cordon of rebel posts extended at this time across the country from Columbus, on the Missis- sippi, to Richmond, on the James river, and with the line thoroughly broken at any one important point, the loyal armies would be let loose to com- mence their southward march into the enemy's territory. Thomas had partially done it at Mill Spring, but at a point that, especially at mid-winter, rendered an advance impossible. But with the Ten- nessee and Cumberland rivers cleared, our gun- boats could move along with the land forces, car- rying all the supplies needed.

The grand movement was fixed for the fore- part of February; and when, on the morning of the 6th, Foote was unmooring from the bank where the fleet had lain all night, several miles below the fort, he told Grant that he must hurry forward his columns, or he would not be up in time to take part in the action, and secure the prison- ers. The latter smiled incredulously. But re- cent rains had made the cart-paths and roads so heavy, that his progress was slow. As he toiled forward, the heavy cannonading, as Foote advanced to the attack, broke over the woods, and rolled in deep vibrations down the shore, quickening his movements. Before, however, the fort was reached, the firing ceased. Grant was perplexed at the sudden termination of the contest; it did not seem possible that the fort had been taken so soon; it was far more probable that the gunboats had fallen back disabled. He sent scouts forward to ascertain the truth, which soon came galloping back with the news that our flag was flying above the fort. The unexpected tidings rolled down the line, followed by long and deafening cheers. Grant, with his staff, spurred forward, and in half an hour rode into the fort, which was immediately turned over to him.

Halleck, who never was anything but a martinet, though conducting war, as he believed, on scientific principles, now wrote to Grant to hold on and strengthen his position, and forwarded intrenching tools for that purpose. But this, Grant had no intention of doing. Fort Donelson, on the Cumberland, some twelve miles distant, was the key to Nashville, and he at once determined to advance against it. Having left a force in command at Fort Henry, to hold it, he, with some fifteen thousand men, struck across the country, while Foote, with six regiments aboard, went round with his gunboats to attack it on the water front.   Floyd commanded the fort, with Pillow and Buckner under him.

The rebel works here covered a series of hills, some of them steep, and a hundred feet high, while in front of them the trees had been felled with the bushy tops pointing downward and outward, through which it seemed impossible that troops could force their way.   Gullies and ravines also obstructed the advance; two streams setting back from the river protected either flank, while batteries crowned every commanding height.   All these, however, were defences independent of the fort itself, which was three-quarters of a mile back of the first breastworks.   It stood near the river, commanding both it and the interior, and mounted, in all, sixty-five cannon, many of them of large calibre.

Twenty thousand men manned and held this strong position.

Grant appeared before it on the 12th—having driven in the rebel pickets—and began to move his army to the right and left, towards the river, to invest the place, and cut off all avenues of escape to the garrison.   This was slow work, and, strange to say, Grant threw up no intrenchments to protect his troops, or serve as rallying points in case of a repulse—a neglect he would not, a year after, have been guilty of.

Foote, with his fleet, having arrived below the

fort before Grant was ready to coöperate with him, he advanced to the attack, hoping, with his gunboats, to reduce it, as he had Fort Henry. But his fleet, after a short, determined contest, was driven off, badly crippled. Grant saw at once that a delay was now inevitable. He thereupon determined to closely invest the place, and wait till Foote could repair his losses, so as to coöperate with the movements of the army. McClernand's division, composed of three brigades, was sent to the south, closing in with his right on the river, so as to bar all egress to the garrison in that direction, while Gen. Smith held a corresponding position below, his left resting likewise on the river. Between these two divisions the army stretched in a huge semi-circle round the works and the fort.

The rebel commanders, finding themselves thus cooped up, saw at once that immediate action must be taken, or they would be starved into a surrender, and they resolved, by a desperate assault all along Grant's line, to cut their way out to the south, towards Nashville. Saturday dawned damp and chill, for the ground was covered with snow, and the soldiers, roused from their wintry couch, moved stiff and shivering to their places in the ranks. Grant, in the meantime, had repaired on board the flag-ship, to consult with the gallant, disabled Foote, and ascertain when he would be ready for a combined attack on the place.

At this critical juncture, the enemy moved out of his works. The main force, estimated at seven to twelve thousand strong, under Pillow, advanced against McClernand's right wing. The other columns moving against the centre, were mere feints to distract Grant's attention, and prevent him from succouring McClernand. Heralded by three commanding batteries, attended by a regiment of cavalry, Pillow struck the right with a force that threatened to sweep it from the field. But the brave Illinoians stood manfully up to their work, and the battle had hardly commenced before it was at its height. The country was wooded, and covered with underbrush, and broken into hollows and ridges, rendering a survey of the field impossible. Our lines extended for two miles around the fort, and this sudden uproar early in the morning, on our extreme right along the banks of the Cumberland, called each division into line of battle. Wallace was posted next to McClernand, on the top of a high ridge, with forests sweeping off to the front and rear.

When the deep and mingled roar of artillery and musketry first broke over the woods, Wallace thought McClernand had moved on the enemy's works. But the latter was making, instead, des-

perate efforts to hold his own against the overwhelming numbers that, momentarily increasing,
pressed his lines, with a fierceness that threatened
his complete overthrow. Finding, at length, that
his troops were giving way, he, at eight o'clock,
sent off a staff-officer at full speed to Wallace, for
help. The latter had received orders from Grant
to hold the position he occupied, in order to keep
the enemy from escaping in that direction, and
dared not move; and so hurried off the courier with
his despatch to headquarters. But Grant not
being there, the messenger kept on to the gunboats,
in search of him. McClernand, wondering that
no help came, and seeing his lines swinging back,
despite the heroic efforts of the commanders,
hastened off another messenger to Wallace, saying that his flank was turned, and his whole
division was wavering. Wallace could wait no
longer to hear from Grant, and immediately despatched Colonel Croft, commanding a brigade, to
his help. Wallace all this time sat on his horse,
anxiously waiting to hear from Grant, and listen-
ing to the steady crash to the right, that made
the wintry woods resound, when there burst into
view a crowd of fugitives, rushing up the hill on
which he stood. The next moment an officer
dashed on a headlong gallop up the road, shouting, "We are cut to pieces." Seeing his whole
line of the third brigade beginning to shake be-

fore this sudden irruption, he ordered its commander to move on by the right flank, he himself
riding at its head to keep it steady.   He had not
gone far before he met portions of regiments in
full retreat, yet without panic or confusion, calling
aloud for ammunition.   He immediately formed
his line of battle, and sent off to the left for help.
The retiring regiments kept on to the. rear, a
short distance, and refilled their cartridge-boxes.
Scarcely was this new line of battle formed, when
the rebels, following up their advantage on the
right, swooped down, confident of victory, full
upon him.   The shock was firmly met, and the
enemy brought to a pause.   Hours had passed,
in the meantime, in which desperate fighting over
batteries ; repulses and advances of regiments
and brigades; shouts and yells, heard amid the
intervals of the uproar, sweeping like a thunder-
storm through the leafless woods, out of which
burst clouds of smoke, as though a conflagration
was raging below; hurrying crowds in all the
openings,—combined to make up the terrific scene
that was displayed that wintry morning on the
banks of the Cumberland.

All this time, Grant, miles away and ignorant
of what was going on, was slowly riding back to
the army, having finished his consultation with
the Admiral.

Suddenly he saw an officer tearing down the

road, on a wild gallop, towards him. Reining up beside his surprised commander, the latter delivered his despatch, and in a few words explained the critical condition of affairs. Grant immediately put spurs to his horse, but had not gone far before he met General Smith, commanding the left. From a brief conversation with him, he at once comprehended the whole matter, and with that sudden inspiration which belongs to true genius, told him to get ready for a general assault on the enemy's works in his front. He then galloped on to the vortex of the battle. As he advanced, a sight met his gaze that would have appalled a less iron-willed, self-reliant man. Crowds of fugitives covered the fields—even those formations that stood firmest were dreadfully disordered —ammunition was gone, the dead and wounded lay thick around, and discouragement and confusion were on every side. He had not arrived a moment too soon. Although explosions of artillery, and volleys of musketry, rising out of the woods, showed that the conflict was still raging, he saw that the force of the blow had been spent, and the enemy was exhausted by the tremendous effort he had put forth. He knew at once, he said, that whichever now first attacked would win, and he resolved to break into a furious offensive. True, his own losses had been heavy—the troops were worn out with the long struggle, and the entire army in a disordered condition. But he found the haversacks of the rebel prisoners that had been captured in the fight packed with rations for three days, and instantly saw through the plan of the enemy.   The bloody contest that had been waged since early in the morning was not for victory, so that the place might be held, but for *escape*.   Said he thoughtfully, "They mean to cut their way out; they have no idea of staying here to fight us." Wheeling, he dashed the spurs into his horse and galloped back to the left, and ordered Smith to move at once on the rebel works.

It was a bold resolution, to give up in a moment the gunboats, which had been the chief reliance— abandon the plan of a combined movement, and stake every thing on one bold throw. Napoleon once said, "A battle often turns on a single thought." It was so in this case. Grant knew from the course the battle had taken all day, that the enemy must be weakest at this point, and most unprepared for an attack, and in order to keep it from being reinforced, he directed McClernand —exhausted and shattered as he was—to recover his lost ground, piled with his own dead, and assault the rebel works on the left from before which he had been driven. Wallace commanded the assaulting columns, composed of the two brigades of Colonels Smith and Croft.   As the brave regiments moved past him, he coldly told them that desperate work was before them. Instead of being discouraged by this, they sent up loud cheers, and "Forward, forward," ran along the ranks. "Forward, then!" he shouted, in turn. Through dense underbrush, over out-cropping ledges of rock, across open stony places, up the steep acclivity, swept by desolating volleys, they boldly charged, or climbed like mountain-goats. Now lying down to escape the murderous volleys, then.rising with a cheer, they pushed on till they got within a hundred and fifty yards of the intrenchments, when the order came to fall back.

In the mean time Smith was in motion. In front of him was an entrenched hill, which commanded the interior of the rebel works. If that were reached, the garrison would be uncovered to batteries planted on the top, and Smith resolved to take it.

Sending a force around to the right, to make a feint, he took three picked regiments—the 2d and 7th Iowa, and 57th Indiana—to compose the storming column, and, riding at their head, ordered the advance. As his eye glanced along that splendid body of men, he felt they were equal to the bloody task assigned them. The bayonet was to do the work this time. Mounting the slope with leaning forms, those brave troops entered the desolating fire, that rolled like a lava-flood adown the height, and pressed rapidly upward and onward. Their

4

gallant leader moved beside them, with his cap
lifted on his sword, as a banner to wave them on.
Grim and silent, with compressed lips and flashing eyes, they breasted the steep acclivity and the
blinding, fiery sleet, without faltering for one instant.   They sternly closed the rent ranks as they
ascended, until at last the summit was gained.
Then the long line of gleaming barrels came to a
level together; a simultaneous flash, a crashing
volley, a cheer, ringing high and clear from the
smoking top, a single bound, and they were over
and in the rebel works.   The flag went up, and
with it a shout of victory that was the death-
knell of Fort Donelson.   Hurrying up his
artillery and supports, Smith fixed himself
firmly in position, and awaited the morning
light to complete the work already more than
half done.

That wintry night the troops on the extreme
right, ignorant of Smith's success, lay down with
their arms in their hands, on the blood-stained
snow, weary, and hungry, and cold, yet resolute,
and prepared for the assault in the morning.
Smith's heroes also bivouacked on the frozen,
crimson ground they had so gallantly won, while
Grant, with his heart relieved of a heavy burden,
took refuge in a negro hut, to snatch a short repose, or ponder on the events of the coming morning.   He knew that he had been near defeat, but

he now felt that victory was sure, and he longed impatiently for the morning to dawn.

At daylight, the roll of the drum and bugle note called the ranks on the right from their frozen bivouac, to prepare for the grand final assault.

Though cold and chill, they sternly closed up their thinned ranks on the blood-stained snow, while not a heart beat faint. No sublimer spectacle was ever witnessed than those gallant men presented, on that Sabbath morning, as they took their position in front of the frowning works of the enemy. Marching from Fort Henry without tents or rations, except such as they could carry in their haversacks—exposed for three days and nights without shelter or fire, and two out of the three to the driving snow or piercing cold, and all the time under fire; yet they stood eagerly waiting the order to launch themselves on the foe.

Smith, down the river, was, at the same time, training his guns on the devoted garrison, and all was ready for the final struggle. At that moment Col. Lauman heard the clear note of a bugle, rising from out the enemy's works, and turning his eye thither, he saw a white flag waving above them. A long, loud cheer went up at the sight, which, taken up by regiment after regiment, as the exciting news travelled along the line, at last reached the troops of Wallace, on the extreme right, just ready to move to the assault. In a moment their caps were in the air, and amid long and repeated cheers, the band struck up triumphant airs, making the wintry Sabbath morning a scene never to be forgotten.

During the night the rebel generals had held a consultation over their desperate condition, in which, after much sharp discussion, it was finally decided that Floyd should hand over the command to Pillow, and he to Buckner, who should surrender the place, while the two former would attempt to make their escape. When this decision was reported to the brigade and regimental officers, some were astonished, while others stormed, and cursed the renegade commanders. A rebel officer thus describes the scene:

"One said, 'It is mean!' 'It is cowardly!' 'Floyd always was a rascal.'

"'We are betrayed!' 'There is treachery!' said they.

"'It is a mean trick for an officer to desert his men. If my troops are to be surrendered, I shall stick by them," said Major Brown.

"'I denounce Pillow as a coward; and if I ever meet him, I'll shoot him as quick as I would a dog,' said Major McLain, red with rage.

"There were two or three small steamboats at the Dover landing. Floyd and Pillow went on board of one of them, taking part of the Virginia brigade with them. This being seen by some of the other troops they became furious and rushed on board, crowding every part of the boat.

"' Cut loose ! ' shouted Floyd to the captain."

The ropes were cut, the boats swung into the stream, and the fugitives steered for Nashville.

Soon after the flag of truce was raised, an officer appeared bearing the following communication from General Buckner :

HEADQUARTERS, FORT DONELSON, *February* 16, 1862.

SIR : In consideration of all the circumstances governing the present situation of affairs at this station, I propose to the commanding officer of the Federal forces the appointment of commissioners to agree upon terms of capitulation of the forces and fort under my command, and, in that view, suggest an armistice till twelve o clock to-day.

I am, sir, respectfully, your obedient servant,

S. B. BUCKNER, Brig.-Gen. C. S. A.

To Brigadier-General GRANT, commanding United States forces near Fort Donelson.

Grant did not want time to consider what answer to make. His blood was up, and he would wait for no mere formalities or spend time in discussing terms, and sent the following short peremptory reply :

HEADQUARTERS, ARMY IN THE FIELD,
 CAMP NEAR DONELSON, *February* 16, 1862.

To GENERAL S. B. BUCKNER, Confederate Army :

Yours of this date, proposing an armistice, and appointment of commissioners to settle terms of capitula-

tion, is just received. *No terms other than unconditional and immediate surrender can be accepted. I
propose to move immediately upon your works.*

I am, respectfully, your obedient servant,

U. S. GRANT,
Brig.-Gen. U. S. A. Commanding.

Buckner, chagrined, but helpless, saw there was
no alternative but submit or see the Union soldiers rolling like the sea over his works, and so he
sent the following note :

HEADQUARTERS, DOVER, TENNESSEE, *Feb.* 16, 1862.

TO BRIGADIER-GENERAL GRANT:

SIR : The distribution of forces under my command,
incident to an unexpected change of commanders, and
the overwhelming force under your command, compel
me, notwithstanding the brilliant success of the Confederate army yesterday, to accept the ungenerous, and
unchivalrous terms which you propose.

I am, Sir, your obedient servant,

S. B. BUCKNER,
Brigadier-General, C. S. A.

Grant, smiling significantly at this reflection
on his generosity and chivalry, mounted his
horse and rode at once to Buckner's headquarters.
The meeting was courteous and frank, for they had
been cadets together at West Point ; and Grant,
mindful of old times, told the latter that he did
not desire to dictate any terms, for the mere purpose of humiliating him, and that the officers
might retain their side-arms, and both they and

the soldiers keep their personal baggage, but every thing else must be surrendered.   Buckner then invited him to breakfast, and, over their coffee, victor and vanquished discussed, good-naturedly, the operations of the past few days. In alluding to the inferior force of Grant, when he first advanced across the country towards the fort, the rebel general said if he had been in chief command, the former never would have reached it as easily as he did.   Grant replied that, if he had been, the army would have waited for re-inforcements; "but," he added, "I knew that Pillow would not come out of his works and fight me, and I told my staff so."   He knew the stuff that his former comrade was made of, and had also some experience in Mexico of the military ability of Pillow.

When, soon after, the prisoners were being put on board steamers, to be carried north, Buckner asked Grant to take a look at his brigade, which had been drilled under his own eye.   The latter went on board the steamer, and was soon the centre of all eyes.   Buckner then made his men a short speech, in which he praised Grant's kind treatment of them, and bade them remember it, if, hereafter, the fortune of war should throw any of his soldiers into their power.

Sixty-five guns, over seventeen thousand small arms, and fifteen thousand troops fell into Grant's hands, as the result of this victory. The loss of the enemy in killed and wounded could only be conjectured, while his own was a little over two thousand. Probably, it was nearly the same in both armies.

Grant's army, though comparatively so weak when he started across the country from Fort Henry, had been heavily reinforced, so that, on the day of battle, he had in the field twenty-seven thousand men. He captured more guns than he had in the siege, for he brought along but eight light batteries, which were not at all suitable for siege operations.

The victory was the most important one that had yet been obtained by our troops, and it electrified the nation. As the exciting news travelled over the land, bells were set ringing, and salvos of artillery fired, and men thought the end of the rebellion to be near at hand. Grant at once became a favorite of the people, and his emphatic reply to Buckner, "*I propose to move immediately upon your works*," was in every one's mouth. It was uttered by some not only to show the character of Grant, and to swell his praise, but as a sarcasm upon military science. Even the Secretary of War, in an absurd letter, used it for this purpose, and for a while it seemed that no commander could retain his position, if he did not throw to the wind all rules of war, and, no matter what the condition of things might be, "move at once upon the enemy's works," wherever found. With Grant, it was no rash determination, based on mere brute daring, but the dictate of true military sagacity. Many afterwards imitated his boldness, but, wanting his wisdom, made sad failures, and sacrificed thousands of lives in vain.

The day after the battle, he issued the following congratulatory order to his soldiers :

HEADQUARTERS, DISTRICT OF WEST TENNESSEE,
FORT DONELSON, *February* 17, 1862.

The General commanding takes great pleasure in congratulating the troops of this command for the triumph over rebellion gained by their valor, on the 13th, 14th, and 15th instant.

For four successive nights, without shelter, during the most inclement weather known in this latitude, they faced an enemy in large force, in a position chosen by himself. Though strongly fortified by nature, all the additional safeguards suggested by science were added. Without a murmur this was borne, prepared at all times to receive an attack, and with continuous skirmishing by day, resulting ultimately in forcing the enemy to surrender without condition.

The victory achieved is not only great in the effect it will have in breaking down rebellion, but has secured the greatest number of prisoners of war ever taken in any battle on this continent.

Fort Donelson will hereafter be marked in capitals on the map of our united country, and the men who fought the battle will live in the memory of a grateful people. By order,

U. S. GRANT,
Brig.-Gen. Commanding.

4*

The fall of Fort Donelson opened Nashville to our forces. When the disastrous news reached the city, the quiet Sabbath morning was turned into a scene of the wildest excitement. The last news from the fort was a despatch from Pillow, the day before, saying "The day is ours," and hence all fears were quieted. Its surrender, therefore, fell on the people, who were quietly assembling for church, like a thunderbolt at noon-day from a cloudless sky. Faces turned pale with affright, men dashed wildly on horseback through the streets, which soon were thronged with excited men and women. Every available vehicle was at once seized ; and the terrified inhabitants, flinging in the few articles they could conveniently carry, hurried off southward, for in imagination they already heard the tread of Grant's advancing legions. The public stores were thrown open, into which the rabble rushed for pillage ; and for twenty-four hours a scene of terror and lawlessness was witnessed that baffles description.

With the fall of Donelson, not only fell Nashville and Bowling Green, but Columbus itself became untenable, and was soon after evacuated.

Thus, without the aid of the fleet, Grant, by one grand and terrible blow, had broken down the whole line of the enemy's defence, from the Mississippi to the Alleghany mountains, and shoved it beyond the State of Kentucky.

CHAPTER V.

DISGRACE OF GRANT.

Halleck's Neglect—His unjust and abusive Despatch to Washington—Failure of his Attempt to injure him with the Government—Grant ordered to Fort Henry—Halleck accuses him of Acting Unbecoming an Officer—Puts Smith in his Place at the head of the Army of the Tennessee—Continues his Persecutions—Noble Conduct of Grant—Denies the Charges made against him—Asks to be relieved from Command till his Conduct can be investigated—Sudden Change in Halleck's Treatment—Attempts to vindicate his Conduct—His Duplicity—Unsuspected by Grant—General Morgan treated in a similar manner—Magnanimity of Grant and Smith—Rumors of Grant's Arrest.

But, from some cause or other, Halleck refused to acknowledge the merits of Grant in this brilliant movement. His congratulatory order to the troops was cold and restrained, giving Grant no especial praise, while, at the same time, he spoke of the necessity of discipline and good order, in a way that implied censure. Whether he was vexed that Grant had refused to stay and fortify himself at Fort Henry, and, acting on his own responsibility, had attacked and taken Fort Donelson, and thus practically demonstrated his superiority in the art of war; or whether angry at being so suddenly eclipsed by a subordinate, it is impossible to say.

At all events, he sent the following remarkable telegram to Washington, which admits of no palliation: "Smith, by his coolness and bravery at Fort Donelson, when the battle was against us, turned the tide and carried the enemy's outworks. Make him a major-general: you can't get a better one. Honor him for this victory, and the country will applaud." Here a commander-in-chief urges the promotion of a subordinate, who had only gallantly carried out the orders of his superior, to major-general, while the commander himself was but a brigadier. It was a most wicked and shameful thrust, but it failed of success, for the Secretary of War recommended instead Grant to that rank, and he was made a major-general, his promotion to date from the day of the surrender of the fort, and "the *whole country*" did "applaud" the act.

On the 27th of the month, Grant went to Nashville to consult with General Buell, who had arrived there with his army from Bowling Green, on future operations. The very next morning he returned, and immediately advised Halleck of it. On the subsequent day he wrote again to Halleck's chief of staff, stating he had forwarded to the former all information of his movements, the condition of the enemy, and his own wants. On

the same day, Halleck sent a despatch directing
him to move his army back to Fort Henry, preparatory to an advance up the Tennessee. Two
days after Grant received it, his columns were in
motion. But the day previous, without waiting
to hear from him, Halleck sent the following telegram to Washington, which, coming from any other
man than he, would be considered a curiosity in
its way. He says, "I have had no communication with General Grant for more than a week.
He left his command without my authority, and
went to Nashville. His army seems to be as
much demoralized by the victory of Fort Donelson, as was that of the Potomac by the defeat of
Bull Run. It is hard to censure a successful
general immediately after a victory, but he richly
deserves it. I can get no returns, no reports, no
information of any kind from him. Satisfied
with his victory, he *sits down and enjoys it without any regard* to the future. I am worn out
and tired by this neglect and inefficiency. C. F.
Smith is almost the only officer equal to the emergency."

Viewed in its various bearings, in what a pitiful light does this present Halleck. In the first
place, it is such a serious offence for Grant, after
opening Nashville, to run up and see what the
movements of the enemy are, and what next is to
be done, that the former must telegraph the fact

to Washington in a tone of complaint. In the second place, he declares that the victorious army is as much demoralized as the army of the Potomac at Bull Run, when he has never seen it, and, as he affirms, can get *no* report, no information of any kind with regard to it. In the third place, after charging Grant with being too active because he went to Nashville to see if he could be of any service, going even beyond the limits of his command, he, in the next breath, accuses him of sitting down and " enjoying his victory," regardless of the future. To cap the climax of this absurd, petulant, false accusation, he, in his warm and comfortable house in St. Louis, complains of *being* "*tired* and *worn* out," while the man who has been winning victories amid hail and snow, is "sitting *down*" and enjoying himself.

But having thus poisoned the minds of those at Washington, he obtained the requisite liberty to strike, and the very next day after this *secret* stab, he sent a despatch to Grant, ordering him to turn over the command of the expedition planned for the upper waters of the Tennessee to Smith, and remain himself at Fort Henry. Complaining that Grant was sitting still, he now determined to see that he should sit still, and see his brave troops, whom he had led to victory, defile away from him under another commander. But instead of uttering any complaint, Grant contented himself with denying that he had ever disobeyed orders, and adds, "In conclusion, I will say, that you may rely on my carrying out your instructions in every particular to the best of my ability." Calm and serene under his disgrace, he is just as ready to help his commander as though the latter were not plotting his ruin. Without envy or mere personal ambition, he congratulates Smith on his promotion, and says that "he deserves it," and he will give him all the aid in his power. Unselfish and noble, he thinks only of his country's welfare. Halleck, however, seems to be under some baleful influence, and continues his persecutions with a pertinacity that is inexplicable. Not content with disgracing him and leaving him to do simply garrison duty, he, two days after he had removed him from command, sent another rebuke, reiterating his old charges.

Resting only a short time, he returns again to his fault-finding, as if he thought the repetition of his accusations would establish their truth. To all of these, Grant replied in the same calm, courteous spirit. In answer to the charge that he failed to report the number of troops under his command, he, in his quiet, straightforward, truthful way, says, "You had a better chance of knowing my strength whilst my command was surrounding Fort Donelson, than I had. *Troops were reporting* daily by your orders, and *were immediately assigned to brigades.*" This was a home thrust, though probably not intended for one, but only as a vindication of himself. It showed that the *looseness* was at headquarters, in not keeping account of the troops sent forward.

Grant, at the first, when he found himself falsely accused, asked to be relieved from duty, and he now repeated the request, and after saying, "There · is such a disposition to find fault with me that I again ask to be relieved from duty until I can be placed right in the estimation of those high in authority."

The simple, unpretending, unsuspicious manner in which he behaves during all this trying period, when he was so unjustly assailed, and finally placed in disgrace, brings out in bright relief some of the most attractive points in his character. Unaccustomed to the tricks and cabals of politicians—totally ignorant in himself of those petty, low ambitions of which rivals are made—apparently wholly unable to comprehend a character which can cover up its duplicity with hypocrisy, he has a simple, almost child-like faith in truth that is marvellous. At first sight, it seems that such an honest, unsuspecting object of persecution can stand no chance against unscrupulous men who work in the dark. He was not, however, to be laid aside—Providence had more and greater work for him to do.

Halleck having, after the 3d of March, for nearly a week kept up a continuous fire on Grant, either directly or through Washington, suddenly turned round, and told him that he could not be relieved from command. He says, with an effrontery that would have taken away the breath from a less calm, immobile man than Grant, *" There is no good reason for it."* No " reason " for relieving a man from command until he can vindicate himself, when he has persistently disobeyed orders—violated the laws of the service in leaving his command without liberty—been guilty of " marauding "—allowed his victorious army to be more demoralized than a routed one, and amid such chaos and amid all the great preparations going on around him, sits quietly down and refuses to do any thing ! No reason for relieving him ! One would think, on the contrary, if all these charges were true, there was quite reason enough for suspending, if not for cashiering him.

After he had shown himself so petulant, and eager to prefer any and every charge against Grant, without stopping to investigate the truth of them, one naturally inquires what could have caused this sudden revolution in his conduct. There had been no trial, no investigation, no new developments. Such a sudden exhibition of criminal leniency right on the top of such eager haste to condemn and disgrace, deserves some explanation. Did the department commander discover that Grant was too deeply implanted in the favor of the Secretary of War and the President, to be thus summarily disposed of—or did he begin to fear that he had acted in a way that would not stand the scrutiny of a court of inquiry, and the blow he had aimed at an innocent head might have a disagreeable rebound? Any other General would have refused to be satisfied with this retraction, and insisted on a court of inquiry, where his vindication might be complete. But Grant, truthful himself, believed in the sincerity of the statements of others, and with that self abnegation which has made him so conspicuous in this generation of self-seekers, replied that he had thought, after the severe censures heaped upon him, that he could not " serve longer without a court of inquiry ; but your telegram of yesterday places such a different phase upon my position, that I will again assume command, and give every effort to the success of our cause. Under the worst circumstances, I would do the same." No matter how deep the disgrace they might unjustly inflict on him, he would " give every effort to the success of the cause." Evidently for the purpose of making Grant believe that he had acted under advices from Washington, and not from his own suggestions and from inclination, he sent him the following correspondence, which on the face of it places Halleck not only in a fair, curious coincidence, but magnanimous light. The first is a letter from the Adjutant-General, sent apparently without any suggestion received from Halleck.

HEADQUARTERS OF THE ARMY, ADJUTANT-GENERAL'S OFFICE.
WASHINGTON, March 10, 1867.

Maj.-Gen. H. W. Halleck, U. S. A., Commanding Dept. of the Missouri, St. Louis:

It has been reported that, soon after the battle of Fort Donelson, Brigadier-General Grant left his command without leave. By direction of the President, the Secretary of War directs you to ascertain, and report, whether Gen. Grant left his command at any time without proper authority, and, if so, for how long; whether he has made to you, proper reports and returns of his forces; whether he has committed any acts which were unauthorized, or not in accordance with military subordination or propriety, and if so, what.

L. THOMAS, Adjutant-General.

Notice here, that the "reports" to which he alludes are, one and all, precisely the charges made in Halleck's extraordinary letter, which we gave a few pages back. The latter now sees, evidently, that he has gone too far, and returns the following answer, which he sends to Grant, to show that *he* had no hand in these serious charges—that what he did was from orders, which he had received from Washington, and that, instead of unjustly accusing him and persecuting him, he had nobly stepped between him and the authorities at

Washington, and, unsolicited, had vindicated his conduct and saved him from a court of inquiry:

HEADQUARTERS DEPT. OF THE MISSOURI,
ST. LOUIS, Mo., March 15, 1862.

Brig.-Gen. Thomas, Adjutant-General of the Army, Washington:

In accordance with your instructions of the 10th inst., I report that Gen. Grant and several officers of high rank in his command, immediately after the battle of Fort Donelson, went to Nashville without my authority or knowledge. I am satisfied, however, from investigation, that Gen. Grant did this from good intentions, and from a desire to subserve the public interests. Not being advised of Gen. Buell's movements, and learning that Gen. Buell had ordered Smith's division of his (Grant's) command to Nashville, he deemed it his duty to go there in person. During the absence of Gen. Grant, and a part of his general officers, numerous irregularities are said to have occurred at Fort Donelson. These were in violation of the orders issued by Gen. Grant before leaving, and probably, under the circumstances, were unavoidable. Gen. Grant has made the proper explanations, and has been directed to resume his command in the field; as he acted from a praiseworthy although mistaken zeal for the public service in going to Nashville, and leaving his command, I respectfully recommend that no further notice be taken of it. There never has been any want of military subordination on the part of Gen. Grant, and his failure to make returns of his forces has been explained as resulting partly from the failure of Colonels of regiments to report to him on their arrival, and partly from an interruption of telegraphic communication. All these irregularities have now been remedied.

H. W. HALLECK, Major-General.

Grant, evidently, was completely deceived by this correspondence, which Halleck transmitted to him. Unsuspicious of double-dealing, and touched by the apparent magnanimous conduct of his superior, he replied: "I most fully appreciate your justness, General, in the part you have taken, and you may rely upon me to the utmost of my capacity for carrying out all your orders." He felt, as he said in the same letter, that "he had not neglected a single duty," but he was willing to let the past go. We can only conjecture what would have been his feelings had Halleck sent with this correspondence, his own letter, dated March 3d (just a week before) to the General-in-chief at Washington. It is a shallow cunning that prompts to such a course as this, and yet leaves the proof of it on record where it is certain, sooner or later, to come to the light.

This treatment, however, is in perfect harmony with that which General Morgan, who held Fort Cumberland, received. Compelled to evacuate the place because Halleck could not or would not either reinforce him or furnish him supplies, he carried his little army for two hundred miles through a desert country, making one of the most memorable marches of the war. Although with ten thousand men, the place had been held in the face of starvation, and the assembling of a hundred thousand troops around it, yet, as its evacuation made the campaign for the occupation of Knoxville and East Tennessee a failure, Halleck wished the blame to rest on other

shoulders than his own, and so ordered an inves·
tigation of the matter, hoping to be able to place
it on Morgan's. But General Wright, whom he
had appointed to conduct it, made a report com·
pletely exculpating Morgan. Yet with this report
before him, Halleck, in his annual report to Congress, intimates that the evacuation was unnecessary, and adds that he has "ordered an investigation." This coming to the notice of General
Morgan, he was indignant, and immediately wrote
to Halleck, demanding a Court of Inquiry, or
Court Martial. The latter, in reply, said that he
had directed General Wright to make an investigation, and if "that was satisfactory," no further
steps would be necessary, and he would be "relieved from all blame." Morgan wrote at once to
Wright, on the subject, when he learned to his
astonishment that the latter had made the investigation, finished his report, and sent it in the
October previous to the report of Halleck to Congress, in which he says he has "*ordered* an investigation," and months previous to his letter to
Morgan, in which he reasserts the action he had
taken, as if the matter was still in abeyance, and
had not, on the contrary, been completed the fall
before.

In what striking contrast to this does the conduct of both Smith and Grant appear. When the
former was placed over Grant, the latter, instead

of indulging in unkind feelings, wrote to Smith a congratulatory letter, expressing his pleasure at his advancement, and saying, " Any thing you may require, send back transports for, and if within my power you shall have it." On the other hand, when Smith heard that Grant had been restored to his old position, he writes a congratulatory letter in turn, expressing his pleasure that he once more had his old command, from which, he says, "he was so unceremoniously and unjustly stricken down."

This whole matter has been wrapped in obscurity, and all kinds of reports concerning it obtained circulation, and the truth has never been fully known until brought to light by Col. Badeau. One of these reports, which was generally credited, was that Grant, soon after the capture of Fort Donelson, was placed under arrest by orders from Washington. Various reasons were given for this summary action, and one was, that Grant was intoxicated on board the flag-ship while the battle was raging.

We now, however, can trace the origin of this generally believed strange report. Halleck, in a letter to him, in which he endeavors to show that he was innocent of the disgrace inflicted on him, says, that he had received an order from McClellan, to arrest him. The question naturally arises, why was not that order, if issued, obeyed ?

But Col. Badeau says, that no such order is on record or can be found in the War Department, and further, that the Secretary of War never heard that such an order was issued. As it never was executed—has never seen the light, and cannot be found in the place where it ought to be, and no remembrance of such an important transaction remains in the War Department, we must be allowed to express a doubt if McClellan ever gave such an order at all.

Ignorant of all this plotting and persecution, the people were sounding Grant's praises the length and breadth of the land, and the swelling tide of public feeling was being felt in Washington, and threatened to sweep away all this nicely balanced machinery and curious network, that had been woven in the dark. It was hazardous to attempt to stem this popular current, and Halleck doubtless felt so, when he concluded to abandon his persecution of Grant, and outwardly, by restoring him to his command, placed affairs on a friendly footing.

CHAPTER VI.

SHILOH.

WHILE Grant was in disgrace, Smith, whom Halleck had put in his place, proceeded up the Tennessee with the army to cut the great railroad near it at Corinth ; but accomplishing nothing of importance, returned to Pittsburgh Landing, on the western bank of the river, and there disembarked a part of his troops. The original and proper plan was to land at Savannah, a few miles lower down, on the opposite side of the river, where the remaining portion of the army did en-

5

camp. The reason given for this change was, that a rapid movement inland, in the desired direction, could be more easily made from that bank than from the other; as the transportation of troops across would necessarily consume a considerable time. This advantage, however, would not weigh against the peril of having the army divided by the river. Probably the fact that the bluff on which the landing was made was admirably fitted for a defensive position, was another reason. Two streams, one north and the other south of it, flowed almost at right angles into the Tennessee, thus rendering it an easy matter for Smith to protect his flanks—in fact, from the flooded state of the banks at this time, making an attack, except in front, almost impossible. Even in this latter direction nature had helped to defend this excellent position ; for Owl Creek ran along a portion of it parallel to the Tennessee river, and emptied nearly at right angles into Snake Creek, which bounded the bluff on the north. But Corinth lay right west, within striking distance, and common prudence required that to make the position secure, strong defences should be thrown up. This, however, was not done—a neglect the more singular, since Corinth, the objective point of the campaign, and the key to the whole railroad system connecting Tennessee and Mississippi, was known to be occupied by the enemy in force.

Halleck, as we have stated, restored Grant on the 13th of March to his command, and four days after the latter took up his headquarters at Savannah, about nine miles below Pittsburg Landing. Nearly half of the army was at the former place, and Grant saw at once the peril of having the two portions nine miles apart, and separated besides by a broad and swollen river. Hence within an hour after his arrival he ordered Smith and McClernand, who commanded the force at Savannah, to proceed at once to Pittsburg Landing. In the mean time, Halleck, hearing of the concentration of rebel troops at Corinth, had directed Buell, in Central Tennessee, to effect a junction with Grant at Pittsburg Landing. His army numbered nearly forty thousand, and the distance from Columbia, his starting-point, to the Tennessee river, was some ninety miles. But it was early spring, and the streams being flooded made it impossible to calculate with any accuracy how much time it would take to make the march.

In the mean time, Halleck telegraphed Grant to avoid battle unless it was forced upon him—in short, to act solely on the defensive, until the arrival of Buell. This was contrary to the judgment of Grant, who thought a blow should be struck at once, before the concentration of the enemy could be effected.

For nearly three weeks the army lay idle here,

while the hostile forces were rapidly accumulating. By the second of April, Johnston, their commander, saw that he must strike before the arrival of Buell, of whose approach he was made aware by his scouts, if he wished to succeed, and he began to feel our line with his skirmishers.

On the 4th, a heavy force appeared in our front, and for a time a serious engagement seemed imminent. Several rebel prisoners were taken, who said that the " Yankees would catch hell soon." Still, this was thought to be an idle threat, and no notice was taken of it. The next day, Grant rode out to the front and investigated the matter. Both he and Sherman came to the conclusion that there was no appearance or probability of an immediate battle. Grant did not return to the landing until after dark. It was raining at the time, and his horse slipping on a log, fell upon him, which lamed him for several days, and caused him a good deal of suffering.

The demonstration of the enemy this day was not confined to our forces at Pittsburg Landing. Lewis Wallace, with Smith's division, five miles farther down stream, reported a heavy force in his direction. The truth was, the enemy was making a reconnoissance with view to an attack. The next day, a heavy column of cavalry pushed boldly up to Sherman's front, yet still he did not think any thing serious was intended, while Grant felt stronger by the arrival of Nelson's division of Buell's army at Savannah. He had been very anxious for the arrival of these troops, and now directed Nelson to take position at a point about five miles from Savannah, and hold himself ready to march at a moment's notice. He himself designed the next day to remove his own head-quarters to Pittsburg Landing—putting it off till then at the request of Buell, who had informed him that he would arrive at Savannah that day.

The next morning, however, came the battle. Johnston had learned by his reconnoissance that our forces had thrown up no entrenchments, but that the flanks were so well protected by streams and ravines, that an attack could not be made there. Hence he determined to move right down in front, in one overwhelming charge. Sherman's division was in advance, near the Shiloh church. On his left, but farther back, McClernand was posted. Then came Prentiss, more up to Sherman's line, while on the extreme left was Stuart, commanding a separate brigade of Sherman's division, and covering the crossing of Lick Creek. Hurlbut was in reserve.

The constant skirmishing for the last few days had put the officers on the alert, and though it was only just daybreak, the horses of many were saddled while they sat down to breakfast. Every thing seemed quiet, when suddenly, as a clap of

thunder, the onset came. Prentiss first caught
the fury of the bursting storm, which soon swept
along the entire front. Not cautiously, as if feeling their way, did the heavy columns come on,
but in dark masses, like fast following waves,
broke over the camps. A scene of indescribable
confusion followed. From the very outset, the
battle on our part was without plan or cohesion,
while the rebel general held his army completely
in hand, and hurled it with skill, boldness, and
irresistible power, on any point he wished to
strike. Prentiss, in the centre, after striving in
vain to bear up against the flood, was surrounded
and compelled to surrender, with some three
thousand or more of his troops. Sherman and
McClernand fought with their accustomed bravery, but they could hold only a portion of their
troops to the deadly work. Stuart was cut off
from the main army, and compelled to fight his
own battle. Cavalry charged hither and thither
over the tumultuous field, riding down our disordered troops; while our batteries were swept by
the hostile flood, and the broken, disjointed army
was borne steadily back toward the Tennessee.
Sherman, awake to the peril of the army, clung to
each position with the tenacity of death, and rode
amid the hail-storm of bullets as though he had
forgotten he had a life to lose. Horse after horse
sunk under him; he himself was struck again

and again ; and yet he not only kept the field, but blazed like a meteor over it. At noon of that Sabbath day, he was dismounted—his hand in a sling,—and bleeding, giving directions to his chief of artillery, while it was one incessant crash and roar all around him. Suddenly he saw, to the right, his men giving way before a cloud of rebels. "I was looking for that," he exclaimed. The next moment the battery he had been placing in position opened, sending death and destruction into the close-packed ranks. The rebel commander, glancing at the battery, ordered the cavalry to charge it. Seeing them coming down, Sherman quickly ordered up two companies of infantry, which, pouring in a deadly volley, sent them to the right about with empty saddles. The onset was arrested, and our troops rallied with renewed courage. Hurlbut moved up with his reserves, and gave Sherman breathing space.

In the mean time, in the very heat of battle, Grant came on a driving gallop to the front, and at once complimented Sherman on the gallant stand he had made. Sherman, in reply, asked for cartridges. "They are on the way," replied Grant. Knowing from the rapid and incessant firing, that he had heard ever since daybreak, that ammunition must be giving out, he had ordered it forward as he hurried to the front.

He and his staff at Savannah, were taking an

early breakfast, preparatory to riding out to meet
Buell, who was near at hand, when the first roar
of artillery arrested his attention. At first he
thought it was only a repetition of the skirmishing
that had been going on for several days. But as
the thunder swelled louder and louder, and peal
after peal shook the shores, he knew that a battle
was raging, and crying, " to horse," galloped down
to the landing. Before starting, however, he despatched a hasty note to Buell, telling him that
heavy firing up the river showed that the army
was attacked. To Nelson, he sent orders to move
his division up opposite Pittsburg Landing without delay. Pushing up the river himself in a
steamer, he stopped at Crump's landing just long
enough to tell Wallace, in person, to be ready to
march at a moment's notice.

As the boat touched the shore at Pittsburg
Landing, the din of battle was terrific, and already
fugitives were flying from the field. When he
reached the front and saw how terrific was the
onset, and that his army was wavering, he at once
sent an aid as fast as he could ride, to Crump's
landing, five miles distant, with orders to Wallace
to hurry his division forward to the field. To Nelson he wrote, "Hurry up your command as fast
as possible. Push forward—boats will be in
readiness to transport you across." Having done
this he addressed himself to the task of keeping

the heavy masses that surged so fiercely up against his shaking line at bay, till those reinforcements could arrive. The field was wooded, with patches of cultivation between, so that it was impossible for him to get any commanding view of it, and manœuvre the army as a whole. In fact, there was no time for it. The rebel attack was so steady and persistent, that each division simply attempted to hold its ground. Grant, smoking his cigar with imperturbable coolness, moved from point to point, along the front, giving such directions as the emergency seemed to require.

As the decimated army, maintaining a determined though shattered front, still kept falling back towards the river, Grant cast his eye anxiously in the direction where the heads of Nelson's and Wallace's columns should appear, but nothing met his gaze but crowds of stragglers fleeing to the rear. Wallace, at least, should have been there long since, but strange to say, his division was wandering about *lost*, though only five miles from the field of battle, whose uproar loaded the Sabbath air.

Though nearly half of his army had melted away—either prisoners, killed, or straggling—the other half still faced the foe, and met his fierce, determined onsets as the rock meets the wave. But this could not last long—he must have reinforcements, or the brave heroes that refused to fly,

5*

but, with every backward step, dealt a staggering blow, would soon be overpowered; and hearing that another of Buell's divisions had reached Savannah, he sent a staff officer, with desperate speed, to him, with the order: "You will move your command with the utmost despatch, to the river at this point, where steamboats will be in readiness to transport you to Pittsburg." But the peril deepening every moment, he could not wait his return, but sent off another officer with the following still more urgent order: "Commanding officer, advance forces, Buell's army, near Pittsburg: The attack on my forces has been very spirited from early this morning. The appearance of fresh troops in the field now, would have a powerful effect, both by inspiring our men and disheartening the enemy. If you will get upon the field, leaving all your baggage on the east bank of the river, it will be more to our advantage, and possibly save the day to us. The rebel forces are estimated at over one hundred thousand men. My headquarters will be in the log building on the top of the hill, where you will be furnished with a staff officer to guide you to your place in the field." Matters were getting desperate, and he counted the moments when the forces, so pressingly needed, would arrive. Still none came; but about the middle of the afternoon, Buell, accompanied only by his staff, rode up the bluff. Reaching

Savannah, and finding Grant gone, while incessant explosions of artillery shook the shore, he
knew a terrific battle was raging, and leaving the
division he was accompanying to follow on, hurried forward alone. The sight that met his gaze
as he landed, astonished him. The banks were
black with fugitives, who crowded down to the
water's edge for safety. His first impression was
that Grant's army was gone beyond recovery unless
it could be placed across the river, and wait till
his own could come up, and he asked, "What
provisions have you made for a retreat?" Grant
replied, "I don't despair of whipping them yet."
Buell now sent off officer after officer, to hurry up
the tired columns. In the mean time, the battle
raged with increased ferocity; while still back
toward the river, yet still facing the foe, slowly retired the diminished columns. Although Johnson
had fallen, he was succeeded by Beauregard, who
saw that but one more success was necessary to
drive our army into the Tennessee—carry the ravine
that covered Sherman's left, and thus in fact the
landing itself. This done, and the battle would
be over. Grant, too, saw this, and put forth a last
desperate effort to prevent it. The gunboats Tyler
and Lexington could now join in the fight, and
their ponderous shells went screaming up this
ravine, bursting with the sound of thunder amid
the astonished enemy, and his frantic attempts to

clear the ravine were without avail. In the mean time, Nelson's division had crossed and formed in line of battle, and poured in a volley. The enemy, exhausted by the protracted struggle, and now met by new foes, sullenly retired, while the shadows of evening stole over the landscape. Soon, darkness wrapped the two armies, that sank to rest on the torn and trampled field.

Grant now felt the heavy burden, that had increased with every revolving hour, lift from his heart. It was evident that nothing more could be done till morning; and by that time he would have forty thousand fresh troops in the field, while his adversary could bring none. That morning, he determined, should witness a terrible retribution for the disaster of the day just ended.

Troops that had marched all day were now, without rest, crossed over, and every preparation made to recommence the struggle at daylight.

Stretching far back in the gloom lay the battle field, covered with the dead and dying, uncared-for—alone with the night. To make it still more appalling, a heavy storm arose, while ever and anon the inky clouds were ribbed with blazing shells that the gunboats sent at short intervals within the enemy's lines. These, at length, set the woods on fire, that, flashing up here and there, cast a baleful light on the murky landscape. The rain fell in torrents, the only-messenger of mercy to the wounded, burning with thirst, that covered the ensanguined field.

Grant, with his strong nature fully aroused, could not think of rest, but amid the driving storm passed from division to division, visiting each commander in turn, and leaving specific orders for the attack, which he had determined should commence with the morning light. His directions were, at daybreak to commence with a heavy skirmish line, and then, leaving no reserve, advance with the entire force and sweep the field.

At length all his arrangements were completed, and near midnight he rode slowly back to the landing, and dismounting, stretched himself on the ground, and with his head resting on a stump, composed himself to sleep. The pitiless rain beat on him, drenching him to the skin, but he only thought of the coming victory. He sought no shelter, but slept as his brave troops slept, uncovered to the storm.

The battle recommenced at daylight, and although wearied out with the struggle of the day before, and outnumbered more than two to one, the enemy fought bravely, and stubbornly contested every inch of ground. Reluctant to give up the victory that had been almost within their reach, they slowly, sullenly retired over the field they had won. But the success on our side was as steady as it had been on that of the other the day before. Our camps were soon once more in our possession, and the disciplined battalions of Buell pushed the enemy back until he was at last forced to retreat to Corinth, leaving Brecken-ridge, with his division, as a rear guard. Colonel Badeau relates the following incident, which is new. He says:

" Near the close of the day, Grant met the First Ohio regiment marching towards the northern part of the field, and immediately in front of a position which it was important to take at that particular juncture ; another regiment to the left was fighting hard, but about to yield—had, in fact, given way. Grant saw the emergency, and instantly halted the passing force on the brow of a hill, the enemy lying in a wood at its base; he changed the direction of the First Ohio, and himself or-dered it to charge, in support of the yielding bat-talion. The men recognized their leader, and obeyed with enthusiasm, and Grant rode along with them in the line of battle, as much exposed as any private in the ranks. The retreating troops on the left took courage at this sight; they stopped their backward movement, closed up their wavering ranks with cheers, and the two regiments swept the enemy at once from the cov-eted spot, thus capturing one of the last important positions in the battle of Shiloh."

Grant, who never seems to know fatigue, wished

to press the retreating rebels still further, but his own troops were too much exhausted, while McCook and Crittenden, whom he appealed to, replied that their soldiers had marched all the day before, and been on the move a great part of the night, and now having fought all day were in no condition to pursue, especially as the rain was falling in torrents, making the fields very heavy; and so he had reluctantly to abandon his purpose, and turn his entire attention to the care of the wounded, of which there were over eight thousand of his own, besides those which the enemy had left behind in their retreat. His total loss was twelve thousand two hundred and seventeen. That of the enemy nearly 11,000.

The next day Beauregard, under a flag of truce, sent the following communication to Grant:

HEADQUARTERS, ARMY OF THE MISSISSIPPI,
Monday, April 8, 1862.

SIR: At the close of the conflict yesterday, my forces being exhausted by the extraordinary length of time during which they were engaged with yours on that and the preceding day, and it being apparent that you had received and were still receiving reinforcements, I felt it my duty to withdraw my troops from the immediate scene of conflict.

Under these circumstances, in accordance with usages of war, I shall transmit this under a flag of truce, to ask permission to send a mounted party to the battle-field of Shiloh, for the purpose of giving decent interment to my dead.

Certain gentlemen wishing to avail themselves of this

to remove the remains of their sons and friends, I must request for them the privilege of accompanying the burial party; and in this connection, I deem it proper to say, I am only asking what I have extended to your own countrymen, under similar circumstances.

General, respectfully, your obedient servant,

> G. T. BEAUREGARD,
> General Commanding.

To Major-General U. S. GRANT, commanding
United States forces near Pittsburg, Tenn.

To this Grant replied as follows:

> HEADQUARTERS, ARMY IN THE FIELD, }
> PITTSBURG, *April* 9, 1862.   }

General G. T. BEAUREGARD, commanding
Confederate Army of the Mississippi,
Monterey, Tenn. :

GENERAL: Your despatch of yesterday just received. Owing to the warmth of the weather, I deemed it advisable to have all the dead of both parties buried immediately. Heavy details were made for this purpose, and it is now accomplished. There cannot therefore be any necessity of admitting within our lines the parties you desire to send on the grounds asked. I shall always be glad to extend any courtesy consistent with duty, especially so when dictated by humanity.

I am, General, very respectfully,
Your obedient servant,
U. S. GRANT, Major-General.

Much has been written about this battle, and of a very contradictory character. It will be readily seen by the above account, that Grant can in no way be held responsible for the location of the army on the east side of the river, for which he was so severely blamed. It is true, he became responsible for its remaining in that dangerous position, but it must be remembered that its removal would be an implied censure, both on his friend Smith, whom he had superseded, (an old soldier, and his commandant at West Point,) and also on his superior, Halleck, who had made no objection to this disposition of the army. Under these circumstances, we do not see how he could well have done differently; besides, neither he nor Sherman expected an attack before the arrival of Buell. There was a grave error committed by the commanders in front, in not throwing up works, and constructing abatis from the trees, of which there was abundance on the spot. Had this been done, the disasters of that day would, in all human probability, have been averted. It is useless to attempt to explain away or excuse this neglect. The attempt to prove that the battle might have been renewed the next day, with any prospect of success, but for the arrival of Buell, is simply absurd; for, with a fresh army of forty thousand men, we only regained the field, nothing more. All the great military names, and all the military science in the country, can never make such an assertion an historic fact. Desaix did not save Napoleon at Marengo, more than Buell did Grant at Shiloh.

The outcry raised against Grant, for being, as it was asserted, surprised and so severely beaten the first day, was great. West, it was terrific. Congressmen and Governors demanded his removal; and it seemed, for a time, as if he would be swept away by the flood of denunciations. All sorts of charges were preferred against him. The more absurd they were, the more they were believed.

Grant, however, had one friend in Mr. Washburn, the Member of Congress from Illinois, who defended him in a noble speech.

Afterwards, when Grant had reached the pinnacle of fame, his friends went just as far in the other extreme, and asserted, and tried to prove that, in the first place, it was a capital plan to have the Tennessee river divide the forces; equally good tactics not to throw up breastworks. In the third place, there was no surprise, although officers were at breakfast when the onset came; and in the last place, that, although Buell's arrival was very opportune, it was not of vital consequence.

The effort to make a man just as perfect and infallible in judgment, at the outset of his career, as he was after years of actual experience, may show kindly feelings, but not common sense. Grant was not like so many of the ignorant, conceited coxcombs who had charge of our troops, and

believed they possessed all needed military knowledge, before they ever set a division in the field.
Like all great men, he could rise to the circumstances in which he was placed, but would not
pretend he never made a mistake.

CHAPTER VII.

CORINTH, IUKA, AND VICKSBURG.

Halleck takes Chief Command—Again disgraces Grant—Uncomplaining Conduct of the latter—Abused by Correspondents of the Press—His calm Reply to one—His quiet, dignified Behavior—Offers Halleck Good Advice—Insulted for it—His Sharp Retort—Evacuation of Corinth—An Excellent Illustration of Halleck's Strategy—Halleck called to Washington—Last Attempt to disgrace Grant—The latter makes Corinth his Headquarters—Order respecting Fugitive Slaves—Severe Order to the People of Memphis—Receives a threatening Letter—Battle of Iuka—Of Corinth—Sends Sherman to Attempt the Capture of Vicksburg—Causes of his Failure—Plans his great Expedition against the Stronghold.

HALLECK shared in the hostile feeling against Grant, and though he did not remove him from the head of his troops, he himself repaired to the field and took chief command, and, in reorganizing the army, gave the latter a position which was regarded by all the officers as one of disgrace. He was nominally second in command; but the army was divided into three corps, commanded by Thomas, Pope, and Buell, with the reserve under McClernand, while Grant's Army of the Tennessee was distributed between the right wing and the reserve, thus actually placing him under Thomas and McClernand. Though these commanders were Grant's subordinates, yet Halleck ignored him in issuing his orders, and even moved his troops without his knowledge. Nothing could be more painful than this position, yet he bore it without a murmur, quietly doing his duty, and leaving it for time, that "sets all things even," to vindicate him.

The camp was crowded with newspaper correspondents, who, having nothing else to do, criticised or praised the various commanders according to their own inclinations. Grant came in for the most unsparing abuse, yet he uttered no complaint, made no defence. Once, and once only, he broke the uninterrupted silence which he seemed determined to maintain. One of the correspondents had denounced him with most unjust severity. The article came under Grant's eye, and while smarting under its false, unscrupulous aspersions of his character, he met the writer. Instead, however, of denouncing him as he deserved, he simply said, " Your paper is very unjust to me, but time will make it all right. I want to be judged only by my acts."

Says another correspondent, " When the army began to creep forward, I messed at Grant's headquarters with his chief of staff, and around the evening camp-fires I saw much of the general. He rarely uttered a word upon the political bearings of the war; indeed, he said little upon any subject. With his eternal cigar, and his head

thrown to one side, for hours he would silently sit
before the fire, or walk back and forth with eyes
upon the ground, or look at our whist-table, now
and then making a suggestion about the play, &c.,
&c.   At almost every general headquarters one
heard denunciations of rival commanders.   Grant
was above this 'mischievous, foul sin of chiding.'
I never heard him speak unkindly of a brother
officer."

When Halleck had completed his preparations,
he began to advance toward Corinth.   If Grant
had not used the spade and shovel enough, the
former now made up for it, and seemed determined to dig his way into Corinth.   If he had
staid away and left Grant in chief command, the
latter would have been in the place before *he* got
half way there.   Grant never would have been six
weeks advancing fifteen miles, as Halleck was.
He, however, made no suggestion, offered no advice, for he was not consulted.   Once, and once
only, he broke his uniform silence, and that was
when the army finally got before the place.   Being
at headquarters when the probability of the enemy
evacuating it was under consideration, his anxiety
overcame his long reticence, and he advised that
an assault should be made by our extreme right,
in front of which he said he believed the enemy's
defences to be weak; and when they were carried,
to swing up the left and sweep the field.   Hal-

leck, in his pompous way, ridiculed the suggestion, and politely intimated that it would be time
for him to give his opinion when it was asked.
This was more than Grant could patiently endure,
and he replied so sharply and sarcastically, that
he expected to be called to account for it, but the
result so demonstrated the justice of his opinions,
that Halleck was quite willing to let it pass unno-
ticed.

At last, on the 30th of May, Halleck declared
that the enemy was about to attack, and drew up
his army of seventy thousand men, and planted his
batteries, to await the coming shock. But it never
came, and when the army finally advanced, nothing
but an empty town and wooden guns were found
to capture. Beauregard had not only got off with
his army, but with all his war material—in fact,
every thing he wanted to carry away. Blank
faces looked on each other as the tidings travelled
down the line, while a faint smile lighted up the
countenance of Grant, at this illustration of Halleck's grand strategy. He saw as clearly as any
one the importance of seizing great strategic
points, but he knew that the mere occupation of
points in such a vast and diversified country as
ours, would never end the war. Armies must be
taken, as well as places. He was too slow once
(at Fort Henry), but ever after he captured men
as well as strategic points. With Fort Donelson,

Vicksburg, and Richmond, he took whole armies.

When the mighty host of Halleck entered the
deserted works of Corinth, Grant rode over to the
defences opposite our right to see if they were
as weak as he had imagined.   Actual observation
proved the correctness of his judgment, and he
saw, with mortification, what a splendid victory
had in all probability been lost to the Union cause.

After a pursuit of the enemy, which proved
barren of results, Halleck broke up his army to
secure some more strategic points, and finally, in
July, was called to Washington, to take the place
of McClellan, where he only repeated over again
the blunders he had committed West.   His last
act, before leaving, was to offer the command
of the Army of the Tennessee to Col. Al-
len, a quartermaster, who had the good sense
to decline it.   It was a fitting culmination to
his career West, that his last act should be an
attempt to further disgrace the only commander
who had shed lustre on his administration, and
won victories, the honor of which he was not
averse to share.

Grant, however, retained his command, and
was directed to make Corinth his headquarters.
But he was unable to initiate any movements
against the enemy, for two divisions of his army
were taken from him and given to Buell, who was

endeavoring to advance to Chattanooga. His chief occupation was to hold the railroad running north from that place and Bolivar, to Columbus —a kind of campaigning not at all suited to one of his aggressive nature. He was more fitted to *open* communications, than to protect those which others had opened. He remained here, however, two months, watching Van Dorn and Price, who constantly hovered around him.

While here, he issued an order, directing that fugitive slaves, coming within his lines, should be employed in the quartermaster's, subsistence, and engineer's departments—also, when by such employment a soldier might be saved to the ranks of the army—as teamsters, cooks, hospital attendants, and nurses.

Memphis having fallen before our gunboats, came also within his jurisdiction, and caused him no little trouble. The inhabitants, though conquered, continued their treasonable practices, and kept up a constant communication and traffic with the enemy South. Ascertaining this, and finding that his leniency only provoked more daring acts of hostility, he at length issued the following severe order :

DISTRICT OF WEST TENNESSEE, OFFICE PROVOST-MARSHAL GEN'L, }
MEMPHIS, TENN., *July* 10, 1862. }

The constant communication between the so-called Confederate army and their friends and sympathizers in the city of Memphis, despite the orders heretofore issued,

6

and the efforts to enforce them, induced the issuing of
the following order :

The families now residing in the city of Memphis of
the following persons, are required to move south beyond the lines within five days of the date hereof :

First. All persons holding commissions in the so-called
Confederate army, or who have voluntarily enlisted in
said army, or who accompany and are connected with
the same.

Second. All persons holding office under or in the
employ of the so-called Confederate Government.

Third. All persons holding State, county, or municipal offices, who claim allegiance to said so-called Confederate Government, and who have abandoned their
families and gone South.

Safe conduct will be given to the parties hereby
required to leave, upon application to the Provost-
Marshal of Memphis.

By command of   Major-General GRANT.

DISTRICT OF WEST TENNESSEE, OFFICE OF THE PROVOST-
MARSHAL GENERAL, MEMPHIS, TENN., *July* 11, 1862.

*   *   *   *   *   *

In order that innocent, peaceable, and well-disposed
persons may not suffer for the bad conduct of the guilty
parties coming within the purview of Special Order No.
14, dated July 10, 1862, they can be relieved from the
operation of said order No. 14, by signing the following
parole, and producing to the Provost-Marshal General,
or the Provost-Marshal of Memphis, satisfactory guaran-
tees that they will keep the pledge therein made :

PAROLE.

"*First.* I have not, since the occupation of the city
of Memphis by the Federal army, given any aid to the
so-called Confederate army, nor given or sent any
information of the movements, strength, or position of
the Federal army to any one connected with said Confederate army.

"*Second.* I will not, during the occupancy of Memphis by the Federal army, and my residing therein, oppose or conspire against the civil or military authority of the United States; and I will not give aid, comfort, or encouragement to the so-called Confederate army, nor to any person coöperating therewith.

"All of which I state and pledge upon my sacred honor."

By command of   Major-General GRANT.

WILLIAM S. HILLYER, Provost-Marshal General.

He also suspended the Avalanche paper for publishing treasonable articles, and finally permitted it to appear again, only on the condition of the withdrawal of the editor who had written them.

His stern treatment of hostile citizens awakened the bitterest feeling against him, and he received threats of vengeance, of which the following letter is a fair example:

SINATORIA, July 16, 1862.

U. S. GRANT:

SIR: We have seen your infamous and fiendish proclamation. It is characteristic of your infernal policy. * * We had hoped that this war would be conducted upon the principles recognized by civilized nations. But you have seen fit to ignore all the rules of civilized warfare, and resort to means which ought to and would make half-civilized nations blush. If you attempt to carry out your threat against the property of citizens, we will make you rue the day you issued your dastardly proclamation. If we can't act on the principle of lex talionis, in regard to private property, we will visit summary vengeance upon your men. You call us guerillas, which you know is false. We are recognized by our Government; and it was us who attacked your wagons at Morning Sun. We have twenty-three men of yours, and, as soon as you carry out your threat against the citizens of the vicinity of Morning Sun, your Hessians will pay for it. You shall conduct this war upon proper principles. We intend to force you to do it. If you intend to make this a war of extermination, you will please inform us of it at the earliest convenience. We are ready, and more than willing, to raise the "black flag." There are two thousand partisans who have sworn to retaliate. If you do not retract your proclamation, you may expect to have scenes of the most bloody character. We all remember the manner in which your vandal soldiers put to death Mr. Owens, of Missouri. ·Henceforth our motto shall be, Blood for blood, and blood for property. We intend, by the help of God, to hang on the outskirts of your rabble, like lightning around the edge of a cloud.

We don't intend this as a threat, but simply as a warning of what we intend to do in case you pursue your disgraceful and nefarious policy towards our citizens, as marked out in your letter of recent date.

Respectfully,

GEO. R. MERRITT.

Grant fortified Corinth, and erected works nearer the town, so that it could be held by a smaller army than the one which occupied it under Beauregard.

The enemy in the meantime kept him constantly on the alert, and finally, in September, Price suddenly pounced upon Iuka, only twenty miles from his headquarters. Murphy, the commander, gave it up without striking a blow in its defence. Added to this threatening movement, Van Dorn was only four days' march from him in the southwest. He at once determined to crush Price before Van Dorn could form a junction with him. Generals Ord and Rosecrans, with eight or nine thousand troops each, were therefore ordered to move by different routes on the place. Rosecrans had a sharp fight with the enemy, but owing to delays and misunderstandings the two forces did not act in conjunction, as Grant had planned and directed, and Price got off with his army.

Grant now put Rosecrans in command of Corinth, making Jackson his own headquarters, as a point more convenient to communicate with his distributed command. This was on the 23d of September. A few days after, he learned that the rebel forces had effected a junction, and under Van Dorn and Price, were moving on Corinth. On the 3d of October they appeared before the place, and though at first Rosecrans was driven back to his works on the north side of Corinth, he at last, with his army of nineteen thousand, overwhelmed and shattered into fragments the rebel forces, nearly forty thousand strong—thanks to the strong fortifications that Grant, with great forecast, had previously thrown up there. His department being thus relieved from immediate danger, and reinforcements arriving in the latter part of the month, he was anxious to take the offensive, and proposed to Halleck to attempt the capture of Vicksburg. The gunboats above, had opened the Mississippi river down to this place, while Farragut's fleet had cleared it below. Between Halleck, however, who seemed to have no fixed opinion, and political management at Washington, affairs did not move on smoothly, and for a while seemed in an inextricable tangle. But at length they assumed shape, and Sherman with four picked divisions was ordered to embark on board steamers, and planting himself suddenly before Vicksburg carry it by assault, while Grant moved inland, in the rear of it, to prevent reinforcements being thrown into the place. Sherman set out on the 20th of December, landed his troops, and moved to the assault. But in the meantime the shameful surrender of Holly Springs, eight miles in Grant's rear, with its garrison and stores, by which his only line of communication with the north was cut off, brought him to halt, and thus enabled the enemy to reinforce Vicksburg to any extent.

Sherman, ignorant of this, hurled his brave troops against the works; but found instead of a weak garrison a powerful army to oppose him. Repulsed with heavy slaughter, he was compelled to reëmbark his army. McClernand superseded him, when the army and fleet moved against Arkansas Post, on the Arkansas river, and took it with its garrison, stores and arms.

The grand expedition against Vicksburg was

now planned, and Grant's department being enlarged so as to cover the Mississippi river to
this place, he concentrated his army, and gathered together his munitions of war, preparatory to
the herculean task which he knew was before
him.   He arrived at Young's Point on the 29th
of January, and assumed command in person.

CHAPTER VIII.

ABOVE VICKSBURG.

GRANT now had a well-appointed army of some fifty thousand men under him, but the grand difficulty was, to get them within striking distance of Vicksburg. The Mississippi is a very crooked stream, winding in and out, often turning almost directly back and flowing northerly in its course. Just above Vicksburg it wheels short about to the left, and runs *north*-east for some five miles, when it abruptly turns back and flows *south*-east. This of course makes a long tongue of land, projecting from the west side, corresponding in shape with the · bend of the stream. This projection is low, compared with the high bluffs of Vicksburg, so that batteries mounted on it would be perfectly commanded by those occupying the high ground opposite. Hence, the place was safe from any attack that could be made from the west side of the river. It must be approached on the west side, or not at all. Its height rendered it impregnable to the gunboats, that could effectively reach only the water batteries. It therefore was evident that it could be assailed only by moving an army down from the north, or up from the south, and thus get in its rear. But north of Vicksburg, the high bluffs run northeast for twelve miles, to the Yazoo River, where they terminate in the commanding eminence called Haines' Bluff. This whole elevated range was strongly fortified. Haines' Bluff, if once taken, would give a foothold from which an army could work its way along the ridge to Vicksburg. Hence, its seizure was the first thing thought of and attempted, but Sherman's failure demonstrated that this must be given up. The only remaining course left, therefore, was to try to get south of the city, and move up behind it from that direction; but as guns of the heaviest calibre commanded the channel for miles, the army could not be carried in transports past it. Hence, the first thing that suggested itself in this dilemma, was to cut a canal across this low tongue of land, wide and deep enough to float steamers through.

The country here was flat and swampy, which made it seem feasible. This had been commenced some time previously, but it was neither wide nor

6*

deep enough to admit the water from the Mississippi, and had been abandoned. To the opening and enlargement of it Grant's attention was first directed, in accordance with orders from Halleck, who said that " the President attached much importance " to it. Four thousand soldiers, besides negroes, were at once set to work. In the mean time, the low, marshy ground on which the troops were compelled to encamp, produced disease, which swept off, or rendered unfit for duty, a great number. They could not even bury their dead in the neighborhood of their encampment. The levee, a high embankment of the Mississippi, that separated them from the stream, furnished the only dry ground, and this was ridged, as far as the eye could reach, with soldiers' graves—a sad and gloomy spectacle to their comrades below, who thus saw themselves hedged in by the dead. Every thing, however, was done for the health and comfort of the men that foresight and care could accomplish. A lady,* sent by the Sanitary Commission, visited the camp and hospitals at Young's Point, to see if any thing more could be done. She obtained · an interview with Grant, who spoke freely of the sanitary condition of the army, and said he had perfect confidence in its administration, but added that he wanted every thing done for the comfort of the men, that could be, and

* Mrs. A. H. Hoge, author of " The Boys in Blue."

offered her every facility in his power to enable her to carry out her benevolent designs. Looking at every thing in a practical, common-sense light, he did not care whether the good was done through the regular military organizations or not, so that the troops were made more comfortable. She told him she would like some cotton, to make "comfortables" for the soldiers, to keep them warm in the damp, chilly atmosphere to which they were exposed. He immediately sat down and wrote an order for five bales. A tug was placed at her disposal, and she was carried wherever she wished to go. After finishing her investigations, she returned to Grant to make her report to him. Among other things, she said she had discovered that incipient scurvy had commenced in the hospitals at Young's Point, and threatened, according to the reports of the surgeons submitted to her, to become wide and sweeping in its ravages, and that it could be arrested only by a free supply of vegetables and acids. Grant immediately gave an order for the transportation of any needed amount of vegetables from the North; saying, quietly, that, under the circumstances, "onions and potatoes were indispensable to the taking of Vicksburg."

When about to leave, she said: "Well, General, what of Vicksburg? What shall I say when I return?" He paused a moment, in thought,

and then replied: "Madame, Vicksburg is ours,
and its *garrison our prisoners*.   It is only a *question of time*.   I want to take it *with as little loss
of life as possible*."   This confident opinion was
not based on any strong faith in the success of the
canal, for he always doubted it.   It was originally
constructed by Gen. Williams, in 1862, but when
the levee was cut, the water did not pour through
it.   Grant had, therefore, a cut made farther up
the river, tapping the original canal, but starting
at a point where the current struck the bank more
strongly and directly.   For two months the soldiers toiled on to complete it, while the country
waited and grumbled.   But just as success seemed
probable, and this branch cut had almost reached
the main canal, a sudden freshet carried away the
dam at the upper end, and the swollen waters rushing in with great violence, tore over and through
the banks, crushing down all barriers in its mad
flow, and turning the whole peninsula into a
marshy lake.   Horses were swept away, and
drowned—soldiers scattered, pell mell, in every
direction, to save their lives—leaving all their tools
and machines to be borne away or submerged in
the flood, and thus the labor of weeks was totally
destroyed.   In the mean time, the enemy, having.
learned what was going on, planted batteries to en-
filade the canal, so that this project, on the completion of which so much had been anticipated, had to

be abandoned. Grant had put so little faith in the success of this canal that, the very next day after he assumed command in person, he gave orders to have another one cut from the Mississippi to Lake Providence, which lay only a mile from the shore, and connecting by a series of bayous and streams with the Red River, which last stream enters the Mississippi between Natchez and Port Hudson. This was to enable him, in case the first canal failed, to coöperate with Banks—an object that the government had very much at heart. McPherson was set to work on this, but after several weeks' labor, it also was abandoned. For a time, it was supposed by some men of ardent imaginations, that it was going to change the whole course of the mighty Mississippi, clear to the Gulf of Mexico, and thus leave New Orleans an inland town. But its turbid current swept on in its old channel, and Grant was at last compelled to abandon all hope of getting below Vicksburg on the *west* side of the river. It shows how thoroughly he had studied the subject, and estimated the difficulties of the task, by his having several different routes surveyed at the same time, so that if one failed there should be no delay in trying another.

Besides the two plans which had now been tried and abandoned, a third one, before they were tested, had been matured. If he failed on the west side, he determined to try the east side, and

for this purpose, had what was called the Yazoo
Pass surveyed by Lieut.-Col. Wilson.

A few miles below Helena, and about a mile
from the river, lies Moon Lake, once the bed of the
Mississippi. A narrow and crooked bayou formerly led into this, through which light craft
sometimes reached the Yazoo—for Moon Lake
connects with the Coldwater river, which flows into
the Tallahatchie, which, in turn, effects a junction
with the Yallabusha—the two forming the Yazoo.
The distance by this route was some two hundred and fifty miles. The short cut, however,
from the Mississippi into Moon Lake, had been
closed up by the State, as, in times of freshets, the
water poured through it in such volume that it
overflowed the surrounding country.

The levee that shut it up was cut on the 2d
of February, and the water rushed through into
the lake,* cutting a channel in two days, wide
and deep enough to admit the largest steamers.
The rebels, however, who were on the watch for this
very movement, now began to barricade the tortuous
channel beyond, with trees and rafts, at every available point.   In one place, this tangled net-work

---

* The plan and main direction of this route may be understood
by referring to the map giving that of Steele's bayou. Both routes
would take the army into the Yazoo above Haines' Bluff. The
only difference was—this one begun up the Mississippi—struck
down farther east, and reached the Yazoo higher up than the last
one undertaken.

of logs and trees extended over a mile in solid mass. Many of the trees were of gigantic size—weighing twenty tons or more, which, according to Col. Badeau's account, " had to be hauled out entire upon the shore by strong cables, while a few of the most buoyant were cut in pieces and fastened along the banks." To add to the difficulties, the rapid rise of the water, from the crevasse at the entrance, submerged the entire country, except along a very narrow strip of land near the shore. The men, in parties of about five hundred, were thus obliged to work in the water, as well as during almost incessant rains. The barriers, however, being removed, and a heavy growth of overhanging timber cut away, the distance from Moon Lake to the Coldwater was finally cleared. But, while Grant's forces were thus diligently engaged in opening one end of the pass, the enemy had gained time to securely fortify below.

On the 15th of February, however, a way was open to the Tallahatchie, and Brigadier-General Ross, with forty-five hundred men, was ordered into the pass. He embarked on twenty-two light transports, preceded by two iron-clad gunboats, and a mosquito fleet, as the light-armored craft suitable for this navigation was called. Lieutenant-Commander Watson Smith commanded the naval force. The difficulty of procuring light transports delayed Ross over a week, but the combined fleet entered the pass on the 24th of February, and reached the Coldwater, twenty-five miles from the Mississippi, on the 2d of March. The Coldwater is over a hundred feet wide, and runs through a dense wilderness, for nearly all its course. The Tallahatchie is a stream of similar nature, and, from its width and depth, no longer susceptible of obstruction by the enemy. Thirty miles below the mouth of the Coldwater, the Tallahatchie affords free navigation for boats two hundred and fifty feet long. When once the expedition reached these rivers, a great part of its difficulties would, it was hoped, be past. The naval commander moved cautiously, running but little faster than the current by daylight, and tying his boats to the shore after nightfall, so that the expedition did not reach the lower Tallahatchie till the 10th of March. This long passage of two hundred and fifty miles, through an almost unbroken forest, was made without the loss of a man. The country being overflowed, the river-banks could not be approached in any force by guerillas or sharpshooters.

Wilson now reported the practicability of the route as a line of important military operations, and Grant determined to prosecute his entire campaign, if possible, in this direction. The idea was to reach the Yazoo river, above Haines' bluff, with the whole army; the distance from Milliken's Bend would have been nearly nine hundred miles. At first, only a single division of troops, under Brigadier-General Quimby, was sent to the support of Ross ; but, shortly afterwards, McPherson, with his whole corps, and an additional division from Hurlbut's command (at Memphis), was ordered into the pass, whenever suitable transportation could be procured. Great difficulty, however, was found in obtaining light-draught steamers fit for the navigation of these narrow and devious streams ; and the reënforcements were, in consequence, delayed at Helena.

Near where the waters of the Tallahatchie meet those of the Yallabusha, the small town of Greenwood is built; a little way above this point, the former stream sweeps to the east for eight or ten miles, and then doubles at the confluence ; while the Yazoo, which is formed by the junction, flows back again to within five hundred yards of the Tallahatchie. At the narrowest part of the neck of land thus created, the rebels had hastily constructed, of earth and cotton bales, a line of parapet running irregularly across from the Tallahatchie to the north bank of the Yazoo. This work they called fort "Pemberton." This fort commanded all the approaches to the Yazoo and the Yazoo itself, while it was built on ground so low that in front of it the land was covered with water for a great distance, thus making a land at-

tack impossible. Resort was therefore had to the
iron-clads, that had worked their difficult way to
this point. An attack was made by them, at long
range, on the 11th of March, without any effect,
and it was repeated two days after, with the same
result, while one vessel was crippled by the guns
of the fort, and some thirty men killed and wounded. It was plain that some new mode of attack
must be devised. The fort was on such low
ground that a rise of two or three feet in the river,
it was thought, would drown out the garrison,
and it was resolved to try to effect it. For this
purpose, the levee of the Mississippi was cut
eighteen miles above Helena—three hundred miles
away—in the hope that the water pouring through
the country would eventually seek the Coldwater
as an avenue of escape, and produce the needed
rise of water. The only result, however, was the
wide-spread inundation of the country, making it
a vast lake and marsh. This route was plainly
impracticable, while to make matters worse, the
enemy began to hurry troops across the country
by a shorter route, to hem in the boats and troops
from behind. In this dilemma; for the double
purpose of making a diversion in favor of Ross,
the commander, and of reaching the same point
aimed at (the Yazoo above Haines' Bluff), another expedition up Steele's Bayou was started.
This left the Yazoo below Haines' Bluff, and pass-

ing through Steele's Bayou into Black Bayou, thence to Deer Creek—through Rolling Fork, across to the Sunflower, and adown this to the Yazoo again. This strange and tortuous route is clearly shown in the accompanying map. The expedition was under the command of Admiral Porter, to be supported by Sherman, who by a short cut across the country was to reach a point on the Rolling Fork about the same time that he did.

Such inland navigation was never before attempted by war vessels. The expedition consisted of four gunboats, four mortar-boats, and four tugs. For thirty miles the little fleet passed up Steele's Bayou, then a mere ditch, to Black Bayou, in which, for four miles, the trees had to be torn out or pushed over by the iron-clads, or the branches cut away, when Porter at last reached Deer Creek. It took twenty-four hours to make these four miles. Some idea of the difficulties of the route may be obtained, when it is remembered that, with the utmost exertion of the crews, the vessels for twenty-four consecutive hours averaged a speed of only about fifty *rods* an hour. Up this stream to Rolling Fork it was thirty-two miles. To the same point by land, it was twelve miles, over which Sherman marched, in order to coöperate with him. The channel was narrow and filled with small willows, which so retarded the progress of the boats that, with his utmost exertions, Porter could average only about a half a mile an hour. At length he got within seven miles of the Rolling Fork, from whence there would be water enough to the Yazoo.

The inhabitants were filled with amazement to see a war fleet sailing through the heart of a country where a vessel of any kind had never before been seen, while the negroes flocked in crowds to the shore to gaze on the unwonted spectacle. But as soon as the Confederate official in that section was informed of the expedition, he gave the alarm, and ordered the torch to be applied to all the cotton along the shore, and Porter was lighted on his strange course by a continuous conflagration.

Negroes were also set to work cutting down trees to arrest his progress, until troops and guns could be brought up. Porter, made aware of the movement, pushed on the tug Thistle, with a howitzer on board, which reached the first tree before it was cut down. The tug then kept on, to keep the way open, but the enemy at length succeeded in getting one large tree across the creek, and thus for a time stopped all further progress. Being now safe from our guns, the negroes, under the orders of their masters, continued to chop down trees, until it was thought that Porter could make no further advance. He, however, by working night and day, chopping and sawing them in two, or hauling them one side, at length cleared the channel, and pushed on until he got within three miles of the Rolling Fork. Here he saw smoke rising over the tree-tops in the direction of the Yazoo, and learned that the enemy was landing troops to dispute his passage. He immediately sent Lieutenant Murphy, with two boat howitzers and three hundred men, to hold Rolling Fork until he could reach it with his boats.

"After working all night," says Porter, "and clearing out the obstructions, which were terrible, we succeeded in getting within eight hundred yards of the end of this troublesome creek; had only two or three large trees to remove, and one apparently short and easy lane of willows to work through. The men being much worn out, we rested at sunset.

"In the morning we commenced with renewed vigor to work ahead through the willows, but our passage was very slow; the lithe trees defied our utmost efforts to get by them, and we had to go to work and pull them up separately, or cut them off under water, which was a most tedious job.

"In the mean time, the enemy had collected and landed about eight hundred men, and seven pieces of artillery (from 20 to 30-pounders); which were firing on our field-pieces from time to time, the latter not having range enough to reach them.

"I was also informed that the enemy were cutting down trees in our rear, to prevent communication by water, and also prevent our escape; this looked unpleasant. I knew that five thousand had embarked at Haines' Bluff for this place, immediately they heard we were attempting to go through that way, and, as our troops had not come up, I considered it unwise to risk the least thing; at all events, never to let my communication be closed behind me. I was somewhat strengthened in my determination to advance no further until reinforced by land forces, when the enemy, at sunset, opened on us a cross-fire with six or seven rifled guns, planted somewhere off in the woods, where we could see nothing but the smoke. It did not take us long to dislodge them, though, a large part of the crew being on shore at the time, we could not fire over them, or until they got on board. I saw at once the difficulties we had to encounter, with a constant fire on our working parties, and no prospect at present of the troops getting along. I had received a letter from General Sherman, informing me of the difficulties in getting forward his men; he doing his utmost, I knew, to expedite matters.

"The news of the felling trees in our rear was brought in frequently by negroes, who were pressed into the service for cutting them, and I hesitated no longer about what to do. We dropped down again, unshipped our rudders, and let the vessels rebound from tree to tree. As we left, the enemy took possession of the Indian mound, and in the morning opened fire on the Carondelet, Lieutenant Murphy, and Cincinnati, Lieutenant Bache. These two ships soon silenced the batteries, and we were no longer annoyed.

"The sharpshooters hung about us, firing from behind trees and rifle-pits, but with due precaution we had very few hurt—only five wounded by rifle-balls—and they were hit by being imprudent.

"On the 21st, we fell in with Colonel Smith, commanding Eighth Missouri, and other parts of regiments. We were quite pleased to see him, as I never knew before how much the comfort and safety of iron-clads, situated as we were, depended on soldiers. I had already sent out behind a force of three hundred men, to stop the felling of trees in our rear, which Colonel Smith now took charge of.

"The enemy had already felled over forty heavy trees, which Lieutenant-Commander Owen, in the Louisville, working night and day, cleared away almost fast enough to permit us to meet with no delay.

"Colonel Smith's force was not large enough to justify my making another effort to get through; he had no artillery, and would frequently have to leave the vessels in following the roads.

"On the 22d, we came to a bend in the river, where the enemy supposed they had blockaded us completely, having cut a number of trees altogether, and so intertwined that it seemed impossible to move them. The Louisville was at work at them, pulling them up, when we discovered about three thousand rebels attempting to pass the edge of the woods to our rear, while the negroes reported artillery coming up on our quarters.

"We were all ready for them, and, when the artillery opened on us, we opened such a fire on them, that they scarcely waited to hitch up their horses. At the same time, the rebel soldiers fell in with Colonel Smith's troops, and after a sharp skirmish fled before the fire of our soldiers. After this we were troubled no more."

Although Porter now met Sherman's advancing forces, he saw it would be folly to attempt to retrace his steps, and so the expedition, after having sailed over a hundred and forty miles, right through plantations and forests, at length found itself once more at the starting-point, and the last attempt to get around Vicksburgh from the north was abandoned, and Grant at once ordered the concentration of all his forces at Milliken's Bend.

CHAPTER IX.

RUNNING THE BATTERIES.

Grant resolves to run the Batteries with his Fleet—Opposed by his Officers—Boldness of the Resolution—Desperate Character of his Plan—Attempt to remove him—Coöperation with Banks—The Army marches below Vicksburgh—Running the Batteries—A thrilling Spectacle—Success—Grand Gulf attacked—Repulse—Its Batteries run—Landing at Bruinsburgh—Energy and Activity of Grant—Superintends every thing—Strikes Inland—Battle of Port Gibson—Grant assumes Command—The Victory—Grand Gulf Evacuated—Entered by Grant.

INSTEAD of being discouraged at these repeated failures, occupying such a long time, until the public patience was well-nigh exhausted, Grant seemed to feel relieved that these unsatisfactory experiments were at last over, for he would now be justified in taking the short bold course, so much more congenial to his tastes, and in harmony with his character. The winter and spring freshets had somewhat subsided, so that the peninsula opposite Vicksburg might be made passable to troops, and he resolved to march his army across it to a point below, while Porter run the batteries with his iron-clads and steamers. Farragut had passed the batteries at Port Hudson, with some of his vessels, so that

7

Grant was able to communicate with him respecting Banks, from whom he found he could expect no support. He was aware that the Government wished him to effect a junction with that officer before Port Hudson, if the latter did not join him, and it is believed by many that he resolved to do so. Except the feeble attempt to open the Red River route, we, however, see no evidence that he ever wished to put himself under the control of that political General. Besides, he knew that Port Hudson was only an appendage to Vicksburg, and to combine all their forces against a mere outwork was unwise. He knew that if Vicksburg was captured, Port Hudson would fall without fighting; but the overthrow of the latter place would have no effect on the former, except to swell the forces that could be brought against it. But by the time this was accomplished, the enemy also would have concentrated forces to oppose them, so that the relative strength of the two would remain nearly the same. Grant, therefore, with his clear perception, saw that Vicksburg was the point where the blow should be struck, and determined, if events justified it, to plant it there. Still, the objections to his contemplated movement were grave, and the difficulties formidable, and the responsibility and risk frightful. He knew the country was filled with clamor against him. Some of his best friends had deserted him.

Governors and members of Congress visited his camp, and went away with dismal stories of his inefficiency ; and everywhere it was said, that he had only obstinacy in the presence of difficulties, without the genius to overcome them. Confidence in him was being lost, and now he proposed to take a step full of peril, not only to himself, but to the army. He was not going to risk a battle to save his reputation, but to put it and the fate of fifty thousand men on a single throw—for with the army once below Vicksburg, defeat was destruction. He would have no base to fall back upon, no line of retreat left open. Victories sudden, rapid, constant, and overwhelming, he must have, or he was lost. Resting, as he was, under a cloud, it required a character of amazing strength, under these circumstances, to venture on such a bold and hazardous course. He might well hesitate, even though some of his ablest officers approved it. But when, as they did, one and all, oppose it, not hesitatingly and doubtfully, but decidedly and emphatically, it seems marvellous that he did not waver.

Sherman, his best and warmest friend, and ablest general, wrote a letter to him urging him not to venture on such a move. McPherson, equally sagacious and beloved, with others, condemned it. Government did not expect it—no one was near by to sustain him in a course fraught with such fearful consequences. Nothing excites our admiration more for this strong, silent man, than to see him thus stand all alone—enemies without, and friends within, standing aloof—while he gazes thoughtfully, sternly, down the fearful abyss into which he has determined to cast himself and his fifty thousand men.

To what a sublime height must he have reached, to be so completely above all surrounding influences of every kind! How clear and penetrating the glance that could see light beyond the darkness that bounded the vision of all others, even the most clear-sighted. Self-poised, self-sustained, equal in himself alone to the great crisis he had reached, he rises before us like some grand column, resting firm on its foundation by mere weight alone. "Call a council of officers before deciding on so hazardous a step," said the sagacious, true-hearted Sherman—but he wanted no council—his determination was unalterably taken, and nothing but positive orders from Government could change it, and no one knows how near those orders came to be issued. The President was beset with men, high in position, warning and beseeching him to remove Grant. One, who had been a firm friend of the latter, waited on Mr. Lincoln, and after reminding him of his past friendship for Grant, said that he must now abandon him. He evidently was not equal to the po-

sition that he occupied, and the good of the country required that he should be sacrificed. The
President heard him through, and then, pausing
thoughtfully a moment, replied: "I rather like
the man. - *I think I'll try him a little longer.*"
What momentous results hung on that little sentence! If it had been, "I'll try him no longer,"
who can calculate the delay, discouragements, and
loss of life that would have followed. Grant,
however, determined that if "a little longer" time
was given him, he would be beyond the reach of
orders from any source, until his fate was sealed.
These might follow him as fast as snow-flakes seek
the earth, yet they would not overtake the tramp
of his victorious battalions, if he were successful—
and if not, they would never find him. He took
no precautions against false accusations should he
fail—left behind no defence to save his reputation.
Silent, calm, and resolute, he gave all his attention to the mighty task before him. It is true,
his most intimate biographer states, that Grant
did not determine at first on the bold course
that he afterwards took—that his object in getting
below Vicksburg was to coöperate with Banks, at
Port Hudson, and help reduce it, when both
armies could move against Vicksburg. But we
see no evidence of this in his movements, and are
inclined to think the statement is made simply because such was the drift of Grant's orders, and

such the wish of Halleck and the President. In the first place, Banks was the senior of Grant, and hence, in that case, would have assumed supreme command, leaving the latter only a subordinate, and, though he would never put his mere personal ambition against the public service, he knew enough of Banks' military education and career, not to place much confidence in his ability. to carry out such an expedition. In this his best officers sympathized with him. Besides, more than a month previous, he had said that he had discovered a good wagon-road across the peninsula, from Milliken's Bend to New Carthage, when the water was low, and added, " My expectation is for some of the naval fleet to run the batteries of Vicksburg, whilst the army moves through by this new route. Once there, I will move to Warrenton or Grand Gulf, probably the latter. From either of these points, there are good roads to Jackson and the Black River bridge, without crossing Black River. I will keep my army together, and see to it that I am not cut off from my supplies, or beat in any other way than a fair fight."

But what had he to do with Black River or Jackson, lying nearly fifty miles directly east of Vicksburg, and nearly three times that distance northeast from the point at which he proposed to land? To march back inland, fighting as he did for a week or more, was certainly an extraordinary way to reach Banks, at Port Hudson, nearly two hundred miles below.   More than this, there was no change of circumstances whatever, after he had passed Vicksburg, to induce him to change his plan, if that was to coöperate with Banks. On the contrary, the changes that did occur were all of a character to make him carry it out ; for he was compelled to go below the point where he had calculated he could cross the Mississippi.   He did not anticipate the necessity of going below Grand Gulf.   The point where he eventually planted his army on the east shore, was so low down as to increase the hazard of the enterprise against Vicksburg, and took him just so far towards Banks. In proportion as he increased the distance he would have to march to get in the rear of Vicksburg, in that same proportion did he give the enemy time to concentrate his forces against him. Hence, it is difficult to see what " circumstances " induced Grant to change his plan, if that plan was to send a corps to Port Hudson.   It is true that Grant had hoped to open an inland communication, by bayous, through which transports could pass, and so his route for supplies be kept open. But, by the time he had got one vessel through, low water made further navigation impracticable and he had to resort to roads and bridges.   But all this took place before he started, and not after he was below Vicksburg.   More than this, all his efforts on the east shore had not been *merely* to get *below* the place, but *behind* it, and there he evidently determined to plant his army.

When Grant had his entire army well in hand, and had gathered from up the river all the yawls and boats he needed, he began his great decisive movement. Porter's gunboats had shown that they could pass the batteries with comparative impunity, and the former resolved to try the experiment of getting transports past also, while he marched his army inland down the river to meet them. It was resolved to test this matter at night, and the plan adopted was, to have the iron-clads move down and engage the batteries, while the transports, under cover of the smoke and darkness, should slip quietly by, near the western shore. It was a desperate enterprise, to which men could not legitimately be ordered, and volunteers were therefore called for. So many offered, that the necessary number had finally to be drawn by lot. Grant resolved to try the experiment first with three transports.

A little before midnight, the gunboats moved from their moorings and dropped silently down the river, followed by the transports. Seven iron-clads engaged the batteries, while the river steamers, towing the barges, attempted to run the gauntlet of their fire for fifteen miles. It was a night of intense anxiety to Grant; for if this plan failed, even his fertile resources could see no way of getting in the rear of Vicksburg. An hour had not elapsed after the boats disappeared in the darkness, before the thunder of artillery shook the shore, followed soon after by the flame of a conflagration, kindled by the rebels, to light up the bosom of the Mississippi. Under its blaze the poor transports lay revealed as distinctly as though the noon-day sun was shining, while the men on board in turn could see the soldiers hurrying through the streets of Vicksburg, and working the guns. They at once became an exposed target to the heavy batteries, the shells of which cut the ropes and rods supporting the chimneys of the boats, burst in the pilot-houses, and among the machinery, and filled the air on every side with their flying fragments. Yet the little fleet steamed rapidly on, hugging the opposite shore, hoping under its shadow and the covering smoke to escape destruction. Grant stood on a transport located just above the bend, and watched the movement with the deepest anxiety. He was within range of the rebel batteries, and shot and shell fell all around him. Yet he never moved, but kept his eyes on the bosom of the stream, now light as day, where his barges moved, mere dark specks on the water.

"Every transport was struck, and two were drawn into the eddy, and ran over a part of the

7*

distance in front of Vicksburg no less than three times. The Forest Queen was disabled by a round shot, and drifted down opposite the lower picket stations, where the gunboat Tuscumbia took her in tow, and landed her just above the crevasse at New Carthage. The Henry Clay also became disabled, and was in a sinking condition soon after coming within range of the upper batteries; she had in tow a barge with soldiers on board, which was cast loose, and floated down the stream. Not long afterwards the boat itself took fire, from the explosion of a shell, and burned to the water's edge, drifting along with the current, a flaming mass. General Sherman was in a small boat, watching the bombardment, and picked up the pilot as he floated from the wreck. The crew pushed off in yawls to the Louisiana side, where they landed, and hid themselves behind an old levee, during the cannonade. After it had ceased, they made their way back through the submerged swamps, to camp."

" The light streamed up from the blazing hull of the Henry Clay, and threw into strong relief against the shadows of night the other transports, and the gunboats at their fiery work. The currents were strong, and dangerous eddies delayed the vessels; the lights glaring in every direction, and the smoke enveloping the squadron, confused the pilots; the bulwarks, even of the iron-clads,

were crushed; and the uproar of artillery, reëcho-
ing from the hills, was incessant. One of the
heaviest guns of the enemy was seen to burst in
the streets of Vicksburg, and the whole popula-
tion was awake and out of doors, watching the
scene on which its destinies depended. For two
hours and forty minutes the fleets were under
fire. But at last the transports and the gunboats
had all got out of range, the blazing beacons on
the hills and streams burned low, the array of
batteries belching flame and noise from the embattled bluffs had ceased their utterances, and
silence and darkness resumed their sway over the
beleaguered city, and the swamps and rivers that
encircle Vicksburg." *

The next night Grant sent down six more
steamers towing twelve coal barges, of which all
but one steamer, and half the barges, got through,
though most were more or less damaged. .

In the mean time, McClernand, by order of
Grant, had taken his corps, which had the honor
to form the advance, and marched across the
peninsula, driving the enemy out of Richmond,
that lay in his route, while the pioneer corps,
under Captain Patterson, made a bridge two
hundred feet long, of the logs taken from the
adjacent houses. The columns marched over, but
the difficulties of the route had but just com-

* Col. Badeau.

menced. "Old roads had to be repaired, new ones made, boats constructed for the transportation of men and supplies, twenty miles of levee sleeplessly guarded day and night, and every possible precaution taken to prevent the rising flood from breaking through the levee and engulfing us." The rebel cavalry were also hovering around, but, being at last driven across Bayou Vidal, McClernand, on the 4th of April, embarked in a skiff, and, accompanied by Osterhaus and his staff, rowed down to within half a mile of Carthage, on the Mississippi river. Fired upon by the enemy, the skiff was brought to a halt, but not until it was ascertained that the levee had been cut, and the water, in three currents, was pouring through, flooding all the country. Capturing a flat-boat, McClernand mounted it with two howitzers, and embarking a party, sent it down to drive the enemy out of Carthage, which they succeeded in doing.

In this march, McClernand constructed nearly two thousand feet of bridging out of material created, for the most part, on the occasion—completing, in three days and nights, the great military road across the Peninsula, from the Mississippi river to a point forty miles below Vicksburg.

Grant's orders to him were to occupy Grand Gulf, expecting that the troops would be embarked at Carthage, and taken down in transports to that point. But this being found impracticable, the only course left open was for the troops to keep on down the river, nearly fifty miles, to Hard Times, building bridges and constructing roads as they marched. This place at length was reached, where the transports were awaiting them to carry them across to Grand Gulf, the spot selected by Grant for landing. But here, again, the rebels had anticipated him, and formidable batteries frowned from the place.

The 17th Corps, under McPherson, had followed close on the heels of McClernand, and Grant, after consulting with Admiral Porter, resolved to make an attempt to carry the works by assault. The plan was, for Porter to move up and silence the batteries, when the troops, which were on transports, would land and finish the work. On the morning of the 29th of April, the Admiral steamed boldly up with his six iron-clads, and for five hours and a half poured in shot and shell—at times running his vessels almost up to the muzzles of the hostile guns. But the works were too elevated to be easily reached from the water, and although he could with his terrible fire drive the men from the guns, he was unable to dismount a single piece. Grant stood on a transport a little distance off, and watched the battle. Porter at length withdrew, having lost seventy-nine in killed and wounded.

Grant then signalled to him to be taken on board the flagship. It was now afternoon, and as time was every thing, he directed the Admiral, with his battered fleet, and carrying the wounded, to run the batteries with the transports that very night, while he disembarked the troops at Hard Times, and commenced his march below. He in the mean time directed the eastern shore to be examined, with a view of ascertaining the locality and state of the roads leading from Grand Gulf back into the interior. The whole country seemed flooded, and he expected to float down the river until he could find high solid ground; but being informed by a negro, that a good dry road led from the shore at Bruinsburg directly back to the bluffs, which were two miles distant, he landed there. In the mean time, he directed Sherman, who had not yet left Milliken's Bend, to make a demonstration against Vicksburg, in order to keep Pemberton, the commander there, from sending reinforcements to Grand Gulf, while he attacked it. This Sherman did; but on the 1st of May, he received orders from Grant, to push on with all possible speed to join him. The latter also directed a battery to be planted at Perkins' landing, and an improvised gunboat stationed there to protect his supplies gathered at that point. He at the same time ordered two more tugs, with two barges carrying provisions, to run the batteries at Vicksburg.

"Do this," he said, "with all expedition, in forty-eight hours from receipt of orders, if possible. This is of immense importance. Should the crews decline running through, call on the commanding officer for volunteers, and discharge the crews." At the same time that he was setting every thing in motion above him, he was marshalling his columns for an immediate advance up the river. He directed the chief commissary of the Thirteenth Corps, still in advance, to issue three days' rations, which were to last five, and not detain the officers drawing them to give vouchers for them, as was customary. Every hour was priceless, and not a moment's delay could be allowed. His strong nature, seemingly so sluggish, now exhibited its inherent strength; and his mind, usually slow in its operations, worked with the rapidity of lightning. He seemed omnipresent, and to embrace the minutest details in his swift, searching survey of his position. Nothing was left to subordinates but to execute his orders, which flew from one to another incessantly. No mistake must be made, and to avoid one he superintended every thing himself, and kept in the advance where he could do it.

He had not transports enough, and gunboats were used as such, to hurry the arriving troops over the river. Tents and wagons he ordered to be left behind till every man was across. His own horse shared the common fate. Subordinates caught the spirit of their chief, and every thing moved as if the fate of the army rested on the next hour. Hence, the shore at Bruinsburg, was a scene of intense activity all day, for it was six miles from the point where the troops were embarked, so that many trips had to be made with his scant transportation, to get them over; but in twenty-four hours all of McClernand's corps and one division of McPherson's were landed, and by sunset, the bluffs, two miles distant, were reached. Grant knew the moment he struck inland, the enemy would penetrate his design, and so that very afternoon McClernand's corps was started off towards Port Gibson, lying to the southeast of Grand Gulf, the occupation of which would uncover the latter place. He did not even wait for the army-wagons to be brought across the river, but with three day's rations moved off at once. Grand Gulf, which he designed to make his base of supplies, must be taken before the enemy at Vicksburg, informed of his intentions, could reinforce the place. He saw that it must be swift marching, quick fighting, sudden and constant victories, or the storm would gather so heavily about him that his advance would be stopped. Hence he ordered as little baggage to be taken as possible, and set the example of retrenchment himself. Washburne, member of

Congress from Illinois, his ever fast friend, accompanied the expedition, and says that Grant took with him "neither a horse, nor an orderly, nor a camp-chest, nor an overcoat, nor a blanket, nor even a clean shirt. His entire baggage for six days was a tooth-brush. He fared like the commonest soldier in his command, partaking of his rations and sleeping upon the ground, with no covering but the canopy of heaven." This shows not only how terribly in earnest Grant at this point was, but also how thoroughly he comprehended the peril of his situation.

McClernand's corps started at three o'clock in the afternoon, and kept up its march till two o'clock in the morning, when it was suddenly brought to a halt by a battery in its path. At daybreak this was reconnoitred.

The rebel commander at Grand Gulf, informed of Grant's movements, had marched promptly out with eleven thousand men, and taken a strong position along some deep ravines, flanked by heavy woods and canebrakes. McClernand, however, deployed his men the best way he could, and advanced to the attack. The first thunder of artillery roused Grant, who was still at the landing, eight miles off, to the peril of a repulse, and ordering McPherson to push on as fast as possible, borrowed a horse (for his own was not yet across), and with only his staff accompanying him, galloped to the battle-field. The moment he arrived, he assumed command, and pressed the rebel position with relentless severity. In a few hours McPherson's columns appeared on the field, when Grant ordered him at once to move a brigade to the help of Osterhaus, on the left, who could make no headway against the enemy. Grant accompanied this brigade in person, and directed it to charge across a ravine on the rebel flank, while Osterhaus should assault in front. It was done with a cheer, and Grant, with a smile, saw the hostile ranks give way, and after a short struggle to bear up against the shock, turn in swift retreat. Position after position was now carried, until the whole rebel army was driven back. The victorious troops followed until darkness shut out every thing from view, when a halt was ordered, at a point only two miles from Port Gibson. Directing that no camp-fires should be lighted, except in the rear, or in deep gullies, and that the artillery be placed so as to command the surrounding country, Grant ordered McClernand to attack the enemy at daybreak. He then sat down and wrote his despatch to Washington by moonlight.

His loss in killed and wounded in this battle was a little over eight hundred; that of the enemy somewhat less, as he was protected by his position. Grant, however, took six hundred and fifty prisoners, and six guns. Bowen, the rebel general, did not wait for daybreak, but decamped in the night across the Bayou Pierre, destroying the bridge behind him. McClernand was at once set to work to rebuild it, which took all day. The next, the third, Grant pushed on the forces under McPherson, who crowded the enemy back, driving them through Willow Springs, a distance of fifteen miles from Port Gibson, and over the Big Black River in such haste, that they had not time to destroy the bridge.

These successes compelled the evacuation of Grand Gulf, and on the same day Grant, taking one of Logan's brigades, and an escort of cavalry, left Willow Springs for that place. He found Porter in possession of it. He had now for three days been almost constantly in the saddle, not having had his clothes off during that time, but snatching his repose when and where he could. Going aboard one of the gunboats, he borrowed a change of linen, and then sat down and wrote despatches till midnight.

CHAPTER X.

THE GREAT MARCH.

A Perilous Resolve—Cuts loose from his Base—Untiring Activity
—Urgent Orders — Sherman's Arrival—His Astonishment—
Grant Marches for Jackson—Address to his Troops—His little
Son accompanies him—Despatch to Halleck—McPherson defeats Johnston—Jackson evacuated—Grant's Son the first to
enter it—Sherman left to destroy Public Property—The Army
marches back toward Vicksburg—Johnston outmarched—Battle of Champion's Hill—Grant with his Boy under Fire—
"The Hill of Death"—Battle of Black River—Before Vicksburg—Sherman's Opinion of the Campaign—Results of it—
Its Resemblance to Napoleon's Italian Campaign.

IT is stated that, up to this time, Grant had not
abandoned the design of establishing himself at
Grand Gulf, and sending a corps to the aid of
Banks. Be that as it may, all his movements
looked in a different direction. A letter which he
here received from Banks, stating that he would
not be at Port Hudson for a week to come, left
no room for further hesitation, if it ever existed.
But instead of pushing directly for Vicksburg,
Grant having learned that a large army was gathering in the interior to reinforce it, which would
make the garrison outnumber his army, he determined to throw himself between the two, and
prevent the junction. At the same time, he wished

to seize Jackson, fifty miles in rear of Vicksburg, and situated at the junction of the railroads by which the garrison was supplied.   It was a bold, perilous movement.   He might not prevent the junction of the two armies, when he would be too feeble to offer battle, while to keep open his communication with Grand Gulf, his depot of supplies fifty miles distant would require half of his army In this dilemma, he took the daring resolution of cutting loose from his base altogether, and with only three days' rations in the haversacks of the soldiers, swing his army at once into the interior, trusting to the resources of the country to furnish the balance of the supplies.   He knew that this step was looked upon with alarm by his best officers.   Not that they feared for themselves, for more loyal, fearless, and gallant subordinates never gathered around a great leader; but they feared failure and ruin to the army, and damage to the common cause.   They therefore respectfully urged him not to attempt it; but he stood firm, though he stood alone.   He knew, moreover, that if his purpose was known to the Government, he would be promptly ordered to face about.   Still, he did not waver a moment.   This quiet faith in himself invests him with a grandeur greater even than his victories.

Without parade, quietly, yet with a resolution fixed as the granite hills, he, at midnight on the

3d of May, mounted his horse, "turned his back on the Mississippi River," and started for the advance. The die was cast; it was now victory or annihilation, glory or disgrace, life or death, with him and his noble army. He knew all this, as he rode on through the deep night, but he felt no misgivings, no regrets. Thoughtful and solemn, as befitting so momentous a decision, he was nevertheless borne up by a serene confidence in the correctness of his judgment. Paralyzed by no forebodings, his mental faculties, instead of being depressed by the weight of responsibility he had taken on himself, were roused into tenfold activity. No orders could reach him now, until it was too late to obey them. Unfettered and free, he was in just the position for which nature designed him, and he went to work with an energy and power that astonish us. The army must be got in hand as quickly as untiring efforts, and work by night and day, could do it; and then he meant his motto should be that of Danton's, "*Audace, audace, toujours audace.*" His staff was now allowed scarcely a moment's rest, and his orders flew from point to point with bewildering rapidity. Sherman was hurried forward with urgent appeals. Hurlbut, at Memphis, was directed to send on a division at once; another was ordered from Milliken's Bend, with directions to march by brigades. At the same time, the road across the peninsula was ordered to be shortened, so that the trains could be pushed forward more rapidly. He also sent a despatch to the commissary at Grand Gulf to issue three days' rations, which must be made to last five, "if not seven, days," without waiting to go through the prescribed forms. A staff-officer was hurried thither with a carte blanche to use Grant's name in any way necessary to rush on the supplies, while the hard-worked commissary was overwhelmed with the questions, "How many teams have been loaded with rations and sent forward? How many wagons have you ferried over the river? How many are still to bring over? What teams have gone back for rations?" and so on. He heard the sound of the mustering hosts, whose junction must be prevented at all hazards, and every hour was pregnant with destiny to him. At the same time, he directed McClernand to sweep the surrounding country for forage, and McPherson to push his reconnoissance up to the outposts of Vicksburg, in order to make the commander there believe that he designed to move directly on the place.

As soon as Sherman's columns got within supporting distance, McPherson and McClernand were pushed forward. Sherman, when he reached Hankinson's Ferry, was amazed at the evidence of hurry on every side. The trains and escorting troops were in confusion, each team hurrying forward without stopping to consider the order of its going. Ignorant of Grant's determination to swing loose from his base, he wrote to him, describing the chaos he had found on the road, and begging him to stop till he could get things arranged more systematically; for, said he, "this road will be jammed, as sure as life, if you attempt to supply fifty thousand men by one single road." To this communication he received the following reply, which must have startled him beyond expression: "I do not calculate upon the possibility of supplying the army with full rations from Grand Gulf. I know it will be impossible without constructing additional roads. What I do expect, however, is to get up what rations of hard-bread, coffee, and salt we can, and make the country furnish the balance. We started from Bruinsburg with an average of about two days' rations, and I received no more from our own supplies for some days; abundance was found in the mean time. Some corn-meal, bacon, and vegetables were found, and an abundance of beef and mutton. A delay would give the enemy time to reinforce and fortify. If Blair was up now, I believe we could be in Vicksburg in *seven days*. *The command here has an average of about three days' rations, which could be made to last that time.* You are in a country where the troops have already lived off the people for some days, and may find provisions more scarce; but, as we get upon new soil, they are more abundant, particularly in corn and cattle. Bring Blair's two brigades up as soon as possible. . . . . . ."

The movements of the several corps and divisions cannot be described with any satisfaction to the general reader. Grant had not proceeded far from Hankinson's Ferry, before he learned that Pemberton was concentrating his troops at Edwards' Station, some twenty-five miles out of Vicksburg, towards which the latter supposed our columns were moving. This caused a change in the order and direction of the march, for Grant was determined to get into Jackson, destroy the stores there, and defeat Johnston, who was hastening towards it, before the latter could effect a junction with Pemberton. Aware of the short rations, heavy marching, and constant fighting awaiting his army, Grant, before leaving Hankinson's Ferry, issued the following stirring address to his troops, which has the ring of some of Napoleon's famous proclamations:

HEADQUARTERS ARMY OF THE TENNESSEE, IN THE FIELD, }
HANKINSON'S FERRY, May 7. }

Soldiers of the Army of Tennessee:

Once more I thank you for adding another victory to the long list of those previously won by your valor and endurance. The triumph gained over the enemy near Port Gibson, on the first, was one of the most important of the war. The capture of five cannon, and more

8

than one thousand prisoners, the possession of Grand Gulf, and a firm foothold on the highlands between the Big Black and Bayou Pierre, from whence we threaten the whole line of the enemy, are among the fruits of this brilliant achievement. The march from Milliken's Bend to the point opposite Grand Gulf, was made in stormy weather, over the worst of roads. Bridges and ferries had to be constructed. Moving by night as well as by day, with labor incessant, and extraordinary privations, endured by men and officers, such as have been rarely paralleled in any campaign, not a murmur or complaint has been uttered. A few days continuance of the same zeal and constancy, will secure to this army crowning victories over the rebellion.

More difficulties and privations are before us; let us endure them manfully. Other battles are to be fought; let us fight them bravely. A grateful country will rejoice at our success, and history will record it with immortal honor.   U. S. GRANT,
                              Brig.-Gen. Commanding.

He set an example of the privations and endurance which he required of his troops. Satisfied with his hard bread and coffee, sleeping on the porch of some house along the road, or wherever he found time to take a little repose, he showed himself impervious to fatigue, and indifferent to ordinary comforts. A little son, only thirteen years of age, accompanied him in this trying, strange campaign, and, though hardly big enough to sit a horse, was seen galloping alongside of his father. Taking the hard fare of the day without murmuring, he slept in his strong arms by night. The stern leader, carrying the fate of the army on his heart, could yet find time to enjoy the prattle of his boy, and the two moved on amid the crowding columns, and into the confused noise of battle, a strange contrast, yet a touching picture, which often brought the tears to the soldiers' eyes.

To McPherson was assigned the duty of pushing forward and seizing Jackson, while the main army was held back to watch Pemberton. The former pushed on in the direction marked out by Grant, who, day by day, changed the details of his main plan according as the movements of the enemy made it necessary. Arriving at Cayuga, he, on the 11th of May, wrote to Halleck, stating his position and purpose, and closed with the following significant sentence: " As I shall communicate with Grand Gulf no more, unless it becomes necessary to send a train with a heavy escort, YOU MAY NOT HEAR FROM ME AGAIN FOR SEVERAL DAYS." He certainly did not wish to hear from him, for he knew the General-in-Chief well, and feared an order to abandon at once his daring movement, which he had no intention of doing. It was well for the country that communication was cut off; for that very day a despatch was flashing along the wires ordering him to return and coöperate with Banks. When it finally reached Grant he *was* returning, though not to Grand Gulf, but to Vicksburg, over the shattered battalions of Pemberton.

McPherson moved forward, and on the 12th

came upon the enemy, numbering five thousand,
posted in a strong position, within two miles of
Raymond. Sweeping these from his path, in a
short, sharp battle, he kept on towards Jackson—
marching on the 14th twelve miles through a
blinding, pitiless storm. At ten o'clock he drew
up his drenched army before the formidable breastworks of the enemy, who were not only strongly
protected, but also out-numbered him heavily.
The storm now broke, and the spring sun shone
forth in all its splendor, making the rain-drops on
the trees and meadows shine like jewels. Awakened by the freshness and beauty, the birds came
out and filled the air with their gay carols, a rain-
bow spanned the heavens, and all combined to
make it a scene of transcendent loveliness. Amid
this peaceful splendor, McPherson drew up his
fifteen thousand bayonets, and riding along the
glittering line on his splendid black charger,
aroused the enthusiasm of his men by a stirring
appeal. As soon as the artillery had got into position and thoroughly searched the hostile works, he
ordered a charge. At first, slowly and with
measured steps, as though on a dress parade,
Croker's whole line moved over the field, closing
up, calmly, the ugly rents made by the rebel artillery, and kept sternly on without returning a shot
till within thirty yards of the works, when a sud
den flash leaped from the ranks, followed by a

cheer that shook the field; and then, with one
bound, they scaled the ramparts and poured like
a resistless flood through the hostile camp, scatter-
ing every thing from their path, and chasing the
flying foe into Jackson.

Grant had by this movement completely deceived Pemberton, who all this time lay at Edwards'
Station awaiting an attack from him.

Not knowing what force Johnston might have
been able to concentrate at Jackson, and its possession being of vital importance to him, Grant
had directed Sherman to follow McPherson, to
aid him if necessary; and his presence at the critical moment on the flank of the enemy hastened
his flight.

McPherson, now moving forward, came, at
length, in sight of the rebel intrenchments and
rifle-pits in front of Jackson. These extended as
far as the eye could reach, and presented a formidable appearance. Grant, in the mean time, had
joined Sherman, and seeing how strong and extensive the works were, directed him to send a
force to the extreme right, to see if a flank movement could not be made in that direction. After
waiting some time to hear the result of this movement, and becoming impatient at the delay, he, accompanied only by his staff and little boy, rode
over to see about it. He found that the enemy
had evacuated the place, and the road leading into

it was clear. He immediately pushed forward, when his son clapped spurs to his horse, and dashing ahead, galloped alone into the capital of the State, the first into it. Grant smiled at his enthusiam, and followed him leisurely.

He was now at the goal of his march westward, in which he had shattered Johnston's army though he had not captured it, as he hoped to do. On the contrary it had escaped to the north, evidently with the intention of coming down on the railroad west of him, and joining Pemberton. This he must prevent at all hazards, and calling his corps commanders around him in the State Hall that afternoon, he gave them their instructions. Sherman's duty was to occupy the town and works, and destroy the railroad track, stores, and property that could aid the enemy.

The night before, Johnston had sent a despatch, by three different messengers, to Pemberton, requesting him to hasten up, and attack Grant's rear so that he might be kept at bay until the troops that were being hurried forward could have time to come up. One of these despatches was sent by a man who was in Jackson as a Union spy, whither he had travelled from Memphis. He took it straight to McPherson, who sent it and the bearer to Grant. The latter, therefore, became fully aware of the enemy's plans, and could act with certainty and promptness. Mc-

Pherson, in consequence, was sent that afternoon back towards Bolton, distant some twenty miles—the nearest place that Johnston could strike the railroad in his march to join Pemberton. To McClernand, who was far in the rear, he also sent a despatch directing him to march in the same direction. His orders were urgent. General Blair, at Auburn, was also ordered to move towards the same point, and the tired columns were soon sweeping over the broken country towards a common centre. The rains had made the roads heavy, and the troops were weary, but they marched cheerfully off.

Pemberton was still at Edwards' Station, where he had called a council of war to decide whether he should obey Johnston's order to move on Grant's rear. At this very time, the latter was being driven from Jackson. Completely deceived by the celerity of his adversary's movements, Pemberton finally determined to act on his own judgment, and by a brilliant movement cut Grant's communication with Grand Gulf. He did not know that Grant had done this for himself long ago, and would be, on that very afternoon and night, bearing down upon him with his victorious columns. He, however, soon discovered his mistake, and reversing his march moved back to Edwards' Station, towards which Grant's army was advancing along three different roads. McClernand was ordered to push Blair's and A. P. Smith's divisions along by the southern road—Carr's and Osterhaus' by the middle road, while Hovey kept along the northern one, which runs direct from Bolton to it.

Smith's advance first came upon the enemy's skirmishers, when firing commenced. Pemberton kept retiring, until by the fierce manner in which he was pressed he found, to his astonishment, that Grant's army was in his front. He then formed his line of battle, with his left resting on Champion Hill, the highest ground in sight. The slopes of this hill were heavily wooded, and seamed with ravines, which made it difficult for troops to advance up them in any order. The top was cleared of all trees and underbrush, thus furnishing a fine position for the enemy's artillery, which, planted there, swept the entire country around.

Pemberton's line of battle extended for four miles, running southward from this crest—his centre being on the middle road from Raymond. Hovey's division came up on the Bolton road in front of the hill. Logan, with two brigades, was to the right of the road, and farther advanced.

Grant labored under great disadvantage in being ignorant of the country, while the enemy was thoroughly acquainted with every foot of it. Nor was this all; the former could not spare time to make thorough reconnoissances nor gradual approaches. Swung out as his army was into the open country, it must keep moving till its base was secured. Besides, delay would give time for the rebel reinforcements to arrive, and combine against him. He must, therefore, not only fight the enemy on unknown ground, but fight him as soon as found. Hence he resolved to wait here only long enough to get a part of his army up, and the rest in supporting distance, before he moved on the enemy's position.

That night two men employed on the railroad came into his lines, and reported Pemberton's forces to be twenty thousand strong. Grant was waked up at daybreak to receive these messengers. He immediately sent back to Sherman, who was finishing the work of destruction at Jackson, to hurry forward to his support, as the entire force of the enemy was immediately in front, and a battle might be brought on at any moment. The despatch was urgent, and in one hour after Sherman received it, the columns of his advance division were in motion. At half past six, a despatch was received from McPherson, asking Grant to come to the front immediately. The latter galloped off at once, and on his way found the road blocked with teams, so that the troops could not pass. These he ordered to be drawn up one side immediately, so as to to give room for the marching columns. Reaching Hovey, he found him drawn up

8*

in order of battle, but he would not let him commence the attack until he could hear from McClernand, moving up on the southern road. Officer after
officer was sent with headlong speed to the latter,
with orders to press on with all haste. "Close up
your forces expeditiously as possible," he said.

The firing which had been kept up between
Hovey's and the enemy's skirmishers all the
morning, increased in fierceness, until by eleven
o'clock the battle was fairly opened. The bald
top of the hill crowned with the hostile batteries,
was evidently the key to the whole position of the
enemy, and hence the great struggle centred here.
McPherson posted two batteries in an advanta-
geous position, and opened a terrible fire upon
it. Under cover of it Hovey pushed boldly forward in the face of a murderous fire of musketry,
and began to mount the tangled slope. Inch by
inch, the irregular line pressed upward, until at
last the height was won, and several guns and
prisoners fell into his hands. But the enemy rallied behind a deep cut in the road, which had been
sunk in the ridge, while Pemberton, informed of
the repulse at this vital point, hurried forward
reinforcements that now came pouring along the
crest with loud yells. These charging with the
re-formed troops on Hovey, bore him back, after a
gallant attempt on his part to hold his ground.
Grant all this time stood on an eminence that was

in range of the enemy's guns, with his little son by
his side, watching the varying fortunes of the fight
with the intensest interest, and wondering at the
unaccountable detention of McClernand. The balls
whistled around them, but he thought only of the
struggle, on the issue of which his fate depended.
If McClernand's four divisions would only come
up, victory would be certain ; and he therefore
again despatched an officer urging him forward.
But this commander was kept back by a small
force, the size of which he could not ascertain in
the thickly-wooded country through which he had
to move. But the heavy roar of artillery, and
crash of musketry in front, would have told him
on a moment's reflection, that the decisive battle
was being fought there, and that the force that
hovered around his advance,.could only be a thin
curtain of troops, whose sole object was to keep
him away from the spot where the great struggle
was going on. Grant's anxiety was becoming
painful, when he saw a brigade of Crocker's, marching rapidly on the field. He immediately sent it
in to the aid of Hovey, who could hardly hold his
own. Thus strengthened, this gallant officer was
able to maintain his ground. The enemy, however, pressed heavily upon him, and the fifteen
thousand men under McClernand were sorely
needed. Again forced to retire, Hovey sent back
for help. But Grant expected every moment to

hear the roar of McClernand's guns to the south, and delayed, for he had no troops to spare. At this critical moment, it seemed that the enemy would win and hold the height. Seeing the danger, Grant at last ordered· two more of Crocker's brigades into the gap between Logan and Hovey, which had been made by the movement of the former farther to the right; while McPherson, with such troops as he could gather, was directed to sweep round to the rebel rear. McPherson moved off at the double quick, while Crocker's brigades charged with a cheer, rolling back the hostile line. But fresh reinforcements kept pouring in from that portion of the rebel line on which McClernand should have been pressing, and the danger of defeat was imminent, when a brigade of Logan's, marching at the · double quick, charged across a ravine in flank and up the hill, carrying an important position and capturing seven guns. In the mean time McPherson had worked so far around to the enemy's rear, that, fearing their retreat would be cut off, they broke and fled, and the battle of Champion Hill was won. Pursuit was kept up till after dark, when the tired troops were halted.

Grant conducted this battle in person, and fought it with only fifteen thousand men. It is easy to see, therefore, what the result would have been, had the other fifteen thousand under McClernand came up in time, as he expected.

Grant's loss in this desperate battle was nearly one sixth of all the force engaged—that of the enemy was about three thousand killed and wounded, and three thousand prisoners. But what was of still more consequence, one whole division, composing Pemberton's right, was cut off from the main army by Grant's pursuit, and never joined it again—thus materially lessening the garrison at Vicksburg.

The hill, for the possession of which this sanguinary struggle had taken place, presented a frightful appearance. Nearly five thousand men had fallen on the narrow spot, and pools of blood stood in the trampled and muddy road, while mangled corpses strewed the summit and sides. Dead and dying horses, and broken artillery carriages, and abandoned arms, helped to swell the horrors of the scene. Friend and foe were heaped together in one "red burial blent." It was a ghastly spectacle, even to the soldiers, and they named it the "*Hill of Death.*"

Grant, with his staff, pushed on with the pursuing column, and actually got ahead of it in the darkness, and had to retrace his steps till he reached it. A house stood near the camp, which Pemberton had used for a field hospital during the day, and was now literally crowded with the dead and dying. No tents or wagons had yet come up, and Grant, with his boy by his side, stretched himself

on the porch, and endeavored to snatch a little repose amid the groans of the sufferers, who lay
bleeding and dying within. That night he received Halleck's despatch of the 11th of May,
ordering him to return and coöperate with Banks;
but the campaign that seemed so daring had been
won. "The subordinate was indeed retracing his
steps, but with victorious banners; no danger now
of rebuke; no more countermands, no more
recalls." Grant had moved so rapidly that Johnston was now hopelessly cut off from Pemberton.
On the very day of the battle, the rebel commander was resting his troops, after performing
the prodigious march, the day before, of ten miles.
While he was thus halting, Sherman was pressing
forward at the urgent order of Grant, and *after
mid-day* made *twenty miles*.

Starting a column in pursuit the next morning, before it was fairly light, Grant came up in
about six miles with the enemy, strongly posted
on both sides of the Big Black river. On the side
nearest him they were encircled by a bayou, with
its extremities touching the river above and below
their position, while on the opposite side arose a
bluff black with batteries. McClernand had
scarcely opened with his artillery, when the gallant Osterhaus was wounded. In the mean time,
Gen. Lawler had crept around to the right, and
then charged over the open ground to the bayou.

Finding a spot wide enough for four men to pass abreast, where the brushwood had not been piled up, the men, flinging their blankets and haversacks on the ground, plunged into the water, and struggling across amid the raining bullets, suddenly appeared in the enemy's rear. Panic-stricken at this unexpected apparition, the rebels, abandoning their guns, fled for the bridge. The troops on the farther side of the river, seeing the fugitives rushing for the crossing, seized with the same panic, set fire to the bridge and fled in wild terror inland. Not half of their comrades had succeeded in crossing, when the bridge was wrapt in flames, effectually barring all passage. A part had at the outset refused to fly, and surrendered where they stood. The remaining part, now finding themselves cut off, while the pursuers were close behind, plunged into the stream, with the bullets raining around them. Officers and men were mingled in the wild struggle for life, many of whom sank to rise no more. Eighteen cannon and over seventeen hundred prisoners fell into Grant's hands in this short conflict.

Pemberton now retreated behind his works at Vicksburg.

Only one pontoon train had as yet reached Grant, and this he had previously given to Sherman, to enable him to cross the Black River farther up, so as to flank, if necessary, the enemy in his position on the river. He desired earnestly to follow up the demoralized enemy, and enter his works in full pursuit; but, the bridges being destroyed, and this, his only pontoon train, being with Sherman on the right, he was compelled to halt till means of crossing could be provided.

Sherman was directed, after crossing, to follow the enemy into the city, if he found it practicable to do so—if not to halt, and place his troops so as to open communication with him the moment he was over the river, when the army, in three columns, would advance at once on the stronghold of the enemy.

The engineers immediately went to work to extemporize floating bridges of such materials as they could lay their hands on. Timber left from the burnt bridge, cotton-gins, and farm-houses in the region, were used for the purpose—one being constructed entirely of cotton bales, fastened together and planked over. Across these shaking structures the troops hurried, and the onward march commenced.

Sherman started at daybreak on the 18th, and by half-past nine was between Vicksburg and Haines' Bluff, on the Yazoo, thus cutting it, and all the forts on that river, from the former place, and causing their hasty evacuation by the garrisons, that were compelled to leave their heavy guns behind them.

Grant was with Sherman when his column struck the Walnut hills. As they rode together up the farthest height, where it looks down on the Yazoo river, and stood upon the very bluff from which Sherman had been repulsed six months before, the two soldiers gazed for a moment on the long-wished-for goal of the campaign, —the high, dry ground on the north of Vicksburg, and the base for their supplies. Sherman at last turned abruptly round, and exclaimed to Grant : " ' Until this moment, I never thought your expedition a success. I never could see the end clearly, until now. But this is a campaign ; this is a success, if we never take the town.' The other, as usual, smoked his cigar, and made no reply. The enthusiastic subordinate had seen the dangers of this venturesome campaign so vividly, that his vision was dimmed for beholding success, until it lay revealed on the banks of the Yazoo ; but then, with the magnanimity of a noble nature, he rejoiced in the victories whose laurels he could not claim." *

McPherson commanding the centre, and Mc-Clernand the left, had moved simultaneously, and by the 19th of May, the three army corps were in position, extending from the Mississippi below, to the Yazoo above Vicksburg, thus completely investing the place.

* Col. Badeau.

After long months of toiling and waiting—after repeated failures, till the enemy laughed in derision at Grant's futile obstinacy, he had at last, by one of the most brilliant military movements on record, succeeded in flinging his strong arms around the Gibraltar of the Mississippi. From the perseverance he had shown from the outset, from the tireless energy with which he had worked undeviatingly towards that single point; from the tremendous blows he had dealt the foe, as he bore swiftly down upon it, he had astonished his own army, and paralyzed that of his adversary.

With his base of supplies now firmly established at Chickasaw landing, at the foot of those fatal bluffs, Grant at once began the siege of Vicksburg.

It was just twenty days since the campaign began. In that time, Grant had marched more than two hundred miles, beaten two armies in five several battles, captured twenty-seven heavy cannon and sixty-one pieces of field artillery, taken six thousand five hundred prisoners, and killed and wounded at least six thousand rebels more. He had forced the evacuation of Grand Gulf, seized the capital of the State, destroyed the railroads at Jackson for a distance of more than thirty miles, and invested the principal rebel stronghold on the Mississippi river. Separating forces twice as numerous as his own, he had beaten first, at Port Gibson, a portion of Pemberton's army; then, at Raymond and Jackson, the troops under Johnston's immediate command; and again, at Champion Hill and the Big Black river, the whole force that Pemberton dared take outside the works at Vicksburg. Starting without teams, and with an average of two days' rations in haversacks, he had picked up wagons in the country, and subsisted principally on forage and rations that he found on the road. Only five days' rations had been issued in twenty days, yet neither suffering nor complaint was witnessed in the command. His losses were six hundred and ninety-eight killed, three thousand four hundred and seven wounded, and two hundred and thirty missing—in all, four thousand three hundred and thirty-five. This is the brief, graphic summing up of this extraordinary campaign, by his military biographer.

As we remarked in a former work, this campaign, in its general features, resembled the famous Italian one of the young Napoleon. There was the same grand design to cut up the enemy in detail, before he could concentrate his overwhelming forces—the same rapidity of movement and cheerful endurance of privations by the troops, the same terrible blows falling fast and rapid as successive thunderbolts from heaven, rending and paralyzing the foe. And as from the high ridge he looked down on the frowning works, with his gallant army resting at their base, he could address his soldiers in almost the language of that incomparable leader. "Soldiers, in a fortnight you have gained six victories, taken twenty-one pairs of colors, fifty-five pieces of cannon, several fortresses, and conquered the richest part of Piedmont; you have made fifteen thousand prisoners, and killed or wounded more than ten thousand men. Destitute of every thing, you have supplied all your wants, * * * * the perverse men who laughed at your distress, and rejoiced in thought at the triumph of your enemies, are confounded and trembling."

CHAPTER XI.

VICKSBURG stands on a bluff that rises between
two and three hundred feet above the Mississippi,
the sides inland sloping and seamed into deep
ravines and gullies.

On the south side, the country was not so
broken, and here the artificial defences were
stronger. Sheltered behind such formidable intrenchments, on which were mounted two hundred cannon, and behind which were massed
thirty thousand men, Pemberton felt himself secure, unless he was starved out.

But, notwithstanding the formidable aspect of
these works, Grant, the very day after he had
completed the investment of the place, attempted
to carry them by general assault along the rebel
line. At 2 o'clock in the afternoon of the 19th,

three vollies of artillery from all the guns which he had been able to get into position, was the signal to advance. The army surged up against the strong defences, only to be forced back at all points.

Grant now determined to give his overtasked army rest for a few days, while he perfected his communications with his supplies, and got his guns into position. In the mean time, he requested Porter to open a bombardment of the city with his mortar fleet, so as to distract the enemy's attention from him. He did so, and the huge shells fell with such destructive force in the streets, that the inhabitants fled to the cellars to hide themselves.

Every thing being finally completed, Grant determined, on the 22d, to make another and more determined attempt to carry the works by storm. Having given explicit instructions to the corps commanders, he sent word to Admiral Porter, on the 21st, that he should assault the city at ten o'clock the next day, and requested him to throw shells from his mortars into it during the night, and the next morning open with all his gunboats upon it, and keep up the firing till half-past ten. Porter opened the drama with his mortars, and all night long the murky heavens were crossed and recrossed with the tracks of the blazing shells, that kept dropping with a continuous thunder-sound into the devoted city. At three o'clock in the morning, Grant opened with all his batteries, and Porter with all his guns, and from river and shore thunder answered thunder in prolonged and deafening peals, till the earth shook with the reverberations, and the heavens were blotted out by the sulphurous clouds that rolled upward above the terror-stricken town. As the day dawned, the sharpshooters picked off nearly every rebel gunner that dared to show his head, so that but feeble response was made to the cannonading, that made every thing tremble. Hoping, by throwing his army in a simultaneous charge on the long line of the rebel works, he could make a lodgment at some point, Grant had all the corps commanders set their watches by his own timepiece, so that the onset might be like the breaking of one mighty wave. He himself took a commanding position near the centre, where he could watch the progress of the columns. At the precise moment fixed upon, the bugles sounded, and the storming parties started forward on a run.

It is impossible to convey any definite idea of this terrific assault, covering as it did so large a space. For miles the storming columns dashed on the hostile works, through a desolating fire of grape and canister, and pressing up the slope, attempted to carry them. But a double rank of soldiers lay behind each ridge of earth, and mowed them down with incessant vollies of musketry.

This, together with the tangled brushwood, and deep and tortuous ravines, rapidly broke up the formations, so that even brigades moved forward only in detachments, and hence the onset lost all its weight. If an outer-work was carried, it was found to be commanded by an interior one, that rendered its occupation impossible. Deeds of unparalled bravery were performed, flags here and there were planted on the counterscarps, and men that could not make headway against the fiery sleet, lay down in the ditches, where hand-grenades were rolled down upon them. In one instance, a part of the Twenty-second Iowa succeeded in crossing the ditch and parapet of a rebel outwork; but, not receiving the support of the rest of the column, could not push farther, nor drive the enemy from the main work immediately in rear. A hand-to-hand fight here ensued, lasting several minutes; hand-grenades also were thrown by the rebels in rear, while the national troops still commanded the outer parapet. Every man in the party but one, was shot down. Sergeant Joseph Griffith, of the Twenty-second Iowa, fell at the same time with his comrades, stunned, but not seriously hurt. On his recovery, he found a rebel lieutenant and sixteen men lying in the outwork, still unwounded, though exposed to the fire of both friend and foe. He rose, and bade them follow him out of the place, too hot for any man to stay in and live.   The rebels obeyed, and calling to the troops outside to cease their firing, Griffith brought his prisoners over the parapet, under a storm of rebel shot that killed four of those so willing to surrender.

He was not yet twenty years old, and Grant promoted him to a first-lieutenancy the next day, for his gallantry.   Afterward, he was sent to West Point, "where he was known as 'Grant's cadet.'"

In another part of the field, General A. J. Smith was ordered by McClernand to get two guns up to the very ditch of one of the rebel works, and he called on five or six batteries successively, but the captains all protested that it was impossible to drag guns by hand down one slope, and up another, under fire.   Smith, however, exclaimed, "I know a battery that will go to h—l, if you order it there!"   So he sent for Capt. White, of the Chicago Mercantile Battery, and told him what he wanted.   White replied, "Yes, sir, I will take my guns there."   And his men actually dragged the pieces over the rough ground, by hand, carrying the ammunition in their haversacks.   One gun was stuck on the way, but the other was hauled up so near the rebel works, that it was difficult to elevate it sufficiently to be of use; finally, however, White succeeded. in firing into the embrasure, dismounting a gun.

9

The gun was then dragged off down the ravine, and, after nightfall, hauled away; but the ammunition being heavy, was left on the field.

But the gallantry of individuals, the desperate determination of storming parties, and the heavy onset of devoted columns, were all of no avail, and hour after hour wore on in the fruitless struggle. The dead and wounded spotted the crimson slopes, or crowded the ditches into which they had pushed, only to fall. The sun was hot, and the wounded that lay bleeding under its burning rays, panted and cried for water. By noon it was evident that the attempt was a failure, and Grant was about to order the withdrawal of all the troops, when he received a despatch from Mc-Clernand, stating that he had gained the enemy's works, and, if he could receive reinforcements, and a vigorous push be made along the whole line at the same time, the place could be carried. Grant doubted it, and rode over to Sherman with the despatch. Soon another came to the same purport, and they kept coming, till by three o'clock Grant had received four, and he therefore reluctantly gave orders for the assault to be renewed. It was made, but the only result was to swell the number of the dead and wounded. Mc-Clernand was mistaken, as Grant thought he was, for he was confident, from his commanding position, that he could have discovered any such success as the former assured him was achieved.

Three thousand men were killed or wounded in this desperate but fruitless assault. The propriety of it has been much doubted. The place was not like a walled town, in the defences of which breaches had been made; or where, on the open ground, men could be massed in solid columns, and by mere weight and reckless sacrifice of life, make their way—but miles of irregular earthworks stretched across the country, that could in no place be approached by a large body of troops well massed together. So that, although thirty thousand men advanced at the same moment, there was no real, heavy onset any where. It was desultory fighting along the whole extended line; besides, the works were intact. The tremendous but short cannonading of the morning, had made no impression on them, while an army of thirty thousand men, instead of a small garrison, defended them.

Gen. Grant gave several reasons for making this assault, the chief of which were, that Johnston was being daily reinforced, and in a few days would be able to fall on his rear; that the possession of Vicksburg would have enabled him to turn upon him and drive him from the State; that its immediate capture would have prevented the necessity of calling for large reinforcements, that were needed elsewhere ; and, finally, that the troops were impatient to possess Vicksburg, and would not have worked in the trenches with the same zeal, not believing it necessary, as they did after their failure to carry the works by storm.

There was great force in all, or nearly all, these reasons, provided there was a fair chance of success—indeed, *probable* success was reason enough of itself, without any other. But the fact that after the most determined gallantry and devotion on the part of officers and men, not the least impression was made. on the formidable works, and that amid all the chances to which every battle is liable, there came not one gleam of encouragement from first to last, shows that a victory was scarcely possible. There is, however, one reason which Grant does not give, which, we think, had great weight with him —*that the government and people would not have been satisfied without his making the attempt.* The spade had fallen into contempt ever since the seige of Yorktown, and after the successful assault of Fort Donelson, was doomed, apparently, to perpetual disgrace, and nothing would satisfy the country but " to move immediately on the enemy's works." Besides, he knew what clamors were raised against him for his slow progress above Vicksburg, and how nearly he came being removed from command for it. His fate had turned on the President's saying, " I think I'll try him a little longer." Four months had already passed, and how could he expect the public patience to hold out, perhaps two months more, unless it was demonstrated practically that it *must*. In a country like ours, where popular feeling has to be so much consulted by the government, and where politics meddles so disastrously in all war movements, it is often necessary to make even useless sacrifices, to prevent mischief. Grant was aware of this, and the fact doubtless had much to do with his attempt to carry Vicksburg by storm. The failure settled the question, and the people, though restive, were compelled to submit again to the old story, week after week, "nothing new from Vicksburg."

Having settled down to the unpleasant conclusion that the stronghold could be taken only by the slow process of a regular seige, Grant set about it at once, with all the vigor and determination of one who meant to push it to the speediest conclusion. Sherman on the right, McPherson in the centre, and McClernand on the south, vied with each other in pushing forward saps, and covered-ways, etc., towards the rebel works. But first, however, the dead had to be removed, that in the broiling sun lay festering where they had fallen. These, with the decaying carcasses of animals that had been driven out of Vicksburg for want of forage, and shot by our soldiers, filled the air with an insufferable stench, which threatened to breed a pestilence in the crowded city. Pemberton therefore asked for a suspension of hostilities till these could be removed. This was granted, and for several hours, officers and men of the hostile armies met, on the most friendly terms, outside of the trenches.

CHAPTER XII.

THE SIEGE.

Perilous Position of the Army—Want of competent Engineers—Labor of Grant—Silence of the Enemy—Wooden Mortars—Progress of the Siege—Famine in the City—Distress of the Inhabitants—They hide in Caves—Explosion of a Mine—Desperate Fighting—The "Death Hole"—Day fixed for the final Assault—Pemberton sees his Condition to be hopeless.

GRANT now perfected his means of support, and sent North for reinforcements. He still was between two armies, and knew the moment that Johnston could assemble a force sufficiently large, he would attempt to raise the siege. Hence he was compelled to erect works in his rear, similar to those which the enemy had constructed in front. Detachments, in the mean time, were sent out to destroy railroads and bridges back of him, as far east as they could well penetrate, while Porter was requested to land marines and sailors to hold Haines' Bluff until troops could be got on; for Grant had no doubt that the first attempt of the enemy would be to take this commanding position. It was also additionally fortified, so that at length a comparatively small garrison could hold it against a large force.

Grant, in the position he now occupied between

two armies, had to be argus-eyed, and show a
sleepless vigilance.   In the meantime, the be-
siegers labored under many embarrassments. The
army was not supplied with siege guns, nor any of
the appliances for conducting siege operations.
Besides, there were but a few skilful engineer officers in the army.   Being mostly volunteers, they
were totally ignorant of the mode of procedure in
approaching elaborate fortifications. Many of the
materials used, also, had to be extemporized on
the spot.   All this increased sevenfold the labors
of Grant, for it made it necessary for him to superintend every thing.   Details which ordinarily are
left solely to subordinate officers, he was compelled to attend to in person.

But still the work went on, and approaches and
covered ways, parallels, saps, and mines, and
trenches, were pushed forward on every side.   In
the meantime, guns were planted, and parapets
lined with sharpshooters, to keep down the rebel
fire, which otherwise would impede the workmen.

Slowly but steadily the army dug its way up
the slope—the total length of all the trenches
reaching, in the end, the enormous distance of
twelve miles.   The enemy made but feeble attempts to obstruct the progress of the work, partly for want of ammunition, and partly because
the moment a gunner showed his head above the
parapets it became a target for a dozen rifles.

This comparative quiet on the part of the besieged greatly facilitated operations. There being no mortars for throwing shells over the hostile parapets, wooden ones were constructed out of hollow logs, firmly bound with iron hoops, which did good service.

By the last of June, Grant had two hundred and twenty guns in position, but amid them all there was but one battery of heavy pieces, that on the right—which had been landed from the gunboats, and was officered by the navy. The rebels countermined at some points, though without energy or skill; but for the most part they lay silent behind their works. This apathy was, doubtless, partly owing to the belief that before Grant's operations could be completed, Johnston would be thundering in his rear, compelling him to abandon them. An occasional sally was made, but none of those desperate rushes which so often in a single night destroy the labor of days; and Grant kept creeping steadily nearer, preparatory to his final spring. The most important advances were made along the graveyard and Jackson roads by trenches, and through the ravines by covered ways. Protected by these, Grant was able to plant two entire divisions within two hundred yards of the rebel works. (He had begun his approaches at the distance of about six hundred yards.)

9*

In the meantime, food getting scarce in Vicksburg, the garrison was put on short rations, and
Pemberton sent word to Johnston of his condition, saying that he could not hold out much
longer. The anaconda, in the popular phraseology
of the day, was tightening his folds day by day,
around the doomed city.   Flour at last got to be
a thousand dollars a barrel, Confederate money;
meal a hundred and fifty dollars a bushel, rum a
hundred dollars a gallon; while mule-meat was
sold at a dollar a pound.   The half-starved
inhabitants, in order to escape the shells and
missiles of destruction that were constantly hurled
from Grant's batteries into the town, took refuge
in caves and holes which they had dug in the
earth.   Gaunt famine stalked along the deserted
streets, and haggard faces glared out of holes in the
ground, while gaping walls and tottering chimneys leaning over the wide-spread ruin, added
increased mournfulness to the scene.   The name-
less dread, the sleepless terror that brooded over
the spot, were enhanced by the almost unbroken
silence that rested on the ramparts.   Scarcely a
gun responded to the ceaseless thunder of Grant's
batteries, and to the beholder, this strange silence
seemed like the stillness of despair.

It was plain that this state of things could not
endure much longer, and mutinous murmurings
among the troops were kept from breaking forth

into open rebellion, only by the declaration to-day, that Johnston's army was marching to their relief, and to-morrow by the promise that rafts and boats should be made out of the timber of the houses, on which they would be floated over to the western bank, and thus escape the pains of surrender.

A few days before the long-deferred crisis came, a mine was exploded under one of the enemy's works. The heads of the saps had reached the hostile lines at several points, and at one on the Jackson road, the mine was carried in for thirty-five feet, when three branch mines were run out, so as to make the explosion more extensive in its effects. Five hundred pounds of powder were placed in each of the branch mines, and seven hundred in the centre one, making in all a ton of powder.

The 25th of June was the day fixed for exploding it, and although the enemy had countermined, he had effected nothing, and at the appointed time it was fired. "The fuse train being ignited, it went fizzing and popping through the zigzag line of trenches, until for a moment it vanished. Its disappearance was quickly succeeded by the explosion, and the mine was sprung. So terrible aspectacle is seldom witnessed. Dust, dirt, smoke, gabions, stockades, timber, gun-carriages, logs—in fact, every thing connected with the fort—rose hundreds of feet into the air, as if vomited forth from a volcano ;" while the surrounding country shook as if in the grasp of an earthquake. A few rebel soldiers were seen to rise bodily into the air, two of whom came down alive within our lines. But most of the troops had been withdrawn, apparently in expectation of the explosion.

At the moment it took place, to add greater terror to the scene, the artillery opened all along the lines.

The crater made was large enough to hold two regiments, and a column of troops which had stood in readiness to take advantage of the explosion, leaped at once into it, and a fierce, desperate hand to hand struggle took place in the opening. The enemy, however, soon retired to an interior line, higher up the slope, and which looked down on our daring troops below. They at once began to hurl down hand-grenades, and roll down lighted boxes of ammunition, which burst with terrible effect among the crowded ranks. McPherson's men threw hand-grenades back, but being compelled to cast them up hill, they labored at fatal disadvantage. They, however, fought and fell where they stood, all the afternoon. When darkness wrapped the wild ruin, detachments from Leggett's brigade relieved each other in holding the crater, and the gloom was incessantly streaked with the fuses of the grenades or volleys of musketry. So deadly was the effect of the missiles of the rebels, pitched from their elevated position, that the soldiers called the crater "the death-hole."

But although death held high carnival in that smoking chasm, all that horrible night our troops grimly held it, and at morning began a covered way, from which other mines could be run.

Grant, the moment he found the troops in possession of the crater, determined to hold it at all hazards, and gave his orders to that effect along the lines. To Ord he wrote :

"McPherson occupies the crater made by the explosion. He will have guns in battery there by morning. He has been hard at work running rifle-pits right, and thinks he will hold all gained. Keep Smith's division sleeping under arms to-night, ready for an emergency. Their services may be required, particularly about daylight. There should be the greatest vigilance along the whole line."

Another mine was sprung on the 1st day of July, opening another huge abyss under a rebel work.

From this time our mines were run in every direction, to open up a path over the demolished works, for the assaulting columns. They at length brought our troops so near the hostile lines, that the workmen on opposite sides could converse. Grant was now so well up, that he knew but a little more demolition of the obstacles before him was needed to make a determined assault successful. He was the more eager to hasten the decisive moment, for he had intercepted despatches from Johnston, informing Pemberton that he was on the way to relieve him—while there were indications that General Taylor, in Louisiana, designed to move up on the west shore of the river. He determined, therefore, to make the final assault on the 6th of July.

Pemberton saw with alarm the coming storm. The despatches of Johnston could not reach him, while he beheld the relentless line of Grant contracting closer and closer around him with each revolving day. The gunboats were thundering against him from the river, new batteries were springing up in his very face, mines were being loaded beneath his feet, the garrison was starving and dying from miasma and exhaustion, the hospitals were crowded with the suffering, men and women in utter despair and want clamoring for relief, and a terrible assault close at hand,—how then could he hold out longer? No troops ever fought more gallantly or suffered more patiently than those had done which he commanded. Why then should he, from mere pride, expose them, weakened and worn out as they were, to all the terrors of an assault. Even if it should be repelled, it would bring no relief to him. The only result would be more mines, increased starvation and death, and then another assault. Grant's sap-rollers were already crowning the heights he had deemed impregnable, and the final hour could not be long delayed.

CHAPTER XIII.

THE SURRENDER.

In this desperate condition, Pemberton was compelled, bitter as it was, to confess that the place must be surrendered. As if he wished to shut out the full extent of the disaster, from which there was no escape, he, on the 1st of July, submitted the following paper to his four division generals, Stevenson, Forney, Smith, and Bowen: "Unless the siege of Vicksburg is raised, or supplies are thrown in, it will become necessary, very shortly, to evacuate the place. I see no prospect of the former, and there are many great, if not insuperable, obstacles in the way of the latter. You are, therefore, requested to inform me, with as little delay as possible, as to the condition of your troops, and their ability to make the marches and undergo the fatigue necessary to accomplish a successful evacuation."

All agreed that an attempt at evacuation was useless, while two unhesitatingly advised a surrender. Pemberton, therefore, on the 3d of July, addressed the following note to Grant:

"I have the honor to propose to you an armistice of — hours, with a view to arranging terms for the capitulation of Vicksburg. To this end, if agreeable to you, I will appoint three commissioners, to meet a like number to be named by yourself, at such place and hour as you may find convenient. I make this proposition to save the further effusion of blood, which must otherwise be shed to a frightful extent, feeling myself fully able to maintain my position for a yet indefinite period. This communication will be handed you, under a flag of truce, by Major-General John S. Bowen."

About ten o'clock he hoisted a flag of truce, and sent Bowen, with one of his staff, to Grant with the proposition. The bearer expressed a desire for an interview with Gen. Grant, but the latter wished to see no subordinate officer, and refused to meet him. Bowen then said, that he thought it would be well for the two commanding generals to have an interview. To this Grant consented, saying that, if Pemberton so desired, he would meet him at three o'clock in the afternoon, midway between the lines in front of McPherson's position. At the same time he sent the following answer to his note: "Your note of this date is just received, proposing an armistice of several hours for the purpose of arranging terms of capitulation, through commissioners to be appointed, etc. The effusion of blood you propose stopping by this course, can be ended at any time you may choose, by an unconditional surrender of the city and garrison. Men who have shown so much endurance and courage as those now in Vicksburg, will always challenge the respect of an adversary, and, I can assure you, will be treated with all the respect due them as prisoners of war. I do not favor the proposition of appointing commissioners to arrange terms of capitulation, because I have no other terms than those indicated above."

At three o'clock one gun was fired, and immediately answered by one from the enemy, the signal agreed upon, if Pemberton desired the interview. In a few minutes the latter rode out of his works, accompanied by Gen. Bowen and Col. Montgomery, while Grant, in the other direction, rode through his trenches, toward a grassy slope that had not been trod by either army. The unwonted spectacle created the most intense excitement in both armies, and the frowning works on either side became black with troops, gazing intently off on the space where the two commanders were slowly approaching each other. The clouds settled low and dark above the landscape, as if symbolical of the fate that hung over Vicksburg.

Just before meeting they dismounted, and advancing on foot, shook hands, addressing each other courteously. Pemberton then inquired of Grant what terms of capitulation would be allowed him. The latter replied, those that he had stated in his letter of the morning. At this, Pemberton drew himself up haughtily, and replied: "If this were all, the conference might terminate, and hostilities be resumed immediately." "Very well," coolly replied Grant, and turned away.

The interview seemed ended; when General Bowen, with less pride and more judgment than his commander, proposed that two officers from each party should withdraw and talk over the matter. Grant said that he had no objection; and the two generals, leaving them to consult, walked up and down in open view, conversing, Grant, as usual, serenely smoking his cigar.

The day was sultry, and the interview took place under a large solitary oak-tree, that stood in the open space. In a short time Grant and Pemberton returned to this tree, to hear the result of the deliberations. The proposition of General Bowen was, that the garrison should march out of Vicksburg with their muskets and field-guns, leaving the heavy artillery behind them. This, Grant at once rejected. The two now entered into a lengthy discussion, in which Pemberton pressed hard for terms that would break, somewhat, the humiliation of his downfall. Grant, personally, felt no disinclination to this, for, devoid of all mere pride of conquest, and averse, from kindness of heart, to the infliction of needless pain, he would naturally prefer to spare the feelings of a humbled foe. But his duty forbade it. No agreement could be had on such a proposition, and, after an hour's duration, the interview closed, and each returned to his lines with the understanding that Grant, after further consideration, should, by ten o'clock, send his ultimatum.

The latter had no doubt what this should be. Still, willing to yield any thing that he could with propriety, he called a council of his officers and submitted the question to them. They almost unanimously agreed on terms, but Grant would not accept them, and he concluded to act, as he had done in all his campaigns and battles thus far, on his own judgment. He therefore sent the following letter:

HEADQUARTERS, DEPARTMENT OF TENNESSEE,
NEAR VICKSBURG, July 8, 1863.

Lieutenant-General J. C. PEMBERTON, commanding Confederate forces, Vicksburg, Miss. :

GENERAL: In conformity with the agreement of this

afternoon, I will submit the following proposition for the surrender of the city of Vicksburg, public stores, &c. On your accepting the terms proposed, I will march in one division, as a guard, and take possession at eight o'clock to-morrow morning. As soon as paroles can be made out and signed by the officers and men, you will be allowed to march out of our lines, the officers taking with them their regimental clothing, and staff, field, and cavalry officers one horse each. The rank and file will be allowed all their clothing, but no other property.

If these conditions are accepted, any amount of rations you may deem necessary can be taken from the stores you now have, and also the necessary cooking utensils for preparing them; thirty wagons, also, counting two two-horse or mule teams as one. You will be allowed to transport such articles as cannot be carried along. The same conditions will be allowed to all sick and wounded officers and privates, as fast as they become able to travel. The paroles for these latter must be signed, however, whilst officers are present, authorized to sign the roll of prisoners.

I am, General, very respectfully, your obedient servant,   U. S. GRANT, Major-General.

On the reception of this, Pemberton called a council of war, and submitted it to them. All but one advised him to accept the conditions offered. He concluded to do so, and late at night sent the following answer: "I have the honor to acknowledge the receipt of your communication of this date, proposing terms of capitulation for this garrison and post. In the main, your terms are accepted; but in justice both to the honor and spirit of my troops, manifested in the defence of Vicksburg, I have to submit the following amendments, which, if acceded to by you, will perfect the agreement between us.   At ten o'clock A. M., to-morrow, I propose to evacuate the works in and around Vicksburg, and to surrender the city and garrison under my command, by marching out with my colors and arms, stacking them in front of my present lines, after which you will take possession.   Officers to retain their side-arms and personal property, and the rights and property of citizens to be respected."

This reached Grant at midnight, and he immediately replied:

" I have the honor to acknowledge the receipt of your communication of 3d July.   The amendment proposed by you cannot be acceded to in full.   It will be necessary to furnish every officer and man with a parole signed by himself, which, with the completion of the roll of prisoners, will necessarily take some time.   Again, I can make no stipulations with regard to the treatment of citizens and their private property.   While I do not propose to cause them any undue annoyance or loss, I cannot consent to leave myself under any restraint by stipulations.   The property which officers will be allowed to take with them will be as stated in my proposition of last evening : that is, officers will be allowed their private baggage and side-arms, and mounted officers one horse each.   If you mean by your proposition for each brigade to march to the front of the lines now occupied by it, and stack arms at ten o'clock A. M., and then return to the inside and remain as prisoners until properly paroled, I will make no objections to it.   Should no modification be made of your acceptance of my terms by nine o'clock A. M., I shall regard them as having been rejected, and act accordingly.   Should these terms be accepted, white flags shall be displayed along your lines, to prevent such of my troops as may not have been notified, from firing on your men.

I am, General, very respectfully,
Your obedient servant,
U. S. GRANT, Major-General U. S. A.

By a singular coincidence, the next morning was the Fourth of July, our great anniversary day, and at ten o'clock the garrison marched out by regiments, and stacked their arms on the grassy slope in front of the works they had defended so long and gallantly, hanging their colors upon the centre. With that downcast look always so sad in a brave soldier's face, they laid off their knapsacks, belts, cartridge-boxes and cap-pouches, and thus shorn of their arms and accoutrements, and leaving their colors behind them, slowly wheeled back into their works. Not a word had been spoken, save the few words of command necessary from the officers in charge, and these were uttered in a low, subdued tone, as one speaks at a funeral. The spectacle would have been mournful if the humbled foe had been an invader; but it was doubly so when it was remembered that they were citizens of a common country, brethren of the same family, and the very soil on which they stacked their arms was their own birthright.

The painful ceremony lasted over an hour, and when it was over, the rebel and Federal officers mounted in haste and swept away towards the city.

Thirty-one thousand six hundred men, on this eventful morning, surrendered themselves prisoners of war, of whom fifteen were generals.

Pemberton, at this time, was at Forney's head-quarters, a stone house, built on the outskirts of the city, with wide verandahs, and almost hid among the tropical trees. Seated in a damask cushioned rocking-chair, he sat with his head bent as if lost in sad reflections, while pride and mortification seemed struggling for the mastery in his swarthy face. Tall, with black eyes and hair, and a full flowing beard, he was a conspicuous object on the verandah, which was filled with officers. It was a hot day, and the doors and windows were all open to let in a little air, through which also stole the triumphant strains of the distant regimental bands. Grant with his staff trotted leisurely towards this house, and dismounting, stepped on to the piazza, and advanced towards the rebel general. All looked up as he entered, and could scarce restrain their surprise, when instead of a tall and commanding form, clad in the rich uniform befitting so grand an occasion, they saw before them a man of small stature, thick-set, and round shouldered, dressed in a plain suit of blue flannel, and with nothing to distinguish his rank but two stars on his shoulders. Pemberton received his salutations coldly, and had not the civility to rise and offer him a chair. His

officers were all seated on the piazza, but accepting their commander's conduct as the rule of
politeness, not one of them offered Grant a seat.
Not even the swords at their side, which he in
his generosity allowed them to retain, could
prompt them to common civility. Among those
officers it is hard to believe that there was not
many who were ashamed of this want of courtesy,
and persisted in it only because the sullen demeanor and discourteous tone of their chief made
them feel that any other course would be displeas-
ing to him.

Thus for five minutes the conqueror stood conversing with his prisoner seated in his richly-
cushioned rocking-chair. This shameful spectacle
was at length more than the gentlemanly feelings
of one of the officers present could endure, and he
rose and offered Grant a seat. The latter, however,
occupied it but a few minutes, when feeling very
thirsty from his hot and dusty ride, he asked for
a drink of water. Not one offered to get it or
ordered a servant to do so; instead, he was cav-
alierly told that he would find some inside of the
house. Passing within, he groped around, and
at last came across a negro, who brought him a
glass. Grant then returned to the piazza, and
finding his seat had been taken in his absence,
again stood and conversed for nearly a half an
hour with his rude captive. Notwithstanding his

10

incivility, Pemberton did not hesitate to request Grant to supply his troops with rations, to which the latter assented, and inquired how many were needed. "Thirty-two thousand," was the reply, which was a surprise to Grant, who had all the while labored under the impression that the garrison did not reach much over half that number.

In the meantime, Logan's division, to which had been assigned the honor of first entering the city, because it had pushed its approaches nearest to the rebel works, came marching along, the bands playing exulting strains. Grant bidding his surly host good morning, mounted his horse, and putting himself at the head of the division, marched into the city, while the pallid inhabitants stole out of their caves to gaze on the strange spectacle. The tattered banners that had been borne over many a fierce battle-field, stooped and rose proudly along the streets, and at last were carried in triumph to the top of the Court House, where their appearance was greeted with cheers. Grant then passed on down to the wharf to visit Admiral Porter, and exchange congratulations with him on their joint victory. The gallant Admiral in his flag-ship, followed by the whole fleet, covered with flags, and the guns firing a *feu de joie* that made the welkin ring, passed down until he came in front of the town, when he rounded to and swept up to the levee. As Grant and his officers stepped on board, from ship and shore went up thundering hurrahs—flags dipped in graceful salutations to the hero, while the heavy guns roared out their wild acclaim.

The meeting between him and the Admiral was of the most cordial kind, and never did Porter's deck witness a gayer or more gladsome sight than it presented at that moment, crowded with the gallant officers of the army and navy, mingling their warm congratulations. After months of unexampled toil against adverse fate, and from many a fierce fight, in which they had been together, it was glorious at last to see the national colors flying from those lofty bluffs.

The interview was long and pleasant, but just before dark Grant again returned to the shore, and mounting his horse, rode back to his old camp in the field, while the soldiers made the nightly heavens above Vicksburg red with fire-works, in commemoration of the Fourth of July. It had been a glorious Fourth to the national troops, and it was thought strange that Pemberton should have allowed the capitulation to take place on a day that would make the victors feel their triumph so much more keenly. In his report he gives the following reason for it :

"If it should be asked why the 4th of July was selected as the day for surrender ? the answer is obvious. I believed that upon that day I should obtain better terms. Well aware of the vanity of our foes, I knew they would attach vast importance to the entrance, on the 4th of July, into the stronghold of the great river, and that, to gratify their national vanity, they would yield then what could not be extorted from them at any other time."

This evinced a considerable shrewdness on his part, and no doubt most of the officers would have granted easier terms on this day than any other.

That night Grant sat down in his quiet quarters, and while the distant heavens were bright with rockets, wrote the following despatch to the Government:

"The enemy surrendered this morning. The only terms allowed is their parole as prisoners of war. This I regard as a great advantage to us, at this moment. It saves, probably, several days in the capture, and leaves troops and transports ready for immediate service." That is all he has to say respecting one of the greatest victories of modern times, not only in the number of prisoners taken, the amount of war material captured, but in the importance of the position obtained, with reference to the final issue of the contest. Nothing could be more unpretending and commonplace. Cæsar, after a great victory, could say, in dramatic conciseness, "Veni, vidi, vici"—Commodore Perry, in similar circumstances, in laconic but triumphant language, "We have met the enemy, and they are ours," while Grant announces a victory greater than either with apparently as little feeling or excitement as he would the fact that he had made for the government a tolerably fair purchase of a drove of army-mules.   This simplicity never deserts him.   Like his imperturbable serenity, it remains the same under all circumstances.

The rank and file of the rebel army exhibited no such feelings as disgraced their commander, but mingled, in the most familiar manner, with the Union soldiers, and could be seen walking arm in arm along the streets, chatting familiarly as old acquaintances.

Seven hundred of the prisoners refused to be paroled, preferring to remain as prisoners.   Even if the relentless conscription respected their parole, they had no desire to serve again, after exchange, in the rebel army.   Pemberton requested Grant to compel them to accept their parole; but the latter declined to interfere in the matter.   He then requested that a portion of his troops be allowed to take arms with them in order to prevent the rest from deserting on the road.   This Grant also declined to do, as not coming within the line of his duty.   He did not care to give the chief reason that actuated him in refusing this request, viz: that he wished the very thing that Pemberton desired to prevent.

It took a few days to complete the paroles, but every thing being at length arranged, on Saturday forenoon, the 11th, the weaponless army, bereft of all its standards, took up its mournful march. Long lines of national infantry extended along each side of the road for some distance beyond the intrenchments, as guards; and between these, with bowed heads, the silent columns slowly defiled. Many had fought from a sense of duty under the standards they now left behind; from the eyes of these the tears fell hot and fast; others turned to take a last look at the works behind which they had battled so long and well, and suffered so terribly, while others, sullen and desponding, marched doggedly on. Their brave conquerors, forgetting their triumph in the feeling of pity for their gallant but misguided countrymen, exhibited none of the victors' pride, and uttered no word of taunt or boast. In dead silence they let them pass, till the last column disappeared around the winding road, and then wheeled, and marched back to their quarters.

The first response that Grant received from Washington, after this great victory, was a rebuke from Halleck for having paroled the prisoners, and ordering him peremptorily not to carry out his agreement, if it had not been already done—fearing, he said, that the enemy would not regard the parole as binding. It is true, he afterwards complimented him highly for his brilliant strategy, but that did not lessen the painful effect of this first rebuke. The people, however, had nothing but plaudits for him. Hoisting of flags, firing of cannon, and deafening shouts, followed the tidings of his great victory the length and breadth of the land, and his name dwelt on every tongue. The victory of Gettysburg, at the same time, swelled the national enthusiasm to the highest pitch; and the shout that rose from the valley of the Mississippi met that which swelled up the Atlantic slope, till the Alleghanies shook with the glad acclaim.

Four days after, Port Hudson fell, thus opening the Mississippi its entire length. This result Grant had anticipated, when he refused again and again Banks' urgent request to send him troops. Once, in reply to a request for ten thousand men, he wrote with an earnestness not usual with him, unless deeply roused. He said: "Our situation is, for the first time during the entire Western campaign, what it should be. We have, after great labor and extraordinary risk, secured a position which should not be jeopardized by any detachments whatever. * * I have ample means to defend my present position, and effect the reduction of Vicksburg within twenty days, if the relation of affairs which now obtains remains unchanged. But, detach ten thousand men from my command, and I cannot answer for the result. * * * I need not describe the severity of the labor to which my command must necessarily be subjected, in an operation of such magnitude as that in which I am now engaged. Weakened by the detachment of ten thousand men, or even half that number, with the circumstances entirely changed, I should be crippled beyond redemption."

He had not spent months to get just where he wanted to be, to risk success by weakening his forces. He knew well that Port Hudson would fall of itself the moment that Vicksburg surrendered. Banks' sacrifice of life before the former place was as useless as the manner of doing it was unwise. Grant was aware that Banks' request was in accordance with the President's wishes, and this fact made him feel the more deeply, but he resolved that nothing but a peremptory order from headquarters should make him relax for a moment the iron grasp he had got on Vicksburg. After its surrender, he received the following letter from the President, acknowledging his mistake:

EXECUTIVE MANSION, WASHINGTON, July 13, 1863.

To Major-General GRANT:

MY DEAR GENERAL: I do not remember that you and I ever met personally. I write this now as a grateful acknowledgment for the almost inestimable service you have done the country. I wish to say a word further.

When you first reached the vicinity of Vicksburg, I thought you should do what you finally did—march the troops across the neck, run the batteries with the transports, and thus go below; and I never had any faith, except a general hope that you knew better than I, that the Yazoo Pass expedition, and the like, could succeed. When you got below and took Port Gibson, Grand Gulf, and the vicinity, I thought you should go down the river and join General Banks; and when you turned northward east of the Big Black, I feared it was a mistake. I now wish to make a personal acknowledgment that you were right and I was wrong.

Yours, very truly,   A. LINCOLN.

Nothing shows the tireless activity of Grant, and the terrible relentlessness with which he clung to and pushed his foe, more than his action on the night preceding the surrender of Vicksburg. Foreseeing clearly that its capitulation was inevitable, he directed Sherman to march back to Jackson and give Johnston battle, and drive him from the Mississippi Central Railroad. He was not a man to sit down for a moment and enjoy victories already won, when others were to be achieved. It was hard for troops that had struggled and waited so long for the overthrow of the stronghold, not to be allowed to witness its downfall, and share in the triumph. But the order was peremptory, and the tired troops started off, followed, soon as the capitulation was signed, by Ord and Steele; and marched back under a hot July sun for fifty miles, over a parched and pestilential country—with no

10*

water but such as could be gathered from swamps, to quench their thirst.

Rebuilding the bridges they had previously destroyed, the army pushed on to Jackson, where Johnston lay strongly entrenched. Holding him here, in the expectation that he would be assaulted, Sherman sent out expeditions in every direction, destroying railroads and rolling-stock and fixtures, while at the same time he gradually extended his lines around the place, till both extremities touched Pearl River. Johnston, now thoroughly alarmed for his safety, decamped in the night, and fled into the interior, destroying the railroad running east behind him, as he retreated. Sherman then slowly marched back, having lost about a thousand men in the expedition.

This finished the campaign of Vicksburg, the total result of which footed up in losses to Grant of killed and wounded and missing, eight thousand eight hundred and seventy-three; to the enemy, of fifty-six thousand, besides the vast destruction of material of war and public property, and the capture of cannon.

CHAPTER XIV.

GRANT's known anti-abolition principles, as distinguished from that party which, in former years,
waged perpetual war on the South, and his
democratic tendencies, so far as he had any politics
previous to the rebellion, caused many to imagine
that he would be entirely opposed to the employment of negroes as soldiers—a measure recently
determined on by the Government. But they
were mistaken. Not merely as a subordinate
was he willing to obey the behests of his Government, but as a wise commander, he saw that
they could be employed with great benefit to the
country—especially in garrisoning places on the
Mississippi, and thus releasing white troops to be
used in the field. Hence, only a week after the

surrender of Vicksburg, he told the Adjutant-
General of the army, that he was "anxious to get
as many of those negro regiments as possible,"
which had been ordered by the Government. He
said, "I am particularly anxious to organize a
regiment of heavy artillerists from the negroes, to
garrison this place, and shall do so as soon as possible." The President had written to him personally on the subject, for he had sanguine expectations respecting the great results of such a
measure—thinking, in fact, that it alone would
destroy the Confederacy. He said, "It is a re-
source, which, if vigorously applied now, will soon
close this contest." Grant did not share these ex-
travagant expectations. He never was carried
away by any mere theory. He viewed every thing
by the light of common sense; and although at the
outset of the war, like thousand of others who
had never studied carefully the history of civil
revolutions, he thought that a few battles would
end it, he had long since abandoned that idea.
He well knew that many fierce conflicts and a long
struggle, were before the country. Neither did he
believe, like the dreamers at Washington, that
emancipation or the employment of negroes
would do it. He looked upon these all only as so
many measures to help forward an end which
could be reached only by hard fighting and decisive victories in the field. The raising of a hun-

dred negro regiments, was to him simply a hundred thousand soldiers added to the army, nothing more nor less. The Southern commanders were inclined at first not to recognize negroes as soldiers, especially those who were runaway slaves, as under their laws they were required to turn them over to their former masters.

Grant did not trouble himself about the logic of the question—a man wearing the uniform of a United States soldier, and fighting under its flag, was entitled to receive the treatment due an American soldier. Hearing that this had not been granted to some prisoners captured at Milliken's Bend, but on the contrary, that they had been brutally hung, he wrote to General Taylor (son of General Taylor, the former President), within whose command the crime was committed, and after reciting the circumstances, said: " I feel no inclination to retaliate for the offence of irresponsible persons, but if it is the policy of any general intrusted with the command of troops, to show no quarter, or to punish with death prisoners taken in battle, I will accept the issue. It may be, you purpose a different line of policy towards black troops, and officers commanding them, to that practised towards white troops. If so, I can assure you that these colored troops are regularly mustered into the service of the United States. The Government, and all the officers under the Government, arc bound to give the same protection to those troops, that they do to any other troops." No pompous declamation here—no windy threats, which so many delighted to indulge in, for the sake of the pleasant sound they would make when reported in the newspapers; but a quiet, calm utterance of his duty, and a settled determination to perform it. He would hang a rebel general with the same serenity that he smoked his cigar, in the discharge of that. General Taylor replied, that he would punish all acts of inhumanity, or that were unbecoming a soldier; but that his Government required its officers to turn over all captured negroes to the civil authority, to be dealt with according to law.

The closing of the Mississippi had been a severe blow to the Western States, whose commerce had formerly been extensive with the South; hence, soon as it was opened, they anxiously desired to open trade with that portion which had surrendered to our arms. This was natural—else, they said, why expend so much time and treasure, and men, if it is to remain practically as much closed to us as ever. Chase, the Secretary of the Treasury, being himself a Western man, felt the pressure of Western opinion, and urged that trade, under certain restrictions, should be allowed within districts occupied by our military forces. This, Grant respectfully but steadily opposed. Though he said he held himself in readiness to obey any order he should receive, he remonstrated against the course, as certain to inflict serious injury on the Union cause. He declared it would be impossible, if trade were once allowed, to prevent the rebels from being supplied with every thing they wanted. He had seen how the thing worked in Kentucky, and he told the Government plainly, that it could not adopt any general rule in regard to trade under which "all sorts of dishonest men would not engage in it, taking any oath or obligation necessary to secure the privilege." Smuggling, he said, would be carried on in spite of the greatest vigilance, which would give the South, practically, the advantage of open commerce. His wise, sagacious counsels, however, were not followed, and his predictions proved true, while the perpetual annoyances to which it subjected him, were almost past endurance. Jews, and unscrupulous speculators of every kind, blockaded his headquarters, often ruffling that serene temper which nothing else seemed able to disturb. Anecdotes are told of the summary manner in which he sometimes dealt with these pestilent fellows, suggestive of any thing but military formality.

Although, immediately after the fall of Vicksburg, Grant sent off troops to Banks, and otherwise weakened his army, still he did not propose to remain idle. A large force could be assembled in a short time, and he thought if a sudden, vigorous blow were struck at Mobile, it could be taken. This would open the whole southern tier of States to our arms, and Grant proposed an expedition against it to Halleck. Meeting with a rebuff, he returned to it again in a few days, declaring that if permission were given him, he felt certain of success. Admiral Porter was of the same opinion ; but no solicitations could move Halleck. He wanted "to clear out western Louisiana," &c., and the result of his grand scheme was, that instead of the capture of Mobile, we had the Red River expedition under Banks, after cotton, which ended so disgracefully, and which come so near destroying our fleet on the Mississippi. Halleck was always inclined to squander our forces in expeditions which, even if successful, were barren of results that bore directly on the issue of the struggle. Grant always believed in striking vital points first, knowing that if the heart was once reached, the extremities would die of themselves ; while Halleck wished to reach the citadel of life by slow approaches.

Lincoln coincided with the General-in-Chief, respecting the Mobile expedition, and wrote to Grant so, and he was therefore compelled reluctantly to give it up, and remain idle at Vicksburg.

Many officers and soldiers, some of them on account of sickness and wounds, and others, whose absence from duty was necessary, obtained short furloughs, and repaired North. Grant, ever mindful of the welfare of his men, issued an order forbidding the steamboats that cleared from Vicksburg for Cairo, from charging the soldiers more than five dollars, and the officers more than seven, for their passage. Regardless of this order, the steamer Hope had taken on board a large number of both—the captain charging them from ten to twenty-five dollars apiece. Grant, hearing of it, immediately despatched an officer, accompanied by a guard, with the order to the captain to refund at once all the money received by him as fare, over five dollars to enlisted men, and seven dollars to officers, or submit to imprisonment for disobedience, and have his boat confiscated. The astonished captain looked first at the order and then at the guard which had been sent down to enforce it, and sullenly paid back the money which he had received in excess of the fare as fixed by Grant. This care of them by their commander, spread like wild-fire among the soldiers, and they made the shore ring with their hurrahs. On being informed of the various impositions practised on furloughed soldiers and officers, by steamboat men, he became very indignant, and said, "I will teach them, if they need the lesson, that the men who have perilled their lives to open the Mississippi river for their benefit, cannot be imposed upon with impunity."

Grant has none of that electric fire, that magnetic sympathy, such as distinguished Napoleon, and made the meanest soldier proud to die for him. There is nothing dramatic about him. He holds the affections of his troops by a different bond—. by an attachment that springs from profound respect for his ability, forecast, and readiness to share all their toils, privations and danger, and a parental care for their welfare.

In the short rest to which he was now doomed by the mistaken policy at Washington, his wife had time to visit him. For weary months, not only he, but his little son, not yet old enough to do without his mother's good-night kiss, had been either sleeping in pestilential marshes, or riding amid the storm of battle, and her heart yearned to see them, and the moment that victory gave her free access to them, she hastened to their embrace. Reaching St. Louis on her way down, her person was recognized, and immediately the hotel at which she stopped was thronged by the excited populace. Bands of music struck up triumphant airs, the multitude shouted the name of Grant, and so great was their enthusiasm, that they refused to leave until she presented herself on the balcony. Leaning on the arm of Brigadier-General Strong, she stood a moment before the sea of upturned faces, and was received with the wildest demonstrations of delight. General Strong returned thanks in her behalf, in a brief speech.

In the mean time, Halleck had ordered Grant to send the Thirteenth Corps, under Ord, to General Banks, at New Orleans, and otherwise assist him in his plan of operations against Texas.

In the latter part of this month, he visited Memphis to look after affairs in that portion of his department, when the citizens asked him to accept the honors of a public dinner. In complying with their request, after thanking them for the honor done him personally, he said :

I thank you, too, in the name of the noble army I have the honor to command. It is composed of men whose loyalty is proved by their deeds of heroism and their willing sacrifices of life and health. They will rejoice with me that the miserable adherents of the rebellion, whom their bayonets have driven from this fair land, are being replaced by men who acknowledge human liberty as the only true foundation of human government. May your efforts to restore your city to the cause of the Union be as successful as have been theirs to reclaim it from the despotic rule of the leaders of the rebellion. I have the honor to be, gentlemen, your very obedient servant, U. S. GRANT.

When the grand event of the evening, the toast to himself, was given, the company were taken quite aback by his declining to make any response —delegating to one of his staff the duty of returning his thanks. He then made the excuse, which has since become a standing one, that he was not accustomed to public speaking. In this, he differs from any other distinguished military man of the country that we know of.

The next day, he started for New Orleans, to see General Banks, who was on the eve of his departure for Texas, in order to learn his plans, and ascertain if he could be of any assistance to him. While there, a grand military review took place in his honor, at Carrollton. "What a magnificent spectacle! What cheers rent the air, when the historic colors of the old Thirteenth Corps dipped to the hero of Vicksburg as he passed along the lines, followed by a brilliant cortege of captains and staff officers, who had great difficulty in keeping up with the general, as he dashed along at a full gallop on a magnificent charger borrowed from Banks." Taking his place under an oak, he reviewed the troops, and it was noticed that, as they passed, he lifted his hat with a deeper reverence to the veteran Thirteenth Corps, bearing the flags that had waved in the storm of every battle from Donelson to Vicksburg. But, before the splendid pageant was over, an accident occurred, that marred the enjoyment of the day, and came near inflicting an irreparable loss on the country.

Though no man possesses a firmer seat in the saddle than Grant, and there is not, probably, a more accomplished horseman in the whole country, yet by a sudden, unaccountable movement in the animal he bestrode, he was unhorsed in a twinkling, and dashed with great violence to the ground. So heavy was the fall, and severe the injuries he received, that he never rose from the bed to which he was carried, for twenty days, and during all that time was unable to change his position. He could only lie on his back, and in this state was eventually carried on board of a boat and transported to Vicksburg. He remained here confined to his bed until the 25th of September, when he was able to hobble about on crutches. Fortunately, this long incapacity for the field occurred in the most favorable time for the country, as he had nothing to do except hold his own in his department, and give orders of minor importance. Banks was carrying out his Texas expedition, Rosecrans, with wavering fortune, was closing up his military career around Chattanooga, while Burnside of the Ohio department, was holding his own at Knoxville. But about the middle of September, Halleck, who had heard that Bragg, from whose hands Rosecrans had just wrested Chattanooga, was being heavily reinforced, telegraphed to Grant to send all his available force to that place. The despatch, however, was delayed on the road, so that it did not reach Grant until the 23d of the month. He was still in bed at Vicksburg, but immediately sent orders to Sherman to start one of his divisions for Chattanooga as speedily as possible. He also stopped a division of McPherson, which was sailing south to reinforce Steele, and directed it to return at once to Memphis, where Hurlbut was in command, while the latter was ordered to send it, with two divisions of his own and what other troops he could spare, to the same point. Grant bent his whole energies to carry out the wishes of Government, and placed all of his army, except what was necessary for garrison duty, at the disposal of Rosecrans. The effort, however, came too late— the battle of Chickamauga had been fought a few days before, and Rosecrans, defeated with heavy loss, was shut up in Chattanooga, and in great peril of total destruction.

Events were hurrying Grant forward to the high command he was destined to reach, faster than the Government proposed. On the last of the month, Halleck, now fully alive to the perilous state of things in the Cumberland department, telegraphed to Grant, that as soon as he was able, he wished him to go to Nashville, and take charge of the movement of troops, that Rosecrans was in such pressing need of. The day before, however, Grant had telegraphed: "I am now ready for the field, or any duty I may be called to perform." He was ready for the field, "or any duty" that his country might require of him, though he was just out of bed, and with difficulty could get about on his crutches. To men of less iron will or energy, this bodily condition would have seemed any thing but readiness for the battle-field.

Two or three days after, he received a despatch requesting him if possible to come to Cairo, the nearest point with which telegraphic communication could be kept up. He immediately started off, and bade, as it turned out, good-bye forever to Vicksburg and the army of the Tennessee—the child of his own raising, the sharer of his adverse fortunes and his glory, and which had become endeared to him by common toils, and dangers, and sufferings, and triumphs. But no defeats or victories to come could ever obliterate the memories that clustered around that place, the capture of which was the culmination of one of the most brilliant campaigns recorded in military annals. And on the spot where stood the oak under which his interview with Pemberton took place, and which soon disappeared, root and branch, as relics of the great event, a monument was reared, on which is inscribed, "To the Memory of the Surrender of Vicksburg by Lieutenant-General J. G. Pemberton to Major-General U. S. Grant, U. S. A., on the 3d of July, 1863."

As soon as Grant reached Cairo, he advised Halleck of his arrival, who in reply telegraphed him to proceed at once to Louisville with his staff, where he would meet an officer from the War Department, "with orders and instructions." The same day he started by railroad, and at Indianapolis met the Secretary of War himself, with an order which consolidated the three departments of Ohio, Cumberland, and his own into one, to be called the Military Division of the Mississippi, and placed him at the head of it, with full power to plan his campaigns without interference from any one. The Government was at last waking up to the fact that had been demonstrated so often that nothing but madness ignored it, that a cabinet or any representation of the civil government could not conduct campaigns in the field. Mistake after mistake had been made, disaster after disaster reached, the blame of which fell on the commanders, but which impartial history will put on men in civil authority in Washington, who undertook to manage that about which they did not understand the first principles.

CHAPTER XV.

Grant's Despatch to Thomas—Puts him in the place of Rosecrans
—Starts for Chattanooga—Has to be carried over rough
places—Gloomy Entrance into Chattanooga—Positions of the
two Armies—Opening up the Channel for Supplies—Hazen's
Expedition—Seizure of Lookout Valley by Hooker—Burnside
threatened at Knoxville—Sherman hurried forward—Grant
resolves to attack the Enemy—Postponement—His Anxiety for
Burnside—Despatches to him—His great Anxiety.

THE Government in placing Grant in supreme
command of all the forces west of the Alleghanies,
gave him the choice of keeping Rosecrans in
command of the Army of the Cumberland, or
of putting Thomas in his place. He unhesitatingly chose the latter. Orders were at once sent
on to Chattanooga, announcing his assumption of
the command of the new military division, and
placing Thomas over the Army of the Cumberland.

Alarmed at the rumors that Rosecrans was
about to evacuate Chattanooga, he sent with the
same orders the following one to Thomas : "*Hold
Chattanooga at all hazards;* I will be there as
soon as possible." The quick response from this
incomparable soldier, was, "*I will hold the town*

11

till we starve." That was enough. Grant knew
that now no power on earth could remove "the
rock of Chickamauga," till he should arrive there.
The man who, with his division alone, single-
handed, could hour after hour hold at bay the
whole rebel host, and save the Army of the Cumberland from annihilation, could be trusted to
keep what human power could retain.

The next day after sending those orders, Grant
took the railroad for Chattanooga. Reaching
Nashville, he telegraphed orders to Burnside, at
Knoxville, to fortify important points at once ; to
Admiral Porter at Cairo, to get a gunboat to
Sherman on the Tennessee, who was pushing his
way across the country ; and to Chattanooga to
Thomas respecting work to be done without delay. From Nashville, he with his staff took
horses and struck across the country. Grant was
still confined to his crutches, but he could ride
on horseback, and the party moved off rapidly
as the roads would permit. These, however, were
in a horrible condition. Poor in the best season,
now at the close of the fall they had been made
almost impassable, in some parts, by the heavy
rains and army wagons. Across swollen torrents
that came roaring down the mountain sides—
struggling over deep gullies and skirting overhanging precipices—the party made its difficult
way along the wreck-bestrewed road. To one in

Grant's helpless condition the difficulties and ob-stacles that met them at almost every step, were peculiarly annoying, for at some points it was impossible to ride with any degree of safety, and the entire party were compelled to dismount and lead their animals carefully over them. Grant, of course, could not use his crutches in these places, and his escort had to carry him across in their arms.

On the last day before reaching Chattanooga, a cold rain set in, drenching him and his escort to the skin. Just as the dark November night closed over the dreary desolate landscape, made still more gloomy and dispiriting by the chilling rain that fell without intermission, Grant, wet, cold, tired, hungry, and bespattered with mud, rode into the beleaguered place. Passing through the gloomy streets to Thomas' headquarters, he was helped from the saddle, and limped wearily under the welcome shelter of a roof.

Never before did a general assume command under more depressing circumstances.

No welcoming shouts of the soldiers, no cheer-ful congratulations of the officers, met him, but instead, gloomy silence and despondent utterances on every side. Starvation had dried up the cur-rents of life in the troops, while from every height the confident enemy looked down upon them, waiting for famine to do the work of the sword.

That was not a pleasant night to Grant ; but after conversing with Thomas till a late hour, he sought the rest he so much needed. Roused by the morning gun, the prospect as he looked out upon the dreary landscape did not tend to remove the sad impressions of the night before, for rebel fortifications overlooking the place, met his eye whichever way it turned.

After breakfast he mounted and rode out with Thomas and the chief engineer, W. F. Smith, to take a view of the situation. The first object was to open up communication with his supplies, so that the army could be fed.

Bragg held the river between Chattanooga and Bridgeport,—the terminus of the railroad from Nashville,—so that Rosecrans was compelled to bring supplies by land, over the Cumberland Mountains, a distance of sixty miles. The roads had became almost impassable, by the fall rains, and the horses had given out, so that the few teams that arrived often came in half empty, for it was impossible to haul them fully loaded over the frightful mountain roads ; until at last the troops were put on quarter rations, and at the time of Grant's arrival had only provisions enough to carry them through one battle. The opening of a channel, therefore, for supplies to reach him, became the first necessity. This was easily done, if the river to Bridgeport, several miles below, could be cleared of the enemy. The arrival of the Eleventh and Twelfth corps from the Army of the Potomac, just before Grant's appointment to the chief command, had enabled Rosecrans to mature a plan for accomplishing this, which the former approved of, and immediately proceeded to carry out.

The Tennessee River, which, as it approaches Chattanooga, is running southwest, when just below, turns abruptly to the south for a long distance, and then turns back and flows directly to the north, when it once more resumes its old course. This great bend incloses a peninsula, called Moccasin Point, from its resemblance to a moccasin, and was held by our troops; but the opposite bank by the rebels, as far down as Kelly's Ferry. Brown's Ferry was between this and Chattanooga; and the great object was to dislodge the enemy so that the road to both these ferries would be under Grant's control. The communication would then be open to Bridgeport, from which a railroad ran to Nashville. The operations at Kelly's Ferry were entrusted to Hooker, who had halted his corps at Bridgeport; and those at Brown's to Chief Engineer Smith. The latter selected Hazen's brigade for the hazardous enterprise assigned to him.

The south shore of the river was so thoroughly defended, that any attempt to throw a force across by pontoon bridges was impracticable. It was therefore determined to float fifty pontoon boats, with twenty-five men and one officer in each, making in all twelve hundred and fifty men, down the stream by night, and effect a landing on the bank, and hold it till a force of some four thousand men, concealed on the opposite shore, could be ferried over. The force would then be sufficiently strong to maintain itself till a pontoon bridge could be laid, over which reinforcements to any required amount could be sent.

On the morning of the 26th, Hazen went down the north shore to a point opposite where the landing was to be effected, and critically examined the locality. To the left of the ferry-house were two hills, which it was necessary he should occupy, on which there was a rebel picket post, and also one in the hollow between them. Having finished his examination, he arranged his plan of operations, attending to every thing personally, as the enterprise was to be a hazardous one. Each boat-load of twenty-five men was to carry two axes, making in all a hundred; and, as soon as the crest of those hills at the ferry was reached, skirmishers were to be thrown out, and the hundred axes at once set to work felling trees to make an abattis. He also selected points on the north bank of the river, where, at the proper time, signal fires were to be kindled, to guide him in effecting a landing. The fifty boats, made of "rough boards roughly nailed together," were divided into four distinct commands, over which tried and distinguished officers were placed, who, after being fully instructed in the duties they were expected to perform, were taken down opposite the ferry; and the points of landing, and the position of the enemy, etc., all pointed out to them. These in turn, just before night, called together the leaders of the separate squads, and instructed them in the parts they were expected to take, and how each was to act in the confusion that must, to a greater or less extent, exist in the gloom and darkness of night, when an attack was to be momentarily expected.

Every thing at last being arranged, the troops were sent to their tents to get an early sleep. At midnight they were awakened and marched to the landing, and stowed away in the boats. All at length being loaded, at three o'clock the silent little fleet pushed off into the stream, and catching the current, drifted downward in the gloom. It was necessary that the utmost silence should be preserved; for, if the enemy got wind of the movement in time, it would be frustrated. Hazen, therefore, with great gratification, saw that the force of the current alone, without the use of oars, would take him to the desired point of landing in time, and consequently passed the order that oars should be dispensed with—and the boats without a sound floated rapidly down the river. After going three miles, they came under the guns of the rebel pickets; but, by keeping in the deep shadow of the opposite shore, and maintaining a profound silence, they were not discovered, and the hostile sentinels slumbered on unconscious of danger, whilst this first step in the overthrow of the rebel army was being taken. There was no moon, and the waters rippling by gave no token of what was going on out on the dark bosom of the stream. The boats passed undiscovered, not only down to .opposite the place of landing, but the advance ones had actually taken to their oars and crossed over, and were within ten feet of the shore before any alarm was given. Seeing several black masses rapidly approaching the shore, the picket on duty hailed, and receiving no answer, fired a volley and sent back the alarm. Hazen, now that secrecy was at an end, shouted out his orders, and the boats were impelled by the strong oarsmen swiftly to the shore. So rapid was the debarkation, and so perfectly did each party perform its separate duties, even in the pitchy darkness, that the signal fires were scarcely lighted on the opposite bank, before the entire command was drawn up in line of battle. The advance was made with equal rapidity and exactness, so that Hazen was in position, his skirmish line out, and the axes ringing

in the woods, before the reinforcement of the enemy—only a little way over the hill—could arrive
to drive him back. A stubborn fight commenced;
but the boats had no sooner disgorged their loads,
than they were rowed swiftly across the river to
take on board the rest of the brigade that stood
waiting, and which quickly crossing, drove the
enemy back. A thousand rebel infantry, with
three pieces of artillery and a force of cavalry,
were stationed here, which was sufficiently strong
to have prevented any landing, had the enemy
been prepared for it. By noon a pontoon bridge
spanned the Tennessee at this point, over which
artillery and troops were soon thundering.

Hooker crossed his force at Bridgeport, and
marched up the opposite shore. Passing swiftly
through a gorge in the Raccoon Mountain, he de-
scended into Lookout Valley, and on the morning
of the 28th, Howard leading the advance, went
into camp within a mile of Brown's Ferry. Geary,
commanding the other portion of the troops, went
into camp about three miles farther down the river. Bragg, as soon as he was informed of these
movements, penetrated their object, and saw, if
they were not arrested, the siege of Chattanooga
would be practically raised. He therefore hurried forward Longstreet, who suddenly, at one
o'clock at night, fell on Geary, and the battle of
Wauhatchie began. Howard, aroused by the

11*

heavy firing, immediately started back to his help, but was stopped on his way by a rebel force posted on a range of hills, which announced its presence by a sheet of fire from its crest. Though the slope was heavily wooded, and the ground entirely unknown to officers and men, he boldly charged up them in the darkness, sweeping them like a storm.

Geary, after three hours of desperate fighting, repelled the attack of Longstreet. The mule-teams, frightened at the nightly cannonade, broke from the teamsters, and dashing towards the enemy with their harness and chain-traces rattling in the night, completed the discomfiture ; for the astonished rebels mistook them for a charge of cavalry, and fled precipitately. Lookout Valley was now Hooker's, and the river open to Bridgeport, so that only nine miles of land transportation over good roads remained—the rest of the way the supplies being brought in boats extemporized by the soldiers.

The road was now clear to Nashville, and Grant could calmly survey his position, and mature his plans.

Missionary Ridge and Lookout Mountain abut on the Tennessee River, the former above and the latter below Chattanooga, and run inland south, converging towards each other, in the form of the letter V. At the apex rises the Chattanooga

Creek, and flows, a noisy stream, into the Tennessee. The space between is the Chattanooga Valley. Here, on the river, and on and among a cluster of knobs or hills, is Chattanooga town. It lies nearer Lookout than it does to Missionary Ridge, and from the top of the former, shells could be thrown into the place. The problem before Grant was simple enough in statement, but whether, under the obstacles that interposed, it could be satisfactorily solved, was another matter. The enemy must be driven from those threatening heights, that, frowning with cannon, looked down on his camp. This was clear; and it was equally plain that it could be done in only one of two ways—by a flank movement, like that of Rosecrans when he drove Bragg out of Chattanooga, or by moving straight "on the enemy's works," and overcome all opposition by sheer hard fighting. The former course, under the circumstances, was impracticable, and Grant saw plainly that nothing was left but the latter. But before this could be attempted, Sherman, who the month previous had started with his force from Memphis, four hundred miles distant, must arrive. Halleck had ordered him to repair the railroad as he advanced, in order that he might bring up his supplies. Grant now directed him to drop every thing, and push on as rapidly as possible.

This was what Sherman wanted to do. The

moment he had heard of Grant's new appointment, he wrote him a letter expressing his delight,
and now, with increased ardor and confidence,
urged on his weary columns.   Grant knew that
the enemy would not give up Chattanooga without a desperate struggle, for they fully appreciated the importance of its possession to them.
They said: "Food and raiment are our needs.
We must have them.   Kentucky and Middle
Tennessee can only supply them.   Better give up
the seacoast, better give up the Southwest, ay,
better to give up Richmond without a struggle,
than lose the golden field, whose grain and wool
are our sole hope."

Bragg, the moment he saw that he had lost his
hold on the Nashville road, determined to compensate for it by driving Burnside out of Knoxville,
nearly a hundred miles away.   Grant, made aware
of this movement, became exceedingly anxious for
the arrival of Sherman, through whom alone he
could checkmate it, and he sent another messenger to him to take his four divisions and hurry on
to Bridgeport.   In the meantime he informed
Burnside of the danger that threatened him, and
gave him specific instructions how to act.   But it
becoming evident that Longstreet would be upon
him before Sherman could arrive, he ordered
Thomas to attack the enemy on Missionary Ridge,
hoping by this course to bring Longstreet back.

He issued his order on the 7th, saying: "The movement should not be delayed later than till to-morrow morning." Knowing the deficiency of horses in the camp, he directed him, if necessary, to take mules from the wagons, and even dismount the officers and press their horses into the service of the artillery. He also telegraphed Burnside of the intended movement to save him. No doubt the case was urgent, and the danger imminent, but subsequent events proved that had the attack then been made, it would have been repelled, and might have been the beginning of greater dis-. asters. Thomas, who had been on the ground longer, and whose anxiety was tempered with more caution, saw this, and declared that it was impossible for him to move until the arrival of Sherman. Destined to be the strongest prop to every commander he served under, he now saved Grant from committing a hasty act. The latter had entire confidence in the commander of the Army of the Cumberland, and recalled the order, leaving Burnside to oppose, as he best could, the force marching against him. He was disappointed, and thought if Thomas had moved as directed, it would have had the effect to recall Longstreet. Perhaps so; but other results of more importance might have followed. His orders were for Thomas to make the attack at the very point where Sherman shortly after made his.

That Missionary Ridge could not have been carried without Sherman's troops, is evident from
the desperate nature of the struggle by which it
was finally won.   Longstreet's fifteen thousand
men recalled and occupying the point where Sher-
men afterwards made a lodgment unopposed,
would, to say the least, have had a serious effect
on the final result.   It is doubtful if Grant would
have given this order but for the anxiety of the
Government for Burnside, and the pressing nature of the despatches from both Halleck and
the President, to see to it that he was not destroyed.   He may have felt, under this pressure, that
it was his duty to make an attempt, even if it
failed.   But to say, in the light of after events,
that the designed movement would have been
wise, and, in the end, successful, is asserting what
facts do not sustain.

Grant's command covered a large territory.
Two armies besides the one under his immediate
control, demanded his most watchful care, while
the opening and guarding of railroads, and bringing up of supplies, were matters of instant and
pressing necessity.   The anxiety for Burnside,
stimulated as it was by constant telegrams from
Washington, was the crowning source of all his
other anxieties.   The critical state of this commander, at Knoxville, whose defeat would lose us
East Tennessee, again made him wish to give wings

to Sherman's army. His active mind ran over the whole line of his long route, and suggested every possible expedient that might prevent delays, and expedite his march. To Burnside, despatch after despatch was sent, sometimes giving specific directions concerning the steps to take in case certain movements were made by Longstreet. One strain, however, ran through them all. "*Don't retreat.*" "Hold on at all hazards," was the burden of his telegrams, "and I will soon make a movement here that will relieve you." One day his language would be: "Hold on to Knoxville," another, "If Longstreet moves his whole *force across the Little Tennessee, cut his pontoons on the stream, even if it sacrifices half of the cavalry of the Ohio army.*"

CHAPTER XVI.

BATTLE OF MISSIONARY RIDGE.

On the 15th of November, Sherman, leaving
his army toiling forward, reached Chattanooga.
The next day, he and Grant, and Thomas, rode
out to examine the ground to be occupied by his
army in the great move now close at hand. Urged
by Grant to hurry up his columns, Sherman returned at once to Bridgeport, rowing the boat
himself a part of the way.

The moment a portion of his troops arrived,
though worn out with their long march, and many
of them barefoot, Grant determined not to wait
for the remainder, but to attack at once, and
issued his orders to that effect to Thomas, at the
same time sketching the general plan of operations.
But it was impossible for Sherman to get his

troops in position in time for the battle, which
Grant had ordered to commence at daylight, Saturday morning. Pushed to the limits of human
endurance, they were toiling over the miry roads,
or a frail bridge of boats at Brown's Ferry, and
could move no faster. Sherman told Grant so,
and the latter reluctantly, the second time, countermanded his order. His usually quiet nature
was roused into painful excitement by these repeated delays, and the imminent peril they caused
to Burnside, until he could no longer preserve his
habitual repose, but broke forth. " I have never
felt such restlessness as I have at the *fixed and
immovable condition of the Army of the Cumberland.*" It was no common anxiety that could
wring such an expression from him.

When he found that it was impossible for Sherman to be up by the time he had appointed, he
fixed the next Sunday morning for the attack.
But a heavy rain-storm set in, deluging the roads;
while the bridge at Brown's Ferry broke down,
so that, though Sherman worked night and day,
he could not be ready even by Sunday morning.
Chafing under these protracted disappointments,
Grant then fixed Monday morning for the attack,
and so advised Thomas. But as if to try his patience to the utmost, the rains so swelled the river,
that the frail bridges over the Tennessee were
swept entirely away, and every thing brought to

a complete stand still. Once more he was compelled to inform Thomas, that farther delay was inevitable.

On the night of the 22d, a deserter from Bragg's army came in and reported that the rebel general was about to evacuate his works. A day or two before, Grant had received a note from Bragg advising him to remove non-combatants from Chattanooga, as he was about to open upon it with his cannon. He, however, paid no attention to it, and now concluded it was intended to mislead him, while a safe retreat was effected. He therefore directed Thomas the next day to make a reconnoisance in force, and feel the enemy's lines, to see if it were so. The battalions were deployed in the bright sunlight, in full view of the enemy, who thought it was a parade. They were, however, soon undeceived — for the imposing columns moved rapidly forward, and though cannon and musketry opened upon them, never paused until the advanced line of the enemy was carried and held. By this unexpected movement, Grant planted himself a mile nearer Missionary Ridge, and occupied Orchard Knob, a valuable position, with the loss of only a little over a hundred men.

At last Sherman's army, with the exception of one division, was up, and Grant determined to strike without a moment's delay. His general plan was to have Sherman with the army of the Tennessee throw itself across the river opposite Missionary Ridge, make a lodgment there, and then assail Bragg's right wing, posted on that extremity of the mountain. Hooker, while Sherman was getting into position, was to carry Lookout Mountain, the other extremity, and be ready to press forward the next day and cut off the rebel retreat, or operate on his left and rear, while Thomas, with his twenty thousand men, at a given signal was to charge straight up the rocky heights and carry them by storm.

It was of the first importance that Bragg should be kept ignorant of Sherman's movement until he had effected a crossing, and Grant, therefore, manœuvred his troops in a manner to make him think an attack was meditated against his left, and so drew his attention in that direction. In the meantime, Sherman's columns, concealed by hills near the shore, passed up the river till they reached Chickamauga Creek, above Chattanooga. In anticipation of this movement, one hundred and sixteen pontoons had been concealed in a stream near by, which, after dark, were floated down into the Tennessee, full of soldiers; and by dawn the next day eight thousand men were on the other shore, and had thrown up a rifle trench as a *tête du pont*. A bridge thirteen hundred feet long was immediately begun, and by one o'clock was shaking to the tread of the hurrying columns. A drizzling rain was falling at the time, which, with the low clouds wrapping the heights, concealed the movement.

By three o'clock, Bragg, to his astonishment, found an army hanging along the sides of Missionary Ridge, on his extreme right. A feeble attempt was made to repel the advance, but the artillery, dragged up the steep ascent, scattered the enemy, and night found Sherman securely planted.

While Sherman was thus securing a lodgment on the rebel right, Hooker was carrying Lookout Mountain on his left. "The ascent of the mountain is steep and thickly wooded; beetling crags peer out all over its sides from the masses of heavy foilage, and, at the summit, a lofty palisaded crest rises perpendicularly, as many as sixty or eighty feet. On the northern slope, about midway between the summit and the Tennessee, a plateau of open and arable land belts the mountain. There, a continuous line of earthworks had been thrown up ; while redoubts, redans, and rifle-pits were scattered lower down the acclivity, to repel assaults from the direction of the river. On each flank were epaulements, walls of stone, and abatis ; and, in the valley itself, at the foot of the mountain, long lines of earthworks, of still greater extent. The entire force, for the defence of the mountain, consisted of six brigades, or about seven thousand men."

In the same drizzling rain and fog that had partially concealed Sherman's movement, Hooker began his march. As he looked up the rugged slopes, he saw that no common task had been assigned him, but it was in just such emergencies that his great qualities exhibited themselves. That cloud-capped summit must be won, and the first step taken toward victory. The bugles sounded "forward," and the columns took up their line of march for the base, and heedless of the iron-storm that beat from above upon them, reached it and began to climb like mountain goats the steep ascent. Sometimes stopped for a moment, but never driven back, they kept unwaveringly on till they entered the low hanging clouds, which suddenly wrapped them from sight. Grant and Thomas, and others down in Chattanooga, gazed anxiously toward the hidden summit, and listened with beating hearts to the crashing vollies and deep roar of artillery that came out of the mysterious bosom of the clouds. Lookout, for the time, seemed famed Olympus on which Jupiter was thundering, or the gods contending in celestial fury. Nought could be seen, and though the heavy explosions of artillery remained stationary, the vollies of musketry seemed to creep nearer and nearer to the summit. At this moment of intense excitement, the fog suddenly lifted, letting down the light of heaven upon the mountain top, and revealing as by magic to the gazing thousands below, a scene of sublime and thrilling interest. There, amid the rocky ledges, in front of the rebel works, stood our gallant troops, their banners mere specks against the sky. The battle was raging furiously, for this was the last foothold of the enemy—driven from the summit, the mountain was Hooker's. The whole army in Chattanooga were witnesses of this strange fight among the clouds, and when at length they saw the enemy driven out of his works, and our banners wave above them, they broke forth into a shout that rent the heavens, and long, loud acclamations surged backward and forward through the valley. But the fighting did not cease till after dark, and the rebel signal-light could be seen waving from the lofty summit to Bragg on Missionary Ridge, while jets of flame pierced the gloom, and the muffled vollies fell faintly on the ear below.

But the height was won; and Hooker at once opened communication with Chattanooga.

Every thing had worked to Grant's satisfaction, and he only waited for the morning light to hurl his sixty thousand men on the rugged heights in his front. During the night it cleared off, and a sharp autumnal·frost rendered the air of that high region still clearer, and gave a darker blue to the deep vault of heaven. The soldiers crowned the hills with camp-fires, revealing to the enemy their position, as well as showing to their friends in Chattanooga the important points that had been gained. At midnight a staff officer of Grant reached Sherman with directions to attack at daybreak, saying that Thomas would also attack "early in the day." Sherman turned in for a short nap, but before daylight he was in the saddle, and riding the whole length of his lines, examined well his position and that of the enemy. By the dim light he saw, to his surprise, that a valley or gorge lay between him and the next hill, which was very steep, and that the farther point was held by the enemy with a breastwork of logs and earth in front. A still higher hill commanded this with a plunging fire, which was also crowded with the foe. He could not see the bottom of the gorge below, and was not able to complete his preparations so as to attack by daylight, as he had been ordered. General Corse was to lead the advance, and before he had fully marshalled his forces, the sun arose in dazzling brightness over the eastern heights, and flooded the scene with beauty. His beams were sent back from tens of thousands of bayonet points, and flashing athwart long rows of cannon, while the increasing light brought out in a grand panoramic picture,

Chattanooga resting quietly below in its amphitheatre of hills. Banners waved along the heights,
and rose over Grant's encampment in the distance,
and all was bright and beautiful. Here and there
a bugle-call and drum-beat gave increased interest
to the scene. But its beauty was soon to change
—those summits, now baptized in golden light,
were to be wrapped in smoke and heave to volca-
nic fires, and strong columns stagger bleeding
along their sides.

Sherman at length being ready, Corse's bugles
sounded the "forward," and the assaulting regiments moved steadily down the hill, across the
intervening valley, and up the opposing slope.
Morgan L. Smith on the left of the ridge, and
Colonel Loomis abreast of the Tunnel, drew a
portion of the enemy's fire away from the assaulting column, which having closed in a death-grapple with the foe, now advanced its banners, and
now receded, but never yielding the position it
had at first gained. Grant could see the struggle
from his position at Chattanooga, and at one time
observing two brigades give way in disorder,
thought Sherman was repulsed; but it was not
so. Corse, Loomis, and Smith, stuck to the enemy with a tenacity that gave him not a moment's
rest. Sherman's position not only threatened the
rebel right flank, but his rear and stores at Chickamauga station; hence the persistency of his at-

tack alarmed Bragg, and he steadily accumulated forces against him that rendered an advance on Sherman's part impossible. Hour after hour the contest raged with terrible ferocity, and the flaming cloud-wrapped heights appeared to the lookers-on at Chattanooga like a volcano in full, fierce action. Grant had told Sherman that Thomas would attack early in the day, but the former watched in vain for the movement. The gallant Corse had been borne wounded from the field, and Grant, fearing that Sherman was being too heavily pressed, sent over to his help Baird's division; but Sherman sent it back, saying he had all the troops that he wanted. Thus, he fought the battle alone all the forenoon, and still the banners drooped lazily along their staffs in front of Chattanooga. He began to grow impatient. In the bright clear air he could look down from his position on the "amphitheatre of Chattanooga," but could discern no signs of the promised movement. Now and then a solitary cannon-shot alone told that the army there was alive; but beyond, toward Lookout, where Hooker was trying to advance, the heavy reverberations of artillery, and dull sound of musketry, showed that he was pushing the enemy. Thus matters stood at three o'clock, when, said Sherman, "I saw column after column of the enemy streaming toward me, gun after gun pouring its concentric shot on us from every hill

12

and spur that gave a view of any part of the ground held by us." The attack of Thomas, which was to be "early in the day," was unaccountably delayed, and what could it all mean, was the anxious enquiry he put to himself. One thing was plain—his exhausted columns could not long stand this accumulation of numbers and concentration of artillery. Grant, too, was anxious. The appearance of Hooker's column, moving north along the ridge on the other flank of the enemy, was to be the signal of assault on the centre; but hour after hour passed by and no advancing banners were seen. The latter had been detained in building a bridge across Chattanooga Creek.

At length, he could wait no longer, and hearing that Hooker was well advanced, and seeing the centre weakened, to overthrow Sherman, he ordered the assault to be made. Sherman, whose glass was scarcely for a moment turned from the centre, now saw with relief a "white line of musketry fire in front of Orchard Knob, extending further right and left and on." "We could hear," he says, "only a faint echo of sound; but enough was seen to satisfy me that General Thomas was moving on the centre."

He *was* moving, but it was now nearly four o'clock in the short autumnal afternoon, and Grant had waited and waited with painful suspense, for Hooker's advance. What was to be done must be done quickly; and, as now, from his elevated knoll, he saw the hostile columns moving swiftly along the ridge toward Sherman, showing that Bragg was weakening his centre to strengthen his right, he knew that the decisive hour had come. The rebel general was repeating the mistake committed by the allies at Austerlitz —making a flank movement in presence of the enemy, and, like Napoleon, Grant at once took advantage of it, and gave the order to advance.

The signal was six cannon shots, fired at intervals of two seconds each. With regular beat, one, two, three sounded, till, as the last deep reverberation rolled away over the heights, there was a sudden resurrection, as from the bowels of the earth, of that apparently dead line. Four divisions of the Army of the Cumberland composed it. A mile and a half of country lay before them to the rifle-pits at the base of Missionary Ridge. First, a belt of open timber, and then a smooth plain, then the rifle-pits at the base of the Ridge—finally, the rocky hill, four hundred feet high to mount, every inch of it swept by artillery and musketry. Passing through the woods, they burst on a double-quick into the open plain. The tempest that now broke upon their heads was terrible. "The enemy's fire burst out of the rifle-pits from base to summit of Mission Ridge; five rebel batteries of Parrots and Napoleons opened along the crest. Grape and canister, and shot and shell, sowed the ground with rugged iron, and garnished it with the wounded and the dead. But steady and strong our columns moved on."

Over their heads, from every commanding fort and hill, our batteries rained a horrible tempest of iron on the rebel works. Under this awful canopy, the glittering lines breasted on a run the fiery sleet that smote them in front, each eye fixed unwaveringly on the rifle-pits at the foot of the Ridge. The sun was now hanging just above the western horizon, pouring its flood of light upon their backs, and shining full in the enemy's faces. As the unclouded rays fell on those twice ten thousand bayonet-points, sweeping in one glittering wave across the plain, the dazzling sheen of light was so terrible, that the rebels in the rifle-pits fled before it in affright, or fell prostrate in the trenches, and let it roll in flashing splendor over them, without firing a shot.

The orders were, that when the rifle-pits were carried, the line should be halted and re-formed for an advance up the heights. But, as the men bounded into them with a shout, they forgot all orders. Their blood was now up, and sending their loud hurrah above the deafening thunder-peals that shook mountain and plain, they began to scale the rocky slope. The fire that opened on them was appalling. It was no longer round shot and shell, but canister, grape, and musketry. Missionary Ridge was a volcano, "a thousand torrents of fire poured over its brink, and rushed together to its base. But the line moves on and up. They cannot *dash* up that rugged acclivity. They dash out a little way, and then slacken; they creep up, hand over hand, loading and firing, and wavering and halting, from the first line of works to the second; they burst into a charge with a cheer, and go over it. Sheets of flame baptize them; plunging shot tear away comrades on left and right; it is no longer shoulder to shoulder; it is God for us all! Under tree-trunks, among rocks, stumbling over the dead, struggling with the living, facing the steady fire of eight thousand infantry poured down upon their heads as if it were the old historic curse from heaven, they wrestle with the Ridge. Ten, fifteen, twenty minutes go by, like a reluctant century. The batteries roll like a drum. Between the second and last lines of rebel works is the torrid zone of the battle. The hill sways up like a wall before them, at an angle of forty-five degrees, but our brave mountaineers are clambering steadily on—up—upward still!"

It was thrilling, maddening to see those wavering banners fluttering alternately high up the steep acclivity, amid flame and smoke. Now one and now another would sink to the ground along the steep, as the bearers were shot down, but the next moment they would gleam aloft again, as gallant comrades seized them, and carried them farther up the slope. The ranks melted rapidly away, but the survivors kept on. Grant gazed, apparently unmoved, at the sight, yet with his whole soul in the struggle. Even the impassable Thomas, as he saw the slow and difficult progress, exclaimed to Grant: " I fear, General, they will never reach the top." The latter merely replied: " Give 'em time, General, give 'em time." At last the crimson, glittering tide reached the crest, and just as the sun was sinking below the western horizon, flooding the heights with his departing rays, it rolled over them, and Grant knew they were won. Then there went up a shout, like the far-off murmur of the sea, and as the muffled sound reached the ear of Grant, his compressed lips wreathed with a smile, and the burden lifted from his heart.

"But the scene on the narrow plateau can never be painted. As the blue-coats surged over its edge, cheer on cheer rang like bells through the valley of the Chickamauga. Men flung themselves exhausted upon the ground. They laughed and wept, shook hands, and embraced; turned round, and did all four over again. It was as wild as a carnival. Granger was received with a shout. 'Soldiers,' he said, 'you ought to be court-martialled, every man of you! I ordered you to take the rifle-pits, and you scaled the mountain!' But it was not Mars' horrid front exactly, with which he said it, for his cheeks were wet with tears as honest as the blood that reddened all the route. Wood uttered words that rang like 'Napoleon's;' and Sheridan, the rowels at his horse's flanks, was ready for a dash down the Ridge with a 'view halloo,' for a fox-hunt."

Bragg and his staff-officers attempted to rally the troops, and form a second line of battle, in vain, and the disordered host fled in affright. Sheridan, from the Ridge, saw the disorganized columns and confused wagon trains surging through the valley below, and pushed fiercely on. A mile in the rear, the road wound along a high hill on which Bragg had planted batteries, defended by a strong force of infantry, to check the pursuit. These now poured a rapid fire into Sheridan's division, but it kept steadily on, and reaching the base, a part began to climb the mountain in front, while Sheridan sent two regiments to flank it on both sides at once. It was now dark, and just as one of these regiments came over the crest of the hill, the moon rose behind it, and the column, with bayonets and banners, was drawn in black, bold relief against the glittering orb.

Hooker, too, was in full pursuit; while Grant, the moment the Ridge was carried, put spurs to his horse and rode to the top, to direct the move-

272 LIFE OF GRANT.

ments, cheered by the excited soldiers wherever he moved. He kept on for a mile or two, but night checked further pursuit, except by Sheridan, that nothing seemed able to stop—and though confused by the darkness and ignorant of the roads, he kept on for seven miles, carrying consternation into the fugitive ranks.

But the bugle sounding recall along and beneath that blood-stained Ridge, arrested the army, and under the bright moon it went into bivouac with cheers, that, taken up by division after division, made that autumnal evening jubilant with glad echoes.

Six thousand prisoners and forty cannon, were the trophies of the victory.

At seven o'clock that night, Grant sat down and wrote the following modest despatch to Halleck :—

CHATTANOOGA, November 25, 1863—7.15, P. M. -

Major-General H. W. HALLECK, General-in-Chief :

Although the battle lasted from early dawn till dark this evening, I believe I am not premature in announcing a complete victory over Bragg.

Lookout Mountain top, all the rifle-pits in Chattanooga Valley, and Missionary Ridge entire, have been carried, and are now held by us. I have no idea of finding Bragg here to-morrow.

U. S. GRANT, Major-General.

From this despatch one would never dream that he had carried every strong position of the enemy, who was now in full flight, miles away; killed, wounded, or captured nearly a fifth of Bragg's entire force, and taken forty pieces of artillery.

Next morning, the pursuit was recommenced, Grant riding with the advanced columns.

Sherman, from his position, also moved forward, and, as he reached the depot of the enemy, found it a scene of desolation. "Corn-meal and corn, in huge burning piles, broken wagons, abandoned caissons and guns, burned carriages, pieces of pontoons, and all manner of things, burning and broken," attested the ravages of war. Along the road, strewed with the wrecks of the fight, he pressed on till night, when, just as he emerged from a miry swamp, he came upon the enemy's rear-guard. A sharp contest followed, but the night closed in so dark that he could not move forward. Here, in the gloom, Grant joined him. The next morning he continued the pursuit; but finding the roads filled with all the troops "they could accommodate," he halted and turned to the east, to break up the communications between Bragg and Longstreet, now before Knoxville.

Hooker also kept on all day, after the fleeing enemy; and Grant would have pressed the pursuit as long as he could have fed his men, but for his anxiety to relieve Burnside. He therefore ordered it to cease, and at once directed Granger,

12*

and soon after Sherman, to march for Knoxville and raise the siege. To the latter, this was assigning a terrible task. It was hard to ask his troops, after a march of four hundred miles, and a fierce battle, and days of pursuit, now to make a forced march of eighty-four miles, in winter, over a broken country. "Seven days before," says he, " we had left our camp on the other side of the Tennessee, with two days' rations, without a change of clothing, stripped for the fight, with but a single blanket or coat per man—from myself to the private. Of course, we then had no provisions, save what we gathered by the road, and were ill supplied for such a march. But we learned that twelve thousand of our fellow-soldiers were beleaguered in the mountains of Knoxville, eighty-four miles distant; that they needed relief, and must have it in three days. This was enough, and it had to be done," and he at once put his army in motion.

Longstreet heard of his approach, and hastily raising the siege, retreated eastward.

The campaign was now ended, and Grant could take a quiet survey of his position. With sixty thousand men, he had driven forty-five thousand from positions that the enemy supposed half of that number could hold forever; relieved all East Tennessee; and firmly established a base for further operations into the interior.

Although the campaign had closed with a thunder-clap, on a narrow strip of mountain, it had embraced a wide field in its progress. It took in the Army of the Ohio, nearly ninety miles distant, in Knoxville; the Army of the Tennessee, hundreds of miles away, toiling through a hostile country; as well as Chattanooga itself. Every thing centered around the single person of Grant, who, at the latter place, was the moving power of the whole.

Having at length gathered the scattered, isolated elements into his single hand, he hurled them in one mighty blow on the enemy, crushing him into fragments. His plan of battle was simple, and carried out like an order for a parade. Right in the presence of the enemy, who could look down on all his movements from his high perch, he laid all his plans, and executed them with the precision of one who is master of fate. And never before was a battle fought in which there were more dramatic scenery and action combined. Mountain heights crowned with the enemy, looking down on quiet camps below; troops fighting above the clouds; Grant, the central figure of the great panorama, standing on a low hill, with three armies thundering and shouting above and around him; the descending sun, flooding all in its departing splendor, are only so many shifting scenes in the mighty drama.

This brilliant campaign, so glorious in its results, lifted Grant to the highest summit of military renown, and stamped him one of the greatest generals of his time. The President, overjoyed at the result, sent the following telegram to him:

WASHINGTON, December 8.

Major-General GRANT:

Understanding that your lodgment at Chattanooga and Knoxville is now secure, I wish to tender you, and all under your command, my more than thanks—my profoundest gratitude, for the skill, courage, and perseverance with which you and they, over so great difficulties, have effected that important object. God bless you all! A. LINCOLN.

CHAPTER XVII.

GRANT now again proposed to the Government
a movement against Mobile, promising to capture
or secure its investment by the last of January;
but his request was refused.

Soon after, he issued the following congratulatory order to the Army:

> HEADQUARTERS, MILITARY DIVISION OF THE MISSISSIPPI,
> IN THE FIELD, CHATTANOOGA, TENN.,
> December 10, 1863.

The General Commanding takes this opportunity of
returning his sincere thanks and congratulations to the
brave armies of the Cumberland, the Ohio, the Tennessee, and their comrades from the Potomac, for the
recent splendid and decisive successes achieved over the
enemy. In a short time, you have recovered from him
the control of the Tennessee River, from Bridgeport to
Knoxville. You dislodged him from his great stronghold upon Lookout Mountain, drove him from Chatta-

nooga Valley, wrested from his determined grasp the possession of Missionary Ridge, repelled with heavy loss to him his repeated assaults upon Knoxville, forcing him to raise the siege there, driving him at all points, utterly routed and discomfited, beyond the limits of the State. By your noble heroism and determined courage, you have most effectually defeated the plans of the enemy for regaining possession of the States of Kentucky and Tennessee. You have secured positions from which no rebellious power can drive or dislodge you. For all this, the General Commanding thanks you collectively and individually. The loyal people of the United States thank and bless you. Their hopes and prayers for your success against this unholy rebellion are with you daily. Their faith in you will not be in vain. Their hopes will not be blasted. Their prayers to Almighty God will be answered. You will yet go to other fields of strife ; and with the invincible bravery and unflinching loyalty to justice and right which have characterized you in the past, you will prove that no enemy can withstand you, and that no defences, however formidable, can check your onward march.

By order,   Major-General U. S. GRANT.

About Christmas he visited Knoxville, to look after matters there in person. In the mean time, he had planned the great raid into Mississippi, known as the Meridian raid. About the middle of January, he returned to Nashville, where he had established his headquarters.

Congress, in the mean time, passed a vote of thanks, and ordered a medal to be struck in commemoration of the great services he had rendered the country.

Notwithstanding Grant desired greatly to carry on a winter campaign, circumstances rendered it impossible. Thomas, at Chattanooga, could not push on through the mountains towards Atlanta, while the impossibility of supplying the army at Knoxville, in the field, if properly reinforced, compelled him to give up his first purpose to move against Longstreet, who still lingered in East Tennessee. Besides, the term for which a large part of the volunteers had enlisted expired this winter, and, in order to induce them to re-enlist, a furlough of sixty days was given them. Hence, no general movement could be set on foot, and Grant contented himself with sending Sherman on his raid into Mississippi, to be supported by a large body of cavalry, starting about the same time from Corinth. The object he had in view may be seen from his orders to Sherman, as indicated in the following letter to Halleck:

"I shall direct Sherman, therefore, to move out to Meridian, with his spare force, the cavalry going from Corinth; and destroy the roads east and south of there so effectually, that the enemy will not attempt to rebuild them during the rebellion. He will then return, unless opportunity of going into Mobile with the force he has, appears perfectly plain. Owing to the large number of veterans furloughed, I will not be able to do more at Chattanooga than to threaten an advance, and try to detain the force now in Thomas' front. Sherman will be instructed, whilst left with these large discretionary powers, to take no extra hazard of losing his army, or of getting it crippled too much for efficient service in the spring."

Sherman started on the 3d of February, and pushed as far as Meridian, sending consternation through the South, that was filled with all kinds of conjecture as to the object and end of his march. The cavalry force destined to accompany him, however, was driven back by the enemy, which embarrassed his movements and shortened his march, so that, after destroying the railroad depots on each side of Meridian for a long distance, he returned.

In the latter part of January, hearing that his eldest son was lying dangerously ill at St. Louis, Grant obtained permission to visit him. His arrival caused great excitement, and a public dinner was tendered him, in a long, flattering letter. Finding that his son had passed the crisis of his disease, and was pronounced out of danger, he accepted the invitation. As the toast to him, the honored guest, was given, the band struck up " Hail to the Chief," and at the close of the strain, the building rocked to the loud hurrahs of the guests. To all this demonstration, Grant simply returned his thanks. Afterwards, when the crowd blocked the streets and asked for him in deafening clamor, he reluctantly appeared on the

balcony of the hotel. His appearance was greeted with the wildest uproar, and deafening calls for
a speech. But he only said, "Gentlemen, I thank
you for this honor. I cannot make a speech. It
is something I have never done, and never intend
to do, and I beg you will excuse me." But the
surging multitude was determined not to be put
off so. It did not believe that a man who could
so coolly face that mighty throng, blandly smoking
his cigar the while, could not make a speech if
he was inclined to, and the shout, "A speech, a
speech, a speech!" rose like thunder from the
streets below. A gentleman beside him said,
General, tell them you can fight for them, but
cannot talk to them. "Some one else must say
that for me," was the quiet reply. But the
clamor swelling, he was forced to open his mouth,
and said in sharp, decided tones, "Gentlemen,
making speeches is not my business, I never did
it in my life—never will ; I thank you, however,
for your attendance here," and retired, much to the
disappointment of the crowd, for, to an American,
a crowd without a speech is a failure. To one who,
at this time, asked him of his political views, he
said: "These are not the times for parties. Indeed, in this crisis there can be but two parties—
those for the country, those for its foes. I belong
to the party of the Union. Those who are the
most earnest in carrying on the war and putting

down the Rebellion, have my support. As a soldier, I obey the laws and execute the orders of all my superiors. I expect every man under me to do the same."

A bill which had been introduced into Congress by Mr. Washburne, to revive the grade of Lieutenant-General, with a view of conferring it on Grant, passed in the latter part of February. The nomination of the officer to hold this high position, never before occupied but by two men, Washington and Scott, belonging to the President, he, in accordance with his own inclinations, as well as the clearly expressed wish of the people, sent to the Senate the name of Grant. He was promptly confirmed. The President at once sent for him to come on to Washington, and he started on the 4th of March, for the capital. The very day he received the intelligence of the high command to which he had been nominated, he wrote the following letter to Sherman, which, with the answer, exhibits both these great commanders in a most attractive light. He says :

DEAR SHERMAN,—The bill reviving the grade of Lieutenant-general in the Army has become a law, and my name has been sent to the Senate for the place. I now receive orders to report to Washington immediately, *in person*, which indicates a confirmation, or a likelihood of confirmation. I start in the morning to comply with the order.

Whilst I have been eminently successful in this war, in at least gaining the confidence of the public, no one feels more than I, how much of this success is due to the energy, skill, and the harmonious putting forth of that energy and skill, of those whom it has been my good fortune to have occupying subordinate positions under me.

There are many officers to whom these remarks are applicable to a greater or less degree, proportionate to their ability as soldiers; but what I want, is to express my thanks to you and McPherson, as the men to whom, above all others, I feel indebted for whatever I have had of success.

How far your advice and assistance have been of help to me you know. How far your execution of whatever has been given you to do, entitles you to the reward I am receiving, you cannot know as well as I. I feel all the gratitude this letter would express, giving it the most flattering construction.

The word *you*, I use in the plural, intending it for McPherson also. I should write to him, and will some day, but, starting in the morning, I do not know that I will find time just now.

> Your friend,
>
> U. S. GRANT, Major-General.

The simple, manly sincerity of this letter—the utter absence of all vanity and egotism—the abnegation of all claims to distinction from his own merits, the generous acknowledgment of the claims and services of others, and the warm, noble friendship it expresses, reveal, as no eulogy could do, the truthfulness, modesty and real grandeur of his character. Sherman replied as follows:

DEAR GENERAL: I have your more than kind and characteristic letter of the 4th instant. I will send a copy to General McPherson at once. You do yourself injustice, and us too much honor in assigning to us too

large a share of the merits which have led to your high
advancement. I know you approve the friendship I
have ever professed to you, and will permit me to con-
tinue, as heretofore, to manifest it on all proper occasions.

You are now Washington's legitimate successor, and
occupy a position of almost dangerous elevation; but,
if you can continue, as heretofore, to be yourself, simple, honest, and unpretending, you will enjoy through
life the respect and love of friends, and the homage of
millions of human beings, that will award you a large
share in securing to them and their descendants a
government of law and stability.

I repeat, you do General McPherson and myself
too much honor. At Belmont, you manifested your
traits—neither of us being near. At Donelson, also,
you illustrated your whole character. I was not near,
and General McPherson in too subordinate a capacity
to influence you.

Until you had won Donelson, I confess I was almost cowed by the terrible array of anarchical elements
that presented themselves at every point; but that ad-
mitted a ray of light I have followed since. I believe
you are as brave, patriotic, and just, as the great pro-
totype Washington—as unselfish, kind-hearted, and
honest as a man should be—but the chief characteristic
is the simple faith in success you have always manifested, which I can liken to nothing else than the faith a
Christian has in the Saviour.

This faith gave you victory at Shiloh and Vicksburg. Also, when you have completed your best preparations, you go into battle without hesitation, as at
Chattanooga—no doubts—no reserves; and I tell you,
it was this that made us act with confidence. I knew,
wherever I was, that you thought of me, and if I got
in a tight place you would help me out, if alive.

My only point of doubt was, in your knowledge of
grand strategy, and of books of science and history,
but, I confess, your common-sense seems to have supplied all these.

Now, as to the future. Don't stay in Washington. Come West: take to yourself the whole Mississippi Valley. Let us make it dead sure—and I tell you, the Atlantic slopes and Pacific shores will follow its destiny, as sure as the limbs of a tree live or die with the main trunk. We have done much, but still much remains. Time, and time's influences, are with us. We could almost afford to sit still, and let these influences work.

Here lies the seat of the coming empire; and from the West, when our task is done, we will make short work of Charleston and Richmond, and the impoverished coast of the Atlantic.

Your sincere friend,
W. T. SHERMAN.

There is a Spartan simplicity, combined with the chivalry of knightly days, in this correspondence. Amid the stern realities of war, the acclamations of the people, and the applause of the great, what a pleasant side-picture this private interchange of feelings between these two great commanders makes. Neither the hardening sights of the battle-field, nor rank, nor emoluments, can change the inborn nobleness of these two hearts; no pride on the one hand, no envy on the other. The love of these two heroes is grander than their heroism.

Grant's arrival at Washington was the signal for the wildest demonstrations of enthusiasm, and at the President's levee, he was lifted on a sofa so that all might see him. These exhibitions annoyed him, and he said, "I hope to get away from Washington, for I· am tired of this show business."

The next day, March 9th, he was summoned to a meeting of the Cabinet. Taking his little son with him, who had ridden boldly by his side all through the Vicksburg campaign, he entered the room, and was introduced by the President to the various members, who then said:

"GENERAL GRANT: The nation's approbation of what you have already done, and its reliance on you for what remains to do in˙ the existing great struggle, is now presented with this commission, constituting you *Lieutenant-General of the Army of the United States.*

"With this high honor devolves on you a corresponding responsibility. As the country herein trusts you, so, under God, it will sustain you.

"I scarcely need add, that, with what I here speak for the country, goes my own hearty personal concurrence."

Grant read from a paper the following reply:

"MR. PRESIDENT: I accept this commission with gratitude for the high honor conferred. With the aid of the noble armies who have fought on so many battle-fields for our common country, it will be my earnest endeavor not to disappoint your expectations. I feel the full weight of the responsibility now devolving on me. I know that, if it is properly met, it will be due to these armies; and, above all, to the favor of that Providence which leads both nations and men."

Never seeking advancement, he made no effort to have his command increased; yet, with a quiet confidence that results from consciousness of strength, he takes the increased responsibility which is forced upon him, without the least hesitation. He neither presents claims, nor offers excuses; neither seeks power, nor shrinks from accepting it.

A greater contrast can hardly be imagined, than the condition he now presented to that of a few years ago. Then an unknown ex-captain, he hesitatingly sought an interview with McClellan, hoping that he might be taken on his staff; to-day, supreme commander of nearly a million of men. From complete obscurity, he, in a few short years, had vaulted to one of the most exalted responsible positions ever occupied by man. Under no other but a republican government could such a marvellous transition have occurred. Still, he had not sprung at once by a mere stroke of fortune into that position. Although so short a period had elapsed since he began his career, he had *fought* his way up to it. Commanding the limited department of Tennessee, his victories had caused an enlargement of the territory under his control. The wonderful campaign of Vicksburg gave him the whole Mississippi Valley as his theatre of action, and placed three armies under his control. The victory of Chattanooga lifted him still higher, and now half a dozen mighty armies were subject to his sway. As he, from this exalted position, cast his eyes around him, what a spectacle met his gaze. Never before had one commander surveyed so vast a field of operations, and looked over such a mighty array, subject to his single control. From the Potomac to the Rio Grande, for five thousand miles, arose the smoke of camp-fires, and stood embattled hosts awaiting his bidding. To aid him in the gigantic task before him, six hundred vessels of war lined the rivers and darkened the coast for twenty-five hundred miles, while four thousand cannon lay ready to open at his command.

The height of power to which he had so suddenly attained, would have made a less strong head dizzy. It, however, produced no change in him. Volunteering no promises, indulging in no vain glory, he quietly surveys the vast field before him —speaking confidently, but only in subordination to the Being who lifts up and pulls down as He pleases.

The work to be done was plain enough. These various and widely-scattered armies must be wielded like a single engine, and brought to bear with their united force on the central, vital portion of the Confederacy, and crush it to atoms.

The people breathed freer as they saw their favorite commander clothed with this more than regal power. The blunders of the Cabinet, the petty, partisan interference of Congress, which, more than the incapacity of the generals, had caused every thing to go amiss, and heaped defeat on the top of defeat, were now done with. A military man, with the power to grasp, and the energy to carry out a great plan, and embrace the field of operations, was at last at the head of the national forces, and it was plain that the day of "quid nuncs" at Washington was over. The mighty power of the North, which had been hurled hither and thither, with such blind energy, was to be held calmly in hand, and made to move like the steady, resistless tide of the ocean, on the audacious Confederacy, which had for so many years lifted itself on the fragments of the Union.

Under him was a group of lieutenants worthy of their great leader. Sherman, Thomas, Hooker, Howard, Hancock, Sedgwick, Slocum, and others, had no peers in ability and military science.

As it was fit, Sherman was placed over the Mississippi division, which Grant's elevation had vacated.

While the latter was maturing his plans, he quietly began to gather the materials necessary to carry them out. Railways groaned under the weight of soldiers returning to their regiments,

13

the rivers were black with transports bearing ordnance and supplies, and the entire North trembled under the mighty preparations going forward.

One of Grant's first acts after his appointment as Lieutenant-General, was to hurry to some conclusion the ill-starred expedition of Banks, already started for the Red River. This was none of his work, but the result of the combined brilliant strategy of Halleck and Stanton. Hence, he, only a few days after he had come into power, sent a despatch to Banks to advance at once to the point he was aiming to reach—Shreveport— but "if he found that the taking of it would occupy from ten to fifteen days—more time than General Sherman had given to his troops to be absent from their command, he would send them back at the time specified by General Sherman, even if it led to *the abandonment of the* main object of the Red River expedition, for this force was necessary to movements east of the Mississippi ; that, should his expedition prove successful, he would hold Shreveport and the Red River, with such force as he might deem necessary, and return the balance of his troops to the neighborhood of New Orleans, commencing no move for the further acquisition of territory, unless it was to make that then held by him more easily held; that it might be a part of the Spring campaign to move against Mobile; that it certainly would be, if troops enough could be obtained to make it without embarrassing other movements—that New Orleans, would be the point of departure for such an expedition." Finally, he directed him to move as quickly as possible. He wanted the blunder consummated speedily, that it might not entangle and embarrass him in the great movements he contemplated. Halleck's system of operations, which was to kill the monster by cutting off his tail and claws, and so work up to the vital part, was over forever; and the coming contest was to be a death-grapple—a last interlocking between the colossal power of the North and the desperate South, from which only one should arise.

CHAPTER XVIII.

As stated in a former chapter, Grant had no faith in the various theories propounded for bringing the rebellion to a close. Troubled with no visionary schemes, he with his strong common-sense, took a practical view of the war, and said that he "was firm in the conviction that no peace could be had that would be stable and conducive to the happiness of the people both North and South until the military power of the rebellion was entirely broken," *i. e.*, the only road to peace lay over prostrate armies.

This fact being established in his mind, the next step was to decide in what way the war should be carried on. First, he said that active and· continuous operations of all the troops that could be brought into the field, *regard-*

less of season and weather, were indispensable;
for though our numerical strength was far superior to that of the enemy, yet we had such a vast
territory to garrison as we advanced, and such
long lines of communication—the greater our
success the longer—to protect, that it cut down
sadly the actual number of troops that could be
brought into the field. But this was not all, he
said; "the armies in the East and West acted independently and without concert, like a balky team,
no two ever pulling together, enabling the enemy
to use to great advantage his interior lines of
communication for transporting troops from east
to west, reinforcing the army most vigorously
pressed; and to furlough large numbers during
seasons of inactivity on our part, to go to their
homes and do the work of providing for the support of their armies." This shifting men from east
to west, and *vice versa*, as pressed in turn by our
armies, and then, during our intervals of rest, while
raising new levies, sending home the soldiers to
cultivate the neglected fields, although requiring
great activity, effected the same purpose as increase of numbers, so that Grant said "it was a
question whether our numerical strength and resources were not more than balanced by these
disadvantages and the enemy's superior position."

Such being his views as he surveyed the vast

field of operations, it was a matter of course that he should at the outset endeavor " to bring the greatest number of troops practicable against the armed force of the enemy, and prevent him from using the same force at different seasons against first one and then another of our armies, and the possibility of repóse for refitting and producing necessary supplies for carrying on resistance." In other words, his plan was to confront all the armies of the enemy with superior ones at the same time, compelling each to stand and fight alone. Moreover, never to leave his presence winter or summer, so that his conscriptions that exhausted the country should keep it exhausted. In the second place, with our greater power, " to hammer continuously against the armed force of the enemy and his resources, until by mere attrition of the lesser with the larger body, the former should be worn out."

It is plain to see that with such a mind governing the campaign there would be fighting—fierce, incessant, deadly, till one or the other army was destroyed.

With these clear, simple, and comprehensive views and plans, there remained only one more thing to settle—the time and manner of bringing the armies into the field.

Although almost all of Arkansas, Louisana, and Texas was in the possession of the enemy, with probably eighty thousand rebel troops scattered through them, yet the Mississippi and Arkansas rivers were so strongly garrisoned that but little trouble was to be feared from them, unless expeditions were sent into the interior. East of the Mississippi we held down to the State of Georgia, and enough of that near Chattanooga to protect East Tennessee. Detached forces also were scattered along the Atlantic coast. We had, besides, three large armies in the field—that of Banks up the Red River; of Sherman at Chattanooga; and Meade in Virginia. The proper plan, therefore, in accordance with Grant's general views, would have been to move these three armies on three vital points simultaneously, and which were clearly indicated by the position of affairs to be Richmond, Atlanta, and Mobile. Charleston had been abandoned, as a probable base of operations, but Mobile, with its river piercing inland north, might be taken, and furnish a better one. Especially if Atlanta was reached—the converging point of the railroads traversing the Southern tier of States—the occupation of these two places would ensure the overthrow of this entire portion of the Southern confederacy. But it soon became evident that the army of Banks could not be used against Mobile for some time yet, and it was therefore left out of the main plan, and Atlanta and Richmond became the two great objective points of the campaign, and the two armies of Lee and Johnston—one on the Rapidan, and the other at Dalton, were to be assailed with all the strength and determination in his power. It is true there were guerilla bands to be guarded against, and a large cavalry force in Mississippi, and troops in the Shenandoah Valley to be looked after. But these were of minor consequence, and Grant resolved that the main rebel armies should be pressed so vigorously that their leaders would find it necessary to call in these detached roving bodies instead of augmenting their force.

His confidence in Sherman made it unnecessary to give him any but general directions. He was to push on to Atlanta, break up Johnston's army, and advance as far into the interior as he could. They had talked over the campaign together, and its main features were perfectly understood by the latter. One thing was of vital importance, that neither rebel army should be allowed to join the other, and thus give to one a sudden preponderance which might prove fatal to the Union army on which this concentrated force might fall. Grant, therefore, in his last written instructions to Sherman impressed this upon him, telling him that if Johnston showed any signs of joining Lee, to follow him up at all hazards, and hang like a sleuth-hound on his track, while he promised that nothing short of impossibility should prevent him

from holding Lee so firmly that he could not succor Johnston.   To Meade, the immediate commander of the army of the Potomac, his directions
were, " wherever Lee goes, go after him."

In operating against Lee and Richmond, Grant
found it impossible to concentrate all the forces
he designed to use.   He could not join Butler
at Fortress Monroe, because he would thus uncover Washington ; neither could he allow Butler
to join him, for that would uncover the department of the latter ; and he therefore determined on
a double movement toward a common centre.
Butler, with his force swelled to some thirty thousand men, was to move against Richmond from
the south, while the army of the Potomac fell upon
Lee along the Rapidan.   Grant's directions to
him were, the moment he received notice to start,
to take City Point at once, and intrench himself
there.   Richmond, he was told to remember, was
his objective point, and that he must hold close to
the south bank of James River as he advanced.
When the rebel army should be driven into the
intrenchments of the capital, then their two armies
could unite and become a unit.   If Butler could
swing around Richmond to the south far enough
to have his left wing touch the James River to the
west, Grant said he would form a junction there.
This would completely cut Lee off from his supplies, and coop him up in his capital.   If he could

13*

capture Richmond, from which he knew Lee had been compelled to draw a great part of the garrison, to do so—at all events plant himself as far up the south bank of the James as he could.   The minor details he left to himself.   It will be seen by these instructions that Grant laid great stress on the success of Butler's movements ; and whether from want of confidence in the latter's ability or from anxiety to impress on him his duty, he says, "I visited him at Fort Monroe, and in conversation, pointed out the apparent importance of getting possession of Petersburg, and destroying railroad communications as far south as possible.   Believing, however, in the practicability of capturing Richmond, unless it was reinforced, I made that the objective point of his operations.   If the Army of the Potomac was to move simultaneously with him, Lee could not detach from his army with safety, and the enemy did not have troops elsewhere to bring to the defence of the city in time to meet a rapid movement from the north of James River."

With regard to the movements of the Army of the Potomac, he said, two plans presented themselves:—one to cross the Rapidan below Lee, moving by his right flank ; the other moving by his left.   Each presented advantages over the other with corresponding objections.   By crossing . above, Lee would be cut off from all chance of ignoring Richmond or going north on a raid. But, he said, "if we took this route, all we did would have to be done while the rations we started with held out; besides, it separated us from Butler, so that he could not be directed how to coöperate. If we took the other route, Brandy Station could be used as a base of supplies until another was secured on the York or James rivers." Of these, however, it was decided to take the lower route. This being the case, it was necessary to guard the Shenandoah Valley, which by this movement would be left uncovered, and the borders of Maryland and Pennsylvania exposed to invasion. To prevent this, General Sigel was placed here with a strong force under his command. This was the outline of the great overland campaign, on the success or failure of which was to depend the establishment or overthrow of the Southern Confederacy.

Grant had determined to move with the opening of spring, but it passed away, and the army remained quiet. The public wondered, and the spell which had so often held motionless the Army of the Potomac seemed unbroken. The old excuse, that it was stuck in the mud, did not satisfy the people. Such was, nevertheless, the fact. The impassable roads of Virginia, in the rainy season, are no myth. This excuse had been often ridiculed, yet it was still a valid one, and, though Grant knew the public was impatient, he knew also that he might as well attempt to move that mighty army, with all its artillery trains, and material of war, through a mortar-bed, as along those clay roads, until they were dried up. The people wondered, but there was at last nothing left them but patience. As, however, the weather brightened, and the ground became hardened, Grant gave the signal, which was waited for from the Tennessee to the James rivers, and three armies arose as one man and moved forward.

More than a quarter of a million of men composed this force, to oppose which the rebel government could not bring into the field half that number. Yet, singular as it may seem, the same belief was as prevalent South, that the coming campaign would end in their triumph, as in the North, that its close would witness their overthrow. It was natural, from the vastness of the preparations on our side, that we should feel confident of success; but no such increase of force furnished ground for hope in the South. In fact, Lee's army, their chief reliance, was not much more than half as large as it was when he invaded Pennsylvania, while Grant's was nearly double to that of Meade's, which opposed it.

Lee, however, did not share in these fond anticipations. He knew how mighty was the force he was about to meet, which uncounted thousands stood ready to back, while he could look nowhere for reinforcements to his diminished army. As a last resort, he looked to heaven for aid, and issued a general order directing that "a day of humiliation, fasting, and prayer" be observed throughout the army. Public services were held by the chaplains in the various regiments, and great solemnity and deep feeling were exhibited. In the meantime he strengthened his position by intrenching his lines, and digging rifle-pits at the fords of the Rapidan, and left nothing undone which could aid him to meet the terrible shock he so well knew awaited him.

Apparently the odds were fearfully against him, for the Army of the Potomac, with the ninth corps under Burnside to support it, made a movable column of about 140,000 men, while Lee had, all told, but little over 54,000. With such numerical superiority, Grant was confident of success if he could get Lee from behind his works, and force him into a field fight. But, if he was always to be the attacking party and fight the enemy in his intrenchments, he needed 60,000 more men to be on an equality with his adversary.

CHAPTER XIX.

THE OVERLAND MARCH.

The March begun—The Rapidan crossed—Lee's Flank turned—
He determines to attack Grant in the Wilderness—A sagacious
Move—First Day's Battle of the Wilderness—Arrival of Long-
street and Burnside—Swift Marching—Second Day's Battle—
Third Day—Headquarters—Grant attempts to move around
Lee's Left to Spottsylvania—The Night-March—The Enemy
arrive first—Grand Assault of the Enemy's Works—Gallant
Charge of Hancock—A Lull—A third Attempt to get between
Lee and Richmond—It Fails—Last Effort to reach Richmond
from the North—Battle of Cold Harbor—Change of Base to
the James River—Attempt to capture Petersburg.

LEE's army stretched for many miles along the
Rapidan river, and held all the crossings in such
force that, as before stated, Grant, encamped at
Culpepper, determined to swing his army off to
the left, and cross it on the enemy's right flank,
and thus compel Lee to come out of his works, or
be cut off from Richmond. On the morning of
the 4th of May the mighty host was set in motion,
and along every road, and across open fields,
spreading over a vast extent of country, the successive divisions swept forward. Sheridan, with the
cavalry, and an enormous train, composed of four
thousand wagons, moved in advance, and reaching one of the fords, hurried across, meeting with

but little opposition. Column following column in seeming endless succession, pressed after him and gained the opposite bank. The army crossed at two fords, Ely's and Germania, some five or six miles apart. It was divided into three corps— the Second, commanded by Hancock, the Fifth, by Warren, and the Sixth, by Sedgwick. Hancock, in front, crossed at Ely's ford, followed by Warren, while Sedgwick crossed at Germania, forming the right. By night it was all over, having marched twelve miles.

Thus the first great step was successfully taken. Crossing a river at different points, with such an immense train, in the presence of a skillful enemy, was a hazardous movement; and the fact that it had been accomplished without loss, relieved Grant from great anxiety; for though he had been compelled to force a passage where an immense wilderness stretched away from the shore, yet a battle had not been forced on him while in marching order, or struggling across the river. Still, he had not outwitted his wary adversary. He had no idea of having a battle thrown upon him in this frightful wilderness, and therefore issued his orders for the march next morning which he expected would take him beyond it, towards Gordonsville, where he would be between the rebel army and Richmond. A few hours would have sufficed to do this. But Lee, who did not know whether Grant would cross above or below him, kept a corps of observation in both directions, while he held his army like a hound in the leash. The moment he found that Grant had left his front and effected a passage of the stream below him, he put his army in motion for the purpose of attacking him while entangled in the wilderness. This was a bold, sagacious movement, and came very near being successful. Instead of falling back when he saw his flank turned, he resolved to break into a sudden and furious offensive. As Bonaparte, when he found himself outnumbered, two to one, by the Austrians, suddenly planted his little army on two causeways in the marshes of Arcola, where numbers gave but little advantage, and every thing depended on the comparative strength of the heads of columns, so Lee resolved to bring on the battle in this wilderness, crossed only by few roads, in which the heaviest shocks must necessarily occur, and shut Grant's vast army up in the dense woods, where massive columns had little weight—the cavalry be totally useless, and his preponderance of artillery of no avail. From Orange Court House, the centre of Lee's position, two parallel roads, a little distance apart, cross this dreary waste, which cut Grant's line of march at right angles. Down these Lee determined to hurl his columns, and strike the army in

flank while struggling through the thick chappa-
ral. He knew this desolate tract well, and how to
avail himself of the advantages it gave him, while
to Grant it was an unknown wilderness.

Lee, in carrying out his plan, hurried off Hill
and Ewell, one by the turnpike and the other by
the plank road, and at the same time sent a dis-
patch to Longstreet, twenty-five miles distant at
Gordonsville, to move up and strike the heads of
our columns with his corps, while the former
generals fell on them in flank. He was made
aware of Grant's movements and designs so early
that the two corps he sent off down these roads
encamped in the wilderness the same night that
Grant did, and were ready to fall upon him at
daylight in the morning.

Johnson's division, forming the advance of
Ewell's corps, was stationed where the road down
which it had come, intersected that along which
the Fifth Corps, under Warren, was advancing
early next day with its lines extending on either
side into the forest.

Two pieces of artillery went thundering along
the road in advance, and coming within range of
Johnson, unlimbered, and poured in a rapid fire.
The infantry pressed on, receiving, as they advanced, a terrible volley without the least sign
of wavering, till they got within close range,
when with a · clang a whole forest of weapons

came to a level, and a sheet of fire swept
through the green forest. Before it the hostile
line gave way for a brief space; but reinforcements coming up, the troops rallied and charged
with such fury that they carried every thing
before them, and captured the two guns. Pressing up their advantage, they drove our advance
back for a mile. In the meantime Sedgwick,
with the Sixth Corps, came sweeping through
the forest on the left, and a sanguinary struggle
took place in his front, and for miles the woods
echoed with the roar of musketry. Artillery was
almost entirely useless, except along the narrow
roads, and the strange spectacle of mighty armies
contending in a tangled forest, where no regular
formations could be maintained, or strategic movement made, was witnessed. Grant hurried up his
divisions fast as he could amid the trees and
stunted pine bushes; and with Meade rode on to
the Old Wilderness tavern. Up to this time he
did not believe that he had Lee's army in front,
but thought it a small force sent out to deceive him
while the main army effected its retreat. It did
not occur to him that the Confederate commander,
when he found his defensive line turned, would,
instead of falling back to a secure position, boldly
cut loose and swing his entire army down upon
him and offer battle. But as he stood by the
solitary building, he soon discovered, by the steadi-

ly increasing uproar, that the enemy was upon him, and there in that gloomy Wilderness he must grapple with him as he best could. He therefore at once recalled the order of march, and prepared for battle. Hancock at this crisis was ten miles distant, down the river, and swift riders were immediately despatched to him to close up quickly as possible. In the meantime the battle deepened, and at length, when Hancock arrived, it swelled into its grandest proportions. He and Warren however were, in fact, separate armies, fighting separate armies, and all day long had but little connection with each other. Grant at the Old Wilderness tavern listened to the uproar, receiving ever and anon reports from his army, which was so shut up in the forest that no portion of it could be seen. No wind was stirring, and the smoke settled amid the foliage, while from out the bosom of the dense woods arose cries and yells and shouts and rolling volleys, in wild and horrid discord. "Back in a ceaseless flow from the line that marks this fierce struggle the wounded and maimed are borne on blankets and litters, telling by their numbers the deadly work going on in advance."

All day long this mad strife went on, and when night closed over the forest and ended it, Grant found himself near the very spot from which in the morning he had started. His advance divisions had been driven back, his loss had been heavy, and nothing gained. "The woods of the Wilderness have not the ordinary features of a forest. The region rests on a belt of mineral rocks, and for above a hundred years extensive mining has been carried on. To feed the mines, the timber of the country for many miles around had been cut down, and in the place there had arisen a dense undergrowth of low-limbed and scraggy pines, stiff and bristling chinkapins, scrub oaks, and hazel. It is a region of gloom and the shadow of death. Manœuvering here was out of the question, and only Indian tactics told. The troops could only receive direction by a point of the compass; for not only were the lines of battle entirely hidden from the sight of the commander, but no officer could see ten files on each side of him. Artillery was wholly ruled out of use, the massive concentration of three hundred guns stood silent. . . Cavalry was still more useless. But in that horrid thicket there lurked two hundred thousand men, and through it lurid fires played; and though no array of battle could be seen, there came out of it the crackle and roll of musketry, like the noisy boiling of some hell-caldron, that told the dread story of death. Such was the battle of the Wilderness." * Still Grant had no thought of retreating; on the contrary,

* Swinton's Army of the Potomac.

he issued orders to have the attack renewed at sunrise next morning.

In the meantime Longstreet was pressing on through the darkness, and his advance reached the battle-field just as Grant moved again to the attack. It was not yet fully deployed into line when the onset came. With such fury was it made, and so desperately did Grant push the attack at this point, that Longstreet was born swiftly back, till his disordered ranks almost reached the spot where Lee stood.

Longstreet knew what fearful results depended on his checking our victorious troops, and put forth superhuman efforts to stem the flood, but was soon borne bleeding from the field. Lee, now thoroughly alarmed as he saw our line sweeping resistlessly down upon his imperilled right, rode himself at the head of a brigade of Texans, and ordered them to follow, intending to lead the charge in person. But instead of shouts at his gallant devotion, there arose one loud remonstrance against the act, and he had to retire, while the whole division, animated by his example, drove so furiously on our advancing columns that they were forced back, losing the ground they had so nobly won.

To meet just such a possible exigency as this, Grant, the very afternoon on which he crossed the Rapidan, sent back to Burnside—who, with the Ninth Corps, was still at the crossing of the Rappahannock River and Alexandria Railroad, guarding the railroad back to Bull Run—to hurry forward. The latter immediately put his army in motion, and, though in his march two rivers had to be crossed and more than thirty miles of broken country traversed, he at this opportune moment led his tired columns on to the field. He had wasted no time, and, as Grant said, "Considering that a large proportion, probably two thirds, of his command was composed of raw troops, unaccustomed to marches and carrying the accoutrements of a soldier, this was a remarkable march." It was remarkable, and must have been even wonderful to draw such a compliment from Grant, who had thoroughly tested the marching powers and endurance of troops.

Thus reinforced, both armies continued the work of slaughter, and all day the battle roared for seven miles through that forest. "There, in the depths of those ravines, under the shadows of those trees, entangled in that brushwood, is no pomp of war, no fluttering of banners in an unhindered breeze, no solid tramp of marching battalions, no splendid strategy of the field Napoleon loved to fight on. There a Saturnalia, gloomy, hideous, desperate, rages confined. The metallic, hollow crack of musketry is like the clanking of great chains about the damned—that sullen yell of the enemy, a fiendish protest of defiance. How the hours lag! How each minute is freighted with a burden that the days would have groaned to bear in other times. Still the sad, shuddering procession, emerging out of the smoke, and tumult, and passion, and passing on; still the appealing eyes, clenched hands, and quivering limbs of human creatures, worse than helpless, whose fighting is over." Thus wore on this terrible day—the opposing lines swaying backward and forward amid the forest, as now one and now the other advanced or was forced back. Since the first great success in the morning, there had been no crisis in the battle—it was simply a long, tiresome slaughter, and when night came, the two armies occupied nearly the same ground they had in the morning. Lee's flank was not yet turned, and to all appearances Grant was checkmated here at the outset. It was evident that this kind of fighting could not last much longer, for there is a limit to human endurance. For two days, now, the troops had been constantly under arms, and most of the time fighting, many having hardly tasted food the whole time.

Thus far Lee had not remained behind his works, but acted steadily on the offensive whenever he could; but now, crippled and exhausted, he took refuge in them. Grant, on reconnoitering early the next morning, ascertained this, and feel-

ing that it would be asking too much of his jaded
troops to require them to carry these intrenchments by storm, resolved, by a sudden march to
the left, to get around Lee at Spottsylvania. But
little fighting occurred during the day, for the
troops on both sides were completely worn out.
In fact, Grant found the soldiers too exhausted to
make the contemplated march, and gave them till
night to rest; and for miles and miles the forest
was black with prostrate sleeping forms. Even
Grant, with all his endurance, was glad of a little
repose, and throwing himself down on the ground,
was soon wrapped in slumber. An eye-witness
thus draws a picture of headquarters this afternoon: "The lieutenant-general here, at the foot
of a tree, one leg of his trowsers slipped above his
boots, his hands limp, his coat in confusion, his
sword equipments sprawling on the ground; not
even the weight of sleep erasing that persistent
expression of the lip which held a constant promise of something to be done. And there, at the
foot of another tree, is General Meade—a military
hat, with the rim turned down about his ears, tapping a scabbard with his fingers, and gazing ab-
stractedly into the depths of the earth through
eye-glasses that should become historic. General
Humphreys, chief of staff—a spectacled, iron-gray,
middle-aged officer, of a pleasant smile and manner, who wears his trowsers below, after the

manner of leggins, and is in all things independent and serene, paces yonder to and fro. That
rather thick-set officer, with closely-trimmed whiskers, and the kindest of eyes, who never betrays a
harsh impatience to any comer, is Adjutant-General Williams. General Hunt, chief of artillery,
a hearty-faced, frank-handed man, whose black
hair and whiskers have the least touch of time,
lounges at the foot of another tree, holding lazy
converse with one or two members of his staff.
General Ingalls, chief quartermaster of the army,
than whom no more imperturbable, efficient, or
courteous presence is here, plays idly and smil-
ingly with a riding-whip, tossing a telling word or
two hither and thither. Staff officers and order-
lies and horses thickly strew the grove."

But that night, after the moon was down, Grant
began his march, Warren leading the advance.
"The fires burned brightly, and at a distance, upon the wooded hillsides, looked like the lights of
a city. Standing upon an eminence, at the junction of Germania, Chancellorsville, and Orange
Court House roads, along which the tramp of
soldiers and the rumble of wagon trains made a
smothered din, one could almost imagine himself
peering down through the darkness on the streets
of a metropolis in peace. Back in the forest,
from the hospitals, from the trees, from the road-
side, the wounded were being gathered in ambu-

14

lances for the long night-journey.   That part of
the army not on the move was slumbering by
fires, waiting for the signal." Lee, who watched
his adversary with sleepless vigilance, knew of this
movement within an hour after it commenced, and
at once hurried off troops by a shorter route,
which, by rapid marching—at one time going on
the double-quick for two miles—reached Spottsylvania first.   Although Warren pushed the
enemy before him, and succeeded in carrying the
first line of breastworks, yet he was finally compelled to retire with the loss of fifteen hundred men.

The next day Sheridan started on his raid to
break up Lee's communications with Richmond.
This, and the two following days, Grant spent in
" manœuvring and fighting, without any decisive
results."   On the 12th, he made a grand assault
on the enemy's lines, and a most terrific conflict
followed.   Our wearied men fought as though
fresh from their encampments.   Bayonet charges
occurred in various parts of the line, and the roar
of artillery, and crash of musketry, and shouts of
infuriated men, conspired to make a scene of terror inconceivable, indescribable.   The carnage was
awful; not less than eight or ten thousand men
falling on our side alone.   Hancock's assault on
Lee's right centre was a brilliant one, and,
though crowned with great success, gave no per-
manent advantage.   His attacking columns were

formed before it was full daylight, and just in the gray of the dawn moved swiftly, and without firing a shot, straight on the ramparts, at whose base stretched a deep, wide ditch. The enemy, never dreaming of such a bold movement, saw, before they were aware of it, the soldiers pouring like an inundation over the works. Rolled back by the sudden and terrific onset, they retreated, fighting, for a mile. Made aware of the frightful disaster that had overtaken them, the rebel generals hurried up supports, and reforming the lines, advanced with the determination to retake the important position. Five times did Lee hurl his army upon it, and as often was driven back. The battle raged here all day with terrific fury, and the ground was literally heaped with the dead. So determined were the onsets, and so close the death-grapple, that the rebel colors and our own would at times be planted on the opposite sides of the same works, "the men fighting across the parapet."

Hancock captured, in this brilliant assault, an entire division, four thousand strong, and thirty guns.

But Grant saw clearly that the strong position of Lee could not be carried by assault, and he found himself again foiled. He had left a dead and wounded army behind him, and had neither got a decisive battle out of Lee, nor compelled him to retreat. Instead, however, of being disheartened, his purpose was more fixed than ever, and he telegraphed back to Washington, "I shall fight it out on this line if it takes all summer," and asked for reinforcements. They were sent, as of old, with trembling expostulations not to leave Washington exposed; but its safety rested not on its garrisons, but on Grant's strong right arm. While these were coming up, Grant changed his base of supplies to Fredericksburg. Two weeks were consumed in this way, and then he resolved to make another effort to get around Lee. Moving off in a simicircle, he aimed for the North Anna river, which, if he could reach first, would place him between Lee and Richmond. In order to conceal this movement, the corps on his extreme right moved back, and marched down behind the main army. When well under way, the one next to it broke off in the same way—so that the right wing became the left, and *vice versa*. But again Lee, who was keenly on the lookout, detected the movement soon enough, and by swift marching, and having a shorter distance to travel, reached that point first; and Grant, finding his position still stronger than the one at Spottsylvania, made no determined effort to take it. Hancock gained some success; and Warren had a short, fierce battle with the enemy, in which Grant said, "I never heard more rapid or massive firing, either of artillery or musketry." The rebel attack was repulsed, but no important advantage was secured; and Grant determined to make one more attempt to swing around Lee and compel him to fight outside of his works, and on the night of the 26th moved by way of Hanovertown. But when, on the 28th, the army reached the place—which was only fifteen miles from Richmond—he found Lee's army drawn up in line of battle and intrenched, ready to receive him. Marching and skirmishing and partial battles now occupied several days; when Grant, having completed his arrangements, fixed the 3d of June for a heavy assault along the whole line. The Eighteenth Corps had in the meantime joined him from Butler's army, which was so "corked up" at Bermuda Hundred as to be of no practical use. The Union line, at this time, extended from Bethesda Church to Cold Harbor, a distance of eight miles. At a given signal it advanced in splendid order, and Grant hoped by one mighty effort to drive Lee across the Chickahominy, and force him into the intrenchments of Richmond. But the rebel host lay behind strong works that could not be carried, although the troops struggled for five dreadful hours at their very base. Completely exposed, they were mowed down with terrible slaughter; while the enemy, sheltered behind his breastworks, suffered but little. The next morning Grant rode along the front to ascertain from the various commanders the actual state of things in their vicinity. He returned, absorbed in thought, for he knew it would be useless to repeat the attack. All that matchless valor and skill could do had been done, and thirteen thousand men had fallen in the long and hopeless struggle; while the enemy, sheltered behind his works, had lost hardly more than as many hundred. Never had a commander or subordinates made more superhuman endeavors, never had the world witnessed such determination and endurance in troops, yet nothing had been gained except in the destruction of life. Grant saw that his last effort had been made for victory in the field, and he must settle down to a long siege, or change his base.

He now proposed to Lee, that while there was no actual fighting, each party might, on notification to the other, succor its wounded and bury its dead. Lee replied that he preferred it should be done through a flag of truce, to which Grant gave his assent.

Finding that Richmond could not be reached over the enemy in this direction, he determined, by a sudden movement, to fling his army over the James River, and seize Petersburg, which Butler had failed to take, laying the blame of defeat on Gilmore.

This, however, was a delicate operation, for the opposing lines were so close that it was hardly to be expected that he could move off, unobserved, such an immense army, without exposing himself to a sudden attack. But concentrating his lines, and throwing up strong works to protect his flanks, he, on Sunday night, the 12th of June, quietly and swiftly changed front, and marched away from the Chickahominy. Smith's corps moved off to the White House and embarked on transports, while the rest of the army struck across the country to the James River, fifty miles away. Passing below the White Oak Swamp, stirring recollections were brought to the army of the Potomac, which two years before fought their way on almost the same line to the point toward which they were now pressing.

Grant broke up his camp and sent off all his immense trains on the 12th. Two days after, on the 14th, Hancock was crossing the James, by ferry, at Wilcox Landing, and the Sixth Corps, by ferry and a pontoon bridge, a little lower down.

This march of fifty-five miles was made without molestation; and the manner in which it was planned and carried out shows the marvellous skill of Grant in handling a large army. He expected to take Petersburg by this sudden movement, and thus advance his lines nearer to Richmond on the south side. The attack was at first successful, and the outer works captured, and the report flew over the land that it had fallen. It ought to have fallen days before, and would if Grant had been on the spot to have controlled Butler, Gilmore, and Smith, in person. But the failure of these officers had caused the enemy to strengthen the fortifications and reinforce the garrison.

CHAPTER XX.

The Overland and Peninsula Routes considered—Reasons against
the Former—" Continuous Hammering "—Grant charged with
having Contempt for all Manœuvres—The Charge disproved—
Distinguished for his Skilful Manœuvres—Compared to Napoleon—Not to blame for the Slaughter in the Wilderness, or the
Error at Cold Harbor—Gloomy Retrospect—Failure of Siegel
and Butler to do their Part—Reason of the great Disparity in
the Losses of the two Armies.

A CORRECT idea of the motives that influenced
Grant to the course he adopted—and the causes
that led to the failure of his plan in its most important features—and the results he actually accomplished, can be obtained only by a careful
review of the campaign from its inception to its
close.

It had lasted forty-three days, and he now
found himself on the spot that McClellan occupied when the Army of the Potomac was recalled
to Washington.

The friends of the latter pointed to this fact, and
inquired, why, if the army was to occupy the
Peninsula at last, it was not transported there at
the outset—as it could have been without the
loss of a man—instead of reaching it, after a

14*

long struggle, and the sacrifice of sixty thousand men?

It seems never to have occurred to these critics to inquire, what Lee would have been doing while this great transfer of the army was being effected. It is assumed that he would have hastened back to the defence of his capital. But this is merely conjecture : for nothing is more evident than that he could have defended Richmond better by marching again into Maryland, or on Washington; for before the heads of his columns were well over the Potomac, Grant's army would have been recalled. But suppose Lee had not made this bold move, and taken instead his army to Richmond, where he did eventually plant it, he could have spared enough troops to threaten Washington, and break up Grant's army; for even after his terrible losses in the battles of the Wilderness, and at Spottsylvania and other places, he was still able to despatch an army twelve thousand strong into the Valley of the Shenandoah, which gathered its harvests, and then crossing into Maryland and Pennsylvania, burned Chambersburg, cut the railroad north of Baltimore, and advanced to the very gates of the National capital. It spread consternation on every side; and although the Nineteenth Corps opportunely arrived from New Orleans, it was not considered strong enough, with all the forces that could be raised in the vicinity, to cope with the rebels, and the veteran Sixth Corps had to be detached from the army of the Potomac, and sent to protect Washington and the neighboring loyal country.

Now suppose that Lee had the twenty thousand men that lay in hospitals, or strewing the battle-fields on the line of his retreat, to add to the twelve thousand he actually sent to the valley of the Shenandoah, swelling the force to thirty or forty thousand men : who does not see that the siege of Richmond must have been raised, and the whole campaign gone over again ? It requires but the simplest arithmetical calculation to determine, if twelve thousand men demanded the presence of two additional corps in front of Washington, how many corps would thirty or forty thousand men have required. Those dead and wounded of Lee's army that cost us so heavily, were, in the crisis of affairs, absolutely indispensable to the defence of Richmond. Lee could not replace them.

But it has been suggested that Grant should have divided his army, and left part to cover Washington, and transported the other half to the Peninsula. We do not see how this relieves the difficulty ; for in case Grant thus divided his forces, Lee would have divided his also, and left twenty-five thousand men in front of Washington, which, if the two corps sent to defeat Early with twelve thousand furnishes the correct ratio of force required, four corps would have been necessary to oppose them. On this supposition, had there been no overland campaign, and hence Lee lost no troops, he would have had within five thousand as many men to defend Richmond as he did have, while Grant would have been weaker by half his entire army. In the light of subsequent events, it is not difficult to see what added embarrassments, protracted delays, if not defeat, would have resulted from this diminution of his force in front of Richmond. As it was, he had quite few enough troops for the task required of him. Hence it is clear, whatever course Lee might have taken, the result to Grant would have been the same had he planted a part, or the whole of his army, on the Peninsula, without first weakening his adversary. It would have been madness to have assailed him in his strong works along the Rapidan. A flank movement, therefore, was the only course left him ; and the Battle of the Wilderness, fearful as it was, became inevitable, and he now had to fight his way to Richmond, or retreat. No one would approve of the latter course—how then could he have done otherwise than he did ? Will any one assert that the army could have been handled with more consummate skill, or fought with more splendid heroism ? He was not to blame for the strong works that hedged his path on every side. The terrific battles and failures of the last three years had caused them to be constructed by the enemy; and when Grant took command, he had got to fight Lee with all these disadvantages against him, or not fight at all. It was this state of things that made him say he meant to win success by "continuous hammering." The phrase has been repeated to prove that Grant possessed no strategy, and relied solely on brute force. To give still greater emphasis to the accusation, he is adduced as evidence against himself. It is said that soon after he took command of the Army of the Potomac, General Meade was one day speaking to him of certain manœuvres that might be executed, when the former interrupted him with "*I never manœuvre.*"

Now we do not wish to question the authority for this statement, but simply say that it was intended either as a rebuke to mere "*martinetism,*" if we may coin the word—or in other words, an expression of impatience at the laying down of some abstract rules as found in the books, and which had no pertinency in the present condition of things; or he did not believe what he said and stated what his acts disproved. Hence, the inference deduced from the utterance of the expression is totally false.

There are two distinct kinds of manœuvres—one

on the battle-field itself, the whole of which the commanding general from a height or tower of observation embraces in a glance, and over which he moves his troops as one moves pieces on a chess-board. Now if Grant's remark applied to this kind of manœuvres, he not only told the truth, but showed his good judgment—that strong common sense which enabled him to make on the spot, if he had never seen them, all the good rules applicable to that particular case, and reject those growing out of a warfare waged on entirely different conditions than the one he was conducting. He had this distinctive quality of greatness, that he *could use rules without letting rules use him.* Napoleon, in those great battles fought on the extended, open, and often unfenced plains of Europe, was accustomed from some elevated position to sweep the entire field with his glass, and handle his army like a single machine. But not a battle of any proportions had been fought in our country on such an open plain, and probably never will be, unless it takes place on one of our western prairies. Our armies met in woods and ravines and thickets, where the commander could see only a small portion of the army at any one time, and much had to be left to the discretion of the corps and division commanders. To speak of grand manœuvres, such as are described in the military works of Europe, as possible on the fields of our conflict, is absurd; and if Grant said he " *never manœuvred*," in reference to such martial displays, we repeat it, he showed his good sense, and deserves praise instead of censure for it. There was no such manœuvring at Antietam, Fredericksburg, Chancellorsville, Gettysburg, Shiloh, Stone River, or Missionary Ridge. It was all square, stand-up, hard fighting—massive onsets and shocks—and Grant doubtless meant to say it had got to be so to the bitter end.

The other class of manœuvres applies to those movements made to get into right position previous to battle; skillful marches by which the enemy is deceived and attacked in an unexpected quarter, or different portions of his army cut up in detail before they can concentrate. These manœuvres, if successful, indicate the highest order of military genius, and Grant plainly had no reference to these in the remark quoted above, for he had won his greatest fame and success by them. It was a battle of manœuvres from the day he passed the batteries of Vicksburg, for a whole month, till he invested the place. With three armies opposed to him, he so manœuvred that they were never able to form a junction and overwhelm him, but, beating them in detail, separated them totally. In fact, so brilliant were these manœuvres, and so rapidly executed, that but for the failure of McClernand to perform the part assigned him at Champion's Hill, Vicksburg would have been reached and invested without a single serious battle. The first campaign of Napoleon in Italy, and that which shut up Mack at Ulm and compelled his capitulation, are considered models for the military student; yet that of Grant in rear of Vicksburg is equal to either of them in boldness of conception and skill and success in execution, and must, when the nature of the country is taken into consideration, be regarded as superior to them.

It is, therefore, as we said, absurd to attempt to prove that Grant did not approve of manœuvring. He thoroughly understood his situation, and in our opinion, and which we think the facts and reasons as presented above sustain, executed the only manœuvre that promised success. His critics confess that there were but three movements open to him—the one he made, a similar one around Lee's left, and last the transportation of his army or a part of it to the Peninsula. That by the left would have required just as much fighting as the one he took, while subsequent events have shown that the transportation of the army to the Peninsula would have been an error. The most terrible slaughter that occurred in his entire march was at the battle of the Wilderness, where it was a contest of mere brute force, but that was not brought on by him, but Lee, and on purpose to *prevent* manœuvring. Grant here acted on the defensive; and when one points to the piles of dead which strewed that gloomy forest, and speaks of butchery, let him remember that the gladiatorial conflict which wrought that destruction was the work of the rebel commander.

Grant's desperate assault on the strong works at Spottsylvania was necessary, unless he abandoned his plan altogether of getting between Lee and Richmond, and is sustained by the soundest military maxims. The only other fearful slaughter which made his enemies at home and abroad stigmatize him as a butcher, was at Cold Harbor—and if he made any mistake in this campaign it was here. The battle was decided in the first ten minutes, and the long struggle that succeeded was undoubtedly a useless waste of life. Grant may have carried his proverbial obstinacy of character too far here, but it was his last hope. He must do this or give up the plan of reaching Richmond from the north, and it was natural that his last effort should be pushed even beyond the limits of good judgment. The attack proved a total failure, and the frightful disparity in the loss of life shows that it should never have been made.

It is true this campaign of fifty-three days summed up sadly. As Grant looked back on the frightful road he had travelled, he could not behold any one success of great importance. On the contrary, his plans had all miscarried —he had not accomplished what he proposed to do. More than this, the two generals who were to coöperate with him had worse than failed in the task assigned them. Siegel, in the Valley of Shenandoah, not only effected nothing, but was terribly defeated and put to rout, while Butler on the James River had succeeded only in "corking himself up" at Bermuda Hundreds. Different results would doubtless have been reached had more competent generals been in their places. But political considerations in Washington, outside of Grant, put them in the responsible positions they held. Especially, if an energetic, able commander had been in Butler's place, Grant would have been saved the sad retrospect, and the discouraging future he now contemplated. Had Sheridan been at the head of the army on the James, he would long before either have been in Richmond, or pressing it so terribly that Lee would have been compelled to retreat precipitately to save it, with Grant thundering in his rear, and sure of a speedy victory. But some insane political necessity kept Butler in command against Grant's wishes, and he failed utterly to do his part in carrying out his commander's plans, and hence at the very outset rendered their execution impossible.

The disparity of loss in this campaign is mentioned as a proof of Lee's superior generalship, but the inference is false. Grant was acting on the offensive, and had to attack the enemy where he found him. Lee kept behind his works except in the battle of the Wilderness, and the ratio of loss between assailants and defenders, where the latter are protected by strong works, has always been considered as about four to one. It is true that the record of our loss in this campaign is a frightful one. In the battle of the Wilderness and up to Spottsylvania, the aggregate in dead, wounded, and missing, was, . . . 29,410

Spottsylvania	10,381
North Anna	1,607
Cold Harbor	13,153
Total	54,551

But this leaves out the losses of the Ninth Corps, except in the last battle. It was not formally incorporated into the Army of the Potomac until after the battle of Spottsylvania, and hence not included in the report of General Meade. If its losses were half as heavy as that of the other corps, the number would swell to the fearful amount of sixty thousand, of whom three thousand were officers, many of them the flower of the Army of the Potomac. The Confederate loss, as

stated by southern officers and writers, was only
18,000. It may have been a little more, but
probably did not reach 20,000. The nature of
the conflict made this disproportion inevitable—
the enemy fighting behind works, except in the
Wilderness. Here the disparity was owing to
a different cause. Several reasons have been
given for it, but in our estimation, the chief
one has been overlooked. Separate reports on
this battle have never been rendered, but we
can approximate very near the truth. Our
loss may be put at about 20,000, while that
of Lee, according to the reports of the rebel
surgeons, was only seven thousand. Yet here
they did not fight behind breastworks, but out
in the woods, like our own men. The inquiry
then naturally arises, How came the loss to be so
unequal? Some have said that it was owing to
the superiority of the Southern troops in the Indian style of fighting that characterized that battle, and to the dull gray color of their uniforms,
which made them less conspicuous objects amid
the foliage than our troops, with their light blue
uniforms. There is doubtless some force in these
reasons, especially the latter one, but we believe
the chief one, although at first it seems paradoxi-
cal, is to be found in our *superiority* of *numbers*.
It must be remembered that the advantage which
numbers give in battle is two-fold—first, the

weight they impart to a charge or onset. The concentration of masses on a given point puts an inferior army at a great disadvantage. Second, numbers allow the extension of lines till they overlap, and hence outflank the enemy. But in the Wilderness Grant totally lost both these advantages. The wood prevented both the concentration of masses on any portion of the rebel lines and any movement to overreach and lap it. Hence Grant's numbers on this battle-field, which was not of his choosing, only furnished a larger mark to fire at. Artillery being out of the question, and the foliage so thick as to render objects at a little distance invisible, the troops, in order to fight at all, had to be in close proximity, actually face to face. But under these circumstances, only about the same number on both sides could fire with any effect among the trees. Hence the firing was, in fact, nearly equal, while the enemy had twice as many men to fire at as we. The tens of thousands that thronged the forest on our side, and could only act as supports, furnished a mark so large that almost every rebel bullet—being fired at so close a range—that escaped a tree, would strike a soldier. Lee knew this would be so, and chose this strange battle-field for the sole purpose of putting the armies on an equality.

There could be no order of battle in this Wilderness, and it was simply like shooting birds in the field, with the advantage on the rebel side of shooting into a large flock instead of a small one, and of course with the same cartridges doing double execution.

CHAPTER XXI.

THE SIEGE.

Disheartening aspect of affairs—Importance of Petersburg—Hunter succeeds Siegel—Wilson's raid—Movement north of the James River—Explosion of a Mine—Defeat of Hunter—Invasion of Early—Despondency—Grant's letter to Washburn—Appoints Sheridan Commander of all the Forces around Washington and in the Middle Department—Checks Sheridan—Finally, bids him " Go in ! "—Effect of Sheridan's Victories—Grant attempts to get around Lee's left—Hancock attacked—Winter operations—Almost a frightful disaster—Atlanta reached—Grant's grief at the death of McPherson—His Letter to the Grandmother—Permits Sherman to cut loose from Atlanta—His views upon it—Is anxious to have Thomas attack Hood—Correspondence—Fort Fisher—Butler's disobedience—Capture of the place—Directs Sherman to come to him by sea—Countermands the order—Schofield ordered East—Stoneman's raid—Expedition against Mobile—Directions to Thomas—Concentric movements—Sheridan's raid—Correspondence with Lincoln—Interview with him and Sherman—Resolves to move.

As Grant, from before Petersburg, surveyed his position, the prospect was gloomy enough. On every side rose strong works—not a single line of them, but successive ones. He was sorely disappointed in not taking Petersburg, and censured those to whom he had given charge of the undertaking. We have not gone into the details of the various efforts to capture it, nor of the one made by Grant after his arrival before it. There has been much recrimination among the officers commanding the expeditions, and contradiction and confusion in the reports respecting the failure even of the last assault.

The place was over twenty miles from Richmond, and its chief importance lay in the fact that its possession would give Grant nearly all the lines by which Lee's army was supplied. Petersburg, therefore, was, to all intents, Richmond itself. Of course it was of the first importance, now that a regular siege was determined upon, to cut off these sources of supply, which could be done only either by extending his lines around the place to the south, or sending off separate forces to do it.

Grant had previously put Hunter in Siegel's place, with directions to break up a branch railroad, running through Staunton, by which quantities of supplies were forwarded in that direction, while Wilson, with a heavy force of cavalry, was sent to cut the railroads south. The latter succeeded in breaking up a portion of them, so that it took the enemy some time to put them in working order again.

Grant, in the meantime, by the various plans he set on foot, kept Lee constantly on the alert, for his blows fell now on one side and now on the other, and often in a most unexpected time and place. He moved a heavy force north of the James River, to cut the railroad "from near Richmond to the Anna River," and some severe fighting took place ; for Lee, made aware of the movement, sent a large force to check it. Anticipating this, Grant ordered a mine, that had been dug in front of the Ninth Corps, to be sprung, and the explosion to be followed by a vigorous assault of the enemy's lines at that point. It came near being a success, and Grant thought that, with a little more promptness in advancing, Petersburg might have been captured. But now a new cause of anxiety arose. Hunter, who had marched triumphantly up the Shenandoah Valley till he lay siege to Lynchburg, was finally, from want of ammunition, compelled to retreat. If he had moved as Grant anticipated, this would not have happened. Forced to return by the circuitous way of Kanawha, he necessarily left the Shenandoah Valley unprotected, and Early, sweeping down through it, crossed the Potomac into Maryland, and threatened Baltimore and Washington. Despatch after despatch, showing the wildest alarm, was now sent to Grant from the Capital, and the President was besought to recall the army from Richmond. But he stubbornly refused to do so, saying that he had implicit confidence in General Grant, and should leave him to take his own course to avert the

15

threatened danger. The latter immediately despatched the Sixth Corps to Washington, which with the Nineteenth Corps, just arrived from New Orleans, proved sufficient to drive the enemy back. As soon as Grant found that Early was retreating, he ordered the troops back to Petersburg for the purpose of making an attack on Lee while weakened by the absence of this force. But before the Sixth Corps left Washington, he was informed that Early was returning down the Valley, and he countermanded the order, and directed it to return to Harper's Ferry.

This unpropitious state of affairs, of course, caused a great deal of anxiety throughout the country, and Grant was overwhelmed with visits from Members of Congress, and other distinguished men, and with letters, all wishing to know his feelings, and what the prospects were of success. The following letter to his friend, Mr. Washburne, clearly sets forth his views at this time of general despondency, and reveals that calm courage and confidence which never forsook him:

"HEADQUARTERS ARMIES OF THE U. S., }
CITY POINT, VA., Aug. 16, 1864. }

"DEAR SIR: I state to all citizens who visit me, that all we want now, to ensure an early restoration of the Union, is a determined unity of sentiment North.

"The rebels have now in their ranks their last man. The little boys and old men are guarding prisoners, guarding railroad bridges, and forming a good part of their garrisons or intrenched positions. A man lost by them cannot be replaced. They have robbed the cradle and the grave equally to get their present force. Besides what they lose in frequent skirmishes and battles, they are now losing from desertions and other causes, at least one regiment per day. With this drain upon them, the end is not far distant, if we will only be true to ourselves. Their only hope now is in a divided North. This might give them reinforcements from Tennessee, Kentucky, Maryland, and Missouri, while it would weaken us. With the draft quietly enforced, the enemy would become despondent, and would make but little resistance.

"I have no doubt but the enemy are exceedingly anxious to hold out until after the Presidential election. They have many hopes from its effects. They hope a counter-revolution. They hope the election of the Peace candidate. In fact, like Micawber, they hope for something to 'turn up.' Our peace friends, if they expect peace from separation, are much mistaken. It would be but the beginning of war, with thousands of Northern men joining the South, because of our disgrace in allowing separation. To 'have peace on any terms,' the South would demand the restoration of their slaves already freed; they would demand indemnity for losses sustained, and they would demand a treaty which would make the North slave-hunters for the South; they would demand pay for, or the restoration of, every slave escaped to the North."

In the meantime, the telegraph wires between him and Washington being often down, frequently causing a whole day to elapse before his despatches could be received by the Secretary of War, he determined to have all the forces in West Virginia, Washington, Susquehanna, and the Middle Department placed under one officer, capable of man-

aging affairs without particular and constant directions from him, and on his recommendation, it
was done.   He then ordered Sheridan to report
to Halleck, for the purpose of being on hand
when he should be appointed to this important
command.   He himself left City Point and visited Hunter, then encamped on the Monocacy, and
after seeing for himself the condition of things,
directed him to concentrate all his forces near
Harper's Ferry.   He no sooner saw the troops in
motion, than he telegraphed to Sheridan to come
on by the morning train, and put himself at the
head of the army.

On the 6th of August, after a conversation
with him in regard to the situation and future
military operations, he returned to City Point,
feeling that the day of blunders in the Shenandoah
Valley was over.   Knowing, however, how fatal
to his operations around Richmond a defeat here
would be, he would not permit Sheridan to bring
on, as he wished, a decisive battle with Early.
But Sheridan was impatient, and confident also
of success, and Grant, feeling that it was important to relieve Maryland and Pennsylvania from
the constant danger of invasion, and at the same
time obtain full control of the Baltimore & Ohio
Railroad, and Chesapeake Canal, at last determined to accede to his wishes.   But, knowing
that Lee's object in manœuvring in the Shenan-

doah Valley was to draw his army away from Richmond, and hence that it was of vital importance that no risk of defeat should be taken, he concluded not to telegraph the permission to Sheridan to bring on a battle, but go on himself and take a minute survey of the position of the two armies. He left City Point in the middle of September, and met Sheridan at Charlestown. The latter was very positive and decided in his views, and Grant said, " he pointed out so distinctly how each army lay : what he would do the moment he was authorized to move, and expressed such confidence of success, that I saw that but two words of instructions were necessary : 'Go in!' I asked him if he could get out his teams and supplies in time to make an attack on the ensuing Tuesday morning. His reply was, that he could, before daylight Monday morning. He was off promptly to time, and I may add, that the result was such that I have never since deemed it necessary to visit General Sheridan before giving him orders."

The latter soon sent Early " whirling through Winchester." His decisive victory put an entirely different face on matters about Richmond, for instead of Grant being called upon for reinforcements for the Shenandoah Valley, Lee was ; and troops that he had designed to operate in the region of Culpepper and Alexandria, had to be forwarded to Early. Thus strengthened, the latter again moved down the Valley, and though beaten again, finally, on the 19th of October, fell on our army before daylight, while Sheridan was absent, and swept its camps like a whirlwind. The timely arrival of Sheridan, however, restored the battle, and the enemy, beaten and routed, was driven from the Valley forever. This overwhelming victory sealed the fate of Richmond. If Early had conquered, more troops than Grant could spare would have had to be sent away from the siege, but now he gathered the reinforcements to himself.

He now determined, if possible, to sweep around Lee's right flank, and get possession of the South Side Railroad, running into Richmond. So, on the 27th of October, he despatched the Second Corps under Warren, and two divisions of the Fifth Corps, with a force of cavalry in advance, to force Hatcher's Run, lying beyond the extremity of his line, on the left. The movement was successful, and the advance got within six miles of the railroad, but Grant, finding that he had been anticipated by Lee, who had erected strong works in his front to bar his further progress, directed the troops to return. He waited until it was reported that the two Corps had formed a junction, when, feeling no further anxiety, he returned to his headquarters. But the report was not true—the gap was not closed, and the watchful enemy dashed into it, and a bloody combat followed. Hancock repulsed him, though with heavy loss.

Butler, at the same time, was directed to move against the enemy on the north side of the James River, but no important results were secured. "From this time forward," says Grant, "the operations in front of Petersburg and Richmond, until the spring campaign of 1865, were confined to the defence and extension of our lines, and to offensive movements for crippling the lines of communication, and to prevent his detaching any considerable force to send South." By midwinter his lines reached Hatcher's Run, while the Weldon Railroad was destroyed for many miles.

But during this winter, so comparatively quiet, an event occurred which came very near ending in a disaster that would have been almost irreparable. Grant makes no mention of it in his report, because it actually affected only the navy, while the naval report takes but little notice of it, because, so far as the navy was concerned, but little harm was done.

Lee, finding that he must abandon all hope of drawing Grant away by operating near Washington, conceived the daring plan of cutting off his communications, and thus starving the army into a retreat. The absence of our war-vessels operating in front of Fort Fisher, furnished an opportunity to do this which seemed to the enemy almost provi-

dential. On the 24th of January, three iron-
clads and three wooden vessels, with a flotilla of
torpedo-boats, came down the James River, intending to run the batteries, take City Point, and thus
cut off the base of supplies for the whole army,
and divide the forces north and south of the
James. A large rebel force was massed north of
the river, to make an overwhelming assault on the
army there, as soon as City Point was reached.
A high tower, erected at the latter place for observation by Grant, was to be set on fire as a signal of success, and at the same time, of attack.
The vessels came boldly down in the darkness, and
it was soon evident that we had nothing on shore
or in the river that could stop their progress, and
consternation seized our army along the banks.
The Onondaga, on guard, retreated down the river
without attempting a defence. By good fortune,
or rather through an over-ruling Providence, the
iron-clads ran aground, and were stopped midway
in their triumphant career. The country did not
know what a narrow escape Grant and his army
had, but the Government did. A committee of
investigation was appointed, and the universal testimony was, that if these vessels had not gone
aground, the siege of Richmond would have been
raised, to say nothing of the disasters that might
have befallen the army. City Point once occupied by the rebels, not a pound of food could

have reached our troops. Grant alone testified that he did not think the disaster would have been irreparable, and he, only on the single ground that he had provisions enough on hand to last, with great economy, two weeks, and by the end of that time he thought the Government would have been able to re-open his communications. On the probable success of outside efforts alone, he testified, he relied for salvation. What fearful issues hung on the simple question, whether those three ironclads could clear the shoals.

But Grant would not have been accountable for the misfortune, had it occurred. The navy alone would have been compelled to bear the blame.

But though Grant's plans had partially failed in his direct operations against Richmond, they had been crowned with complete success in other portions of the extended field. Sherman had, during the summer, pushed his triumphant way to Atlanta. Grant's delight at his success was marred, however, by a sad event—the death of his dearest friend, McPherson, who fell in one of the battles before the place. When the sad news reached him his strong nature gave way, and bursting into tears, he exclaimed, "The country *has lost one of its best soldiers, and I have lost my best friend.*"

McPherson's grandmother, aged eighty-seven

15*

years, hearing that Grant, when told of his death, retired to his tent and wept, wrote him a letter. To this the latter sent the following tender, touching response:

HEADQUARTERS ARMIES OF THE U. S.,
CITY POINT, VA., Aug. 10, 1864.

Mrs. Lydia Slocum:

MY DEAR MADAM: Your very welcome letter of the 3d instant has reached me. I am glad to know that the relatives of the lamented Major-General McPherson are aware of the more than friendship existing between him and myself. A nation grieves at the loss of one so dear to our nation's cause. It is a selfish grief, because the nation had more to expect from him than from almost any one living. I join in this selfish grief, and add the grief of personal love for the departed. He formed, for some time, one of my military family. I knew him well; to know him was to love. It may be some consolation to you, his aged grandmother, to know that every officer and every soldier who served under your grandson felt the highest reverence for his patriotism, his zeal, his great, almost unequalled ability, his amiability, and all the manly virtues that can adorn a commander. Your bereavement is great, but cannot exceed mine.

Yours truly,   U. S. GRANT.

Sherman, having captured Atlanta, wrote to Grant asking permission to let Hood alone, and march across the country to Savannah. Grant, in reply, asked him if it did not look as if "Hood was going to attempt the invasion of Middle Tennessee, using the Mobile and Ohio, Memphis and Charleston roads, to supply his base on the Tennessee river, about Florence or Decatur.

If he does this, he ought to be met and prevented from getting north of the Tennessee river. If you were to cut loose I do not believe you would meet Hood's army, but would be bushwhacked by all the old men, little boys, and such railroad guards as are still left at home. Hood would probably *strike for Nashville*, thinking that by going north he could inflict greater damage upon us than we could upon the rebels by going south. If there is any way of getting at Hood's army I would prefer that, but I must trust to your own judgment." With that prescience which distinguishes the great commander, he here traces out the exact course that Hood afterwards took. But Sherman still urged that he might be permitted to strike across the country, saying, " Hood may turn into Kentucky and Tennessee, but I believe he will be forced to follow me." Grant's forecast was the truest, and his plan unquestionably the safest and best if any other commander than Thomas had been left to take care of Hood. He, however, finally gave his consent in the following despatch: " Your despatch of to-day received. If you are satisfied the trip to the sea-coast can be made holding the line of the Tennessee river firmly, you may make it, destroying all the railroads south of Dalton or Chattanooga as you think best."

It was his original design to have Sherman

push through to the sea-coast, and thus cut the Confederacy in two; but his plan was to have him hold Atlanta, and get through by garrisons stationed all along the railroad—Atlanta being the base—but not destroy it and cut loose entirely, as he did.

When Hood finally started north, Grant said he was going to his certain doom; and that if he were directing his movements, he would not alter them.

When the rebel army finally appeared before Nashville, in the latter part of December, Grant became very anxious to have Thomas attack him at once.

But though the latter was to all appearance ready to take the field, he was sadly deficient in cavalry. He wished not only to defeat Hood, but to have the means of pursuing him when beaten. Grant finally telegraphed him that he wished him to move at once upon the enemy, and he replied that he was not ready. Grant sent back word that he had more confidence in him than any other man, and to take his own time; still, he would like to know the reasons of his delay. But Thomas, determined that in no way should these reasons leak out on the road, did not give them.

Grant, fearing that Hood would leave Nashville and cross the Cumberland into Kentucky, felt so impatient at Thomas' delay, that he left City Point and started west, to superintend matters in person. He never could stay away from any point, whether in battle or out of it, when the danger was pressing. But when he reached Washington, he met the despatch of Thomas announcing his victory. "I was delighted," he says; "all fears and apprehensions were dispelled." He, however, still thinks that it would have been better, had Thomas attacked Hood before he had time to fortify; but says in his frank, generous way, "his final defeat of Hood was so complete, that it will be accepted as a vindication of that distinguished officer's judgment." This victory, and Sherman's triumphant entrance into Savannah, lighted up the winter to Grant at City Point, and made him see clearly the approaching end of the struggle.

The capture of Fort Fisher was another bright gleam above the horizon. In the first expedition against this stronghold, Grant, in furnishing the land forces, designated Weitzel to command them; but they being taken from Butler's army, he, of course, sent his instructions through the latter officer. These did "not order an assault, but said, the first object is to close to the enemy the port of Wilmington, which as yet had not been done." But Butler never gave these instructions to Weitzel at all; and the latter told Grant he was

not aware of their existence until he saw them in
Butler's official report of the failure of the expedition.

Butler quietly pocketed them, and coolly took
command himself. Grant says, "I had no idea
of General Butler's accompanying the expedition
until the evening before it got off from Bermuda
Hundred; and then did not dream but that
General Weitzel had received all the instructions,
and would be in command." He thought, he
said, "that he was going to witness the effect of
the explosion of the powder boat." Grant's in-
dignation was aroused at this bold contempt of
his orders and breach of military discipline that
deserved a court martial, and soon after put Ord
in his place.

Porter, who would not retire from before the
fort, after Butler withdrew the army, wrote to
Grant that it could be taken; and so the latter
sent another force, under General Terry as commander. This expedition succeeded, and Wilmington soon after fell.

Sherman having reached Savannah, Grant
sent a despatch to him, in which he gave directions "that after establishing a base on the sea-
coast, with necessary garrisons to include all his
artillery and cavalry, to come by water to City
Point with the balance of his command." But
finding it difficult to get ocean transportation, and

seeing that it would take two months to bring the army on, he changed his mind and thought Sherman might, perhaps, better operate from where he was. But in the meantime he received a letter from him sketching his daring plan of marching up by land, and forming a junction with him before Richmond. His confidence that he could do so pleased Grant, and he immediately sent back a despatch directing him to carry out his own plan.

The total rout of Hood in Tennessee removed all danger from the enemy in that quarter, and released the troops under Thomas so that they could be used elsewhere, and Grant now ordered Schofield, with the Twenty-third Corps, numbering twenty-one thousand men, east, for the purpose of making an advance inland—either from Wilmington or Newbern, toward Goldsboro', to coöperate with Sherman's movements. Helping to reduce the former place, Schofield was directed to make it his base of operations, while another column pushed inland from Newbern. In addition to this, Grant directed Thomas to send Gen. Stoneman with a large cavalry force across the mountains into South Carolina, to destroy railroads and material of war, and at the same time release our prisoners at Salisbury, N. C. But Sherman's rapid march north caused a change in this plan, and Stoneman was directed to operate against the railroad toward Lynchburg. This concentric movement of various forces shows the comprehensiveness of Grant's mind, and the remorseless energy and determination with which he pushed his adversary. The heavens were gathering blacker than midnight above Lee, and it thundered all around the horizon.

While thus concentrating his own forces, Grant, in order to prevent the enemy from doing the same by bringing up reinforcements from the extreme South, ordered Canby, who had relieved Banks, to organize an expedition against Mobile. "This," Grant wrote to Thomas, "will attract all the attention of the enemy, and leave an advance from your stand-point easy. I think it advisable, therefore," he said, "that you prepare as much of a cavalry force as you can spare, and hold it in readiness to go South." He designed to have this force push deep into Alabama, destroying the rebel communications, and dispersing and capturing detached bodies of the enemy.

The armies East and West under his hand had not proved a balky team, but had pulled steadily together, and were now, at a rapid pace, nearing the goal.

From this brief sketch of the various plans of Grant and the movements he set on foot during this winter, how like a single machine our vast and scattered forces appear in his grasp! Separated by thousands of miles—lofty mountains and broad rivers intervening,—yet all like so many wheels obeying a central force till one could almost count the days when the iron walls would close forever around Confederacy.

Success now did not depend on any great pitched battle, though it might be hastened by one. It was secure, whether that was fought or not. There was a mathematical certainty about it that must have been appalling to Lee. Grant's movements were like the finger on the dial-plate of a clock, moving round with a uniform, steady motion, until the given hour is reached, when the relentless hammer will strike.

In order to assist Sherman, who was comparatively weak in cavalry, Grant, while these various movements were being set on foot, directed Sheridan, who also was foot-loose in the Shenandoah Valley, to push on to Lynchburg, and after destroying the railroad and canal, endeavor by heading the streams to reach Sherman toiling up from Savannah.

Sheridan, with twenty thousand cavalry, started on the 27th of February, and pushed on to Lynchburg; but the enemy burning the bridges over the James River, he could not get across, and so, after destroying every thing within his reach, moved down the north bank of the stream toward Richmond—causing the wildest consternation in the capital. Columns were at once hurried off to meet this new danger, but Sheridan sweeping swiftly across the country reached the White House in safety. After resting here awhile, he crossed the James River and joined Grant.

Every thing now was moving but the Army of the Potomac—Sherman was at Goldsboro', Canby thundering at the gates of Mobile, while two cavalry expeditions were afoot, one pushing into Alabama, and the other towards Lynchburg. Grant saw that the time to strike, at last had come. In the meantime the President visited him at headquarters. Not expecting to do so, he sometime previous wrote him the following encouraging letter :

"*Lieutenant-General Grant :*

"Not expecting to see you before the spring campaign opens, I wish to express, in this way, my entire satisfaction with what you have done up to this time, so far as I understand it. The particulars of your plans I neither know nor seek to know. You are vigilant and self-reliant; and, pleased with this, I wish not to obtrude any restraints or constraints upon you. While I am very anxious that any great disaster or capture of our men in great numbers shall be avoided, I know that these points are less likely to escape your attention than they would be mine. If there be any thing wanting which is within my power to give, do not fail to let me know it. And now, with a brave army and a just cause, may God sustain you.

"Yours, very truly,   A. LINCOLN."

Touched with this mark of confidence, Grant returned the following frank, characteristic reply :

"*The President :*

" Your very kind letter of yesterday is just received. The confidence you express for the future, and satisfaction for the past, in my military administration, is acknowledged with pride. It shall be my earnest endeavor that you and the country shall not be disappointed. From my first entrance into the volunteer service of the country to the present day, I have never had cause of complaint, have never expressed or implied a complaint against the Administration, or the Secretary of War, for throwing any embarrassment in the way of my vigorously prosecuting what appeared to be my duty. Indeed, since the promotion which placed me in command of all the armies, and in view of the great responsibility and importance of success, I have been astonished at the readiness with which every thing asked for has been yielded, without even an explanation being asked.

" Should my success be less than I desire and expect, the least I can say is, the fault is not with you.

" Very truly, your obedient servant,

" U. S. GRANT, Lieut.-General."

Sherman also came up from Goldsboro', to consult with him about his plans. The latter told him the army was about to move around Lee's right—to turn Petersburg, and assist Sheridan, who would be sent with a strong force of cavalry to destroy the South Side and Danville railroads, and thus cut off Lee's supplies. He therefore directed him to march north towards Dinwiddie Court House, to coöperate with this movement. The latter hurried back, while Grant issued his orders for his army to move.*   He had, as he says, "spent days of anxiety lest each morning should bring the report that the enemy had retreated the night before." His various movements had been organized at such vast distances, thus giving premonitions of their character so long beforehand, that he felt that a skilful commander like Lee, would not remain to be cooped up in Richmond and starved to death, but retreat in time to effect a junction with Johnston operating against Sherman. If he succeeded in this, a new campaign would have to be organized, and hence new delays become inevitable.

There has never been given a satisfactory explanation for Lee's strange conduct in madly clinging to Richmond until escape was impossible. Doubtless one great reason was, consciousness of his inability to hold his army together the moment it was put on the march from the abandoned capital.

* Vide Appendix.

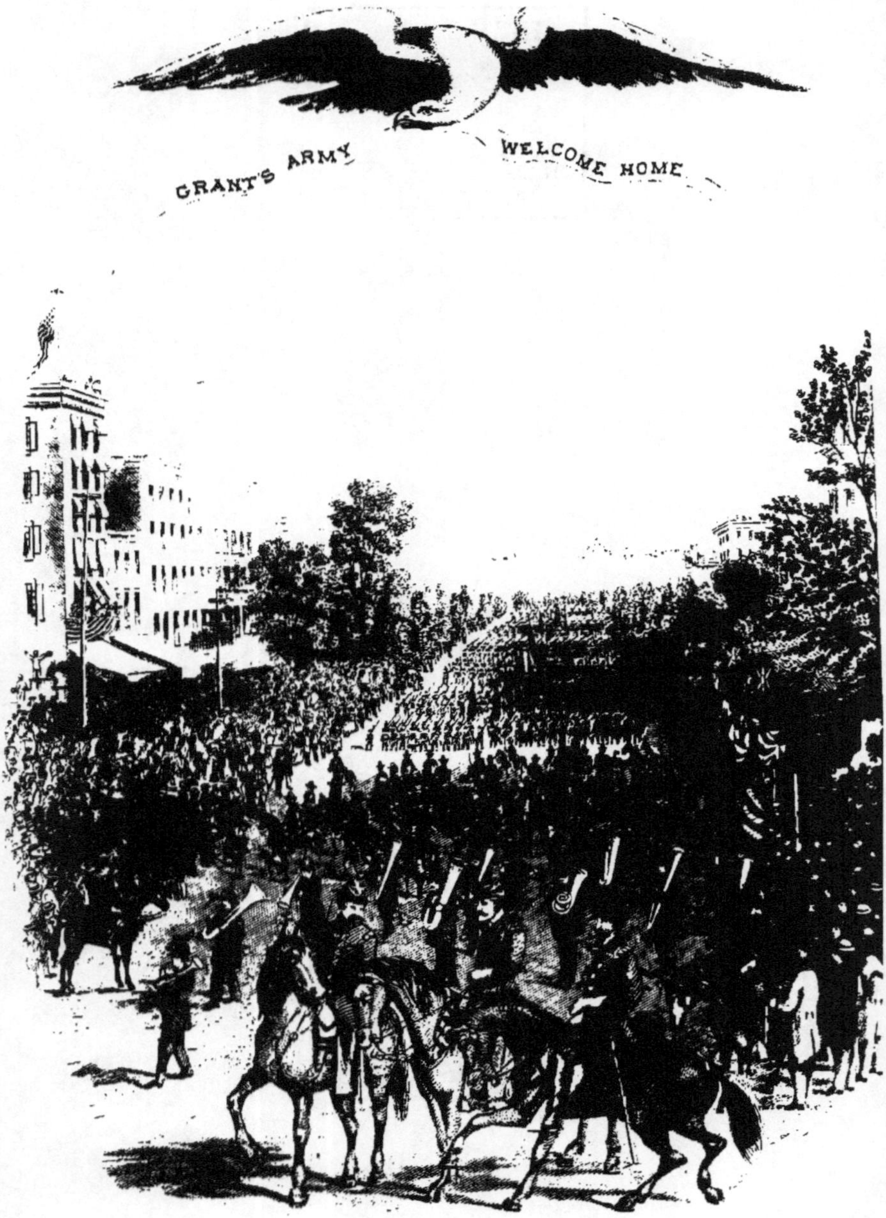
GRANT'S ARMY
WELCOME HOME

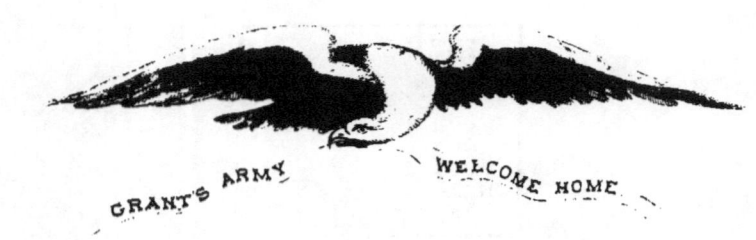

CHAPTER XXIII.

THE LAST GREAT MOVEMENT.

GRANT'S order to Meade for the great final movement was dated March 24th. By a singular coincidence, the very next day Lee assumed the offensive, and made a bold dash on Grant's lines South of the Appomattox River, and directly in front of the Ninth Corps, and actually broke through, carrying Fort Steadman, and turned its guns upon our troops. But the force on either flank held its ground, while the .rebel soldiers could not be induced to leave the breastworks to charge again our broken lines. Reserves being brought up, they were driven out, and their own intrenched picket-line seized and held, though Lee made desperate efforts to retake it.

This bold attack of Lee was the last expiring blow of a dying man, and must have been made with the desperate feeling of a gambler when he stakes his last dollar; for the three or four thousand men he lost here he could illy spare. Four days after, Sheridan moved off to execute the task assigned him, while the Fifth and Sixth Corps followed after. That night he was at Dinwiddie Court House, with the infantry well up, and Grant saw himself in a favorable position " to end the matter," as he said, and he wrote to Sheridan that " he *felt like it*," and therefore to abandon his raid on the railroads for the present, and, instead of cutting loose from the army, as he had directed him to · do, to coöperate with it, and push on around the enemy to his rear. For two days it now rained incessantly, turning roads and fields into a quagmire, and making it well-nigh impossible to move any thing on wheels. The next day, however, Sheridan advanced to the neighborhood of Five Forks, where he found the enemy in force, while everywhere along the new line occupied by the infantry, the same state of things existed. Grant seeing this, and knowing that if he had been correctly informed of the strength of Lee's army, he could not man properly his extended lines, reaching from Richmond to his present extreme right—he determined therefore to push his own line no farther to the left, but detach one corps with Sheridan to turn the rebel flank, while he moved boldly to the assault in front, and " end the matter."

More or less fighting now occurred, to get in proper position; but on the 1st of April Sheridan, with the aid of Warren, captured the position at Five Forks, with all the artillery and five or six thousand prisoners. The remainder of the force, instead of falling back on the main army, turned westward, and, panic-stricken and demoralized, fled in every direction. Thus, at one fell blow, Lee saw his right wing " violently wrenched from his centre." He was aroused as by a thunder-clap at the fatal news. Grant received Sheridan's despatch that evening, and knowing what a terrible blow it was to Lee, feared he would retreat in the night-time, and falling on Sheridan as he did so, overwhelm him. He therefore instantly started off Miles' division to reinforce him, while he ordered all the guns in position to open on the works in front, and keep up the bombardment till four o'clock in the morning, at which time the assault was ordered.

At the appointed hour, the attacking columns moved gallantly forward, and Wright and Ord carried every thing before them on their side. Parke broke the main line in his front, but could not carry the inner one, while Gibbon got possession of two strong works. But inner works were still held, where the enemy rallied—and amid shouts and yells, and roar of cannon, and vollies of musketry, a terrible conflict went on, especially around Fort Gregg, until Sheridan, swooping down from the left, and a force sent by Meade from the front of Petersburg, closed in in that direction, shut down like the door of fate on the diminished garrisons, when they broke and fled in confusion.

EVACUATION OF RICHMOND.

These successes around Petersburg settled the fate of Richmond, and Lee sent a despatch to the War Department to have every thing in readiness to evacuate it. It is a curious fact that the inhabitants were totally ignorant of the terrible struggle which had been going on for the last three days between the two armies. The latest news from the front was that Lee, in a night attack, had defeated Grant with heavy loss—hence they were wholly unprepared for the appalling tidings that awaited them. "John M. Daniel, editor of the Richmond *Examiner*, died that day, under the delusion that such a victory had been won, and John Mitchell, who wrote his obituary in the papers, expressed the regret that the great Virginian had passed away just as a decisive victory was likely to give the turning-point to the success of the Southern Confederacy."

Davis was at church, when a messenger entered the aisle, and walking rapidly up to the pew in which he sat, handed him a slip of paper containing Lee's despatch. Outwardly it seemed a slight event, but it struck deep as a bullet and as deadly, into the heart of the rebel president. Though with a strong effort he mastered his emotions, his cheek blanched at the terrible tidings; for he knew it to be the handwriting on the wall.

The services had hardly closed, when it was evident from the faces of the few people seen in the quiet streets, that ominous tidings were in the air. The church-bells pealed their Sabbath tones as usual—the breath of spring stole softly in from the distant fields, and all was peaceful as the day of rest should be. Still, a strange sense of coming evil began to be felt; for rumors were afloat of some dire impending calamity. At length these began to assume shape, and white lips whispered in incredulous, astonished ears, that the city was to be given up to the enemy. Some smiled in unbelief, some laughed outright, at the absurd report; while even to the believing it seemed hardly possible, as they heard the bells sweetly chiming, and saw women and children wending their way in tranquil security to church, that conquering battalions were about to shout along those streets. But officers galloping through them, and the din of preparation

16

going on in various quarters, soon dispelled all doubt; and then disorder and tumult swelled along every avenue. The change from the deep repose of Sabbath to the wild alarm and uproar that followed, was appalling. Crowds, heaving in fierce agitation, poured along the streets—army wagons, loaded with boxes and trunks, drove furiously towards the Danville Depot; pale women and ragged children streamed after, going they knew not whither; excited men filled the air with blasphemies, while the more desperate surged up around the commissary depots, awaiting the signal for pillage. There was no order—no attempt on the part of any one to enforce it. Says one of their own writers: "The only convocation, the only scene of council that marked the fall of Richmond, took place in a dingy room in a corner of the upper story of the Capitol Building. In this obscure chamber assembled the city council of Richmond, to consult on the emergency, and to take measures to secure what of order was possible in the scenes about to ensue. It appeared to represent all that was left of deliberation in the Confederate capital. It was a painful contrast to look upon this scene, to traverse the now almost silent Capitol House, so often vocal with oratory and crowded with the busy scenes of legislation; to hear the echo of the footstep, and at last to climb to the dismal show of councilmen in the remote room, where a half dozen sat at a rude table, and not so many vacant idlers listened to their proceedings. At the head of the board sat an illiterate grocer, of the name of Saunders, who was making his last exhibition of Southern-spirit; and twenty-four hours thereafter was subscribing himself to some very petty Federal officer, '*most* respectfully your *most* obedient servant.' Here and there, hurrying up with the latest news from the War Department, was Mayor Mayo—excited, incoherent—chewing tobacco defiantly; but yet full of pluck, having the mettle of the true Virginia gentleman, stern and watchful to the last, in fidelity to the city that his ancestors had assisted in founding, and exhibiting, no matter in what comical aspects, a courage that no man ever doubted."

Such is the picture of the *official* proceedings that dignified the downfall of the haughty rebel capital. Humiliating as it is, it stands out in bright relief as contrasted with the scene that took place outside of the building. There the strong hand of military power was at last withdrawn—the breathless fear of unsparing despotism gone—the last restraint even of common humanity removed, and wild terror held high carnival in the doomed capital, over whose dwellings arose a fearful and confused murmur—the prelude of the coming storm. The excitement and tumult growing fiercer as evening drew on, the mayor attempted

to restore order by calling out two regiments of
militia and establishing patrols, and destroying
all the liquor in the stores and warehouses; but
militia and patrols, as soon as darkness closed
over the city, became swallowed up in the mad-
dened throng that surged unchecked through the
streets. The gutters ran with liquor, and drunken,
frenzied men reeled, with hideous blasphemies on
their lips, along the side-walks that were loaded
with broken glass and the contents of pillaged
stores. Wild cries of distress mingled with the
horrid oaths that made night hideous, and the
city became a scene of horror and terror indescribable. But as if this were not enough, General
Ewell, commanding Lee's rear-guard north of the
James, blew up the iron-clad vessels in the river;
and before the earthquake shock had hardly
passed away, the three bridges that spanned the
stream were ablaze, ribbing the darkness with
their long lines of flame. The next moment, four
huge tobacco warehouses were wrapped in fire,
shooting murky clouds of smoke and fiery sparks
into the heavens. The neighboring houses caught
fire; and the conflagration passing all control,
raged unchecked along the streets, and roared like
the ocean over the abandoned city. As the light
fell on the terror-stricken or ferocious faces of the
yelling crowd, it seemed as if the infernal depths
had vomited up its inhabitants.

But while this frightful scene was going on in the city, outside, the air was filled with strains of music. Weitzel, who commanded our forces on the north side of the James, in front of whom was Ewell's rear-guard, had been directed by Grant to make as great a demonstration as possible. He, therefore, as night closed in, set all his regimental bands playing. Ewell ordered his own to respond; and hour after hour the melodious strains echoed through the night, presenting a strange contrast to the savage yells and tumult within. But at midnight the music suddenly ceased, and Ewell quietly withdrew; while Weitzel gazed in astonishment and doubt on the lurid heavens above the Capital.

When morning broke he found that the enemy in his front was gone, and he immediately sent forward a body of horse to reconnoitre.

The sun was a little over an hour high when these troopers, forty in number, appeared in Main street. Suddenly the cry of "Yankees!" "The Yankees are come!" swept in wild clamor up the street, the upper end of which was choked with a crowd of men, women, and children—some with carts, others rolling along barrels, or staggering under the weight of plunder.

As the shout of "Yankees" smote their ears, these rushed away in terror, cursing and trampling on each other in savage fury. The troops

walked their horses till they reached the corner
of Eleventh Street, when they broke into a trot
for the Public Square, and riding straight up to
the Capitol planted their guidons on its top, where
they fluttered proudly in the breeze. A few
hours later, the heads of Weitzel's columns appeared in the streets. Says a lady who witnessed
the entrance: "Stretching from the Exchange
Hotel to the slope of Church Hill, down the hill,
through the valley, up the ascent to the hotel, was
the array, with its unbroken line of blue, fringed
with bright bayonets. Strains of martial music,
flushed countenances, waving swords, betokened
the victorious army. As the line turned at the
Exchange Hotel into the upper street, the movement was the signal for a wild burst of cheers
from each regiment. Shouts from a few negroes
were the only response. Through throngs of sullen spectators, along the line of fire, in the midst
of the horrors of a conflagration increased by the
explosion of shells left by the retreating army,
through curtains of smoke, through the vast aerial
auditorium convulsed with the commotion of
frightful sounds, moved the gay procession of
the grand army, with horse, music, and bright
banners, and wild cheers. A regiment of negro
cavalry swept by the hotel. As they turned the
street-corner they drew their sabres with savage shouts, and the blood mounted even in

my woman's heart with quick throbs of defiance."

Meanwhile the conflagration raged with unchecked fury. The entire business part of the city was on fire—stores, warehouses, manufactories, mills, depots, and bridges, covering acres of ground, were in flames, while the continuous thunder of exploding shells added ten-fold to the horrors of the scene. All during the forenoon, flame and smoke and showers of blazing sparks filled the air, spreading still further the destruction until every bank, every auction store, every insurance office, nearly every commission house, and most of the fashionable stores, were a heap of smouldering ruins. The atmosphere was so choking that " men, women and children crowded into the square of the capital for a breath of pure air ; and one traversed the green slopes blinded by cinders and struggling for breath. Already piles of furniture had been collected there, dragged from the ruins of burning houses, and in uncouth arrangements made with broken tables and bureaus, were huddled women and children with no other resting-place in Heaven's great hollowness." Deep apathetic silence visited the city at night after the fire had burned itself out, and clouds of black smoke like a funeral pall hung over the smouldering ruins.

CHAPTER XXIII.

THE RETREAT AND SURRENDER.

The Pursuit—Swift Marching—Sheridan's Victory over Ewell—Lee cut off from Burkesville—Endeavors to reach Lynchburg—Grant's Letter to Sherman—Lee leaves the Highway, and takes to the Thickets—Headed off by Sheridan—Grant addresses a Note to Lee asking him to surrender—The Reply—Correspondence—Lee resolves to cut his way through Sheridan's Cavalry—The Attempt abandoned—Lee seeks an Interview with Grant—Description of the Meeting—The Surrender of the Army agreed upon—The Surrender—Grant visits Washington—The President tells him a Dream—Is sent down to receive the Surrender of Johnston—The Army starts for Home—Grand Review in the Capital.

WHILE this terrific scene was being enacted in the rebel capital, the fugitive president was fleeing for his life, and the disorganized army of Lee was crowding along the highways and fields to escape the remorseless pursuit of Grant. Leaving to others the glory of entering the rebel capital, the latter was in the saddle guiding and urging on his victorious columns.

Lee's great object now was to get to Danville, from whence he could easily effect a junction with Johnston, near Raleigh. On the other hand, Grant's great object was to cut him off from that

point, and Sheridan was pushed on toward Burkesville, the junction of the railroads, while the Second
and Sixth Corps were sent on to his support.

The race between Lee's and Grant's armies was
a desperate one; the former marched swiftly along
the north bank of the Appomattox, and the latter
the south, both heading for Burke's Station, fifty-
three miles from Petersburg, where the South-
side and Danville Railroads intersect. If Grant
reached it first, Lee's chances of escape were well
nigh hopeless, and he knew it. But the former
had the inside track. From the Rapidan to Richmond, a year before, Lee had it. Matters were
reversed now, and Grant was not the general to
let this advantage be lost; so the two armies
strained forward, Sheridan all the while harassing
the rebel flank. Lee's army marched for life, ours
for victory. Our army, by putting forth herculean efforts, and marching as wearied men never
marched before, reached it first, and Lee was cut
off from Danville by that route. On Thursday
afternoon, with the assistance of the Fifth and
Sixth Corps, Sheridan completely cut off and captured Ewell's entire column of nine thousand men,
seven general officers, fifteen field-pieces of artillery, twenty-nine battle-flags, and six miles of
wagon-trains.

After reaching Burkesville, General Meade,
with the greater portion of the Army of the Po-

16*

tomac, took up the pursuit on the north side of the railroad; while Sheridan's cavalry and Ord's Twenty-fourth Corps moved rapidly along the south side, Sheridan being constantly on Lee's flanks, frequently compelling him to halt and form line of battle, and as often engaging him, cutting off detachments, picking up stragglers, capturing cannon without number, and demor-alizing the enemy at every stand. On Friday, at Farmville, sixteen miles west of Burkesville, a considerable engagement occurred, in which the Second Corps participated largely and suffered some loss. Lee, however, was compelled to con-tinue his retreat. At High Bridge, over the Ap-pomattox, he again crossed to the north side of the river, and two of our regiments, the Fifty-fourth Pennsylvania and One Hundred and Twen-ty-third Ohio, which were sent there to hold the bridge, were captured by a strong rebel cavalry force. The railroad bridge at this point, a very high and long structure, was burned by the enemy. "Lee now headed directly for Lynch-burg, in the hope of reaching a point where he could move around the front of our left wing, and escape toward Danville by a road which runs di-rectly south from a point about twenty miles east of Lynchburg. But his rear and flanks were so sorely pressed that he was compelled to skirmish nearly every step, and to destroy or abandon an immense amount of property, while Sheridan was rapidly shooting ahead of him."

Grant having received a despatch from the latter requesting his presence, mounted and hurried to the front. On the 5th, he had written to Sherman, saying: "Sheridan is up with Lee, and reports all that is left—horse, foot, and dragoons—at twenty thousand men, much demoralized. We hope to reduce this number one-half. I shall push on to Burkesville; and if a stand is made at Danville, will, in a very few days, go there. If you can do so, push on from where you are, and let us see if we cannot finish the job with Lee's and Johnston's armies."

He had said at the outset, when he started from Culpepper Court House, near the Rapidan, that he meant to follow Lee wherever he went; and he was now doing it, and would do it, if it took him to the Gulf of Mexico.

All next day the pursuit was kept up, and the fighting continued; while, like a hunted stag, with the cry of the eager pack drawing nearer and nearer every moment, Lee strained forward with the mere wreck of his army. But the foe was everywhere—the country on every side swarmed with Grant's troops; and on the 7th the sore-pressed, disheartened army turned off the main roads, and toiled through dense thickets of oak and pine, that were here and there crossed only by a

wood road or path.   It marched this day without
much molestation, except now and then it was
startled by Sheridan's bugles, as his bold troopers
dashed on the meagre trains.   The next day it
struck a main road and marched rapidly till dark,
when it quietly went into camp.   No foe was in
sight—the air no longer echoed with Sheridan's
bugles, and to all appearance the way was clear
to Lynchburg.   During the night the general officers held a consultation on the condition of affairs,
and the proper movements to be made in the
morning.   But before they had come to any conclusion, the boom of Sheridan's cannon in front
startled them like a sudden thunder-peal; for it
told them that the road to Lynchburg was blocked
up by the enemy.   Ord was to the south, so that
they were cut off in that direction; while Meade
was thundering in the rear.   It was plain there
was no way of escape, unless they could cut a
road through Sheridan's cavalry.

In the mean time Grant, who knew that Lee
would soon be enclosed in his net, had two days
before addressed him the following note:

APRIL 7, 1865.

General R. E. Lee, Commanding C. S. A.

GENERAL: The result of the last week must convince
you of the hopelessness of further resistance on the part
of the Army of Northern Virginia in this struggle.   I
feel that it is so, and regard it as my duty to shift from
myself the responsibility of any further effusion of blood,

by asking of you the surrender of that portion of the Confederate States Army, known as the Army of Northern Virginia.

Very respectfully, your obedient servant,

U. S. GRANT,

Lieutenant-General, Commanding Armies of the United States.

To this Lee sent the following answer:

APRIL 7, 1865.

GENERAL : I have received your note of this date.

Though not entirely of the opinion you express, of the hopelessness of further resistance on the part of the Army of Northern Virginia, I reciprocate your desire to avoid useless effusion of blood, and therefore, before considering your proposition, *ask the terms you will offer, on condition of its surrender.*

R. E. LEE, General.

To Lieutenant-General U. S. GRANT, commanding Armies of the United States.

Whether he believed there was any hope of escape, or whether he spoke of still resisting in order to get better terms, it is impossible to say. He may not have been aware that Sheridan was at that moment sweeping around his front, cutting off his escape to Lynchburg; for the day he sent this note was the one on which his army was marching through the thickets without much molestation, except from some detachments of cavalry that caused but little alarm. The next day, however, he had a clearer, more correct idea of his condition; for the thunder of Sheridan's guns in front told him, in language too plain to be misunderstood, that his case was hopeless. His army had dwindled down to less than ten thousand men, bearing arms—though there were nearly double that number who had thrown away their muskets, and become mere stragglers, scattered through the woods—and it was evident that those which still kept in the ranks must disband and scatter also, or surrender.

The following was Grant's reply:

APRIL 8, 1865.
To General R. E. Lee, Commanding C. S. A.

GENERAL: Your note of last evening, in reply to mine of same date, asking the conditions on which I will accept the surrender of the Army of Northern Virginia, is just received.

In reply, I would say that, *peace being my first desire, there is but one condition that I insist upon,* viz. :

That the men surrendered shall be disqualified for taking up arms against the Government of the United States until properly exchanged.

I will meet you, or designate officers to meet any officers you may name, for the same purpose, at any point agreeable to you, for the purpose of arranging definitely the terms upon which the surrender of the Army of Northern Virginia will be received.

Very respectfully,
Your obedient servant,
U. S. GRANT,
Lieutenant-General, Commanding Armies of the United States.

Lee's response was hardly as " frank " as he pretends, unless he refers to the mere form of surrender, or to his *own* personal surrender, for the " emergency " he speaks of, had certainly arisen.

The very haste with which he answers Grant's note, and his anxiety to know what terms he will offer, shows that he feels it has.   He says :

APRIL 8, 1865.

GENERAL : I received, at a late hour, your note of to-day, in answer to mine of yesterday.

I did not intend to propose the surrender of the Army of Northern Virginia, but *to ask the terms* of your proposition.   To be frank, I do not think the emergency has arisen to call for the surrender.

But as *the restoration of peace should be the sole object of all,* I desire to know whether your proposals would tend to that end.

I cannot, therefore, meet you with a view to surrender the Army of Northern Virginia ; but as *far as your proposition may affect the Confederate States forces under my command, and tend to the restoration of peace,* I should be pleased to meet you at 10 A. M. to-morrow, on the old stage-road to Richmond, between the picket-lines of the two armies.

Very respectfully,
Your obedient servant,
R. E. LEE, General C. S. A.

Grant, perfectly certain that Lee could not now escape, was unwilling that another brave soldier should be sacrificed through false pride or foolish obstinacy, and determined to lose no chance of bringing the matter to a peaceful termination, and hence replied :

APRIL 9, 1865.

General R. E. Lee, Commanding C. S. A.

GENERAL : Your note of yesterday is received.   As I have no authority to treat on the subject of peace, the meeting proposed for 10 A. M. to-day could lead to no

good. I will state, however, General, that *I am equal-
ly anxious for peace with yourself;* and the whole
North entertain the same feeling. *The terms upon
which peace can be had are well understood. By the
South laying down their arms, they will hasten that
most desirable event, save thousands of human lives, and
hundreds of millions of property not yet destroyed.*
Sincerely hoping that all our difficulties may be set-
tled *without the loss of another life,* I subscribe myself,
Very respectfully,
Your obedient servant,
U. S. GRANT,
Lieutenant-General United States Army.

The very day on which this was sent, Lee had
resolved to make a last attempt to cut his way
through Sheridan's force. Gordon, to whom this
perilous task was assigned, marched off with his
thinned, disheartened division to execute it, when
to his surprise he found that heavy masses of
infantry supported the cavalry. Seeing at once
that the attempt would only expose his men to
butchery, he abandoned it, and sent a despatch
to Lee announcing the fact. The latter in the
mean time had ridden to the rear in hope of meeting Grant, but failing to do so, addressed him the
following note:

SUNDAY, April 9, 1865.

GENERAL: I received your note of this morning, on
the picket-line, whither I had come to meet you, and
ascertain definitely what terms were embraced in your
proposition of yesterday with reference to the surrender
of this army.
I now request an interview in accordance with the

offer contained in your letter of yesterday for that purpose.   Very respectfully,
                              Your obedient servant,
                                   R. E. Lee, General.
To Lieutenant-General Grant, Commanding United States Armies.

Grant, as soon as he received it, sent the following letters, which came just in time for a flag of
truce to be raised in front of Gordon's troops, and
prevent a charge of Sheridan's cavalry, which was
already drawn up and waiting the sound of the
bugle to dash down.

                              Sunday, April 9, 1865.

General R. E. Lee, Commanding C. S. A.

Your note of this date is but this moment, 11 50
A. M., received.

In consequence of my having passed from the Richmond and Lynchburg road to the Farmville and Lynchburg road, I am at this writing about four miles west
of Walter's church, and will push forward to the front
for the purpose of meeting you.

Notice sent to me, on this road, where you wish the
interview to take place, will meet me.

                    Very respectfully,
                         Your obedient servant,
                              U. S. Grant, Lieutenant-General.

                    Appomattox Court House, April 9, 1865.

General R. E. Lee, Commanding C. S. A.

In accordance with the substance of my letters to
you of the 8th inst., I propose to receive the surrender
of the Army of Northern Virginia on the following
terms, to wit:

Rolls of all the officers and men to be made in duplicate, one copy to be given to an officer designated by me, the other to be retained by such officers as you may designate.

The officers to give their individual paroles not to take arms against the Government of the United States until properly exchanged, and each company or regimental commander sign a like parole for the men of their commands.

The arms, artillery, and public property to be parked and stacked and turned over to the officers appointed by me to receive them.

This will not embrace the side-arms of the officers, nor their private horses or baggage.

This done, *each officer and man will be allowed to return to their homes,* not to be disturbed by United States authority so long as they observe their parole and the laws in force where they reside.

Very respectfully,
U. S. GRANT, Lieutenant-General.

These terms were at once accepted, in the following short, direct reply:

HEADQUARTERS, ARMY OF NORTHERN VIRGINIA,
April 9, 1865.

Lieutenant-General U. S. Grant, Commanding U. S. A.

GENERAL : I have received your letter of this date, *containing the terms of surrender of the Army of Northern Virginia,* as proposed by you. As they are substantially the same as those expressed in your letter of the 8th inst., *they are accepted.* I will proceed to designate the proper officers to carry the stipulations into effect.

Very respectfully,
Your obedient servant,
R. E. LEE, General.

Grant immediately rode forward to meet Lee.

The latter, at this time, was resting under an apple-tree, with a single member of his staff beside him, when Col. Babcock, of Grant's staff, rode up and said, that if Gen. Lee remained where he was Gen. Grant would soon meet him, as he was coming along that road. Lee immediately directed Col. Marshall, his aid, to find a suitable place in which to receive Grant. The Colonel hailed the first inhabitant he saw, a Mr. McLean, and was directed by him to a vacant house near by, which was partly in ruins. He refused to receive the Union commander in such a dilapidated building, when McLean offered his own residence, a farm-house a little way off. Here, in a plainly furnished sitting-room, Lee received Grant, who was accompanied by several staff officers and generals. The meeting was frank, courteous, and without ceremony. Lee wore his sword, which Grant observing, said, " I must apologize, General, for not wearing my sword—it had gone off with my baggage when I received your note." Lee bowed, and at once entered on the business that had brought them together, and asked Grant to state in writing, if he preferred it, the terms on which he would receive the surrender of the Army of Northern Virginia. Grant immediately sat down by a table, and with a common lead-pencil wrote the following note :

APPOMATTOX COURT HOUSE, April 9th, 1865.

General R. E. Lee, Commanding C. S. A.:

In accordance with the substance of my letter to you of the 8th inst., I propose to receive the surrender of the Army of Northern Virginia on the following terms, to wit:

Rolls of all the officers and men to be made in duplicate, one copy to be given to an officer designated by me, the other to be retained by such officers as you may designate.

The officers to give their individual parole not to take arms against the Government of the United States until properly exchanged; and each company or regimental commander to sign a like parole for the men of their commands.

The arms, artillery, and public property to be parked and stacked and turned over to the officers appointed by me to receive them. This will not embrace the side-arms of the officers, nor their private horses or baggage. This done, each man will be allowed to return to their homes, not to be disturbed by the United States authority, so long as they observe their parole and the laws in force where they may reside.

Very respectfully,

U. S. GRANT, Lieut.-Gen.

He handed this to Lee, who read it carefully, and then asked the construction to be put on "private horses," as most of the cavalrymen owned their horses. Grant replied, that they must be turned over to the Government. Lee acknowledged that it was just, when Grant said that he would instruct his officers to let those men who owned their horses retain them, as they would need them to till their farms. The

conqueror, in the very moment of his highest triumph, by a single sentence brings up a quiet
picture of peace, and already begins to prepare
for turning the "sword into a ploughshare."

While this document was being copied, which
took some time, as there was but one inkstand in
the house, Grant and Lee conversed familiarly,
each inquiring about old army friends.   In casu-
ally alluding to the business before them, Lee said
that he had two or three thousand Federal prisoners on hand, and he was afraid he had not
rations to supply them.   Sheridan, who was
present, immediately replied: "I have rations for
twenty-five thousand men."

When Grant's paper was copied, Lee directed
Col. Marshall to write a reply, the substance of
which he gave him.   The latter began with, "I
have the honor to reply to your communication
of, &c."   Lee scratched all this out, and wrote
simply and soldier-like: "General, I have received your letter of this date, containing the terms
of surrender of the Army of Northern Virginia as
proposed by you.   As they are substantially the
same as those expressed in your letter of the 8th
inst., they are accepted.   I will proceed to designate the proper officers to carry the stipulations
into effect."

Thus ended the interview of that memorable
Sabbath — Palm Sunday — between those two

great actors in the frightful drama that had just closed. On the one side was the Virginia gentleman, with the courtly bearing of the old school, and standing over six feet high—head and shoulders above all around him. On the other, the Western representative man—short, thick-set, and broad-shouldered, self-possessed and natural as in his own camp. There was no theatrical display or language from beginning to end. Simple, un-assuming, straight-forward and manly, they both went through the eventful interview, so painful to one, in a manner that became them. The change that comes over Grant in the moment of victory is very marked. While pressing towards it, he is relentless as fate, and blow follows blow with un-paralleled fierceness. But when it is achieved all the warrior suddenly disappears, and you see only a kind-hearted, simple, unassuming man, more intent on sparing the feelings of his conquered foes than occupied with his own triumphs. The inter-view being over, Lee mounted his horse and rode thoughtfully back to his headquarters. The deed was irrevocably done—the Confederacy, which had put forth such superhuman efforts for the last few years, was dead forever—the mighty structure lay in ruins, and the land was strewed with its wreck.

Grant, as he rode away, felt that his work was also done—but it was a work of accomplishment, not of destruction—of glory enduring, not of disgrace and sorrow.

Three days after, the Army of Northern Virginia had its last parade, and marched by divisions to a spot near the Court House, and there silently stacked their arms, took off their accoutrements, and piled together their flags. About 25,000 men, more than half unarmed, all that were left of Lee's great army, then turned towards their ruined, wasted homes. Grant, with that true magnanimity and delicacy that have always characterized him, was not present at the final surrender. Prompted by the same spirit, he never made a formal entry into the hostile capital, as other conquerers would have done. Avoiding all pomp and show, he was content with having finished the work assigned him. Never did a warrior in the height of triumph wear honors so meekly.

Grant now hastened to Washington, and on the 14th, the day on which the President was assassinated, attended a cabinet meeting. During a pause in the discussions, the President turned to him and asked if he had heard from Gen. Sherman. Grant replied that he had not, but expected every hour to hear that Johnston had surrendered to him. "Well," said Mr. Lincoln, "you will hear very soon now." "Why do you think so?" asked Grant. "Because," said he, "I had a dream last night, and ever since the war began

I have invariably had the same dream before any important military event occurred. I dreamed that I saw a ship sailing very rapidly, and I am sure it portends some important national event."

The very next day, Johnston, having learned the fate of Lee, proposed an armistice to Sherman, offering, on certain conditions, to surrender. The Government disapproving of both, sent Grant down to take control of matters, who, offering substantially the same terms granted to Lee, the army was surrendered. During this very week Mobile fell, and now almost as rapidly as messages could be transmitted the rebel forces in every section of the country laid down their arms.

The army, its great work being done, now took its joyful, triumphant march for home. But before those brave troops melted away into the common mass of citizens again, it was determined that they should once more pass in review before their great leaders, in the capital of the country. It was a noble spectacle, as with the President, and cabinet, and foreign ministers around him, Grant looked down on those bronzed veterans who had moved at his bidding, and been the instruments to execute his will, as he pressed the hosts of rebellion back, and rescued the Republic from destruction. For two days the mighty army marched past him, and his eye kindled as the old banners that had waved amid the storm of Donelson, Shiloh, and Vicksburg, and Missionary Ridge, dipped proudly to him. Great and touching memories clustered around them, for they marked the steps of the wondrous path he had trod for the last four years. Soldiers and officers had become endeared to him by a common toil, a common danger, and a mutual triumph. They had never failed him in the hour of deadly peril. Brave hearts were they all, who had stood shoulder to shoulder with him on many a hard-fought field. On every drooping banner his eye rested with pride, for not one had been disgraced—on the contrary, they were covered all over with noble inscriptions, the mere mention of which, was a history of their gallant deeds. Although the air was tremulous with triumphant music, and shouts to the chief rocked the heavens, yet amid all this adulation and excitement, a sad and mournful feeling filled his heart, as the swiftly-marching columns disappeared in the distance, for they were parting forever. But over all, swelled emotions of joy, that the Union was saved —the country rescued from ruin, and a happy, united people would ere long forget the past, in the enjoyment of peace and prosperity.

17

CHAPTER XXV.

THE life of Grant since the war, furnishes but
little exciting, though important material for the
biographer. Unobtrusive in peace as he was
modest in war, he has avoided mixing in the political contests of the day, steadily refusing to give
the sanction of his great name to any mere party
measure.

He has shown the same well-balanced character amid the fierce and warring passions of men
that he did in the strife and tumult of battle.
He shared with President Lincoln in that freedom
from bitter animosity to the South, for the untold
evils it had brought on the country, which swayed the feelings, and controlled the actions of so

many, in and out of power. Not that he felt less the fearful crime that had been committed, or was less shocked at its results, but that he was too great and noble to live in the foul atmosphere of revenge and hate, and was too far-seeing a states-man, and too pure a patriot, not to deprecate continued animosity and wider separation. He felt that if South and North were ever again to form a Union, a union in reality and not in name, by-gones must be by-gones, so far as the common safety and justice would permit. Had President Lincoln lived, there is no doubt but that they would have moved in perfect harmony and accord in the work of reconstruction. But the tragical death of the President turned the kind feelings of too many in the North into gall and wormwood; for in their grief and passion they forgot to be just, and the act of one madman was construed as the act of the entire South. Grant, though no one was more shocked and grieved than he, showed that superiority to surrounding influences that made him always so calm and self-poised in the heat of conflict—even when every thing was tossing in wreck and ruin around him.

In this respect he is one of the most remarkable men in history. Though possessing a kind heart, the contagion of sympathy, or passion, like the panic of officers and men in battle, never warps his clear judgment or prevents his seeing the right.

When under the influence of the excited state of feeling arising out of the horrible tragedy, an indictment of treason was found against Lee, like a true soldier, who will no sooner allow his honor than his sword to be tarnished, he promptly interposed, saying, that it was contrary to the express stipulations of the surrender at Appomattox Court-House, which declared that none of those who had laid down their arms were to be molested so long as their conduct was peaceable and orderly. So when the President consulted him on his amnesty proclamation, Grant was entirely opposed to that provision which excluded from its benefits all officers from a brigadier-general up. He said that those, of whatever grade, who had belonged to the regular army, and hence been educated by the General Government, should be excluded; but he could see neither the propriety nor justice of excluding a volunteer, who by his bravery and talents had risen to the rank of general, and yet pardoning one who, though he tried, failed to get higher than a major or colonel. Every man of common sense will acknowledge that he was right. He was also opposed to the property distinction, by which all persons worth over twenty thousand dollars were deprived of the benefits of the amnesty. It could not but seem strange, that, of two neighbors living side by side, and who had been equally active in the rebellion, one worth but fifteen thousand dol-

lars should be pardoned, and the other, because
he happened to possess five thousand more, should
not be. But it seemed proper that there should be
a limit somewhere, and as the same objection
would hold good wherever it was placed, he afterwards changed his mind, and approved of it.

The President consulted him much respecting the
proper course to pursue towards the rebel States,
but he steadily refused to be mixed up in civil
matters—he simply urged, and urged strenuously,
that some kind of government should be adopted
at once. As a military commander, it would
have been natural for him to suppose that military rule would be better until the chaotic state of
affairs should partially cease. But like Washington, he believes that almost any government is better than a military despotism—that even great dis-
orders are preferable to it. His views on this point
show him to be more of a statesman than those
who have exercised the civil power.

The well-known magnanimity of his character
caused many prominent rebels, especially officers
excluded by the amnesty proclamation, to apply
to him to obtain their pardon ; and when the case
seemed a proper one for the Executive clemency,
he never refused.

As this fact came out on his examination before
the impeachment committee of Congress, many
at first thought he had been guilty of too great

leniency; but as each case was investigated, the
simple statement of facts was all the defence
necessary. He had not made a single mistake
that even his opponents could use; while the
spirit he exhibited, caused many of his enemies
at the South to change their feelings toward him.
The uniform correctness of his judgment under
all circumstances, is one of the most remarkable
traits in his character.

The reception he met with, as he moved from
point to point in the country, showed the un-
bounded love felt for him by all classes. At New
York, tens of thousands crowded the City Hall
to shake hands with him; while he stood amid
the rush and crowd, quietly smoking his cigar,
just as he had been accustomed to do under the
blaze of batteries and amid the tossing ranks of
war. At Boston, determined efforts were made
to get a speech out of him, but in vain. The
same reticence and unobtrusive manner characterized him throughout the Presidential tour across
the country, at the time of the inauguration of
the monument to Douglas in Illinois. He lived
and moved in a political atmosphere, and it
seemed impossible that a man could talk at all,
unless he expressed his opinion on politics; but
not a word escaped him. Once, some persons
tried to entrap him, when the sudden waking-up
of the lion taught them that impassibility was

not always stolidity. He was a much greater personage than the President; and the immense crowds that gathered on the way to welcome the distinguished party, gave their longest, loudest cheers to Grant.

But perhaps the most imposing, if not the most enthusiastic reception he ever received, was at the last Sanitary Fair, held in Chicago. The expectation of seeing him and Sherman, and other distinguished officers, had brought an immense crowd together; so that "Union Hall" was packed with ten thousand people, when, heralded by a salute of a hundred cannon, and escorted by General Hooker, the honorary president of the fair, and other distinguished men, he entered the door-way. The moment he appeared, a choir selected for the purpose, struck up "The Red, White, and Blue." But the pealing melody had hardly commenced when it was drowned, lost, in the enthusiastic, wild hurrahs that shook the building—cheer following cheer, like successive billows; while long lines of waving handkerchiefs and bright eyes, gleamed above the dark mass, like sunlight on the waves. As the tumult subsided, Grant stepped forward, but before he could open his lips the building again shook with the thunders of applause. He gazed calmly on the excited, mighty multitude, and as soon as there came a lull in the storm, said: "Ladies and gentlemen, as I never make a speech myself, I will ask Governor Yates to return the thanks I should fail to express." Governor Yates then came forward, and closed a short, exciting address with, " and, fellow-citizens, I am here to-day to say that the proudest reflection that thrills the heart of this brave soldier and General, is, that we have gloriously triumphed. That our nation is preserved, that our government has been maintained, and that we have our free institutions for us and our posterity forever."

The citizens of Galena, his place of residence before the war, received him under triumphal arches.

During the war, a person on one occasion remarked to him that his name had been mentioned in connection with the presidency. He laughingly replied, that if he ever run for an office, he hoped it would be for mayor of Galena, so that he might have a sidewalk built from his house to the railroad depot. This the citizens had built; and now over one of the green arches were the words, " General, the sidewalk is built."

Everywhere the same enthusiastic welcome attested how deeply he had implanted himself in the affections of the people.

Though grateful for these spontaneous, unstinted expressions of love and respect, yet all public ovations wearied him, and he was glad to get back to his legitimate work—reducing the army, and distributing the various portions of it as the public exigencies required.

Such conflicting reports were circulated respecting the condition of the South, that the President sent him to inquire into it. He did so, and his report showed that superiority to outside influences, and calm, dispassionate, just judgment that has ever distinguished him from other men.

True to the man who had so nobly stood by him during the war, when the President removed Sheridan from command in New Orleans, he remonstrated against it.

He had shown himself a great general, and he was at length to exhibit those rare executive and administrative faculties which are not always combined with military ability.

Last year, 1867, the President removed Mr. Stanton, Secretary of War, and put Grant as Secretary *ad interim* in his place.

Though Stanton, when he confined himself to the special, appropriate duties of his department, was generally conceded to be one of the ablest Secretaries of War we ever had, yet Grant, though a novice, and hurried without previous preparation into the place, excelled him in every particular. Although as General-in-Chief he had all the departments under his charge, some of which, especially the Southern, caused him much anxiety and trouble, yet the administration of the office

17*

was complete and perfect. Nor was this all—he immediately entered on the work of retrenchment. One would think, burdened as he was with the two-fold duties of the office and those belonging to him as General, and knowing, too, that his occupation of it was only transient, that he would have been quite content to have kept things going on in their old channels. But instead of this, his first act was to seize the pruning-knife, and not rashly, but wisely, he cut down the expenses of the department millions of dollars.

His report at the opening of Congress, gives a clear, compact statement of the military situation, unburdened with theories and recommendations of his own. Stating facts so that Congress could act intelligently, was better than any mere personal opinion. Though wishing to reduce the expenses of the Government as much as possible, he would not even recommend the discontinuance of the Freedmen's Bureau. Although the expenditure had been over $3,000,000, yet he says: "No recommendation is made at the present time respecting the continuance or discontinuance of this Bureau. During the session of Congress, facts may develop themselves requiring special legislation in the premises, when the necessary recommendations may be made."

In this single sentence, one can see the reason for his strange reticence on political questions. "*Facts may develop themselves,*" is the key to this silence that has offended so many. Senator Wade once said that he tried to get his political views, but when he talked politics Grant *talked horse*. The leaders of both parties for a long while denounced or sneered at this want of an opinion, or fear of expressing it, as they termed it. No man, they said, was fit to be President who had not fixed, decided opinions. In ordinary times one naturally has fixed opinions on matters that divide parties, but in the chaotic state of the South no man could tell what new phase it would present, requiring consequently a corresponding change in measures. Grant, however, was unmoved either by expostulations, entreaties, or threats. He never in war laid down a campaign in all its details; certain outlines were fixed, but he changed his plans and marches and battles as circumstances changed; and he wants to be left free to act correspondingly in civil matters. He has not sought the nomination for the Presidency—has not even said he would accept it if tendered him. He has said distinctly that he did not wish to be President, and in that he shows his wisdom; for that high office is not only beset with untold annoyances, but is of short duration, while the position he holds as Lieutenant-General is far more desirable in itself, and lasts for a lifetime. He has said moreover, if he should accept the office, it would

be from the same motive that prompted him
to accept command in the army—to serve his
country.   The position, high or low, is of second-
ary consequence—he must see first how he can
be of benefit to the country in occupying it.
And we believe that, if any political party attempts to hamper him with platforms of mere
measures that will prevent his acting as he
shall deem the public interest requires, he will
refuse to be President.   If a few leaders expect
him to be a mere machine, the wires of which
they pull, they have grievously misunderstood
his character.   His main views he never con-
ceals.   His platform is broad as his character.   The restoration of the Union to peace
and prosperity is its foundation.   How pitiful
do mere factions appear when contrasted with
this single-hearted, lofty patriotism.   To the careful reader of history, no truth is plainer than that
factions can never bring the country out of its present chaotic, perilous condition.   If the people
cannot rise to the high level that Gen. Grant
occupies, and from which he will not be forced by
threats or flatteries, then we must add our name
to the long, sad roll of Governments that have
fallen before contending factions.

We are not speaking of Gen. Grant politically,
but historically—defending him from the attacks
that have been made on him.   As a man, whether

President or not, we assert that his course is right, his example noble, and one that ought to be followed.

The people of a country may have their prejudices or passions played upon by unscrupulous political leaders, till their judgments are warped, and misguided action follows. But the hour of disenthralment will surely come, and the true, unselfish patriot will receive the eulogies of those who traduced him. The laurels he deserved in life, sometimes, alas; fall only on his grave, or the grave of the republic; yet, Time, in the end, vindicates the right.

CHAPTER XXVI.

AMID the bitter feeling of party that has characterized Congress and distracted the country for the last three years, it seemed impossible that Grant could draw up a report of the condition and wants of the South, or afterwards act as Secretary of War, without having abuse from one side or the other heaped upon him. But so free was he from all mere party bias himself, so sincere and apparent his desire for truth, and so simple and straightforward his whole conduct, that even party rancor was compelled to silence. This fact alone is the highest encomium on his integrity and ability that can be pronounced.

But that such a prominent figure as he, could forever remain in that vortex of passion and party hate—Washington—where plots and counterplots, and threats, and flatteries, and cunning, and falsehood have full scope, without in some way being drawn into it, was impossible. Filling the office of Secretary of War with marked ability and integrity, it turned out that he was not put there for those qualities, but to take the cross-fire of the President and Senate, or, in other words, be a rock on which both should hammer while settling their personal quarrel.

But when the Senate, on its assembling, refused to sanction the removal of Stanton, Grant quietly vacated the office. This was the signal of a storm. It was stated that Grant had agreed not to give up the office, but compel Stanton to resort to legal measures to get it, and thus compel the Tenure of Office bill to be taken to the Supreme Court, where its constitutionality could be decided. The papers teemed with rumors and assertions affecting, as Grant said, "his personal honor," and a correspondence ensued between him and the President, in which they stand diametrically opposite in regard to certain facts that took place in a Cabinet meeting where the question of Stanton's reinstatement by the Senate was discussed.

The entire correspondence is too long to be inserted here. The following, however, is substantially the version of the affair as given by Grant:

" When the question came up as to what course should be pursued in case the Senate did not concur in the suspension of Stanton, Grant replied

that he thought Mr. Stanton would have to appeal to the courts to reinstate him; adding, however, that should he change his views on this
point he would inform the President. Subsequently, after closely examining the terms of the
Tenure of Office bill, he came to the conclusion
that he could not, without violating the law, refuse to vacate the office of Secretary of War the
moment Mr. Stanton was reinstated by the Senate, even though the President should, which he
did not do, order him to remain. He therefore
notified the President of the decision to which he
had come on this point. The President urged in
reply that, as Mr. Stanton had been suspended,
and Gen. Grant appointed under authority granted by the Constitution, and not under any Act of
Congress, Grant could not be governed by the
Act. Grant rejoined that the law, whether con-
stitutional or not, was binding upon him until set
aside by the proper tribunal. So matters stood
for some days, until Mr. Stanton, with whom
Gen. Grant had held no communication, reassum-
ed the duties of his office, when Grant, who no
longer considered himself to be Secretary of War,
was requested by the President to attend a Cabinet meeting on the 14th of January."

At this meeting the President on his part affirms
that Grant acknowledged "that he had agreed
either to hold on to the post until the courts

otherwise decided, or to resign before the Senate had taken action;" that after the promise was given, he agreed to another conference, but did not attend; that the members of the Cabinet coincided with him in his views, &c.

Grant, in reply, denies the correctness of this statement of the matter *in toto.* Astonished at the explicit charges of the President, he adds: " You know that we parted on Saturday, the 11th ult., without any promise on my part, either express or implied, that I would hold on to the office of Secretary of War *ad interim* against the action of the Senate; or, declining to do so myself, would surrender it to you before such action was had; or that I would see you at any fixed time on the subject." After going on to say that for him to have pursued any other course than the one he did, would have been in violation of law, and subjected him to fine and perhaps imprisonment, he concludes: " When my honor as a soldier and integrity as a man have been so violently assailed, pardon me for saying that I can but regard this whole matter, from beginning to end, as an attempt to involve me in the resistance of law, for which you hesitated to assume the responsibility, and thus to destroy my character before the country. I am, in a measure, confirmed in this conclusion by your recent orders directing me to disobey orders from the Sec-

retary of War, my superior and your subordinate."

To meet this direct denial of Grant, the President then gave the versions of the several members
of the Cabinet with regard to this arrangement
between Grant and himself. Welles, McCulloch,
and Randall, say that in all "important particulars, the President's statement accords with their
recollection of the conversation." Mr. Browning
gives a more lengthy statement, and says distinctly, that the last interview closed with the
understanding between Grant and the President,
that no *definite conclusion had been reached;* but
that they would have another conference, which,
however, never did take place. He also makes
the following remarkable admission: "I did not
understand General Grant as denying nor as admitting these statements [of the President as to
what had previously passed between them] in the
form and full extent to which the President made
them. His admission was rather indirect and
circumstantial, though I did not understand it to
be an evasive one." Mr. Seward states, that at this
meeting Grant remarked, by way of explanation
for his not attending the proposed conference: "I
was engaged on Sunday, the 12th, with General
Sherman, and also on Monday, in regard to the
War Department matter, with a hope, though he
did not say with an effort, to procure an amicable

settlement of the affair of Mr. Stanton; and he still hoped that it would be brought about."

Enough of this is given to show the points at issue between the President and Grant, and the character of the testimony by which the former sustains his statements. This testimony, it seems, is contradictory. Mr. Browning, though more circumstantial and detailed than the others, does not corroborate the President in his strong, explicit assertions respecting the promise made by Grant. This one fact, it seems to us, furnishes the key to the solution of the whole discrepancy. It exhibits, it seems to us, a blind partisan spirit rather than a calm judgment, or proper respect, for either party to assert, as so many of the adherents of each do, that one or the other is guilty of a direct falsehood. It is evident, from the want of emphatic direct testimony, such as a court of law would demand (the whole being a sort of " general recollection "), as well as from the fact that they " recollect" on some vital points differently, and different from the President, that the whole matter was nothing more than *a general understanding on both sides*. Whether Johnson hesitated to press an explicit agreement, lest Grant's suspicions should be aroused and he refuse point blank to take any part in the transaction at all, or the latter declined to bring the matter to the same definite conclusion from disinclination to come in direct conflict

with his commander-in-chief, is of little consequence.   Let the causes be what they may, the
fact is evident from the testimony and the correspondence, that while the "understanding" on
either side might have been this or that, there
was no actual agreement entered into.   Now
any impartial man who is at all acquainted with
human nature, knows how easily two parties, each
looking at things from his own stand-point, can
come to diametrically opposite conclusions respecting how much the other was compromised
in a general conversation.   Any business man
understands this.   But if great disappointment
succeeds on one side, this general understanding
always becomes downright assertion.

The President was bitterly disappointed, and
hence felt keenly, and, regretting that he had not
acted more promptly and definitely, naturally
concluded that Grant had deceived him.

But, independent of all this, every just man
must admit, without argument, that one single
act, utterly at variance with the whole life and
character of a man, can never stand against
him without the strongest and most positive
and impregnable testimony.   Now, if there is
one thing that distinguishes Grant above all other
men, it is that he is incapable of low cunning,
underhand plotting, hypocrisy, and deceit.   He
has never been charged with or even suspected of

these; and to say that such loose testimony as that furnished by the Cabinet makes him such a character in this solitary case, is neither just nor honorable. Besides, there is a single fact that seems to be entirely overlooked, which completely disproves the charge. All agree that he endeavored to get Sherman to help him prevail on Stanton to resign, and thus relieve the President and the country of the shameful, humiliating affair. This does not look like low conspiracy against the President, but the act of a friend of all, and of the country. Judging Stanton by himself, he thought there was little doubt that as soon as he had won the victory over the President, his own delicacy and regard for the peace of the country would prompt him to resign. That he was mistaken, does not affect the purity of his motives. The act surely shows that he was not guilty of hypocrisy, but wanted to adjust the matter peaceably and to the satisfaction of all parties.

At all events he did right. He would have been untrue to himself had he allowed the President to make a cat's-paw of him—involve him in lawsuits, and subject him perhaps to imprisonment, and doubtless to odious legislation. His duty was to keep aloof from such strifes as were here intended to be forced upon him.

Another cause of complaint against Grant has been, that he refused to sustain Hancock, whom the President put over the military department

of Louisiana, in place of Sheridan. That Hancock is an upright man, and too elevated in sentiment and principle to let partisanship affect his
action, no one who knows him will doubt. It is
equally plain that his action which Grant refused
to approve, was intended to serve the public welfare; but it nevertheless was the exercise of
military over the civil authority, which Grant
always condemned, unless there was absolute
necessity in the case. Moreover, Hancock himself had taken this ground when he assumed command of the department, and been extolled by the
enemies of Grant for it. Yet these very persons,
who had declaimed loudest against the military
despotism exercised over the South, complained
of Grant for refusing to sanction it. The whole
matter is comprised in the following statement of
Grant, and at the same time reveals the spirit
that animated him. He says: "The office of Recorder of the City of New Orleans is elective by
the people; but in case of a vacancy it is made
the duty by law of the Boards of Aldermen and
Assistant Aldermen, in joint meeting, to elect
viva voce a person to fill the vacancy. The office
of Recorder of the Second District of New Orleans was, by the Supreme Court of Louisiana,
adjudged vacant; and the City of New Orleans
was ordered to be notified to proceed according to
law to elect a Recorder for said district, which

judgment was made final January 20, 1868. In pursuance of this order of the Court, the Board of Aldermen and Assistant Aldermen met in joint session on the 4th of February, 1868, to elect a Recorder for said Second District. At this session was read a communication written by Capt. Chandlee, Assistant Secretary of Civil Affairs, and purporting to be by your direction, inviting attention to the first and second sections of the Supplementary Reconstruction Act of Congress, passed July 19, 1867, and to paragraph two, Special Order No. 7, from Headquarters Fifth Military District, dated March 28, 1867. At the date of this communication, namely, January 25, 1868, and before any action of either branch of the Council had been had relative to the election therein referred to, you were absent from the City of New Orleans, in the State of Texas. This communication did not in terms forbid the election; neither did the sections of the Act to which it referred, except as it might be inferred from the second section, wherein the District Commander is empowered, under certain restrictions, to fill vacancies occasioned by death, resignation, or otherwise. Section nine of this Act, as well as the original Reconstruction Act of March 2, 1867, recognizes the right of the State and municipal authorities to appoint and elect officers under certain restrictions and limitations; but the exercise of this right is subject to the authority of the District Commander. Subsequent to the issuing of Special Order No. 7, referred to, and during the administration of Gens. Sheridan and Mower, the City Council of New Orleans did in some cases fill vacancies in corporation offices under the provisions of section 24 of the city charter of New Orleans in the same manner as is provided for filling the vacancy in the office of Recorder, and after you assumed command the office of City Attorney was filled under the same authority and in the same manner. No exception was taken in any case by any of the District Commanders to such action. On assuming command of the district, you announced in General Order No. 40, of November 29, 1867, that it was your purpose to preserve peace and quiet in your command, and that as a means to this great end you regarded the maintenance of the civil authorities in the faithful execution of the laws as the most efficient under existing circumstances; also, that when the civil authorities are ready and willing to perform their duties the military power should cease to lead, and the civil administration resume its natural and rightful dominion. Under this statement of facts the City Council of New Orleans might reasonably have presumed it to be their right and duty, especially under the order of the Court, and your Order No. 40, to fill the vacancy in the office of Recorder, as it appears they did from your report of this case, dated February 15, 1868. The same facts, too, in connection with the printed report of their proceedings, embraced in your report of February 15, preclude the presumption of any intended contempt of the military authority by the members of the City Council."

Although in very many cases it would evidently be for the best for a one-man power to step in and prevent the wrong contemplated by officers who had been elected by the people; yet Grant believes that in a republican government there is but one course to pursue—let the people remedy their own wrongs by removing those who have abused their confidence. Indeed this is the only course that can be pursued in a republic—any other is despotism.

In the work now completed we have followed General Grant from his early boyhood—when, the son of a poor tanner, he commenced life in the West—to the present time, when he stands at the head of our armies, and is the most prominent candidate mentioned in connection with the Presidency. That life which has embraced so many and various scenes and fortunes, is singularly blameless, and should it pass on into the vortex of partisan hate and be subjected to the trying tests of a heated political contest, will still remain untarnished.

18

HIS CHARACTER.

We think that the main points of his character are clearly revealed by his own acts.

His courage is undoubted, though it is not of that fiery, chivalric kind which dazzles the public eye. He is not borne up in action by the enthusiasm and pride of the warrior; but apparently unconscious of danger, makes battle a business, which is to be performed with a clear head and steady nerves. His coolness in deadly peril is wonderful. What we once said of Marshal Ney applies forcibly to him. "In battle he could literally shut up his mind to the one object he had in view. The overthrow of the enemy absorbed every thought within him, and he had none to give to danger or death. Where he placed his mind he held it, and not all the uproar and confusion of battle could divert it. He would not allow himself to see any thing else than the one object in view, and hence was almost as insensible to the dangers around him as a deaf and dumb and blind man would be. He himself once expressed the true secret of his calmness, when, after one of those exhibitions of composure amid the most horrid carnage, an officer asked him if he *never* felt fear, he replied: 'I *never* had time.' This was another way of saying, that fear and danger had nothing to do with the object before him, and, therefore, he would not suffer his mind to rest on them for a single moment." This wonderful power of concentrating all his faculties on a given point, is strikingly characteristic of Grant. In tenacity of will, also, he is like Ney, *who would not be beaten;* and in the last extremity rallied like a dying man for a final blow, and then planted it where the clearest practical wisdom indicated. Like Ney, too, he is naturally of a sluggish, indolent nature, which requires great crises to thoroughly arouse.

We cannot better express our views of this last peculiarity of Grant, than by repeating what we once before said of him. There are some men in this world possessing immense mental power, who yet, from mere inertness, pass through life with poor success. Lighter natures outstrip them in the race for wealth or position, and the strength they really possess is never known, because it has never been called out. It never *is* called out by ordinary events. They were made for great emergencies, and if these do not arise, they seem almost made in vain; at least these extraordinary powers appear to be given them in vain. Grant is one of these. He is like a great wheel, on which mere rills of water may drop forever without moving it, or if they succeed in disturbing its equilibrium, only make it accomplish a partial revolution. It needs an immense body of water to make it roll, and then it revolves with a power and majesty that awes the beholder. No slight obstructions then can arrest its mighty sweep. Acquiring momentum with each revolution, it crushes to atoms every thing thrust before it to check its motion.

One would naturally think that such a character would pay but little attention to mere detail, contenting itself with general instructions and movements. But this is not so with Grant. When once awaked to action, his whole being is alive, and he wants to be omnipresent. Thus, in the campaign of Vicksburg, he was constantly performing the duties of subordinates, fearing that unless he personally superintended every thing his plans would miscarry. Nothing escaped his memory, or inspection. Hence, he was often on the picket line all alone, endeavoring to ascertain, from personal inspection, more of the enemy's position and plans than he could obtain from the reports of his officers. On one of these occasions he came near falling into the hands of the enemy. It was at Chattanooga, while he was preparing for the battle of Missionary Ridge. Wishing to get a nearer view of the enemy, he often rode out on the picket line, and once happened to be on the eastern bank of Chattanooga creek, when a party of rebel soldiers were drawing water on the other side. They wore blue coats; and, thinking they were his own men, Grant asked them to whose command they belonged. They answered, "Longstreet's corps;" whereupon Grant called out: "What are you doing in those coats, then?" The rebels replied: "Oh! all our corps wear blue." This was a fact, which Grant had forgotten. The rebels then scrambled up on their own side of the stream, little thinking that they had been talking with the commander of the national army.

Another striking peculiarity of Grant is his correctness of judgment under adverse circumstances and conflicting views. Sherman once told him that he thought he would fail in "grand strategy," but he found that his strong common sense supplied the place of the study of this science. This is but another way of saying that Grant's judgment is so correct that he seldom fails to do the right thing under whatever new circumstances he may be placed. His confidence in this judgment is wonderful—not the confidence of self-conceit, but of conscious power. He never hesitated to assume any responsibility. In his final campaign against Vicksburg he acted against the advice of every officer whom he consulted, and against the known views of the General-in-chief and the President. Not only was it conceived by himself alone, but in carrying it to its successful termination he never called a council of war.

The victories he has won are evidence to the whole world of his great ability as a military leader; but he has also shown a remarkable power in one respect that has hardly been commented upon—the power of handling large armies. Napoleon declared that not more that one or two generals beside himself in all Europe, could manœuvre a hundred thousand men on the field of battle. Grant did more than this; and the manner in which he handled the Army of the Potomac on the route from the Rapidan to Richmond, was more astonishing than the winning of a great battle. The way he swung it from Spottsylvania to the North Anna, without having his flank crushed in, and from thence to the Pamunkey, and, last of all, from the Chickahominy, for fifty miles, across the James, to Petersburg, right from under the nose of the enemy, and yet never be attacked, shows a capacity in wielding enormous forces possessed by few men in the world.

In this change of base to James River, in the presence of the enemy, he exhibited the skill of a great commander as much as in any battle he ever fought.

Napoleon says a change of base is " the ablest manœuvre taught by military art." This proof of Grant's great ability is one that cannot be appreciated by those who never made military movements a study. Hence President Lincoln, in summing up Grant's character, entirely overlooked the power of combination—the mental breadth, comprehensiveness and administrative power which he possessed, and put foremost that which was really a subordinate quality. He says: "the great thing about Grant, I take it, is his perfect coolness and persistency of purpose. I judge he is not easily excited—which is a great element in an officer, and he has the *grit* of a bull-dog! Once let him get his teeth *in*, and nothing can shake him off." Now it is unquestionably true of Grant that he possesses the characteristics here mentioned. But these alone can never make a great general. Obstinacy without the ability to plan and control, fails as often as it succeeds. So coolness and self-possession will not avail unless connected with mental activity and the power to take in, comprehend, and mould the tossing, conflicting elements around him. Thought often wins battles more than the sword.

In this connection it is pleasant to give the views of an intimate, beloved friend, now no more—McPherson. A noble man himself—universally beloved and esteemed for his private, as for his public qualities, those views possess rare value:

"Lieutenant-General U. S. Grant I regard as one of the most remarkable men of our country. Without aspiring to be a genius, or possessing those characteristics which impress one forcibly at first sight, his sterling good sense, calm judgment, and persistency of purpose, more than compensate for those dashing, brilliant qualities which are apt to captivate at a first glance. To know and appreciate Gen. Grant fully, one ought to be a member of his military family.

"Though possessing a remarkable reticence as far as military operations are concerned, he is frank and affable, converses well, and has a peculiarly retentive memory. When not oppressed with the cares of his position, he is very fond of talking, telling anecdotes, &c.

"His purity of character is unimpeachable, and his patriotism of the most exalted kind. He is generous to a fault, humane and true, and a steadfast friend to those whom he deems worthy of his confidence, and can always be relied upon in case of emergency."

What McPherson says of his patriotism and purity of character, knowing him as long and intimately as he did, should alone outweigh all the charges that party hate or personal passion may bring against him.

We are told that "he that ruleth his spirit is greater than he that taketh a city." Gen. Grant has shown that he can do this. Taking cities is not an uncommon exploit; but this thorough control of one's self, under the most unfavorable circumstances, is little short of a miracle. He has not been betrayed into a foolish word or act, or indulged in an angry expression, or exhibited a revengeful spirit towards his enemies. He has never sought promotion, indulged in no recriminations under slanderous charges, nor used his power to humble an enemy. Though so far above the people in position, he feels as one of them, and wears his honors as but few of our poor fallen race can wear them. It is these qualities that, though so undemonstrative himself, make him universally beloved.

Time will increase, instead of diminish that affection, and, side by side with Washington, his great services and great patriotism will remain like two marble columns to commemorate his fame.

————o————

Since the first edition of the present work was published, General Grant, as then anticipated, has been elected President of the United States, and is now a candidate for a second term. Although at that time there was no doubt of his integrity of purpose and sincere desire to secure the prosperity of the country, there was some fear that his entire disconnection from politics, from his youth up, might lead him into some errors. But in this respect his record compares favorably with the best statesmen who have gone before him. When he first assumed high command in the army, General Sherman said he feared that he would fail through want of knowledge of "grand strategy," but that his strong common-sense more than made up for any deficiency in the study or experience of this branch of military science. So in his political career as head of the

* Eight pages are here added to make up for the omission in paging the engravings.

18*

nation, that same common-sense has proved to be wiser than the statesmanship that has surrounded him and often crippled his efforts. It is seen, now that the hostile parties are arrayed against each other; that had his views been honestly carried out by those on whom the responsibility rested, the opposition to-day would scarcely have a plank out of which to make their platform. The Tenure-of-office bill, which was an outrage, he at the outset asked Congress to repeal. The same spirit which prompted him to treat the conquered Lee with a kindness that displeased many of his most ardent admirers, and also called forth those memorable words, "Let us have peace," made him desire and advise in his first message a general amnesty. That it was not done is certainly not his fault. After four years of delay, Congress at the last moment endeavored to retrieve its error, and reluctantly acknowledged the superior statesmanship of their chief. Reform in the civil service was another crying evil, and this, too, he has persistently urged. The reduction of the public debt he has constantly kept in view, while he has never endeavored, from any personal consideration, to force the country into an attitude with a foreign nation, contrary to the expressed wish of the people. A man must be judged by what he tried to do, and if left alone would have done, and not by what he failed to do through the lack of that assistance which he had a right to expect, and without which he was powerless to act. Impartial history will do him that justice which partisanship never renders.

APPENDIX.

———•••———

HEADQUARTERS ARMIES OF THE UNITED STATES,
WASHINGTON, *June 26th*, 1865.

Hon. E. M. Stanton, Secretary of War:

SIR: I have the honor to transmit herewith a full and complete return of the battle of Belmont, Missouri, fought Nov. 7, 1861, which I would respectfully ask to have substituted in the place of my report of that action of date Nov. 19, 1861, made to Gen. S. Williams, Assistant Adjutant-General to the General-in-Chief.

Very respectfully, your obedient servant,

U. S. GRANT, Lieutenant-General.

Referred to the Adjutant-General for publication with the accompany report.

E. M. STANTON, Secretary of War.

June 27, 1865.

HEADQUARTERS DISTRICT SOUTHEAST MISSOURI,
CAIRO, ILL., *November 17th*, 1861.

GENERAL: The following order was received from Headquarters Western Department:

ST. LOUIS, *Nov.* 1, 1861.

Gen. Grant, Commanding at Cairo:

You are hereby directed to hold your whole command ready to march at an hour's notice, until further orders; and you will take particular care to be amply supplied with transportation and ammunition. You are also directed to make demonstrations with your troops along both sides of the river toward Charleston, Norfolk, and Blandville, and to keep your columns constantly moving back and against these places, without, however, attacking the enemy.

Very respectfully, &c.,

CHAUNCEY McKEEVER,

Assistant Adjutant-General.

At the same time I was notified that similar instructions had been sent to Brig.-Gen. C. F. Smith, commanding Paducah, Ky., and was directed to communicate with him freely as to my movements, that his might be coöperative.

On the 2d of the same month, and before it was possible for any considerable preparation to have been made for the execution of this order, the following telegraphic despatch was received:

ST. LOUIS, *November* 2, 1861.

To Brig.-Gen. Grant:

Jeff. Thompson is at Indian Ford of the St. Francis River, twenty-five miles below Greenville, with about three thousand men. Col. Carlin has started with force from Pilot Knob. Send a force from Cape Girardeau and Bird's Point to assist Carlin in driving Thompson into Arkansas. By order of

Maj.·Gen. FREMONT.

C. McKEEVER, Assistant Adjutant-General.

The forces I determined to send from Bird's Point were immediately designated, and Col. R. J. Oglesby, Eighth Illinois Volunteers, assigned to the command, under the following detailed instructions:

HEADQUARTERS DISTRICT SOUTHEAST MISSOURI, }
CAIRO, *November* 3d, 1861. }

Col. R. J. Oglesby, Commanding, &c., Bird's Point, Mo.:

You will take command of an expedition consisting of your regiment, four companies of the Eleventh Illinois, all of the Eighteenth and Twenty-ninth, three companies of cavalry from Bird's Point (to be selected and notified by yourself), and a section of Schwartz's Battery, artillery, and proceed to Commerce, Missouri. From Commerce you will strike for Sikeston — Mr. Cropper acting as guide. From there go in pursuit of a rebel force understood to be three thousand strong, under Jeff. Thompson, now at Indian Ford, on the St. Francis River.

An expedition has already left Ironton, Mo., to attack this force. Should they learn that they have left that place, it will not be necessary for you to go there, but pursue the enemy in any direction he may go; always being cautious not to fall in with an unlooked-for foe too strong for the command under you.

The object of the expedition is to destroy this force, and the manner of doing it is left largely at your discretion; believing it better not to trammel you with instructions.

Transportation will be furnished you for fourteen days' rations and four or five days' forage. All you may require outside of this must be furnished by the country through which you pass. In taking supplies you will be careful to select a proper officer to press them, and require a receipt to be given, and the articles pressed to be accounted for in the same manner as if purchased.

You are particularly enjoined to allow no foraging by your men. It is demoralizing in the extreme, and is apt to make open enemies where they would not otherwise exist.

U. S. GRANT, Brigadier-General.

Col. J. B. Plummer, Eleventh Missouri Volunteers, commanding at Cape Girardeau, was directed to send one regiment in the direction of Bloomfield with a view to attracting the attention of the enemy.

The forces under Col. Oglesby were all got off on the evening of the 3d.

On the 5th, a telegram was received from headquarters, St. Louis, stating that the enemy was reinforcing Price's army, from Columbus, by way of White River, and directing that the demonstration that had been ordered against Columbus be immediately made. Orders were accordingly at once given to the troops under my command that remained at Cairo, Bird's Point, and Fort Holt. A letter was also sent to Brig.-Gen. C. F. Smith, commanding at Paducah, requesting him to make a demonstration at the same time against Columbus.

To more effectually attain the object of the demonstration against the enemy at Belmont and Columbus, I determined on the morning of the 6th, to temporarily change the direction of Col. Oglesby's column towards New Madrid, and also to send a small force under Col. W. H. L. Wallace, 11th Illinois Volunteers, to Charleston, Mo., to ultimately join Col. Oglesby. In accordance with this determination, I addressed Col. Oglesby the following communication :

CAIRO, Nov. 6, 1861.

Col. R. J. Oglesby, Commanding Expedition :

On receipt of this, turn your column toward New Madrid. When you arrive at the nearest point to Columbus from which there is a road to that place, communicate with me at Belmont.

U. S. GRANT, Brigadier-General.

Which was sent to Col. Wallace with the following letter :

CAIRO, Nov. 6, 1861.

Col. W. H. L. Wallace, Bird's Point, Mo. :

Herewith I send you an order to Col. Oglesby to change the direction of his column towards New Madrid, halting to communicate with me at Belmont from the nearest point on his road.

I desire you to get up the Charleston expedition ordered for to-morrow, to start to-night, taking two days' rations with them. You will accompany them to Charleston, and get Col. Oglesby's instructions to him by a messenger, if practicable, and when he is near enough you may join him. For this purpose you may substitute the remainder of your regiment in place of an equal amount from Col. Marsh's. The two days' rations carried by your men in haversacks will enable you to join Col. Oglesby's command, and there you will find rations enough for several days more should they be necessary. You may take a limited number of tents, and at Charleston press wagons to carry them to the main column. There you will find sufficient transportation to release the pressed wagons.

U. S. GRANT, Brigadier-General.

On the evening of the 6th I left this place on steamers, with McClernand's brigade, consisting of the 27th Regiment Illinois Volunteers, Col. N. B. Buford; 30th Regiment Illinois Volunteers, Col. Philip B. Foulke; 31st Regiment Illinois Volunteers, Col. John A. Logan; Dollins' Company Independent Illinois Cavalry, Capt. J. J. Dollins; Delano's Company Adams County Illinois Cavalry, Lieut. J. R. Catlin. Dougherty's brigade, consisting of the 22d Regiment Illinois Volunteers, Lieut.-Col. H. E. Hart; 7th Regiment Iowa Volunteers, Col. J. G. Lanman; amounting to 3,114 men of all arms, to make the demonstration against Columbus. I proceeded down the river to a point nine miles below here, where we lay until next morning, on the Kentucky shore, which served to distract the enemy and lead him to suppose that he was to be attacked in his strongly fortified position at Columbus.

About two o'clock on the morning of the 7th, I received information from Col. W. H. L. Wallace at Charleston (sent by a messenger on board steamer *W. H. B.*), that he had learned from a reliable Union man that the enemy had been crossing from Columbus to Belmont the day before, for the purpose of following after and cutting off the forces under Col. Oglesby.

Such a move on his part seemed to me more than probable, and gave at once a twofold importance to my demonstration against the enemy, namely: the prevention of reenforcements to Gen. Price, and the cutting off of the two columns that I had sent, in pursuance of directions, from this place and Cape Girardeau in pursuit of Jeff. Thompson. This information determined me to attack vigorously his forces at Belmont; knowing that, should we be repulsed, we could reëmbark without difficulty under the protection of the gunboats. The following order was given:

ON BOARD STEAMER BELLE MEMPHIS, }
Nov. 7, 1861—2 o'clock A. M. }

SPECIAL ORDER:— The troops composing the present expedition from this place will move promptly at six o'clock this morning. The gunboats will take the advance, and be followed by the 1st brigade, under command of Brig.-Gen. John A. McClernand, composed of all the troops from Cairo and Fort Holt. The 2d Brigade, comprising the remainder of the troops of the expedition, commanded by Col. John Dougherty, will follow. The entire force will debark at the lowest point on the Missouri shore where a landing can be effected in security from the rebel batteries. The point of debarkation will be designated by Capt. Walke, commanding naval forces.

By order of
U. S. GRANT, Brig.-Gen.
JOHN A. RAWLINS, A. A. G.

Promptly at the hour designated we proceeded down the river to a point just out of range of the rebel batteries at Columbus, and debarked on the Missouri shore. From here the troops were marched, with skirmishers well in advance, by flank for about one mile towards Belmont, and there formed in line of battle. One battalion had been left as a reserve near the transports. Two companies from each regiment were thrown forward as skirmishers, to ascertain the position of the enemy, and about nine o'clock met and engaged him. The balance of my force, with the exception of the reserve, was promptly thrown forward, and drove the enemy foot by foot, and from tree to tree, back to his encampment on the river bank, a distance of over two miles. Here he had strengthened his position by felling the timber for several hundred yards around his camp, making a sort of abatis. Our men charged through this, driving the enemy under cover of the bank, and many of them into their transports in quick time, leaving us in possession of every thing not exceedingly portable.

Belmont is situated on low ground, and every foot is commanded by the guns on the opposite shore, and, of course, could not be held for a single hour after the enemy became aware of the withdrawal of his troops. Having no wagons with me, I could move but little of the captured property, consequently gave orders for the destruction of every thing that could not be removed, and an immediate return to our transports. Tents, blankets, &c., were set on fire and destroyed, and our return march commenced, taking his artillery and a large number of captured horses and prisoners with us. Three pieces of artillery being drawn by hand, and one by an inefficient team, were spiked and left on the road; two were brought to this place.

We had but fairly got under way when the enemy, having received reinforcements, rallied under cover of the river bank and the woods on the point of land in the bend of the river above us, and made his appearance between us and our transports, evidently with a design of cutting off our return to them.

Our troops were not in the least discouraged, but charged the enemy and again defeated him. We then, with the exception of the Twenty-seventh Illinois, Colonel N. B. Buford commanding, reached our transports and embarked without further molestation. While waiting for the arrival of this regiment and to get some of our wounded from a field hospital near by, the enemy, having crossed fresh troops from Columbus, again made his appearance on the river bank and commenced firing upon our transports. The fire was returned by our men from the decks of the steamers, and also by the gun-boats, with terrible effect, compelling him to retire in the direction of Belmont. In the meantime Colonel Buford, although he had received orders to return with the main force, took the Charleston road from Belmont and came in on the road leading to Bird's Point, where we had formed the line of battle in the morning. At this point, to avoid the shells from the gunboats that were beginning to fall among his men, he took a blind path direct to the river, and followed a wood road up its bank, and thereby avoided meeting the enemy, who were retiring by the main road. On his appearance on the river bank a steamer was dropped down and took his command on board, without his having participated or lost a man in the enemy's attempt to cut us off from our transports.

Notwithstanding the crowded state of our trans-ports, the only loss we sustained from the enemy's fire upon them, was three men wounded, one of whom be-longed to one of the boats.

Our loss in killed on the field was eighty-five, three hundred and one wounded, (many of them, however, slightly,) and ninety-nine missing. Of the wounded one hundred and twenty-five fell into the hands of the enemy. Nearly all the missing were from the Seventh Iowa regiment, which suffered more severely than any other. All the troops behaved with great gallantry, which was in a degree attributable to the coolness and presence of mind of their officers, particularly the Colo-nels commanding.

General McClernand was in the midst of danger throughout the engagement, and displayed both cool-ness and judgment. His horse was three times shot under him.

Colonel Dougherty, of the twenty-second Illinois volunteers, commanding the Second Brigade, by his coolness and bravery, entitles himself to be named among the most competent of officers for command of troops in battle. * * * *

In pursuance of my request, General Smith, commanding at Paducah, sent on the 7th instant a force to Mayfield, Kentucky, and another in the direction of Columbus, with orders not to approach nearer, however, than twelve or fifteen miles of that place. I also sent a small force on the Kentucky side toward Columbus, under Colonel John Cook, 7th Illinois Volunteers, with orders not to go beyond Elliott's Mills, distant some twelve miles from Columbus. These forces, having marched to the points designated in their orders, returned without having met serious resistance.

On the evening of the 7th, information of the result of the engagement at Belmont was sent to Colonel Oglesby, commanding expedition against Jeff. Thompson, and order, to return to Bird's Point by way of Charleston, Missouri. Before these reached him, however, he had learned that Jeff. Thompson had left the place where he was reported to be when the expedition started (he having gone toward New Madrid or Arkansas), and had determined to return. The same information was sent to the commanding officer at Cape Girardeau, with directions for the troops to be brought back that had gone out from that place.

From all the information I have been able to obtain since the engagement, the enemy's loss in killed and wounded was much greater than ours. We captured one hundred and seventy-five prisoners, all his artillery and transportation, and destroyed his entire camp and garrison equipage. Independent of the injuries inflicted upon him, and the prevention of his reinforcing Price, or sending a force to cut off the expeditions against Jeff. Thompson, the confidence inspired in our troops by the engagement will be of incalculable benefit to us in the future. Very respectfully, your obedient servant, U. S. GRANT, Brig.-General.

Brigadier-General Seth Williams, Assistant Adjutant-General, Washington, D. C.

General Sherman's letter to Grant previous to entering on the campaign below Vicksburg, in which he tries to dissuade him from undertaking it, and of which we spoke in the body of the work, Col. Badeau says, was never preserved, and he was therefore indebted for a copy of it to General Sherman himself. It is probably the paper that the former is said to have handed back to him after the fall of Vicksburg. It shows what kind of opposition Grant had to encounter in venturing on that extraordinary campaign, and how fearful the responsibility he dared to assume.

GENERAL SHERMAN TO COLONEL RAWLINS.

HEADQUARTERS FIFTEENTH ARMY CORPS, }
CAMP NEAR VICKSBURG, *April* 8, 1863. }

Col. J. A. Rawlins, A. A. G. to General Grant:

SIR: I would most respectfully suggest, for reasons which I will not name, that General Grant call on his corps commanders for their opinions, concise and positive, on the best general plan of campaign. Unless this be done, there are men who will, in any result falling below the popular standard, claim that their advice was unheeded, and that fatal consequences resulted therefrom. My own opinions are:

1. That the Army of the Tennessee is far in advance of the other grand armies.

2. That a corps from Missouri should forthwith be moved from St. Louis to the vicinity of Little Rock, Arkansas, supplies collected while the river is full, and land communication with Memphis opened *via* Des Ark on the White, and Madison on the St. Francis rivers.

3. That as much of Yazoo Pass, Coldwater, and Tallahatchie rivers as can be gained and fortified be

held, and the main army be transported thither by land and water; that the road back to Memphis be secured and reopened; and as soon as the waters subside, Grenada be attacked, and the swamp road across to Helena be patrolled by cavalry.

4. That the line of the Yallabusha be the base from which to operate against the points where the Mississippi Central crosses Big Black above Canton, and lastly where the Vicksburg and Jackson Railroad crosses the same river.

The capture of Vicksburg would result.

5. That a force be left in this vicinity, not to exceed ten thousand men, with only enough steamboats to float and transport them to any direct point. This force to be held always near enough to act with the gunboats, when the main army is known to be near Vicksburg, Haines' Bluff, or Yazoo City.

6. I do doubt the capacity of Willow bayou (which I estimate to be fifty miles long and very tortuous) for a military channel, capable of supporting an army large enough to operate against Jackson, Mississippi, or Black river bridge; and such a channel will be very valuable to a force coming from the west, which we must expect. Yet this canal will be most useful as the way to convey coals and supplies to a fleet that should navigate the reach between Vicksburg and Red river.

7. The chief reason for operating *solely* by water, was the season of the year and high water in Tallahatchie and Yallabusha. The spring is now here, and soon these springs will be no serious obstacle, save the ambuscades of the forest, and whatever works the enemy may have erected at or near Grenada. North Mississippi is too valuable to allow them to hold and make crops.

I make these suggestions, with the request that General Grant simply read them, and give them, as I know he will, a share of his thoughts. I would prefer he should not answer them, but merely give them as much or as little weight as they deserve.

General Grant's order for the guidance of the army when below Vicksburg:—

HEADQUARTERS DEPARTMENT OF THE TENNESSEE,
MILLIKEN'S BEND, LA., *April* 20, 1863.

Special Order No. 110.

* * * * * * *

VIII. The following orders are published for the information and guidance of the "Army in the Field," in its present movement to obtain a foothold on the east bank of the Mississippi river, from which Vicksburg can be approached by practicable roads.

1. The Thirteenth Army Corps, Major General John A. McClernand commanding, will constitute the right wing.

2. The Fifteenth Army Corps, Major General W. T. Sherman commanding, will constitute the left wing.

3. The Seventeenth Army Corps, Major General James B. McPherson commanding, will constitute the centre.

4. The order of march to New Carthage will be from right to left.

5. Reserves will be formed by divisions from each army corps, or an entire army corps will be held as a reserve, as necessity may require. When the reserve is formed by divisions, each division will remain under the immediate command of its respective corps commander, unless specially required for a particular emergency.

6. Troops will be required to bivouac till proper facilities can be afforded for the transportation of camp equipage.

7. In the present movement one tent will be allowed to each company for the protection of rations from rain; one wall tent for each regimental headquarters, one wall tent for each brigade headquarters, and one wall tent for each division headquarters. Corps commanders having the books and blanks of their respect-

ive commands to provide for, are authorized to take such tents as are absolutely necessary, but not to exceed the number allowed by General Orders No. 166, A. G. O. Series of 1862.

8. All the teams of the three army corps, under the immediate charge of the quartermasters bearing them on their returns, will constitute the train for carrying supplies and ordnance, and the authorized camp equipage of the army.

9. As fast as the Thirteenth Army Corps advances, the Seventeenth Army Corps will take its place; and it, in turn, will be followed in like manner by the Fifteenth Army Corps.

10. Two regiments from each army corps will be detailed by corps commanders, to guard the lines from Richmond to New Carthage.

11. General hospitals will be established, by the medical director, between Duckport and Milliken's bend. All sick and disabled soldiers will be left in these hospitals. Surgeons in charge of hospitals will report convalescents, as fast as they become fit for duty. Each corps commander will detail an intelligent and good drill officer, to remain behind to take charge of the convalescents of their respective corps; officers so detailed will organize the men under their charge into squads and companies, without regard to the regiments they belong to; and in the absence of convalescent commissioned officers to command them, will appoint non-commissioned officers or privates. The force so organized will constitute the guard of the line from Duckport to Milliken's bend. They will furnish all the guards and details required for general hospitals, and with the contrabands that may be about the camps, will furnish all the details for loading and unloading boats.

The movement of troops from Milliken's bend to New Carthage will be so conducted as to allow the transportation of ten days' supply of rations, and one-half the allowance of ordnance required by previous orders.

12. Commanders are authorized and enjoined to collect all the beef cattle, corn, and other necessary supplies on the line of march; but wanton destruction of property, taking of articles useless for military purposes, insulting citizens, going into and searching houses without proper orders from division commanders, are positively prohibited. All such irregularities must be summarily punished.

13. Brigadier-General J. C. Sullivan is appointed to the command of all the forces detailed for the protection of the line from here to New Carthage. His particular attention is called to General Orders No. 69, from Adjutant General's office, Washington, of date March 20, 1863.

By order of
Major-General U. S. GRANT.
John A. Rollins, Assistant Adjutant General.

Grant has been more bitterly assailed by General McClernand, a former friend and brother officer, than by any other man—his hostility growing out of his removal from the command of his corps before Vicksburg. It is but just to the former, therefore, that the public should know the reasons of that removal. These are fully shown in the following order and correspondence:—

CONGRATULATORY ORDER OF GEN. McCLERNAND.

HEADQUARTERS THIRTEENTH ARMY CORPS, }
BATTLEFIELD IN REAR OF VICKSBURG, *May* 30, 1863. }

General Orders, No. 72.

COMRADES: As your commander, I am proud to congratulate you upon your constancy, valor, and successes. History affords no more brilliant examples of soldierly qualities. Your victories have followed in such rapid succession, that their echoes have not yet reached the country. They will challenge its grateful and enthusiastic applause. Yourselves striking out a new path, your comrades of the Army of the Tennessee followed, and a way was thus opened for them to redeem previous disappointments. Your march through Louisiana, from Milliken's Bend to New Carthage and Perkins's plantation, on the Mississippi river, is one of the most remarkable on record. Bayous and miry roads, threatened with momentary inundation, obstructed your progress. All these were overcome by unceasing labor and unflagging energy. The two thousand feet of bridging which was hastily improvised out of materials created on the spot, and over which you passed, must long be remembered as a marvel. Descending the Mississippi still lower, you were the first to cross the river at Bruin's Landing, and to plant our colors in the state of Mississippi below Warrenton. Resuming the advance the same day, you pushed on until you came up to the enemy near Port Gibson, only restrained by the darkness of night. You hastened to attack him on the morning of the 1st of May, and, by vigorously pressing him at all points, drove him from his position, taking a large number of prisoners and small-arms, and five pieces of cannon. General Logan's division came up in time to gallantly share in consummating the most valuable victory won since the capture of Fort Donelson.

Taking the lead on the morning of the 2d, you were the first to enter Port Gibson, and hasten the retreat of the enemy from the vicinity of that place. During the ensuing night, as a consequence of the victory at Port Gibson, the enemy spiked his guns at Grand Gulf, and evacuated that place, retiring upon Vicksburg and Edwards' Station. The fall of Grand Gulf was solely the result of the victory achieved by the land forces at Port Gibson. The armament and public stores captured there are but the just trophies of that victory.

Hastening to bridge the south branch of Bayou Pierre, at Port Gibson, you crossed on the morning of the 3d, and pushed on to Willow Springs, Big Sandy, and the main crossing of Fourteen-mile creek, four miles from Edwards' Station. A detachment of the enemy was

19

immediately driven away from the crossing, and you advanced, passed over, and rested during the night of the 12th within three miles of the enemy in large force at that station.

On the morning of the 12th, the objective point of the army's movement having been changed from Edwards' Station to Jackson, in pursuance of an order from the commander of the department, you moved on the north side of Fourteen-mile creek towards Raymond.

This delicate and hazardous movement was executed by a portion of your numbers under cover of Hovey's division, which made a feint of attack, in line of battle, upon Edwards' Station. Too late to harm you, the enemy attacked the rear of that division, but was promptly and decisively repulsed.

Resting near Raymond that night, on the morning of the 14th, you entered that place—one division moving on to Mississippi Springs, near Jackson, in support of General Sherman, another to Clinton, in support of General McPherson—a third remaining at Raymond, and a fourth at Old Auburn, to bring up the army-trains. On the 15th, you again led the advance towards Edwards' Station, which once more became the objective point. Expelling the enemy's pickets from Bolton the same day, you seized and held that important position.

On the 16th, you led the advance in three columns upon three roads, against Edwards' Station; meeting the enemy on the way in strong force, you heavily engaged him near Champion Hills, and, after a sanguinary and obstinate battle, with the assistance of General McPherson's corps, beat and routed him, taking many prisoners and small-arms, and several pieces of cannon.

Continuing to lead the advance, you rapidly pursued the enemy to Edwards' Station, capturing that place, a large quantity of public stores, and many prisoners. Night only stopped you.

At day-dawn, on the 17th, you resumed the advance, and early coming upon the enemy strongly intrenched in elaborate works, both before and behind Big Black River, immediately opened with artillery upon him, followed by a daring and heroic charge at the point of the bayonet, which put him to rout, leaving eighteen pieces of cannon and more than a thousand prisoners in your hands.

By an early hour on the morning of the 18th, you had constructed a bridge across the Big Black, and had commenced the advance upon Vicksburg.

On the 19th, 20th, and 21st, you continued to reconnoitre and skirmish until you had gained a near approach to the enemy's works.

On the 22d, in pursuance of the order of the commander of the department, you assaulted the enemy's defences in front, at 10 o'clock A. M., and within thirty minutes had made a lodgment, and planted your colors upon two of his bastions. This partial success called into exercise the highest heroism, and was only gained by a bloody and protracted struggle. Yet it was gained, and was the first and largest success achieved anywhere along the whole line of our army.

For nearly eight hours, under a scorching sun and destructive fire, you firmly held your footing, and only withdrew when the enemy had largely massed their forces and concentrated their attack upon you.

How and why the general assault failed, it would be useless now to explain. The Thirteenth Army Corps, acknowledging the good intention of all, would scorn indulgence in weak regrets and idle criminations. According justice to all, it would only defend itself. If, while the enemy was massing to crush it, assistance was asked for, by a diversion at other points, or by reën-forcement, it only asked what in one case General Grant had specifically and peremptorily ordered, namely, simultaneous and persistent attack all along our lines until the enemy's outer works should be carried; and what, in the other, by massing a strong force in time upon a weakened point, would have probably insured success.

Comrades, you have done much, yet something more remains to be done. The enemy's odious defences still block your access to Vicksburg. Treason still rules that rebellious city, and closes the Mississippi River against rightful · use by the millions who inhabit its sources and the great Northwest. Shall not our flag float over Vicksburg? Shall not the great Father of Waters be opened to lawful commerce? Methinks the emphatic response of one and all of you is, " It shall be so? " Then let us rise to the level of a crowning trial! Let our common sufferings and glories, while uniting us as a band of brothers, rouse us to new and surpassing efforts! Let us resolve upon success, God helping us! I join with you, comrades, in your sympathy for the wounded and sorrow for the dead. May we not trust —nay, is it not so—that History will associate the martyrs of this sacred struggle for law and order, liberty and justice, with the honored martyrs of Monmouth and Bunker Hill!

JOHN A. McCLERNAND,
Major-General commanding.

GENERAL SHERMAN TO COLONEL RAWLINS.

HEADQUARTERS FIFTEENTH ARMY CORPS, }
CAMP ON WALNUT HILLS, *June* 17, 1863. }

Lieutenant-Colonel J. A. Rawlins,
  A. A. General Department of the Tennessee:

SIR: On my return last evening from an inspection of the new works at Snyder's Bluff, General Blair, who commands the second division of my corps, called my attention to the enclosed publication in the *Memphis Evening Bulletin* of June 13th instant, entitled "Congratulatory Order of General McClernand," with a request that I should notice it, lest the statements of facts, and inference contained therein, might receive credence from an excited public.

It certainly gives me no pleasure or satisfaction to notice such a catalogue of nonsense, such an effusion of váinglory and hypocrisy; nor can I believe General McClernand ever published such an order officially to his corps. I know too well that the brave and intelligent soldiers and officers who compose that corps will not be humbugged by such stuff.

If the order be a genuine production, and not a forgery, it is manifestly addressed, not to an army, but to a constituency in Illinois, far distant from the scene of the events attempted to be described, who might innocently be induced to think General McClernand the sagacious leader and bold hero he so complacently paints himself.

But it is barely possible the order is a genuine one, and was actually read to the regiments of the Thirteenth army corps, in which case a copy must have been sent to your office for the information of the commanding general. I beg to call his attention to the requirements of General Order No. 151, of 1862, which actually forbids the publication of all official letters and reports, and requires the name of the writer to be laid before the President of the United States for dismissal.

The document under question is not technically a letter or report, and, though styled an order, is not an order. It orders nothing, but is in the nature of an address to soldiers, manifestly designed for publication for ulterior political purposes. It perverts the truth, to the ends of flattery and self-glorification, and contains many untruths, among which is one of monstrous falsehood.

It substantially accuses General McPherson and myself with disobeying the orders of General Grant, in not assaulting on the 19th and 22d of May, and allowing, on the latter day, the enemy to mass his forces against the Thirteenth army corps alone. General McPherson is fully able to answer for himself; and for the Fifteenth army corps I answer, that on the 19th and 22d of May, it attacked furiously at three distinct points the enemy's works, at the very hour and minute fixed in General Grant's written orders; that, on both days, we planted

our colors on the exterior slope and kept them there till
nightfall; that from the first hour of the investment of
Vicksburg until now, my corps has been far in advance
of General McClernand; that the general-in-chief, by
personal inspection, knows this truth; that tens of thousands of living witnesses beheld and participated in the
attack; that General Grant visited me during both assaults, and saw for himself, and is far better qualified
to judge whether his orders were obeyed than General
McClernand, who was near three miles off; that General McClernand never saw my lines; that he then
knew, and still knows nothing about them, and that
from his position he had no means of knowing what
occurred on this front.

Not only were the assaults made at the time and
place, and in the manner prescribed in General Grant's
written orders, but about three P. M., five hours after
the assault on the 22d began, when my storming-party
lay against the exterior slope of the bastion in my front,
and Blair's whole division was deployed close up to the
parapet, ready to spring to the assault, and all my field-
artillery were in good position for the work, General
Grant shewed me a note from General McClernand,
that moment handed him by an orderly, to the effect
that "he had carried three of the enemy's forts, and
that the flag of the Union waved over the stronghold
of Vicksburg," asking that the enemy should be pressed
at all points, lest he should concentrate on him. Not
dreaming that a major-general would at such a critical
moment make a mere buncombe communication, I
ordered instantly Giles A. Smith and Mower's brigades
to renew the assault, under cover of Blair's division, and
the artillery deployed as before described, and sent an
aide to General Steele, about a mile to my right, to convey the same mischievous message, whereby we lost
needlessly many of our best officers and men.

I would never have revealed so unwelcome a truth
had General McClernand, in his process of self-flattery,
confined himself to facts in the reach of his own obser

vation, and not gone out of his way to charge others for results which he seems not to comprehend.

In cases of repulse and failure, congratulatory addresses by subordinate commanders are not common, and are only resorted to by weak and vain men to shift the burden of responsibility from their own to the shoulders of others.

I never make a practice of speaking or writing of others, but, during our assault of the 19th, several of my brigade commanders were under the impression that McClernand's corps did not even attempt an assault. In the congratulatory order I remark great silence on that subject. Merely to satisfy inquiring parties, I should like to know if McClernand's corps did or did not assault at two P. M. of May 19th, as ordered. I don't believe it did, and I think General McClernand responsible.

With these remarks I leave the matter where it properly belongs, in the hands of the commanding general, who knows his plans and orders, sees with an eye single to success and his country's honor, and not from the narrow and contracted circle of a subordinate commander, who exaggerates the importance of the events that fall under his immediate notice, and is filled with an itching desire for "fame not earned."

With great respect,
Your obediant servant,
W. T. SHERMAN,
Major-General commanding.

GENERAL MCPHERSON TO GENERAL GRANT.

HEADQUARTERS SEVENTEENTH ARMY CORPS, ⎫
DEPARTMENT OF THE TENNESSEE, ⎬
NEAR VICKSBURG, MISS., *June* 18, 1863. ⎭

Major-General Grant,
commanding Department of the Tennessee :

GENERAL: My attention has just been called to an article published in the *Missouri Democrat* of the 10th instant, purporting to be a congratulatory order from Major-General John A. McClernand to his command.

The whole tenor of the order is so ungenerous, and the insinuations and criminations against the other corps of your army are so manifestly at variance with the facts, that a sense of duty to my command, as well as the verbal protest of every one of my division and brigade commanders against allowing such an order to go forth to the public unanswered, require that I should call your attention to it.

After a careful perusal of the order, I cannot help arriving at the conclusion that it was written more to influence public sentiment at the North, and impress the public mind with the magnificent strategy, superior tactics, and brilliant deeds of the major-general commanding the Thirteenth army corps, than to congratulate his troops upon their well-merited successes.

There is a vaingloriousness about the order, an ingenious attempt to write himself down the hero, the master-mind, giving life and direction to military operations in this quarter, inconsistent with the high-toned principle of the soldier *sans peur et sans réproche.*

Though "born a warrior," as he himself stated, he has evidently forgotten one of the most essential qualities, viz., that elevated, refined sense of honor, which, while guarding his own rights with jealous care, at all times renders justice to others.

It little becomes Major-General McClernand to complain of want of coöperation on the part of other corps, in the assault on the enemy's works on the 22d ultimo, when twelve hundred and eighteen men of my command were placed *hors du combat* in their resolute and daring attempt to carry the positions assigned to them, and fully one-third of these, from General Quimby's division, with the gallant and accomplished Colonel Boomer at their head, fell in front of *his own lines,* where they were left, after being sent two miles to *support him,* to sustain the whole brunt of the battle, from five P. M. until after dark, *his own men being recalled.*

If General McClernand's assaulting columns were not immediately supported when they moved against the enemy's intrenchments, and few of the men succeeded in getting in, it most assuredly was his *own fault*, and *not* the fault of *any other* corps commander.

Each corps commander had the positions assigned to him which he was to attempt to carry, and it remained with him to dispose his troops in such a way as to support promptly and efficiently any column which succeeded in getting in.

The attack was ordered by the Major-general commanding the department to be simultaneous at all the points selected; and precisely at the hour, the columns moved, some of them taking a little longer than others to reach the enemy's works, on account of the natural and artificial obstacles to be overcome, but the difference in time was not great enough to allow of any changing or massing of the enemy from one part of the line to the other.

The assault failed, not, in my opinion, from any want of coöperation or bravery on the part of our troops, but from the strength of the works, the difficulty of getting close up to them under cover, and the determined character of the assailed.

Very respectfully, your obedient servant,

JAMES B. McPHERSON, Major-General.

BRAGG'S REPORT OF BATTLE OF CHATTANOOGA.

HEADQUARTERS, ARMY OF THE TENNESSEE, DALTON, GA, *November* 30, 1863.

SIR: On Monday, the 23d, the enemy advanced in heavy force, and drove in our picket line in front of Missionary Ridge, but made no further effort. On Tuesday morning early, they threw over the river a heavy force opposite the north end of the Ridge, and just below the mouth of the Chickamauga, at the same time displaying a heavy force in our immediate front.

After visiting the right and making dispositions there for the new development in that direction, I returned towards the left, to find a heavy cannonading going on from the enemy's batteries on our forces occupying the slope of Lookout Mountain, between the crest and the river. A very heavy force soon advanced to the assault, and was met by one brigade only—Walthall's, which made a desperate resistance, but was finally compelled to yield ground—why this command was not sustained is yet unexplained. The commander on that part of the field, Major-General Stevenson, had six brigades at his disposal. Upon his urgent appeal, another brigade was despatched in the afternoon to his support, though it appeared his own forces had not been brought into action, and I proceeded to the scene.

Arriving just before sunset, I found we had lost all the advantages of the position. Orders were immediately given for the ground to be disputed until we could withdraw our forces across Chattanooga creek, and the movement was commenced. This having been successfully accomplished, our whole forces were concentrated on the Ridge, and extended to the right to meet the movement in that direction.

On Wednesday, the 25th, I again visited the extreme right, now under Lieutenant-General Hardee, and threatened by a heavy force, whilst columns could be seen marching in that direction. A very heavy force in line of battle confronted our left and centre.

On my return to this point, about eleven A. M., the enemy's forces were being moved in heavy masses from Lookout, and beyond to our front, whilst those in front extended to our right. They formed their lines, with great deliberation, just beyond the range of our guns, and in plain view of our position.

Though greatly outnumbered, such was the strength of our position, that no doubt was entertained of our ability to hold it, and every disposition was made for that purpose.

During this time they had made several attempts on

our extreme right, and had been handsomely repulsed with very heavy loss, by Major-General Cleburne's command, under the immediate direction of Lieutenant-General Hardee.

By the road, cross (*sic*) the ridge at Rossville, far to our left, a route was open to our rear. Major-General Breckinridge, commanding on the left, had occupied this with two regiments, and a battery. It being reported to me that a force of the enemy had moved in that direction, the general was ordered to have it reconnoitred, and to make every disposition necessary to secure his flank, which he proceeded to do.

About three and a half p. m., the immense force in the front of our left and centre advanced in three lines, preceded by heavy skirmishers. Our batteries opened with fine effect, and much confusion was produced, before they reached musket range.

In a short time the war of musketry became very heavy, and it was soon apparent that the enemy had been repulsed in my immediate front.

Whilst riding along the crest, congratulating the troops, intelligence reached me that our line was broken on my right, and the enemy had crowned the ridge. Assistance was promptly despatched to that point under Brigadier-General Bate, who had so successfully maintained the ground in my front, and I proceeded to the rear of the broken line to rally our retiring troops and return them to the crest to drive the enemy back. General Bate found the disaster so great that his small force could not repair it.

About this time I learned that our extreme left had also given way, and that my position was almost surrounded. Bate was immediately directed to form a second line in the rear, where by the efforts of my staff, a nucleus of stragglers had been formed upon which to rally.

Lieutenant-General Hardee, leaving Major-General Cleburne in command on the extreme right, moved towards the left, when he heard the heavy firing in that direction. He reached the right of Anderson's division just in time to find it had nearly all fallen back, commencing on its left where the enemy had first crowned the ridge. By a prompt and judicious movement, he threw a portion of Cheatham's division directly across the ridge, facing the enemy, who was now moving a strong force immediately on his left flank. By a decided stand here the enemy was entirely checked, and that portion of our force to the right remained intact.

All to the left, however, except a portion of Bate's division was entirely routed, and in rapid flight—nearly all the artillery having been shamefully abandoned by its infantry support.

Every effort which could be made by myself and staff, and by many other mounted officers, availed but little. A panic, which I had never before witnessed, seemed to have seized upon officers and men, and each seemed to be struggling for his personal safety, regardless of his duty or his character.

In this distressing and alarming state of affairs, General Bate was ordered to hold his position, covering the road for the retreat of Breckinridge's command; and orders were immediately sent to Generals Hardee and Breckinridge to retire their forces upon the depot at Chickamauga.

Fortunately, it was now near nightfall, and the country and roads in our rear were fully known to us, but equally unknown to the enemy.

The routed left made its way back in great disorder, effectually covered, however, by Bate's small command, which had a sharp conflict with the enemy's advance, driving it back. After night, all being quiet, Bate retired in good order—the enemy attempting no pursuit.

Lieutenant-General Hardee's command, under his judicious management, retired in good order and unmolested.

As soon as all troops had crossed, the bridges over the Chickamauga were destroyed to impede the enemy, though the stream was fordable at several places.

No satisfactory excuse can possibly be given for the shameful conduct of our troops on the left, in allowing their line to be penetrated. The position was one which ought to have been held by a line of skirmishers against any assaulting column ; and wherever resistance was made, the enemy fled in disorder after suffering heavy loss. Those who reached the ridge, did so in a condition of exhaustion from the great physical exertion in climbing, which rendered them powerless; and the slightest effort would have destroyed them.

Having secured much of our artillery, they soon availed themselves of our panic, and turning our guns upon us, enfiladed the lines both right and left, rendering them entirely untenable.

Had all parts of the line been maintained with equal gallantry and persistence, no enemy could ever have dislodged us; and but one possible reason presents itself to my mind, in explanation of this bad conduct in veteran troops, who had never before failed in any duty assigned them, however difficult and hazardous.

They had, for two days, confronted the enemy, marshalling his immense forces in plain view, and exhibiting to their sight such a superiority in numbers, as may have intimidated weak minds and untried soldiers.

But our veterans had so often encountered similar hosts, when the strength of position was against us, and with perfect success, that not a doubt crossed my mind.

As yet I am not fully informed as to the commands which first fled, and brought this great disaster and disgrace upon our arms. Investigation will bring out the truth, however, and full justice shall be done to the good and the bad.

After arriving at Chickamauga, and informing myself of the full condition of affairs, it was decided to put the army in motion for a point further removed from a powerful and victorious army, that we might have some little time to replenish and recuperate for another struggle. The enemy made pursuit as far as Ringgold, but was so handsomely checked by Major-General Cleburne and Brigadier-General Gist, in command of their respective divisions, that he gave us but little annoyance.

Lieutenant-General Hardee, as usual, is entitled to my warmest thanks and high commendation for his gallant and judicious conduct during the whole of the trying scenes through which we passed.

Major-General Cleburne, whose command defeated the enemy in every assault on the 25th, and who eventually charged and routed him on that day, capturing several stands of colors and several hundred prisoners, and who afterwards brought up our rear with great success, again charging and routing the pursuing column at Ringgold, on the 27th, is commended to the special notice of the government.

Brigadier-Generals Gist and Bate, commanding divisions, Cumming, Walthall, and Polk, commanding brigades, were distinguished for coolness, gallantry, and successful conduct, throughout the engagements, and in the rear-guard on the retreat.

To my staff, personal and general, my thanks are specially due for their gallant and zealous efforts, under fire, to rally the broken troops and restore order; and for their laborious services in conducting successfully the many and arduous duties of the retreat.

Our losses are not yet ascertained; but in killed and wounded, it is known to have been very small. In prisoners and stragglers, I fear it is much larger.

The chief of artillery reports the loss of forty pieces.

I am, sir, very respectfully,

Your obedient servant,

BRAXTON BRAGG, General commanding.

General S. Cooper,
Adjutant-General C. S. A,, Richmond.

General Grant's order respecting the last great move of the Army which ended in the surrender of Lee.

CITY POINT, VA., March 29, 1865.

GENERAL :—On the 29th instant, the armies operating against Richmond will be moved by our left for the double purpose of turning the enemy out of his present position around Petersburg, and to ensure the success of the cavalry under General Sheridan, who will start at the same time, in his efforts to reach and destroy the South Side Railroads.

Two corps of the Army of the Potomac will be moved at first in two columns taking the two roads crossing Hatcher's run nearest where the present line held by us strikes that stream, both running towards Dinwiddie Court House.

The cavalry under General Sheridan joined by the division under General Davies, will move at the same time, by the Weldon road and the Jerusalem plank road, turning west from the latter before crossing the Nottoway, and west with the whole column before reaching Stony Creek. General Sheridan will then move independently, under other instructions which will be given him. All dismounted cavalry belonging to the Army of the Potomac, and the dismounted cavalry from the Middle Military Division not required for guarding property belonging to their arm of the service will report to Brigadier-General Benham, to be added to the defences of City Point. Major-General Parke will be left in command of all the army left for holding the lines about Petersburg and City Point, subject of course to orders from the commander of the Army of the Potomac. The Ninth Army Corps will be left intact to hold the present line of works so long as the whole line was occupied by us is held. If, however, the troops to the left of the Ninth Corps are withdrawn, then the left of the corps may be thrown back so as to occupy the position held by the army prior to the capture of the Weldon road. All troops to the left of the Ninth Corps will be held in readiness to move at the shortest notice by such route as may be designated when the order is given. General Ord will detach three divisions, two white and one colored, or so much of them as he can and hold his present lines, and march for the present left of the Army of the Potomac. In the absence of further orders or until further order is given, the white divisions will follow the left column of the Army of the Potomac, and the colored divisions the right column. During the movement, Major-General Weitzel will be left in command of all the forces remaining behind of the Army of the James.

The movement of troops from the Army of the James will commence on the night of the 27th instant. General Ord will leave behind the minimum number of cavalry necessary for picket duty in the absence of the main army. A cavalry expedition from General Ord's command will also be started from Suffolk, to leave there on Saturday, the 1st of April, under Colonel Sumner, for the purpose of cutting the railroad about Hicksford. This, if accomplished, will have to be a surprise, and therefore from three to five hundred men will be sufficient. They should, however, be supported by all the infantry that can be spared from Norfolk and Portsmouth as far out as to where the cavalry crosses the Blackwater. The crossing should probably be at Unitee. Should Colonel Sumner succeed in reaching the Weldon road he will be instructed to do all the damage possible to the triangle of roads between Hicksford, Weldon and Gaston. The railroad bridge at Weldon being fitted up for the passage of carriages, it might be practicable to destroy any accumulation of supplies the enemy may have collected south of the Roanoke. All the troops will move with four days' rations in haversacks and eight in wagons. To avoid as much hauling as possible, and to give the Army of the James the same number of days' supply with the Army of the Potomac, General Ord will direct his commissary and quartermaster to have sufficient supplies delivered at the terminus of the road to fill up in passing. Sixty rounds of ammunition will be taken in wagons and as much grain as the transportation on hand will carry after taking the specified amount of other supplies. The densely-wooded country in which the army have to operate making the use of much artillery impracticable, the amount taken with the army will be reduced to six or eight guns to each division, at the option of the army commanders.

All necessary preparations for carrying these directions into operation may be commenced at once. The reserves of the Ninth Corps should be massed as much as possible. Whilst I would not now order an unconditional attack on the enemy's line by them, they should be ready and make the attack if the enemy weakens his line in their front, without waiting for orders.

In case they carry the line, then the whole of the Ninth Corps could follow up so as to join or coöperate with the balance of the army. To prepare for this, the Ninth Corps will have rations issued to them same as the balance of the army. General Weitzel will keep vigilant watch upon his front, and if found at all practicable to break through at any point, he will do so. A success north of the James should be fo 'owed up with great promptness. An attack will not be feasible unless it is found that the enemy has detached largely. In that case it may be regarded as evident that the enemy are relying on their local reserves principally for the defence of Richmond. Preparations may be made for abandoning all the line north of the James, except inclosed works—only to be abandoned, however, after a break is made in the lines of the enemy.

By these instructions a large part of the armies operating against Richmond is left behind. The enemy knowing this may, as an only chance, strip their lines to the merest skeleton, in the hope of advantage not being taken of it, whilst they hurl every thing against the moving column and return. It cannot be impressed too strongly upon commanders of troops left in the trenches, not to allow this to occur without taking advantage of it. The very fact of the enemy coming out to attack, if he does so, might be regarded as almost conclusive evidence of such a weakening of his lines, I would have it particularly enjoined on corps commanders, that in case of an attack from the enemy, those not attacked are not to wait for orders from the commanding officer of the army to which they belong, but that they will move promptly and notify the commander of their action. I would also enjoin the same action on the part of division commanders when other parts of their corps are not engaged. In like manner I would urge the importance of following up a repulse of the enemy.

U. S. GRANT, Lieutenant-General.

Major-Generals Meade, Ord, and Sheridan.

THE BOYS IN BLUE;

OR,

HEROES OF THE RANK AND FILE,

COMPRISING

Incidents and Reminiscences from the Camp, Battle-Field and Hospital,
with Narratives of the Sacrifice, Sufferings and Triumphs

OF THE

SOLDIERS OF THE REPUBLIC.

Mrs. A. H. HOGE,

ASSOCIATE MANAGER OF THE NORTH-WESTERN BRANCH OF THE U. S. SANITARY COMMISSION, CHICAGO

WITH AN

Introduction by Thomas M. Eddy, D. D.

Able writers have described the campaigns which resulted in the overthrow of the Rebellion, and the lives of the Generals and officers who planned the manœuvres of our armies have been written, but as yet poor Justice has been done to the Soldiers who made the reputation of these generals, and who fought the battles and gained the victories for which the leaders have received nearly all the credit. In this volume—which its talented author, Mrs. A. H. HOGE, has appropriately and happily called "THE BOYS IN BLUE; or, HEROES OF THE RANK AND FILE,"—this oversight is partially remedied; partially, we say, for language can never do full justice to the gallantry, the heroism, and the undaunted bravery of the Private Soldiers. As a leading spirit of the North-Western Sanitary Commission, as a faithful nurse in the camp, in the hospital, and in the field, Mrs. HOGE, witnessed nearly all the important operations of our armies in the South-West, first under Grant and afterwards under Sherman. In this volume she takes us directly among the "Boys in Blue," and tells us in simple, earnest, but glowing and eloquent language, of the sacrifices and suffering through which they passed to win their grand triumphs.

The story Mrs. HOGE narrates is one of the most thrilling interest. She confines herself to incidents which passed under her own observation, and these she weaves together with wonderful skill and effect. The private soldier who survived the war will find his own experiences reproduced in this deeply interesting volume; and the thousands who mourn a son, brother or father as among the victims of rebel hate will equally welcome the work, not only as a souvenir of the struggle so full of tender memories for them, but as a record, which, by commemorating the services of the "Boys in Blue," worthily supplements the more ambitious histories which the war has produced.

Numerous Steel and Wood Engravings—all executed in the highest style of the art—illustrate the incidents which Mrs. HOGE so graphically describes, and makes the volume artistically one of the most attractive of its class.

The work is sold by Agents, and will be comprised in one handsome volume of nearly Five Hundred Octavo Pages, with numerous Illustrations from original designs by Nast, Momberger and others,

AND DELIVERED TO SUBSCRIBERS IN

Neat and Substantial Binding, Extra English Cloth,	-	-	$3 00	
Extra English Cloth, Beveled Boards, Gilt Edge,	-	-	3 50	

Disabled Soldiers, Soldiers' Widows, and Energetic Men and Women are Wanted in every Township and Village of the Country to introduce this Work into every Family.

E. B. TREAT & CO., Publishers, 654 Broadway, New York.

www.ingramcontent.com/pod-product-compliance
Lightning Source LLC
Chambersburg PA
CBHW031047110726
47900CB00003B/839